Karen Restaino began her writing career as a playwright with her debut stage play, a Victorian period drama, *A Guinea Too Much*, being successfully performed at the Mansfield Palace Theatre in 2003 and her TV drama, *Age Concerned*, shortlisted for Channel 4's *The Plays The Thing* in 2006. The mother of four returned to education shortly after studying for a BA in Theatre Studies at the Rose Bruford College in Sidcup, South London, then went on to attain a PGCE in her home town of Sheffield at Hallam University.

Since then, Karen, now 54, and a grandmother with five grandchildren, had a burning desire to return to writing. *The Ringmaster* is her first novel, which incorporates her fascination with the art of Theatre with a love of storytelling.

Karen Restaino

THE RINGMASTER

AUSTIN MACAULEY PUBLISHERS™

LONDON * CAMBRIDGE * NEW YORK * SHARJAH

A CIP catalogue record for this title is available from the British Library.

ISBN 9781398452725 (Paperback)
ISBN 9781398452732 (ePub e-book)

www.austinmacauley.com

First Published 2023
Austin Macauley Publishers Ltd®
1 Canada Square
Canary Wharf
London
E14 5AA

Thank you:

Roz, Don, Max and Mini and Grandchildren: Bells, Mia, Lucca, Matty and Issy.

Vito, for your patience and care.

Mum, Kathleen, for your support and encouragement.
Dad, Wilfred, for providing me with the storytelling gene

Barry Heath, for the pen and paper! FYI, Sam and Quirimisu are in here somewhere!

Austin Macauley, for believing in me!

While some actual geographical locations set the scene, all persons and events represented in this book are fictional.

Circus Franconi 1937

A Circus appeared like a snake, gliding silently down from the High Peaks into the Hope Valley. As it descended the hills like a multi-coloured string of beads, a majestic melody drifted towards the sleepy village of Castleton. As the Circus approached, emanating from its convoy of horse-drawn wagons and carriages was an air of vibrant expectation. At its flanks, a modest number of otherworldly people danced along to shimmering trumpeters in an explosion of petals, fluttering scarves and banners. The fanfare was not just a spectacle for a grand entrance into the Hope Valley and the village of Castleton but rather a celebration, a festival of life and art, methodically rehearsed with the precision of a Roman Legion returning home triumphant from battle. The whole ensemble had been choreographed for stimulation, to arouse imagination, stir up intrigue and strategically designed to create misalliance in the souls of even the most conservative of village folk. Trailing behind the procession were elaborately dressed horses and carriages decorated in beautiful bright fabrics, trimmed exotically with ribbons of red and green, golden silks and laces woven in a silvery gossamer thread. Goaded by its handler, a sullen lion wearing a heavily rusted harness swung its head from side to side, nodding and growling at the passing crowd. A line of followers slowly increased as local villagers trotted along behind. Children were incredibly intrigued to discover where the excitement would take them. They cheered when the lion flew at a sleek leopard in its silver harness. A golden-haired African boy riding bareback on a jewelled elephant waved down at the chattering children as they ran alongside the lumbering beast, dodging the animal's carelessly placed footsteps that fell clumsily beside them, while daring to pat the beast's hind legs before running off to a safe distance. Comic acts took up the rear, bounding in with juggling tricks and cartwheels, sending un-expecting children scuttling from the monstrous elephant's strides. Bare-chested, sun-baked Circus men blew kisses to adoring women as they lined the main road to see them strutting by like peacocks. Exotically dressed women in silver bangles and amethyst necklaces danced alongside mysteriously painted carriages, showering crowds and narrow cobbled streets with wildflowers, handpicked along the way: petals, berries, moss and leaves. Long swishing skirts seductively revealed smooth, toned calves and jingling bells about delicate ankles, drawing interested men from their work. The Circus, graceful, mysterious and skilled, elaborate and explosive, introduced itself to the quiet village of Castleton, bringing bewilderment, excitement and awe. Its exit left behind a hum of gossip, anticipation and much to do preparation.

Georgia's Home 2020

As Len's Volvo pulled up at the front of High Oakham Cottage, gravel spitting from beneath its wheels like ball bearings as it slowly ground to a halt, he declared with pride and conviction, "Home sweet home!" He leaned back, removed his glasses and yawned, "Do you need to yawn so loudly?" Georgia was tired and hungry, after being stuck on the M1 for hours. Tutting under her breath, she unclipped her seatbelt, sat up slightly and peered over the dashboard.

"So? What do you think?" Len asked without looking at her.

Georgia glanced over at her father and then turned back to the windscreen to wipe away the condensation with the palm of her hand.

In all its glory, the cottage stood silent, dark, abandoned and mysterious, "It looks damp."

Len thought the tiny particles of quartz and feldspar that cement each stone together appeared to shimmer in the early evening rain. Sighing, he breathed on his glasses, wiped them on his sleeve and put them back on. "They certainly don't make houses like this anymore." He folded his arms across his chest. "It's solid; built from sedimentary rock, a composition of sand-sized grains of mineral and ancient organic material. It would have been quarried locally at least over two hundred years ago. Oh yes, she's certainly got some history in her old bones."

Georgia laughed. "I know enough from years of your long, boring geography lessons to know that the space between the sand grains are made of a rich matrix of silt and clay."

"Ah, so you did learn something?"

"– And judging by how the lime cement between each stone is severely eroded, the whole building must be really damp."

"Hmm, well, it's quite possible. She's going to need some TLC, that's for sure."

"Just like us then?"

"That was the plan from the start, wasn't it?

Georgia couldn't help thinking before Len switched off.

the Engine, plummeting the whole building into a pitch-black void, how had time not eroded it away; judging by the shininess of the rain upon the quartz, the cottage must have once shone amazingly in the sunlight. Breaking the silence, Len opened his door to climb out, leaving Georgia to tug at her bag; somehow, it was stuck beneath the passenger seat. Finally, pulling it free, she climbed out exhausted. A woman's face suddenly appeared out of the darkness, inches from her nose. Georgia jumped slightly and let out a muffled, pathetic yelp that made her feel instantly embarrassed. "Oh my God, you made me jump!"

"Oh, sorry, I didn't mean to startle you." The woman's hair, dripping wet and lank, clung to her sallow cheeks like damp straw as she grinned widely and stepped a little nearer to shake Georgia's hand. "It's me." She dropped her head strangely to one side and narrowed her eyes inquisitively. "Where have you been?"

"Travelling up from London. Have you been waiting long?" Georgia gave a quick furtive glance down to the woman's boots and wondering why she was wearing a skirt that practically swept the ground on a night such as this, hardly water-resistant or warm against the freezing cold. She couldn't help but notice that the saturated coat the woman was wearing was clinging to her like a wet bin liner, revealing her pitifully thin form beneath. Seemingly unencumbered by neither rain nor cold, the woman smiled again, lifted a shaky hand to her mouth and dragged wet hair from her lips. She stepped back, allowing Georgia to alight with a relative amount of grace and dignity, "Thanks," she said, closing the car door behind her. "I'm exhausted." Sighing heavily at the prospect of having to entertain a complete stranger in a house she hadn't yet seen herself, Georgia quickly glanced over at Len, beckoning an answer to the burning question she had in her mind; 'who the hell is this', but Len had already walked away and was now standing with his back to them, stretching, yarning and rocking his hips back and forth.

"It's me, Rebecca." the woman said, with a sarcastic laugh as if she had read Georgia's thoughts somehow. Georgia couldn't help but notice the woman reeked of farm animals, stagnant water and bonfires as she leaned forward to extend another welcoming hand. Instinctively, she wanted to push her away, but instead, she smiled politely, leant back on her heels ever so slightly and turned a cheek to inhale a breath of fresh air discretely. Thankfully, the woman took another step away, allowing Georgia just enough time to regain some personal space. Exhaling quickly, Georgia gave the woman a wide berth and then dropped her bag on the ground; took the woman's hand and shook it with enthusiasm. With the woman's cold hand clasped in hers, Georgia distinctively noticed that her smile was sliding crooked as though it was an effort to keep it going. When the woman's eyes grew suddenly narrow again, Georgia wondered if she was mocking her. "Sorry, have we met before?"

The woman glanced up suddenly and gave a little smile,

then sighed as if she was greatly disappointed in what she saw before her. Georgia, dying to know who the woman was, and trying not to appear rude, looked to her father again, hoping he would offer some information as to why she was here to greet them upon their arrival.

Len, now walking around the circumference of the car, stared over the dry-stone walling to the distant, dark woodland. Georgia, following his gaze, glanced across the lane and fields beyond, then whispered in his ear. "Who is she? What is she doing here?"

Georgia's initial reaction to High Oakham Cottage was one of horror. "This place is nothing like I had imagined, Dad."

Glancing up at the property, she couldn't help thinking the place she was now supposed to call home for the rest of her life, or at least for the foreseeable future, was somewhat disappointing. "Do you think we've made a colossal mistake, Dad?"

Rebecca cleared her throat, reminding Georgia that she was still, in fact, very present. Georgia felt the urge to say something,

verbalise anything, just to fill the awkward silence between them.

"It's dark," she said finally, turning to Rebecca and rubbing her hands together to generate warmth. "No street lights, I see?"

They both gazed around as Georgia tried hard to not show her contempt. Rebecca held out a wet, shaky, cold hand again.

"Here, allow me!"

It took Georgia a moment to realise that the woman was only offering to take her bag; she declined, shaking her head.

Not wanting to leave the woman's hand outstretched and hanging, she quickly clasped it in hers and shook it. "I am sorry, I'm Georgia, by the way, forgot to say. I can manage, thanks. Pleased to meet you, Rebecca." The woman retained the handshake that tad bit too long for Georgia's liking. It caused her blood to stir with mistrust and made the situation feel even more intense. "I bet nights are long out here?" Georgia said finally. She pulled her hand free, lifted her bag from the ground, flung it over one shoulder and moved away; then, shivering, zipped her jacket up to her chin, something she would never do in London, then followed her father to the rear of the car.

Both girls watched in silence as Len popped open the boot with the fob on his key ring and began removing boxes and cases, lining them in neat rows in the gravel. "I'm guessing there's loads of work to do then? The place looks really rundown!" She watched Rebecca bend down to pick something up from the ground. To Georgia's surprise, no one responded; her words seemed to just drift away into the darkness. Len suddenly snapped from behind the boot of the car, "Georgia, grab a box, will ya? Come on, help!" He looked up momentarily before burying his head to search for the most essential items that could not wait until morning. He began gathering them together like they were about to be stolen at any moment and pushed them into another larger box made of transparent Perspex. Heaving the heavy container free of the boot and resting it momentarily upon one raised knee, Len reached up to close the boot with his free hand. Georgia heard the car's central locking system beep as Len locked it with the fob and pushed his keys into his back pocket. Georgia turned to Rebecca to see what she was doing. Seeing her struggling with something heavy, she instinctively reached to offer assistance.

"Here, let me take that!" She tried to prise the item from the reluctant woman but gave up when she realised she wasn't going to release it.

"I'm here to help," Rebecca said as she hurried towards the path that led to the cottage. Georgia quickly took up a box, which was really heavy. She guessed it must contain a collection of her father's old Geography books that he had accumulated during his time working at the University. While gripping the heavy box, she followed Rebecca to the gate. Rebecca held it open with her foot and waited for Georgia to catch up.

"Thanks."

"I brought milk, a few logs and eggs."

Rebecca pushed her way through the broken gate that hung loosely on one hinge. "That is very kind of you, thanks." Georgia turned, expecting her father to respond with a similar sentiment, but was shocked to see he wasn't following them as she had thought.

"Well, we are neighbours." Rebecca was saying.

She stopped by the door waiting for someone to unlock it. When Georgia caught up with her finally, she realised Rebecca wasn't holding a box but rather a very traditional wicker basket.

"Love that! Is it vintage?"

Rebecca moved the basket from one arm to the other,

threading her arm through the handle and clutching its sides tightly to support the weight of its content. She turned slowly to respond to Georgia and was about to tell her about the basket when her mouth dropped open. Georgia looked over her shoulder to see what the woman was staring at. "What? What is it?"

Rebecca let out a piercing scream. Georgia yelled and spun on her heels. "My God, what is it?"

A sudden rush of wind whipped up around them, carrying rain like tiny needles of ice that painfully penetrated their skin, leaving them both drenched within seconds. All Georgia could think to do was run back to the car when strangely, Rebecca's screaming stopped, cutting off like a car siren terminated in the dead of night, leaving a cold, stark, eerie silence. Georgia stood rigid. She found herself weirdly hugging the box she was carrying, her mouth still open, wondering what the hell had just happened but was too shocked to ask.

"You took her," Rebecca whispered.

"What?"

Rebecca's eyes were burning straight through Georgia.

"You took my baby."

"I took who?" Believing that Rebecca must be talking to someone else, instinctively, Georgia turned to see who but found no one there in the darkness. She didn't hesitate a moment longer; she dropped the box she was carrying and ran back towards the car.

Rebecca was calling after her,

"Janey loved those kittens!"

Rebecca's words trailed off in the wind as Georgia left her standing alone by the door. Heading back up the path, Georgia leapt over a grass verge into bushes and suddenly stumbled, confused in the darkness. Running in a blind panic she had somehow changed direction.

Now, so overwhelmed with fear, her heart raced painfully off beat. She tried to shout out for her father through the emptiness, but her words flying out like flares, alerted no one to her rescue. Len had disappeared; it was like the very darkness itself had engulfed him. The wind and rain were pressing against her so fiercely that she felt she could barely hear her thoughts. Discovering a clearing, Georgia began aimlessly, wading through freezing cold water and mud until she eventually found a courtyard around the rear of the building. Georgia realised the area beyond the garden was nothing but marshland, and the water around her ankles seemed to be getting deeper. A river nearby had broken its bank, causing the river to surge past the cottage, over the back yard and beyond the lane and adjoining fields. It became apparent that the raging water had engulfed the seemingly derelict property at the rear and was lapping around the barn. Georgia could hear the creaking and cracking of the wooden structure under the water's tremendous force and quickly deduced that the building would probably be swept away by morning. Not sure how she had found her way around to the rear of the property, but her thoughts suddenly returned to the whereabouts of Rebecca. Glancing around, she saw her racing up behind, so close yet strangely way off in her peripheral vision. She felt sure she should be further away, yet two images were split in half, refracting like a stick in the water. Georgia glanced up; clouds above were sailing at breakneck speed across the moon, illuminating the cottage and courtyard through the veil of rain in a haunting wash of uranium blue. Realising there was nowhere left to run, she stopped to catch her breath. Her chest was heaving painfully with exhaustion. Rebecca appeared before her, rising slowly as if from the ground itself until she was looming over with her, clothes now in rags, wringing wet and torn, thrashing mud up into Georgia's face. Then, leaning in slowly, she began breathing out words that Georgia could not comprehend. Georgia tried hard to shield her eyes and face with her hands but could smell that rancid aroma again: rotting vegetation, stagnant water and cold, wet earth. Droplets of mud and grit splashed up from the hem of Rebecca's skirt, hitting the back of Georgia's throat as she lay motionless. She threw her arms up around her head for protection as more voices could be heard over the sound of the raging river, furtively whispering to each other, low-pitched and mumbled. Georgia could see boots splashing in the water around her between the fingers covering her eyes. More people were approaching now, gaining in numbers and growing louder as they drew closer, splashing the cold, murky water over her freezing body with their boots as they stomped in agitation. Petrified, Georgia sensed her body growing rigid with the cold. Then a strong waft of paraffin rose thick in the air. Daringly, she lifted her head to see where the smell was coming from. Hundreds of lamps shone around the courtyard, painting the sharp rain with a flickering hue of golden-yellow against the darkness. Georgia's fears were confirmed; Rebecca was no longer alone. Anger and wrath emanated from the gathering crowd. It was apparent, whoever these people were, instinctively, Georgia knew, they were a lynch mob of dead souls.

Hope to Mam Tor 2020

Jake Franconi's boots, segged with Yorkshire Hobnails, stopped strolling along an ancient bridleway; his hand-carved walking stick jabbed at the ground beside a ravine that dramatically fell away from the high peak known locally as Mam Tor into the valley of Castleton below. Dwarfed by Derbyshire's abundance of Ling heather and golden-brown bracken, a small amount of Bell Heather quivered gently on the fringe of the bridleway as a Red Admiral Butterfly flicked from stem to stem quite out of season. A young Grouse nestling unseen in the undergrowth, equally camouflaged by its rusty red plumage, was disturbed. It vocalised its annoyance with an undulating whirring sound that gave Jake the impression of a two-stroke Engine similar to his old 1987 Yamaha Banshee. The bird fluttered inelegantly into the air in panic, struggling to gain height against a north-westerly front slowly sweeping in over the darkening, rugged peaks. A fresh early spring breeze not only brought with it spits of cold sideways rain, but the silhouette of a Circus snaking down the valley below. The ringtone of Jake's phone suddenly split the eerie silence with a tinny rendition of a song by Ace of Base, 'Don't turn around.' "Yeah! What?" Jake snarled at his brother, Joshua, down the phone. "I know! I can see them from here! Looks like a vintage Circus or a Steampunk rally or something. It's exactly what we need. Yeah, I'm really pissed off. I would have liked us to be the first to have them in town, but what am I supposed to do about it now? Joshua? Josh! You there, mate?" Losing the signal, Jake walked further along the track until the signal bars slowly climbed back up to three; he stopped and waited for his brother to call again. Jake and his brother Joshua had moved to Derbyshire only five years earlier. Looking, they told their bank manager when applying for a substantial loan to buck the trend in quirky, liberated, modern bars and restaurants selling craft beers and vintage recipes in remote rural areas. Following their Great-grandmother's move to a local care home a year or so earlier, the two boys had inherited the responsibility of her substantial estate, which is tucked away in the High Peaks of the

Derbyshire hills, somewhere between the quaint village of Castleton and the pretty nearby village of Hope. At first, it was agreed that the boys should sell up, share what profit there was to have and enjoy their inheritance, but then, upon visiting the site, they had a change of heart and decided to turn the place around and convert it into a lucrative business. Luckily, the bank agreed and granted the loan. The first twin born, Jake believed he knew enough, or at least a little of what they would require to make the business tick over. When they moved into the buildings on the farm's estate, they had high hopes of renovating and opening their successful rural bar and restaurant almost immediately. They then decided to add a working craft outlet with a mill, a small farmstead with a farm shop and visitor centre, and so upon receipt of the loan, work started immediately but took an additional two years for planning and an extra year to complete the first phase of their renovation project. Their exciting new venture evolved slower than expected, and their dream of becoming wealthy entrepreneurs was far from a reality. By all accounts, the boys knew they had their work cut out in trying to drag the Franconi brand kicking and screaming into the 21st century, but it didn't help that they were known locally as the infamous Franconis' who was rumoured to have once been associated with the famous Circus disaster, a story shared in many a book and local folktale. Over the years, the story of the disaster had taken on more sinister and somewhat sombre lore, which according to Jake, could either help or hinder their plight.

"It adds to that 'Po di qualcosa di diverso!" Jake told Faye, his Great-grandmother. He frequently spoke to her in his Great-grandfather's foreign tongue to preserve that precious side of his heritage before it was lost; after all, knowing she had been a well-travelled Circus performer who had once spoken several languages, he didn't want her to forget either.

"Yeah, having a history gives us a backstory, even if it is sinister. It helps create intrigue and sets us apart from other restaurants and bars." Joshua delighted in reminding his Great-grandmother, but she wasn't too impressed.

Faye glanced up, biting down on the temple arm of her glasses; she sighed at the intrusion, then put her glasses back on. "If you say so, boys." She nodded, flicked the creases from the newspaper she was reading before being rudely interrupted and returned her attention to the crossword.

"It will become a rambler's oasis, Gran!" Growing frustrated at her lack of enthusiasm, Joshua began tapping his thighs agitatedly.

Jake placed a reassuring hand on his brother's arm. "It's okay, mate. We've printed leaflets, Gran, look. Show her, Josh."

Joshua pulled a leaflet from his satchel and presented it with a huge smile. "Fresh off the press, Gran." The off-white glossy A3 double-sided advert was elegantly designed with a golden-brown font that flashed in the harsh strip lighting that ran along the centre of the ceiling in the dining room, where Faye was now forced to live with twenty other residents, most infirm or with varying levels of senility. Faye looked up, took the leaflet and read-aloud – "Tempting Victorian Dishes and Sweets, Camp Coffee and Items from that Yesteryear. Hmm, very nice, dear."

"See, Gran, how the text wraps around the image of our Showman's Traction Engine? Do you recognise it?"

Glancing back down, Faye flicked the leaflet over. She took a while to re-read each element, giving it closer scrutiny, then sighed and handed it back. "Hmm, lovely, Joshua."

"You've seen the plans, haven't you, Gran?" Jake began rolling out reams of drawings and blueprints. "We've painstakingly designed all the outbuildings to include a Victorianesque Confectioner, Milliners, Ironmongers, Tobacconist, Butcher, Gift Shop."

"It's a handcrafted only gift shop, isn't it, Jake?"

"Yeah, we only sell goods made in our own workshops, Toys, Jewellery, etc." Jake and Josh tried to keep their grandmother abreast of everything, but lately, she was only interested in the profit margin, nothing more.

"And we have a collection of Steam Engines now, Gran." Joshua pointed to the area on the blueprint where the Engine Emporium was situated. Josh was proud to announce his contribution. "It's a Steam Engine Museum."

Jake smiled at his brother's show of pride. "It's the crowning glory, isn't it bro?"

"Took us a long time to decide where to house the collection. It was my idea, wasn't it, Jake?"

"They look great, mate; really help capture the overall theme."

"My Engines help give a snapshot into industrial life during that period. The Hamlet looks real now, like it's frozen in time." Josh took great pride in pointing this out to his Great-grandmother. "And the collection looks cool on the menus and printed stationery, doesn't it?" Josh wafted the leaflet under Faye's nose again.

"Yes, it all looks very impressive, Joshua." Faye folded the newspaper and removed her spectacles. "Hmm, yes, I see the point to it all, but are you making any money?"

Jake sighed inwardly, thrust his hands into his pockets, and walked to the window. Looking out over the grey, wet car park on the ground floor below, a memory of his childhood fluttered vaguely before him; he glanced over his shoulder and saw that Joshua had gone into the kitchen, reserved, according to the sign on the door for 'staff only.' Jake knew once Joshua found a sink, he'd be in there for ages washing his hands a million times before being satisfied that they were clean.

Jake walked back to Faye's table and sat. "Hey, Josh, don't be hours in there, okay!"

Faye smiled knowingly and placed her hand gently over Jake's. "You're good to him, Jake."

Jake didn't say anything; he just looked down at his boots and nodded.

The boys were close, not through similarities or shared interests, but Joshua's need for individual support. Since childhood, Joshua had been a square peg in a round hole, different and somewhat problematic. Being responsible for his twin brother made life difficult sometimes. It had always been hard for Jake to leave his brother's side. Forming relationships with others had never come easy to Joshua, so as his twin brother, Jake took this burden upon himself and felt a moral obligation to be eternally responsible for him. Fighting off bullies and tormentors had become second nature to Jake and somewhat of an occupational hazard, which seemed to be getting more challenging the older they got, but as professional partners, they were, and Jake would be the first to admit, a really great team. Jake took the rough with the smooth, and Josh took each obstacle in his day-to-day life on the chin. Life was a constant battle for the twins, whose natures couldn't be more poles apart, but the problems it caused came with the territory.

"The Hamlet is looking great. It's really shaping into the Victorianesque mini-village that we envisioned, Gran. It's finally showing life from both perspectives like we wanted; both rich and poor."

Faye nodded. It wasn't entirely true, and Jake knew she could tell. His Great-grandmother was never one to suffer fools gladly. Jake and Joshua's vision of workers wearing an assortment of social uniforms from fine aristocratic attire, maids in traditional white and black, cooks in the kitchen in their flour-dusted aprons, working tirelessly over boiling pots and pans were never employed because there was no demand for them. Nor the need for labourers in rags working over screeching looms and oily Engines. The endless stream of rambling visitors, who were supposed to scramble either on foot or by cycle from the village of Hope through Hope Pinfold and up over the old railway bridge, passing through the Hamlet on route to the infamous Mam Tor, never made it. There was no flocking of walkers, cyclists, runners or otherwise, and indeed, no rush of tourists seeking to be enthralled, fed or watered as expected. So, to the locals, the brotherhood of dreamers became the brotherhood of losers. Even on the grand opening, the boys had been described in the Derbyshire News as likely lads, whose idea of opening a retro-themed Oasis in the middle of nowhere was fanciful, if not somewhat off the shelf, especially given that there had been no one trading up on those high peaks, other than sheep farmers for over one hundred years. This hadn't put the boys off. Instead, they hoped the news article would create intrigue no matter how negative it sounded. When it became apparent that their dream business was somewhat of a washout, they blamed the unseasonably wet weather and turned their hands to what they knew best. Joshua became known locally as the go-to guy for fixing traction Engines, tractors and old motors, which was keeping them afloat, while Jake returned his hand to carpentry, building and any other odd job he could pick up along the way.

Georgia's Home (Continued) 2020

Georgia awoke from the weirdest dream she'd ever had. The sound of her father's phone buzzing on the dashboard startled her. She took in her surroundings before sitting up, yawning and stretching.

"Awake?"

"Yeah. I am now! Where are we?" She yawned again and glanced over the distance fields and forests that lined the M1.

"Hardwick Hall junction 28 or 29. Not too far now."

Disconnecting the phone from the USB port, she read the name flashing on the screen: "Marlow and Brown Estates?"

"Congratulations on your new property, Mr Franconi!"

The voice on the phone blurted in a broad Derbyshire accent.

"Er, sorry?" Georgia said, glancing over at Len. "This is Georgia, Mr Franconi's daughter. He's driving at the moment. Can I help? Actually, I'll put you on speaker."

Len was nodding excitedly and smiling from ear to ear.

"Hello!" He winked at Georgia, then returned his eyes to the road.

"Hello, Mr Franconi. Sorry for calling while you're driving. Are you safe to speak?"

"Yes, yes, on hand's free, fire away!"

"We have the keys ready for you in the office. You may call and collect them any time before 5:00pm today."

Len checked the time on the dash. "What time do you close there, darling?"

"Around five."

"Oh, we're still driving from London. I'm afraid we're about an hour away, just pulling off the M1 now, so we'll probably miss you."

"Would it help if I met you at the property? I really don't mind; High Oakham Cottage is on my way home. We're practically neighbours, you see."

The lady laughed. "I'll be passing your farm around six if that helps?"

Len looked at the clock on the dash again and nodded at Georgia. "That would really help, wouldn't it, G? We'll be arriving around that time according to the sat-nav, so yeah, sounds good!"

"Great, no problem then, I'll meet you there."

"Yes, yes, thank you! Thank you very much! We'll see you there."

Georgia leaned over, plugged the phone into the USB port and set it back on the dash. Len pressed resume on the sat-nav and let out an excited "Y-e-s!" He gave a long sigh and drummed his fingers on the steering wheel. "That estate agent," he said, "has been absolutely great! They've all been amazing in that office."

Georgia, still shaken from her strange dream, yawned and nodded. "Who knew buying a farm at auction over the phone would be that easy; I can't believe you did that without seeing it. Mum would be turning in her grave." She laughed and turned to look out over the fields.

"You know me, I like a gamble?"

"Taking ridiculous risks, you mean?"

"I told you, this place is fantastic. You're going to love it. Anyway, what we got to lose, nothing!"

Georgia glanced over her shoulder at all the stuff piled in the back of the car. "You're probably right," she said.

"About what?"

"Having nothing to lose, I mean, everything we own is literally in this car, and it's all just a pile of shit!"

Len looked at her disapprovingly, then glanced back at the road ahead.

"Oh no…" Georgia began rummaging through a box on the back seat.

"What? You forgotten something?"

"Remember that butterfly Mum bought me in the glass jar?"

"The Red Admiral, yeah, you forgotten it?"

"No, it's here," she lifted the jar into the light, examined it, and held it up for Len to see. Len glanced over the rim of his glasses briefly.

"She brought you that because symbolically, a Red Admiral butterfly is supposed to represent a powerful spirit or soul, just like you."

"I vaguely remember her saying something like that."

Len laughed. "Superstitions surrounding Butterflies vary among cultures around the world; while some believe they symbolise danger others say they are evil, so take your pick."

Georgia quickly ran a google search on her phone. "They are thought of as elemental. Apparently, some believe they are closely connected to the life force in each of us. If you come into contact with one, it can be a sign to follow your dreams and take a risk. It can also be seen as a visit from a person who has passed away – someone who knew how to love deeply."

"Well, that's a load of old codswallop, but the Butterfly is the most beautiful as far as the Arthropod species go."

"Not this one. Not anymore." Georgia tossed the jar over the seat and watched it bounce from the box and roll off. "Its wings have broken off." Len grimaced at the thought of the black, wingless bug. Georgia pulled a coke from her bag and relaxed back into her seat to drink it.

"Hey, G! Wake up!"

Georgia jumped. "What…?"

"A local builder!"

"What?"

"Grab a pen, get their number down."

Georgia sat up, rubbing her eyes. "Did I just fall asleep again?" She pulled a phone from the back pocket of her jeans and got ready to punch in the numbers as Len slowed the car down and pulled in tighter to the Hawthorn hedge, and eased up to the rear of the van, which in his opinion, was parked just a little too far out on a blind bend.

The only tool left in this van is my brother, do not steal him! I need him to work to pay your benefits. Tel: 01433 835783

Len read the message on the van and laughed. "Brilliant! These jokers will come in handy. Tap that number into your phone, will ya! Got it?"

"Yep."

"Good."

Moments later, spotting an area where the Hawthorn hedge split, Len indicated, pulled in and parked up in front of the builder's van, then slipped off his seat belt, relaxed, took off his glasses and rubbed his eyes. Georgia looked to her left and realised they were no longer on the motorway but high up. The road below appeared to snake down into a dip. The scenery was a vast sea of rolling hills and valleys of green.

"That's Hope Valley down there." Len stretched and yawned.

"Tired?"

"No, not really, just relieved. We're here. We're home!"

"No way!" Georgia sat bolt upright in her seat, slipped her shoes on and peered around.

"Stay here." Len climbed out of the car.

'Where you going?" Georgia sprang out and crowded after her father. She scrabbled up the grass verge practically on her hands and knees. "Why have we stopped here?"

Len stood beside a dry-stone wall; it trailed off in all directions for miles, snaking up and down the valley and away into the distance below.

"My family were farmers down there." Pointing off somewhere vague, Len leaned over the wall and peered down the hill slope.

"I know." Georgia had no idea where he was pointing; to appease him, she pretended to look interested. She pulled her phone from her back pocket and checked for messages, but the mobile data didn't work.

"Yorkshire's that way, Nottinghamshire and Derbyshire are over there –" Len was still pointing in all directions – "and in that direction –"

Georgia followed his gaze. "Huh-uh. I have no internet. Why have we stopped here?"

"– Sheffield is that way. Oh, and Manchester is over there, and Nottingham…."

"I know; Nottingham is over there. I get it!"

Len gave a 360-degree turn to look out over the horizon.

"They're all the largest and nearest cities here, close enough for you to visit when you want to go shopping with your friends."

"Great, except I now no longer have friends because they are one hundred and fifty miles away in London, which is in that direction, if you remember?"

Len watched as Georgia began walking back to the car. She was hoping he'd follow. She stopped and waited for him; leaning against the car, she began scrolling her phone again, trying to reconnect it to the net. "Can you unlock it?" She shouted to Len, "It's freezing." Shivering, she pushed her arms up inside the sleeves of her jacket. "And it's starting to rain!" She looked over at a guy standing a little away by the quirky builder's van.

He was on his phone, too, pacing back and forth.

Hope to Mam Tor (Continued) 2020

Joshua Franconi stopped pacing and leaned against his van. The side of the high vehicle offered shelter from the fresh evening breeze that was beginning to whip up around his legs. He repeatedly punched his brother's number into his mobile phone and waited for a dialling tone. While waiting for a response, he took a crunchy bar from his jacket and tore it open with his teeth. As he bit down, he looked to the right, saw Georgia watching him and nodded. Still stood by the Volvo waiting for her father to open it, she gave a weary nod back and then dropped her eyes to the road, following its grey ribbon-like curve until it disappeared around the blind bend. Still waiting for his brother to respond, Joshua read the writing on the side of his van. He didn't really know why he was reading it because he'd read it a million times before: The only tool left in this van is my brother – Jake had scrawled his brother's name in the grime months ago, and there it still remained for all to read, Josh Franconi.

"Come on, you fucker, answer it!"

Joshua tried reconnecting with Jake for over ten minutes but kept losing connection. It wasn't until his brother walked into a live zone upon the High Peak that his phone found a signal and began buzzing in his pocket.

"Where are you, pub?"

Joshua didn't really like pubs, and Jake knew it. "Bet you're supping a pint right now, aren't you crafty little…?"

"No! No, I'm not actually! Where are you?"

"Told you, I'm out walking! I'm still looking for that old path, which is supposed to link the village to our place, but since no one seems to know where it is, how can we advertise it as a new route?"

Jake looked around for gaps in the thick undergrowth and clumps of coarse heather. "It looks like it's grown over if ever there was one. I thought, if we found the alternative route that's supposed to exist, it might bring walkers up here."

"Will they come, though, Jake? There are already excellent routes, but no one comes."

"Well, I think they'll come; if not for the challenge of finding a new route from us to Mam Tor, they'll come to escape the crowds on the old routes, surely? Where are you anyway?"

"On Edale Road heading towards Castleton. I've checked the gate; see if Mark's locked it again."

"Has he?"

"I think so. There's some girl and bloke there, so I can't get to it, but it looks locked."

"Right! As I was saying, that Circus or Steampunk Rally was apparently in Bakewell yesterday. It's supposed to be moving to Hope or Castleton after that."

"It's Castleton, I think. I saw posters up in the village."

"Ah, so you have been to the pub?"

"No, I haven't!"

Jake was pulling Joshua's leg, as he always did at every opportunity.

"It's doing its rounds, I guess."

"Sounds like it. Nikki told me she saw it advertised in the village, so I went to have a look. She said she saw it packing up earlier over in Bakewell."

There was silence. Then Jake sniffed and spoke shakily as though he was running. Joshua could hear the wind rushing over his phone. "You were supposed to book them!"

"I know. Well, it's too fucking late now, isn't it? What's the point of us inviting them to the Hamlet?"

"What do you mean? We could still have them at our place! Nikki said the Traction Engines are being hauled."

"They aren't. It looked to me like the Engines were all travelling."

"Ah, so they're travelling? Wow!"

"Yeah. I could just about make one or two out with my binoculars. It's a sight to see, mate? You'd love it! How many are there actually, did Nikki say?"

"She said there were quite a few. Why didn't you book them when we spoke about it? I thought you said you had?"

"Well, I didn't; I forgot. It's too late now anyway. If everyone in the village has seen the spectacle already, the novelty will have worn off."

"Yeah, of course! No one will travel to the Hamlet to see a Circus and Steampunk Rally if they've already seen them in the village."

"Unless, like I said, we get a celebrity involved."

"We can't afford that."

"It's an idea, mate, definitely something to think about."

Joshua stared over at Georgia, who was now talking to the older man. They were both hanging over the gate, looking out over the fields.

"We need to do something drastic to be honest." Jake said, his voice suddenly sounding robotic.

"What? You're breaking up!"

"I said, I think the restaurant will have to go. If it wasn't for the extra cash I'm picking up and the salvage work you're doing, we'd have gone under already. We're broke, mate. I don't know how long we can keep afloat!"

"I know."

"And Gran don't take us seriously anymore." Jake faded off momentarily.

"Hello, Jake?" Joshua moved over to the right a bit to try to reconnect.

"Yeah, I'm still here."

"Ask the bank again; they listen to you."

"I can't go back to them. We can't afford more bank repayments anyway; too expensive."

"For fuck's sake!"

"Don't get upset, mate. It's okay, honest.

"What are we gonna do, Jake?"

"Derbyshire will not beat us, mate, don't worry! We'll get involved in the Castleton Rally and use the opportunity to advertise the Hamlet. We'll organise a mini Steampunk festival of our own up here. We'll involve a few of your Engines, local Crafties; they love any excuse to set out their wares. It'll be okay, mate, you'll see. Get some of your dealer friends to help; they'll have contacts you can tap into. You know a few Steamheads; you can call them and get them on it. We'll make it work, bro. Don't worry. In the meantime, keep doing what you do, fix up your Engines and tractors, and I'll step up the building work. It's just for a little longer. We'll make it work, mate."

"We're running out of options, aren't we, Jake?"

"No, not yet. Wait, I can see the Circus again! They're in the valley now."

"Who? Where are you?"

"Eastside. The Engines are in convoy, traditional like."

"Are you joking?"

"No, it's definitely a convoy."

"I can't see them. Nikki said there are a few Gypsy caravans, a traditional setup."

"I've seen those guys before in Ashbourne with Gran years ago."

"Nikki sent a few photos. Here I'll send you one." Josh began searching the gallery on his phone until he found a photo of a traditional Circus with wagons and carts. He tapped send and waited for Jake to respond.

"Got it?"

"They look great, don't they?"

"Fuck it, yeah, they're perfect. I'll get um booked, Joshua, don't worry. We'll find the money somehow."

"Okay!"

"See ya in a bit, yeah? By the way, never mind, see you later."

"What? Speak!"

Jake dug his walking stick into the ground, whistled for Ollie, his Border Collie, and descended towards the village. "Granny Faye doesn't know."

"About what?"

"Everything! She doesn't know how broke we are. She thinks we're doing okay. Don't tell her; she'll go mental."

"I won't."

"Honestly, don't say anything. Don't even mention the money side of things."

"I won't!"

"You know what she's like with her temper? She's our Great-gran, but sometimes I swear to fucking god."

"I know! I love her and all that, but....."

"I know, me too, bro."

"Joshua, fuck me!"

"What?"

"I've just seen – I swear to god, I just saw this, well, there was a kid!"

"And?"

"Well, I watched her come towards me, and I swear to god –"

"– What?"

"She was about, I dunno, five-six maybe."

"So?"

"I swear to god, Josh, this kid had no fucking feet!"

"What?"

"Think I just saw a ghost!"

"You don't believe in ghosts."

"I don't."

"Where is she now?"

"Gone! She literally disappeared."

Georgia's Home (Continued) 2020

Georgia climbed the gate and leaned over to peer down into the valley. "Dad, do you see that?" She looked over at the guy now climbing back into his van.

"What is that, a Circus?"

"Indeed, looks like it, an old fashioned one. It's like going back 80 years; how lovely. Look, they've even got a Showman's Engine, now that's not something you don't see every day. Just look at that! It's an old Burrell."

"Amazing!"

"They're heading for one of the towns nearby, I suspect."

"Which one?"

"Dunno, they're heading in the wrong direction for Bakewell or Buxton. I wonder if they're going to Castleton?"

The builder's van parked just under 100 meters away suddenly zoomed past them. Len tutted as he watched it take the blind bend on two wheels.

"Speaking of Hope, I hope his building work is better than his driving. Did you get his phone number?"

"Huh-uh."

"Well, indeed, you don't see that every day; an old-fashioned Circus with Gypsy wagons and an old Showman's Engine."

"Aw, how cute."

There was a long pause as they watched the Circus disappear along the road beneath the valley. Len sighed and stretched, "It's nearly summer, but you can still feel winter snapping at your heels."

"Okay, shall we go then, Dad?"

Len seemed to have gone off into a trance.

"When I was a lad, I loved the end of summer. It was a busy affair around these parts."

Georgia sighed loudly and couldn't help thinking how Northern he sounded suddenly. This wasn't the way she had imagined arriving at her new home.

Georgia had dreamed of pulling up to a quaint cottage in the middle of a forest with a roaring fire waiting, a Grandfather clock ticking away in the corner, and a cat curled up on the hearth. She glanced down at her new Converse All-Stars, which were now covered in wet grass stains and mud and gave them a quick wipe on the backs of her legs.

"I only remember that –" Len continued – "because food suddenly became more interesting, stews, preserves, cheeses, apples and chestnuts, not to mention the wonderful mushrooms. Oh, and the pies! And indeed, lots of people helping out around the place, many more than usual, would be roaming about the Farm, coming and going, working the land, you know, potato picking, all sorts."

Georgia followed Len's gaze across the valley. Crows flew in droves over the dipping hills and treetops, and a buzzard fluttered aimlessly in one spot before suddenly swooping down to jab at the ground below.

"All this land before it dips into the valley," Len pointed. Georgia nodded, her teeth clattering in the cold. "All belonged to the farm we now own."

"Really?"

Even the evident plume of frozen breath, which rose from her words like speech bubbles, didn't alert him to an urgent need to get back in the car.

"My grandad, your great-grandad of course, Leo, would have had this waist-high in wheat by Harvest time, between mid-July and September, then he'd burn it off, flat-black. He'd set fire to an oily rag, attach it to the back of his plough and drag it up and down this valley, burning it off to a cinder ready for his winter crops."

"Can we get back in the car, Dad?"

Len stood in silence, imagining the blackened chard ground before him and, for a while longer, watched as the early evening rain washed the greyish-blue hills with a coating of fine purple mist. The strip of low-lying fog appeared to be slowly creeping down into the small distant village of Hope. "Every dream begins with a dreamer," Len said, stretching his arms above his head and taking a deep breath. He turned to seek approval from Georgia and leaned against the gate. Then yawning, he thrust his hands into his pockets.

"Yappari!" Georgia said, rolling her eyes.

"Yappari? Is that another one of your new words?"

Georgia rolled her eyes again.

"Soon as I saw this place," Len said, nodding, "I knew we just had to have it, G."

"Dad, it's nearly six O'clock" Georgia put her arm through Len's and snuggled into his strong shoulder. "Come on, we need to go."

"Since your mum passed, I think we've grown closer."

"We need each other, that's why."

"I'd blame myself at the end of my days if I didn't give us a fresh start. Coming here has fulfilled my father's prophecy and your mum's dream. She always wanted trees and a veg patch in her garden, but we never had the land."

"We never had a garden, let alone land! So now you impose their wishes onto me."

"Really? Is that how this feels to you?" Len's face grew serious.

"I'm sorry, Dad. I'm just not sure how I am supposed to find work out here, let alone make friends and meet someone."

"Oh, don't be silly; you will!"

"I'm going to find it difficult, Dad; I must say, there's nothing here! This dream of finding a remote farm in the Derbyshire hills is a dream of yours, not mine, not really! And remember, I'm only doing this to end your drinking and bad habits!"

"Bad habits?"

"The gambling, don't act innocent."

Like a teenage version of himself, Len rolled his eyes and tried to avoid the statement by glancing skywards just as a star streamed across the inky void above them. Georgia followed his gaze. They both let out a gasp.

"Aw, did you see that?"

"Indeed, I did."

"Was that a sign?"

"A good omen, I hope."

"Me too!"

"Look, more stars popping out between the clouds."

Len squeezed his daughter's arm. "Things will be different here, I promise! Remember," he said, "the beauty of nature and our appreciation of it brought us here, not other people's hopes and dreams."

"We need to go, Dad. We're supposed to be meeting that lady for the keys."

The moon now resembled a blade, a slither of sharp, shiny silver slicing its way out of the night sky, casting shadows over Castleton's highest Peak, known locally as the Shivering Mountain. Mam Tor loomed in the distance, crawling out of the earth, stretching and arching its back like a giant serpent; it seemed to stir something in Georgia that she didn't recognise, a sudden sense of belonging, familiarity.

"Have I been here before?"

"Not to my knowledge. Now, will you let me have a wee or what?" Len laughed and pulled his arm free from his daughter's.

"Sorry, you didn't say!"

"Why do you think I've been standing here all this time?"

"I thought you were being... I don't know...all nostalgic."

"Well, you just had to ask why I'm hopping from one foot to the other."

"I thought you were freezing, like me?"

As Georgia rushed back to the warmth of the car, giggling into the cold night air, she stopped suddenly. A tractor was approaching on the grass verge.; she wondered why she hadn't heard it. It was close and coming up on the left side of the tight road with its headlights on full beam. Len turned and stood back to allow the beast of a machine to mount the grass verge and inch towards the gate. Both Len and Georgia stood, mouths gaping as the tractor ground to a clunking, choking halt. The farmer flung open the cabin door and climbed out, half pressed into the bushes and Hawthorn hedgerows; he yelled, "Alright!"

"Hiya," Georgia answered, then realised her response sounded very southern.

"Evening," Len said, standing back to allow the farmer to unlock the padlock on the gate.

The chain slid off and clattered against the steel. As the farmer climbed back up on the tractor, he shouted over his shoulder, "Give it a push for me, pal, will ya, ta!"

Len hastened to the gate, gave it a push, and then stood back to allow it to swing open under its weight.

"Okay, buddy!"

"Thanks, youth. Admiring the view, are ya?" He laughed and nodded over the field.

"My land actually, just acquired it. Reckon that's us, over there. Can just about make out the roof of our place." Len sounded fiercely proud.

"You've bought the old cottage, have ya? We must be neighbours then?" The farmer climbed back down from the tractor, wiping his hand on his jeans; he walked over, offering his hand for Len to shake. "Sorry about that, mate, didn't release who you are. Name's Price. We've farmed this land for near on four generations. My old man's grandad won your place in a poker game, if you can believe that? He sold it on for a tidy profit. Well, anyway, there's a bit of history for you. I'm glad I met you, actually. I'll come to your place to remove my Engine from your barn. The old man who lived there let me use it to do the Engine up, but then he got taken to hospital and died. Someone locked it up, and no one seems to know who!" He laughed and returned to the tractor. "Unless, of course, you fancy winning the Engine back in a hand? We Prices are notorious for our tables in this village! Anyway, if there's anything you need to know, we're all a friendly lot here, so don't be afraid to give us a shout!"

"Thanks!"

The farmer stopped to light a cigarette.

Turning to Georgia, Len lowered his voice to a whisper.

"I'm not amused by that comment, not really."

"What comment?"

"The story about the Engine. It wasn't mentioned in any paperwork I've been privy to."

"Should it have been?"

"Well, I read nothing relating to an Engine in the sale of the farm, nor was it mentioned in the auction catalogue. If it was stored in the barn, it should have been mentioned. How do I know it belongs to him?"

"You'll be frequenting the Traveller's then?" The farmer wafted out a match and flicked it into the bushes. "It's the pub in the village, Traveller's Rest?" He drew deeply on the cigarette and blew a halo of smoke into the early evening sky.

"I intend to frequent them all soon as I get settled."

The farmer laughed. "I think you're supposed to be meeting my Mrs? She said she was on her way to hand over keys to that place. Ask her about the Engine, and she'll explain. She's the local estate agent around here. I'll give her a ring; let her know you're here."

The farmer climbed back into the cabin, made a brief call on his mobile, then hung his head out the window and waved.

"Mrs is at the place already, said she'll wait for you. When you're settled, all the pubs in the village are worth a visit; there's seven, so you've got one for every day of the week!" He chuckled, turned his head back into the cabin, nodded, and switched on the Engine before moving off slowly.

"See you in the Traveller's, mate!"

Georgia looked at Len; his eyes seemed to be sparkling with joy. Len waved his hand at the tractor as it inched by and shouted. "I am a bit of a gambling man as it happens."

"Well then," Georgia said to Len, "Sounds like you've already settled in."

The tractor began its manoeuvre between the narrow space of the gate posts and the wall.

"You're in, pal," Len shouted as he waved the vehicle through and then closed the gate behind it. Georgia was embarrassed.

"Do you wonder how he ever managed to get his tractor in the field before you arrived, Dad?"

"Shut up," Len was smiling and still waving as the tractor ground its way over the field. He gave a little jiggle and jangled the keys in his pocket. A hand waved back from the cabin as Len and Georgia watched it continue its journey towards a herd of cows huddled together where the field appeared to slope away.

"You'll have to wait until we get to the cottage for that wee; you can't do it while he's watching."

Georgia returned to the car, relieved to be finally climbing into the passenger seat. Len dropped into the seat beside her and turned on the Engine. "And, no," he said, glancing over his right shoulder before indicating to pull out, "before you ask, I'm not going to start gambling again!"

Home Sweet Home High Oakham 2020

A small black Citroen with 'Marlow & Brown Estates' blazed in red times new roman was parked in the top lane. There was no gate at that entrance, just a rough dirt track leading down to the cottage and barn. The rear door was nearer though to the actual cottage, but according to local land searches and details in the auction pack, the whole lane leading to the place at the rear of the property was once prone to flooding. Being aware of this, Rebecca Price of Marlow & Brown Estates took no chances. She parked on the main road and waited with the car Engine running and full beams lighting up the dirt path just in case the Franconis should arrive from the front lane. She didn't want to miss their arrival but didn't wish to be alone in that dark lane either, car or no car. She remained poised for some time, with the car Engine running intermittently. It was beginning to get really dark, and Rebecca was ready to drive at breakneck speed away from there if she needed to. Since childhood, she had always known High Oakham Cottage was that spooky place at the foot of the hill. After nearly an hour of waiting, her hospitality level on behalf of Marlow & Brown had well expired. She was tired, hungry, cold and conscious that Mrs Hall, her babysitter, would be so offended if she took the liberty and made her wait an extra half hour, especially since her son James was so overactive. She glanced at her watch and imagined how naughty he would be around this time. He always seemed to get worse at night. Though not yet professionally diagnosed, she guessed her son exhibited classic signs of extreme ADHD. Rebecca stepped out of the vehicle and dialled her mobile; the word HOME glowed on the screen of her Apple but yielded no answer.

"Crap!" She had one last walk up and down the lane, wrapped her coat around her tightly, and hurried back to the car. She wiped the steam from inside the windscreen and looked down towards the cottage with a sense of unease. As she stretched, yawned and looked at her watch again, a child appeared in the pool of light emitting from the headlamps. The child stood before the car for a fraction of a second, then was gone.

It was nearly six-thirty when Len's Volvo finally pulled up in the farm's front yard and slowly ground to a halt.

After opening the passenger door, Georgia tugged her bag free from beneath the seat and began climbing out.

"Hello…"

A woman's face appeared inches from her nose. She wore a black woollen two-piece that seemed to drape around her shoulders like it was wet. Smiling, the woman stepped back from the car and waited for Georgia to climb out of the vehicle.

Georgia glanced over at Len to say, Who the hell is this? But he had already gotten out of the driver's side and was stretching, groaning and rocking his hips back and forth.

"I'm Rebecca," the woman said, leaning back towards Georgia to offer her hand.

"Georgia! Box!" Len snapped from somewhere around the back of the car. He buried his head in the boot and unloaded more boxes and suitcases.

Confused, Georgia looked around to see what boxes he was referring to, then seeing Rebecca holding something heavy in her arms, automatically assumed he meant that one, so politely offered to take it from her.

"Oh, sorry, let me take that!"

"It's fine, go ahead. I'm here to help." Rebecca turned away and headed off up the path towards the cottage.

Feeling a vague sense of déjà vu, Georgia grabbed another box from the floor and hurried after her.

"Have we met? Thanks for your help, by the way."

"Oh, no problem. I brought milk, a few sticks of wood and eggs." Rebecca pushed open the small broken garden gate with her foot.

"That's kind of you." Georgia looked about for Len expecting him to respond to the lady too, but he wasn't behind her as she had thought.

Rebecca sighed. "Well, we are neighbours."

As Georgia caught up with her, she realised she wasn't holding a box but a traditional vintage-style wicker basket. She had her arm threaded through it and clutched its sides tightly to support the weight of its content. As they reached the cottage, she turned slowly and was about to speak when Len, clearly rushing to get into the house, passed Georgia on the path, nearly knocking her off her feet. He was carrying a heavy Perspex box containing kitchen utensils and food items from their old house. "Excuse me, love," Reaching in between Georgia and Rebecca, he pushed on the cottage door with his shoulder and stopped to watch as it creaked open to reveal a dark, empty space that smelled damp and musty. Len waved in the air to beckon the girls inside. Rebecca placed a hand on Georgia's arm and gently pulled her to one side. Georgia noticed the coldness of her icy cold fingers penetrating through the arm of her leather jacket.

"Keep the barn locked," she whispered.

"Alright. Why?"

Rebecca bent down and began rummaging through the contents of the basket she had been carrying.

"Why, why do I need to keep the barn locked?"

"We have a barn!" Len exclaimed excitedly as he stepped inside.

Without looking back, he edged his way into the darkness, dropping the plastic box over the threshold, as he did so, then stood back to make a grand gesture.

"Our first step into our new home and new life." He flung open his arms wide. "Ta-dah…Oh, allow me…" he said, taking yet another step back, hands waving over the doorstep like a Jester's rolling bow.

Tentatively, both girls stepped inside. Rebecca and Georgia entered almost together, shoulder to shoulder. Georgia noticed that Rebecca's complexion appeared glowing, almost translucent in the moonlight. Feeling yet another intense episode of deja-vu even more potent than the last, Georgia wanted to blurt it out and get it off her chest, but dared not for fear of ridicule. Len's opinion on such topics was far from her own, and also, she didn't quite know how she should verbalise the experience anyway, especially in front of an estate agent, who would be used to going into old buildings. Len, already inside now, was searching around for a light switch. "Come in, come in," he said as he fumbled in the dark. "Help find a light switch, will you?"

The smell of damp and rot suddenly hit Georgia's nostrils, making her think of churches and graveyards. She whispered beneath her breath.

"What are we doing here? What the…!" Something darted into the darkness.

Len jumped, "Georgia, bloody hell, you made me jump! What's wrong?"

"Something is moving."

"Where?"

"There… in the corner! Oh god, it's not a rat, is it?"

"Where? I don't see anything!"

Eyes goggling, Georgia tried to point through the darkness to indicate where she thought she had seen movement and hoped Len would make sense of it.

"Aw, you're getting excited about nothing."

Len was stumbling around frantically, searching the walls for a light switch.

"Kittens! Dad it's kittens!"

"Where…I don't see anything, Georgia!"

Georgia held light from her phone and illuminated a basket by the hearth. "Look! They are so cute!" To his astonishment, Len turned to find Georgia peering into a basket, which really did appear to contain tiny balls of squirming fluff.

"How on earth is that possible? How have they got in here? This place was supposed to have been empty for months."

"Maybe there's been a mistake."

"Obviously, there's been a mistake! Someone is clearly still living here. The door, of course, that explains why the door wasn't locked!

"Hello! …Wo-o-o-!" Georgia said sarcastically.

"Shh, Georgia! Obviously, there's someone here? Get the light on, come on, help me find it!"

The two began searching.

"We should just use this place as a holiday cottage, Dad. Like we planned? We should build a new place with the life insurance when it comes through, you know, further up the hill. We can live in a caravan or something until the new house is built. Would we need planning, Rebecca?"

Georgia stopped suddenly and looked around. "Where is she? Where's Rebecca?"

"Who?"

"Rebecca!"

Georgia spun on her heels. "Where has she gone?"

"Who are you talking about?"

"The woman from the estate agent? Rebecca!"

"Who the hell is Rebecca?"

"She was here a minute ago… when we arrived?"

"The estate agent? I didn't see her. Why didn't you tell me! I thought she didn't turn up. Unless it was her who opened the door! Well, of course, it must have been her! There'll be some keys in here somewhere. She's obviously dropped them off."

"Well, I guess so; that makes sense."

Len scratched his head and considered where the agent would have left keys for the cottage.

"She bought eggs and milk!"

"Did she? Why didn't I see her?"

"She was already here, Dad, when we got out of the car!"

Len was still trying to make sense of it all.

"Wait a minute, she was standing by the door when you opened it, and you watched us both step inside; of course, you saw her!"

"I honestly didn't see her!"

"Yes, you did! She said she brought eggs and wood…we spoke to her."

The light came on, and Len stood smiling smugly.

"It's here, look, by the door." He switched the light on and off several times to demonstrate, then took his coat off.

"I didn't see any woman, and I certainly don't remember anything about eggs and kittens. I am starving; I do know that!" He walked towards the only other door in the room.

"Bring that box in, will ya? It's got milk, tea and sugar in it. Let's get the kettle on. This has got to be the kitchen."

Len pushed the door open as Georgia went to the front door to retrieve the box and followed him into the kitchen. When she got in there, Len was looking around. Georgia put the box down on the side and began unpacking its contents. "Are you sure you didn't see that woman, Dad? When we pulled up in the car, she stood right there." She demonstrated the proximity that Rebecca had placed her face next to hers with her hand. "She practically climbed in the car with me; she was weird. She said she was called Rebecca and...."

Len shrugged, scratched his head again and delved into the plastic box. "Here, have biscuit. I didn't see her love." Crumbs spat from his lips. He wiped them away on the back of his hand and delved into the box again for milk. "I did wonder who you were talking to though G. Kettle! Here we go. Get that on! I'm gagging."

He opened a tiny door in the far corner of the kitchen and ran up a narrow-whitewashed stone stairwell that appeared to lead up into a dark void above them. Georgia could hear his boots creaking around above her head on the floorboards.

She opened the back door and looked out into the darkness and beyond the misty fields.

Len reappeared at the foot of the stairs with a great wide smile.

"No goldilocks sleeping in my bed."

"What about mine?"

"Nor yours."

"Thank god for that!"

"If the door was open when we arrived, does that mean we have no keys to lock up?"

"Indeed, now there's a point. Where do you think your friend put those keys?"

"How are we supposed to lock up if we don't find any? It's a bit irresponsible, don't you think?" Georgia laughed, "Told you that woman was weird." She laughed again. "I can't believe you didn't see her."

"Well, I didn't."

"She was so weird." Georgia held the kettle under the tap, which thankfully yielded good freshwater, then after plugging the kettle in, she left the room.

She began picking up kittens one by one, kneeling down as she placed each one in her lap. Len leaned around the door and smiled. "Don't get too attached; they're going tomorrow"

"Aw, no, Dad, please. They look too young to me. If we separate them from their mother, she might reject them."

Thinking simultaneously, they both stopped, turned and scanned the room.

"Where is the mother?"

They both laughed.

"Someone's feeding them."

"Yeah, but who?"

The grey glow from a single bulb lit the room dimly, leaving the corners in a dark shadow.

Georgia took off her jacket. "Don't know why I'm taking my coat off; it's freezing here." Georgia stood up and went a bit dizzy for a minute. She put the jacket back on again.

Len went back into the kitchen. Georgia, feeling uneasy and not wanting to be alone, followed.

"So, this... this the utility room?"

"No, Georgia, it's definitely a kitchen, hence the cooker and the sink."

"I thought it might be the utility room or even a cupboard, judging by its size!"

"What do you want?" Len was laughing. "There's a sink, a freezer, an automatic washing machine!"

"Automatic washing machine! Aw, well then, now you're talking!" She still mocked him when she brushed the old net curtain back over the sink to peer outside. "Wow, overload on mod cons in this house!"

She examined the dark space outside and wonders where the toilet might be. "Hope I don't have to go outside for the loo."

"There's a tumble dryer!" Len announced. "And, here it is… yes, a boiler." Len tinkered with a few dials and buttons on the clattered-out model, hidden in a cupboard beside the window. "Great, it's a conventional boiler, a vented system, hot water tank, cold water tank and header tank, probably in the loft. These things live forever. Looks like it was installed in the '80s."

"I bet it's not been serviced since then either."

"It's probably never broken down or needed any expert attention. These old boilers are really that good! And, yes, it works!"

Water began thundering through the pipes.

"Okay, not sure if it should make that noise, though."

"Indeed, maybe not."

"Should you actually switch that thing on? It might explode."

"Sounds like it's exploding already." Len pressed his ear against it.

Georgia stuck her head around the door and shouted into the dimly lit living room. "Rebecca, is this boiler safe? Oh, by the way, could we please have our keys back."

Len laughed. "Yes, keys would be good."

Georgia laughed as she crossed the room and stuck her head in a small cupboard in a recess beside the fireplace.

"Rebecca? Oh, it's a cupboard; I thought it might be your bedroom, Dad! Phew, god, it stinks like a graveyard in there!"

She closed the door and leaned back against it.

"For Christ's sake!" She yelled out and waved her arms above her head. Len came in to find her freaking out in the centre of the room, trading punches with a thick dusty spider's web. He casually glanced up over his silver-framed glasses, then returned his attention to the boiler in the kitchen. He walked around and pulled on the back door. "There's a key in this door! Oh, but wait, yep, the lock's broken."

"Oh, yeah, I know about that," Georgia shouted as she wiped cobwebs from her face and returned to the kitchen. "I broke it!"

Len pushed his glasses onto the top of his head and rattled the lock until it dropped to pieces in his hand. He turned, walked towards Georgia with pieces of the lock tightly gripped in his palm and handed them to her. Georgia stood dazed as Len dropped loose springs and nuts and bolts into her hands and then cupped her fingers around them.

"Then you can fix it."

"I don't know how to do that!"

"Well, you had better hang on to those pieces until you find someone who can." Len placed his glasses back on his nose and went into the living room. "I'll get a locksmith in the morning."

Georgia heard him shout something about not having a signal on his phone.

"So," she said as she followed him around the living room. "What do you think about the place?"

Len leaned against the fireplace, looking down at the kittens with a mug of tea in his hand. He looked tired.

"What about you?" He burped and then took a sip of his tea.

"Odd and very old."

"What's odd? Don't lose those pieces; put them somewhere safe."

Georgia looked at the pieces of metal in her hand and dropped them down on the mantle above the fire. "That woman, she was definitely weird!"

"Who?"

"That Rebecca! The farmer's wife or estate agent, or whoever she was… she literally just disappeared."

"She's not here now, that's for sure."

"She vanished! Here one minute, gone the next."

"Have a look to see if she's left keys?"

"No, she hasn't. I've looked! Do you know who she reminded me of?"

"No."

"That book"

Len drew up a dusty old chair and sat down. "What book?"

Georgia had her father's full attention now.

"This woman keeps appearing, right?"

"In the book?"

"Yeah, in the book I studied, remember?"

"Go on!" Len took another sip of tea. "You mean that Henry James story don't you, The Turn of the Screw?"

"Yeah, I read it for GCSE."

"I read it for your GCSE, you mean. Yes, I remember it!"

"Well, that book I was supposed to read."

Len nodded. "You made me buy the movie, so you didn't have to read it."

"It was scary."

"No, it wasn't."

"It was! Too scary to read."

"You mean you were too lazy to read it."

"It was an 1898 horror novella.

"Novella? Listen to you!" Len laughed into his cup.

"See, I did learn something."

"Yeah, but did you ever read it?"

"No, but you're missing the point."

"You were supposed to read the story so that you could get to grips with the Victorian style of writing, and the whole purpose of reading was to understand the way narratives were structured then, as a Gothic fiction."

"I formulated an opinion and an argument; that's what I was supposed to do. I think the governess was delusional, and the book was crap?"

"So, you believe the ghosts in the house didn't really exist?"

"What did you think?"

"Were the ghosts only a figment of her imagination then?"

"Hmm, let me think, yeah, absolutely, she was a crazy bitch, but that's not the point…that woman…the one you didn't see tonight, even though I know you did…clearly!"

"Georgia, I swear, I didn't see that woman here tonight. Nor did I speak to her like you did."

"Could she have been a ghost?"

"Ghosts don't leave milk and eggs, G, or feed kittens!"

"True! So, you did hear her say milk and eggs?"

"No, but there is milk and eggs in the kitchen."

"Really! Where?"

"In a basket on the side!"

Georgia spun round. "So, she was real then? I knew it!"

Len let out a stifled laugh. "You thought she was a ghost a minute ago."

"No, I said the governess in the book was delusional. I didn't think she was a ghost! Obviously, she couldn't have been a ghost if she had left milk!"

"She must think I was so rude."

"Was she here as the farmer's wife, the estate agent, or just because she was a nosey bitch-neighbour."

"Will you stop using that word? I don't care in what capacity she was here; she left food!"

"Exactly! So, why didn't you see her?"

"No idea; I was too busy getting stuff out of the car. You should have introduced me to her. I feel quite rude; what must she be thinking?"

"So, I'm glad we've established that she was no ghost?"

"No! Don't be silly."

"Aren't folk funny around here?"

Len looked at the kittens by the hearth and scratched his head. "Yeah, I guess they are. I'll get that locksmith out tomorrow. Better to be safe than sorry. We'll get all these locks changed."

Len went into the kitchen, lifted the kettle and filled it back up. "Want another cuppa; yours is cold." As yellow ooze dripped from the faucet, he turned on the tap and stood in horror. Suddenly the tap shook violently as it released cleaner water that hit the sink with such velocity it drenched him before he could turn the tap off again. "And a plumber!" He wiped his face dry on the sleeve of his jumper.

Georgia opened a cupboard door, threw back her head and laughed. "Help, Dad!"

Len leapt across the room to offer assistance. Together they closed the door again before it completely fell off its hinges.

"And a joiner!"

The light bulb above their heads suddenly popped, tripping all the electrics out in the building. Plunged instantly into cold darkness, Len and Georgia stood in silence, unable to see each other let alone their own hands in front of their faces.

Georgia breathed out into the cold room, "And an elec…"

"– Don't even say it!" Len's voice faded off somewhere in the darkness. He lit a match, which created a tiny pool of warm light around his face. A sudden gust of ice-cold wind extinguished the flame and shook the cottage to its very core. They both laughed.

High Oakham Cottage Within
These Four Walls 2020

Buried on the outskirts of Hope in the heart of the Derbyshire Peak District, a candle flickered in the upstairs window of the Cottage known locally as High Oakham. Its warmth emanated into the damp air as the rain pattered relentlessly against the tiny warped glass panes. The oil-rich candle's scent wafted a delicate plume of fresh Cotton Linen and Lavender, bringing a sense of comfort and belonging to Georgia as she unpacked in what used to be Amy's room. She knew that because the name Amy scratched ever so lightly in the glass of a gorgeous Victorian mirror that stood over the fireplace in the corner appeared to add further distress to the plate, adding, Georgia suspected, even more value to the antique, she was sure.

Suddenly, the candle extinguished, and the temperature plummeted as though someone had just opened a freezer. A dark shape appeared from the shadowy recesses of the low hung beams, growing silently. Unbeknown to Georgia, the figure had been hiding in the corner for

quite some time before it began emerging; sliding down the wall from the ceiling, Georgia switched on the bedside lamp and quickly snapped the curtains closed across the blackness beyond. She clasped the radiator to see if it was working—it was. As she stepped from the window, a piece of newspaper between the old thread-bare carpet and the yellowing skirting board caught her eye.

'The Ringmaster—Derbyshire News'

High Oakham Cottage has long been used for nothing more than a place where strangers pass through. Until more recently, purchased by a seemingly innocent family at the start of the New Year, the Cottage, steeped in history and folklore, is now set to be returned to a family abode.

"This family," said one neighbour, "obviously has no local knowledge. Who else would buy a property with such a grim history? A curse is reported to reside within the shadowy crevices of the locally mined sandstone walls. According to locals, an evil so pure emanates from the very fabric of the building itself; so vile and terrifying is this demon that any poor, lonely soul wandering through falls victim to its curse. Locals say the house feeds upon lonely souls. They believe anyone passing through High Oakham with a broken heart is said to be lost to the house already. According to local folklore, the house became cursed following the death of farmworker Abraham Morten who, on the 01st November 1666, was the last person in the village of Eyam to die of the Bubonic plague. Fourteen months before his death, he and a group of friends were said to have taken to the streets of Eyam on a warm sleepy afternoon to rehearse a play for the Wakes, a week-long religious Festival. The troupe performed a reconstruction of a Mystery Play that foretold plague and pestilence. The plot describes how due to the villagers' immorality and sinful behaviour, they would fall victim to the epidemic as a penance for their sins unless they change their wicked ways. The peaceful folk of Eyam had been so appalled with Abraham's dramatic portrayal of them that he became known as the troupe's evil Ringmaster. Soon after this portrayal of pestilence and suffering, the village fell ill. The Black Plague silently crept around the village, killing 260 residents: men, women and children. Everyone knew the disease had begun 14 months earlier, around the time of Abraham's rehearsal. It was believed that a bale of cloth, sent to Eyam from London, where the disease had already killed thousands of inhabitants, had been sent to a Mr Alexander Hadfield, the village tailor. He had been requested by Abraham to create costumes for his troupe as they prepared to perform their Mystery Play in full costume on Wakes Week, but unknown to Mr Hadfield, the damp cloth contained fleas carrying the deadly disease. George Viccars, a visitor to the village, had been planning on performing in Abraham's Mystery Play and so offered to help the Tailor make the costumes for the performance. As the Tailor's new assistant, he was said to have opened up the cloth and, noticing it was damp, hung it to dry before the fire, unwittingly stirring up the disease-ridden fleas hidden within it. Sadly, George was one of the first to die and never left the village again, but one Troupe member did. The man had been a performer at the Finsbury Fields Play House in London before coming to settle in the village of Eyam, but following the death of Abraham and George, there was no other left to blame for the disaster, so fast becoming their scapegoat, and now known as the new Ringmaster, he was forced to run away with his wife and daughter to the Hope Valley. When survivors from Eyam discovered he was living in High Oakham Cottage with his family, a lynch mob tracked him down, hung him by the neck, and then killed his wife and daughter in the barn along with the family's horses. It is said that the Ringmaster still remains in the barn seeking vengeance against his archenemies, plotting the ultimate finale as a comeuppance against the pack of rivals, the good people of Eyam. No matter what nature of a machine is stowed away in the barn, the Ringmaster's restless soul inhabits it, and no one can ever destroy him.

…As the saying goes, the show must go on…and on and on...

"Wow!"

"Yeah, crazy, eh?"

"How weird is that!"

"I know!"

"That is not the history of Eyam, at all!"

"I know!"

"That is the grossest misinterpretation of actual events I have ever heard…who wrote that?"

Georgia shrugged and flicked the paper around to search for an author's name. "So, you think there is no truth in it, then?"

"Absolutely not! Utter tosh! Where did you find it?"

"Upstairs."

"Propaganda! I think that's a real attempt by some local Airbnb to sabotage this holiday home, when it was a holiday home of course."

"But, you hear about supposedly haunted hotels being really busy."

"Indeed, indeed, could have been written by a previous owner"

Georgia held up the article, which didn't appear too old. "By the way, it's freezing upstairs. I thought you'd got the radiators working?"

"I did. I'll call someone out tomorrow. Let me take a look at that –"

Georgia handed over the fragile piece of paper and watched her father's facial expression as he scanned the print. He lifted his glasses.

"This part about some unwitting innocent family buying the place, I think that's us…!"

"I think so too!"

"So, it couldn't have been printed that long ago?"

"Guess not."

"Have you googled it?"

"Not yet."

"I'll do it; I'm interested to find out who wrote it."

"Okay, I'll leave it with you."

The curved electric lamp placed thoughtlessly between six low solid oak beams cast a grey light around the room. Abruptly, dizziness struck Georgia. She became acutely aware of a presence pressing around her and looked about the room nervously. She zipped up the fastener on her fleece and, as if physically drained, flopped in a chair beside Len. Len was too busy reading and re-reading the article to notice the colour drain from his daughter's cheeks. He placed the paper in his jeans pocket and tried to fix the bolt he had taken from the back door.

"I'm going back up to my room."

Len didn't respond; he just looked over his glasses when Georgia began climbing the stairs. Creaking along the corridor, upon reaching her room, she thought she saw shadows beneath the door, as though there was movement inside. She took a step back before pushing it open with her foot. The air felt dense and damp inside like it had rained heavily there. She lay upon the bed and waited for thoughts to come and go. She wanted to take off her Converse All-Stars, but not mustering the strength, she wrapped the quilt over one shoulder, closed her eyes, rolled over and slowly drifted off.

She fell into a deeply relaxed state as she lay on the bed, eyelids flickering. In that warm, soft place between awake and sleep, she distinctly remembers thinking perhaps the journey from London had somehow disturbed her, though she wasn't usually upset by travel. Her mind began floating away as if some distant seasonal memory had awakened deep in her subconscious. She wondered, what would it be thinking if the so-called 'resident evil' was watching her right now? What would it feel about Len? But then, sleep pressed heavy upon her, and she suddenly felt too tired to care.

Sensing the rise and fall of her own chest, slowly, sleep carried her off to somewhere strange yet wonderfully familiar and from the dark recesses of the room, she sensed someone was there with her. Like the article suggested, whoever it was felt her sadness, her heartache. Even if she wasn't aware of it herself, Georgia's profound sense of loss was all-enveloping, and on occasion, she thought she was going to suffocate. Of course, she made sure that no one knew of this, not even her father, but somehow, as she lay wrapped in her thoughts, she was aware that the house understood her grief.

Upon arriving at High Oakham, Georgia told herself repeatedly that this house could never be a permanent place for her.

'I need to get away from here,' she thought this the entire time she was there and wondered what Len would say if he knew how she felt.

Remembering home, her mind suddenly raced back to the vivid streets of London, the smells, the sounds of the city and the screaming sirens, the memory of them still ringing in her ears as she suddenly woke with a start. She rose warily upon one elbow, rolled across the bed and with her face pressed against the window, listened to the silence beyond. A white patch of breath slowly spread up the tiny panes of glass as she stared out at her reflection. Pale and distorted by the mirrored effect the blackening sky behind the glass created, the face staring back, though familiar as her own, was not one Georgia recognised anymore. She studied her attire with a semiconscious awareness that her garments did not portray what she actually felt inwardly. Why wear Converse All-Star sneakers? Sure, their versatility meant she didn't need to care about anything else she was wearing – not that much – everything else just seemed to match because Converse are so iconic, cool and they look eternally classic with anything, but now they seemed too youthful, in a way that made her feel childish almost. Her jeans – nothing wrong with those; her legs and thighs were still slender, so they 'felt' natural, but the T-shirt-sweatshop manufactured, with a meaningless logo that wasn't cheap to buy just made her feel detached from the deep, sensuous feelings she knew that person in the window was harbouring. The woman in the reflection looked older than the girl she knew she was. Her eyes, in particular, had somehow lost something quite profound and fundamental, though time had washed away their youthful shine and vibrancy and somehow, they had lost her soul. Georgia was gone.

Georgia snapped the curtains closed and flopped back down on the bed. As soon as she closed her eyes, vivid, bright images began formulating in her mind. A place she did not wish to leave, somewhere far, far away from the crowds of London, far from the noise and the echoes. Georgia felt like she was being pulled through time to somewhere strangely familiar. This place, she suddenly recognised, was High Oakham Cottage. Familiarity seemed to be securely wrapping itself around her like a blanket, bringing warmth, a feeling of love, and an overwhelming sense of belonging; this is home, she thought.

Evil filled every space of the room, and though she couldn't fight it, Georgia sensed its presence and knew it was pulling her inch by inch through the veil of time to a place where she knew she had once belonged.

Hearing whispers, though distant, Georgia tried to focus, they were garbled, immortal words fluttering vaguely down the generations, instinctively, she knew this. She felt surrounded, her body too weak and heavy to fight; she allowed herself to drift away.

A hot summer's day filled every corner of her mind. Warm sunshine shrouded the dimensions from where the modern High Oakham Cottage ended and the old High Oakham Cottage began. Slowly, as the haze faded, the story started to unfold.

It was one of those still, close afternoons when it feels like everyone has been strangely abducted by some unseen entity. Georgia now slept upon the place where she thought she once lay many generations before. In the sunlight, she could see High Oakham Cottage on a hill with a distant haze creeping slowly across the fields, bringing the threat of late afternoon thunder and sweet, warm rain. The sensation of gentle wisps of warmth beneath the soles of her feet ignited a distant memory as she ran barefooted down the sun-baked stone path leading towards the Cottage with a child by her side; she neared the door and said,

"We have been far away from this place for too long."

The child reached for her hand. "But now we are home."

Georgia suddenly found herself looking down upon her own form. It had been laid out, prepared in some crude way, with the child by her side, ready for a quick burial. The long white shroud clinging to her deathly white frame was dripping slimy and putrid.

She was then drawn to her own reflection in the window. The eyes staring back were barely visible through long strands of straggly, wet hair, black and soulless, like the eyes of a great white shark. Her skin, what was remaining of it, was rotted and decomposed.

Whispering voices of those who travelled through High Oakham came to the forefront of her mind telling her in a mash-up of foreign tongues.

"Eravamo tutti innocenti."

"Soyons entendus, nous sommes innocents."

"muéstrale lo que hizo."

"et redde ei."

"gadewch inni gael ein clywed, rydym yn ddieuog."

"We were innocent!"

Then her journey back in time began again; back to a time when no one spoke; to a time when all lips were sealed, and heads hung low for fear of retribution, acquisition and punishment, despite the pretence of innocence and morality.

Dan's Circus Franconi
Castleton 1937

The convoy of wagons had barely halted when Jacamo alighted carrying a small jug of stale Ale. He strode over the field like a banshee on the warpath, flicked his cigarette into the grass and, without raising an eye towards his brother Danielle, removed his cap and waved him down.

"Bro, quick word!"

"Can't it wait?"

"No, come on, get down!" He didn't wait for his brother to question his actions further.

"Bringing the Circus to Castleton without even sending out the advance man? Mio fratello, cosa stai pensando?"

It also shocked others, even though they had all been fully aware of their route for the past two weeks.

"We thought we were going on further than here; I dunno, to either one of the cities or towns? What's wrong with Sheffield, Manchester, Stockport, or even Bakewell?"

"We aren't ready. Jack, a small site mid-season will give us some breathing space. You want to prepare for the bigger fairs, Appleby and Cambridge?"

Dan climbed down from the Wagon and secured the horse's reins.

"Give us time to prepare, recuperate, rest up the animals, maybe even claw back some losses."

"What, here?"

"Well, look, Goose Fair will soon be upon us. We'll survive the season and be ready for the start of the new season next year if we prepare for it now. We can get to the Goose Fair less than a week from here."

"Vaffancullo!" Jack thumped the Wagon.

Dan snapped in his defence and grabbed his brother's shoulder. "We've a reputation to uphold, bro; come on! There are too many things wrong with equipment to go on pushing our luck. What if there's an accident or something? Then what...? Eh, then what? Anyway, I've business to attend to."

"Where, here?"

"Yeah!"

"Like what?"

"Stuff, you know?"

"No, I don't know."

"Look, we need to talk."

"I'm listening!"

"Bro, come on later, you know, in private."

"Won't be a later if you don't tell us what's going on!"

"These back to back menageries we've been doing are taking their toll. I've found this site out of the limelight where we can get the tent up, do a few matinee shows, make repairs, and get stuff done without making too much noise. We might even make some spare cash—then we can get back on the road and back on our feet without ruining our reputation, that's all I'm saying."

"We won't have a reputation if we hideaway in these backwaters performing for niente."

"He' has a point." One of the small folk said as he walked past with bundles of hay for the horses.

Jack spun around and shot him a look. "Whose fucking side are you on?"

"Geographically, I mean..." the little guy began saying as he ripped out clumps of hay and began feeding it to Dan's horse,

"Castleton is the best location. It's popular with visitors." He stopped what he was doing and pointed out over the hills. "And it's situated between Snake Pass, connecting Stockport, Manchester and Sheffield, and like he said, it's on route to Bakewell over yon as well, so, I think it's a good site."

"And it's only for a week or two," Dan interjected.

"Maybe he's right, Jack." Another Josser whispered gingerly.

"Smaller townships are always hungrier for fun," Leo sidled over. He wedged between his two brothers and gently prised them apart with his hands on their chests. Leo was the largest of the three triplets, a rare but lucrative asset to be a part of in the Circus trade; Leo was very similar in appearance but not in nature. None of the three brothers was. Initially, upon meeting them all together, the three boys could never be set apart until being in their company for a short while and recognising that their varying personalities define them drastically. Leo's extreme seriousness made him appear older. He was the most diverse, evident through his personality, mannerisms and expressions alone. He occasionally wore a rough black beard and carried a sizeable portly stomach, which added years in comparison to his brothers, who, adversely, shared a leaner, athletic physique. Only those close to Jack and Dan could decipher one from the other; their personality traits and disposition could sometimes mirror each other.

"Folk think niente of walking five or ten miles for the Circus, and they let kids out of school early around these parts. They don't do that in cities. We can do afternoon shows easy." Leo maintained pressure between the chests of his brothers and kept them apart.

Jack sniffed and relaxed back slightly. "There was no mention of stopping at this shit hole, though," he said. "No one told me we were stopping here."

"Nor me," Leo said, eyeing Dan with a discontented look. He took another breath and leaned in.

"Liar! You knew about this?" Jacamo suddenly turned to Leo, pointing his finger practically in his face.

Leo pressed between the boys and lifted his chin towards Jack, "Aha, okay then, what if I did?" He lied; he didn't but wanted to see how Jack would respond.

"Now, now, ladies, that's enough." Faye strolled over, laughing. "You boys, you're worse than children. So, what does it matter if we stop here for a few days. I'm sure as hell ready for a break.

"Well, no one told me!" Jack said, fuming. Like a child to its mother, he turned to his wife, seeking sympathy. "Everything should come between my boys and me first, everything!"

"See, this is where I get confused," Dan said, spitting into the grass.

"What?" Jack snapped in retaliation, spitting out the brown soddened baccy he had been chewing most of the day.

"Why should I discuss everything with you?" Dan looked at Faye and shrugged. "He opposes everything I say? Faye lowered her eyes to the ground and shook her head.

"Do you pay the bills? Is your name the only one written on the side of those wagons?"

Jack thrust his finger up in Dan's face. "You know what I mean, bro. We have an agreement." He glances over at the wagons where Dan was pointing.

"Why didn't we send out the advance man, eh? At least people would know we're here?"

A small guy stepped up in Jack's defence, "Yeah!"

Faye laughed.

"Talk Denarii before you go planning jumps behind our backs." The small guy shouted. He nodded at Jack searching for encouragement.

Dan just smirked at him, looked at Jack and shook his head. He began climbing back up into the Wagon he'd driven for the past two days and threw his cap on. He looked around at the faces of those who had now gathered in support of Jack. A few women too, the usual suspects, descending ranks to slum at Jack's mercy. Jack was nodding over at his comrades, his smug face turning towards them for their vote of confidence. Then he took a step back, threw the jug of Ale up to his mouth, and quenched the back of his throat.

Leo pushed his hands into his pockets and walked off. Drawing his eyes up to his brother, Leo wondered if Dan had felt it too. He'd known for quite some time of the covert meetings between his brother Jacamo and the rest of the Jossers and had sensed unrest brewing for weeks. He had wanted to warn him sooner but feared he'd stir something up that would potentially pass over if they'd had a few good runs, but they hadn't. No one had been paid in weeks. That perhaps had been Dan's mistake.

Leo had been widening his eyes at his brother whenever he picked up a fly comment or sarcastic note and hoped Dan would hear it too or pick up on his warning signs.

"I know!" Dan said to Leo, without even looking at him. "Of course, I knew it was coming."

Dan had sensed it bubbling under the surface weeks ago, but hadn't said anything either. He had just been waiting, wondering when it all would kick-off.

He took up the reins and was ready to move on. Everything Jack had been saying behind his back with all the Jossers for weeks, both Dan and Leo knew; they knew every word of his well-oiled rhetorical bullshit that he comes up with at least once a year, like magma sitting under the chamber of a volcano, year in, year out. It had now reached its highest melting point with the effect of a subsequent violent eruption. He knew he was the only member of the Circus who had not yet heard the crap about to be unleashed from Jack's mouth, but he'd heard it all before anyway.

Dan wondered how many hours his brother had been sat in boozers with these drunken jossers, firing them up, encouraging them to revolt against him, while he fiddled off with some young lad he'd picked up as they all argued amongst themselves.

"Impressive," Dan said, laughing to himself. "It must be nearly a year since my brother last self-elected himself the head of this Circus, and still no other has had the notion of challenging him for it."

Dan looked at Leo and smiled. "Always makes me laugh." Even though Leo sensed this coming and was emotionally prepared, like Dan, he still felt betrayed, as he always did. Leo smiled back at Dan, thrust his hands in his pockets and kicked the turf.

Dan couldn't help thinking and tried hard to hold back his tongue; Jack is nothing but a drunken perverted Joey with a weakness for young lads, and even though he is one of the beloved triplets, he couldn't hide the fact that everyone knew. Lucky for him, as a closeted man caught up in a double life, his work in the Circus enabled him to jump from town to town to avoid the nick.

Dan stood up in the Wagon to take a higher vantage point with pacifiers prepared while waiting for his brother to kick off. Dan needed a minute to remind himself that he was still the head of the family, not just by choice, not even by birth, but by his infamous ability to be a better business mind. He knew his trade; his father before him taught him well-entrusted him with the business, and the others had then agreed that he was the best man for running the business. The other brothers brought their specialities to the table, which helped contribute to the show's overall success.

"Do you agree, most class me a fair and genteel leader," he said finally, looking down at his brothers from the Wagon.

"You fill the old man's boots respectfully; why?" Leo asked.

"I know my letters, business sense isn't bad, and some have likened my managerial skills to a board room officer."

"Okay," Leo laughed. "On occasion, everyone knows you can bare your teeth, especially against Jack and me; hey Jack, do you agree? Don't know if that makes you the best board room officer, though, bro, eh? Don't even know what that means. What are you getting at?"

Jack stood perplexed. He took a long drink from the jug and wiped his face across the back of his arm.

"Well, our brother Jacamo-Jack here, Jack-the-lad, or whatever his name is nowadays, needs to remember—the one thing, the one thing… and this needs to be clear to everyone!" Dan's voice rose as he looked around at all those slowly gathering.

"My position here is head of this Circus. The position is fast becoming unbearable, not for me personally, but for him!" Dan pointed down at his brother and laughed.

Jack was snarling now as he stared up at this brother.

"And…" Dan continued, "…it always baffles me how he gains such respect from you lot?"

Even though Jack was part of the Circus family and an actual owner of the business in every sense, he worked well, but most of the working Jossers, both physically and mentally, were more astute. Even the most simple-minded observer could see that he was a drunken idiot and nothing more than a Josser himself, so how they were always so easily agitated by such a weak leader totally baffled both Dan and Leo. Yet, somehow, Jack's rhetoric commanded respect and got the same delusional suckers to substitute their intellect for his brainless babble.

"Isn't the threat of war enough to turn any man's hair grey?" Dan shouted. "They say it's coming any day soon, but we are probably one of the few Circuses lucky enough to avoid it. And this, you know, so why go disturbing the apple cart now?" Dan shouted across the field. "In fact, lucky isn't the word. I at least appreciated that. The last war saw this Circus working in the forest collecting wood for the trenches when men younger than us were dying for their country! Our forefathers avoided being killed and shot because they stuck together. I'll see no one getting drafted to fight a war that has nothing to do with us!"

There was a chorus of cheers from the crowd.

"Many Circuses had their animals taken away, forced to disband, and good free travellers, who have known nothing but the great outdoors and the luxury of freedom from birth, were forced to join up!"

More cheers of agreement.

"The reputation our forefathers uphold with their horses enabled them to avoid being drafted. Our fathers celebrated together when they were granted an exemption for their skills with the horses in the forests. I say we work together to keep up that reputation, especially as another war is looming around the corner as we speak. It will come, my friends, it will come, mark my words! So, I am asking you now, stand with me—remain here at this site, gain strength, rest up the animals, clean up our acts and then…and only then, will we be ready to go to the larger towns and cities and regain our outstanding reputation. Let's make sure, for the sake of our wives and children, we never allow them to take away our freedom! Who's with me?"

Jack corrugated a stern frown at Dan, seething he made ready to blast his brother and regain the crowd's affection.

"Look!" Jack shouted, turning to his comrades.

"Bro, I'm not being outcast here when I put m' neck out to speak up," he shouts louder. "All's we want to know is how much you're gonna pay us for working this hole. It's all well and good preserving a reputation, but will we be getting paid for it? You say all the great things, bro, about reputation and freedom, but we still need to eat! We know war is looming; we don't need to be reminded by you!" Jack expands his arms to make reference to the crowd and their surroundings. "We aren't stupid! But working a shit hole like this isn't going to feed our starving wives and kids? Why are we here? What are we here for? If it isn't for the denarii, bro, what's in it for us?"

"Like I said," Dan replied. "I have reasons for coming here; you all need to trust me."

"What cut of the take are we in it for?" Jack repeated.

We're not just wanting a payoff; we're talkin' a cut t' cherry pie bro, by Christ, we're no mud show, we're family. We're all family!"

Rallying cries from the men in the crowd echoed through the valley. "Agree?" Jack shouted, turning to his Jossers for support.

"Well!" Dan said, smiling. He lifted his cap in jest. "Not sure you're thinking of the best terms for yourselves; often after expenses, there's nothing left of the pie—and yet, you have always got paid. I usually go without…and you too bro, as you are my brother and co-owner of the business. Remember how it works, bro, since you always seem to forget."

Dan scratched his nose. "See, your terms might not be the best for you or your men in the long run—yes, you need money—denarii, denarii, we all do!"

There was a universal murmur among the men and women.

Jack made a sort of reverence to them by throwing open his arms again. "Denarii! That's all we need to know! What's your cut—what's ours!"

"Really, still? Okay then!"

A little person, who goes by the name Stout, hobbled over.

"Before we lift another finger, we need to know what the hell you were thinking bringing us to a place like this when there are better sites up yon? Under any terms, and if there'll be nothing left for any of us, why are we here? No one will turn up out here; it's too far. Look at it! There's nothing here!" He took a step forward to rally the strong crowd of little folk. A Joey, one of the youngest nephews on Stout's side, thrust his hands up in the air and stepped forward, nodding. "Yeah, there's nowt here!"

"Denarii," Jack repeated, rubbing his fingers together at Dan. "We ain't lifting a finger until you can guarantee it!" They all agreed with a kind of mumbled grunt in unison.

"Or else we don't pitch no King Poles!" Stout's nephew shouted. More rallying cries of agreement filled the air.

Suppressing a smile, Dan was disappointed; he also found them mildly amusing. He hoped they'd got better at it by now, but no; same old argument, same old faces.

He hesitated a moment longer; as he stood in the miserable gloom of the early evening greyness, he wondered, if only momentarily—why? Why hadn't they all moved on? Why were they all still there, picking out imperfections like the sediment clouding up the whiskey they always had money to buy and would drink copious amounts of while plotting and planning a mutiny. This was not a life for the oppressed—the millstone that binds them to grind and toil; this was the 'Vita Di Circo-Circus life; Franconi life.

Dan sniffed, then shrugged off his doubts and announced, "Okay, don't blame ya," he said. He grabbed a cloth bag from his satchel and leapt down from the Wagon to level with them. "Winter's around the corner, what with war looming and all…. Everything we own in these wagons is all on the blink. The last time we put up the tent we had problems, agreed, remember? It's not gonna take a few days to put this show back on the road, as we'd like, and you know it, it's gonna take so much more than we can all well afford. So, if you're still planning to see out the rest of this season with the Circus Franconi, I suggest you trust me, let me do my job while you do yours. I've done this work all my life; I know some of you were around even then, but…" Dan looked at no one in particular as he began walking through them.

He heard disconcerted whispers among ranks. A notorious Strong Man known ironically as Wee with coarse, wild rusty hair whispered to his mate in earshot of Dan, "Yeah, but, did we make a good enough impression when we came through, cos without the advance man out there, I'm not even sure the villagers know we are here!"

"I reckon a few good folks know we are here. Don't worry about that." The Strong Man's mate responded.

"Yes, cooperation," Dan thought, gesturing with a discrete thump of his fists, one in the other. He was winning them back, 'cooperation', he echoed again in his thoughts.

Now at least they were talking to each other. There is no more abstract situation between Jacamo and Jossers, authentic debates with real voices speaking up, questioning, and wondering—a substantial discussion evolving, one with options, opinions, and solid ideas. His people were starting to talk to each other. Dan felt assured that while every thought was on the surface, positive actions could only be generated, and he knew it was down to him to make that happen. Sneaky revenge and evocative threats never lead any man to do anything good or constructive. Positivity all the way, that's what was needed. The Great War didn't kill men nor conflicting ideals, but the likes of Jacamo urging them to jump in on their clever conspiracy theories did, and Dan, having made a decision to bring the Circus to some remote place in Derbyshire, was all Jack needed to create the perfect one.

"Why would Dan want to harm his own business in times that were already difficult to stay afloat unless he was hell-bent on depriving his men of a living." Dan heard someone say.

Jack might have taken the perfect moment to form the ideal conspiracy, but Dan held one last card up his sleeve. The cloth bag he held in his hand dropped by his side. He shook it before letting it fall to the ground.

"I was going to sell these to raise the money for your wages," he shouted, "but since you are all so desperate for denarii, you can take them as they are. Not sure how much you'll get for them." He held the corner of the bag and let it tip open onto the wet grass. Twenty golden fob watches—pacifiers—fell in a tangled heap; cheap by no means, but they came less than twenty wage packets for a winning hand at the table.

"An advance...one for each family!" he began tossing watches over to familiar faces. "Here! I was gonna wait till the end of the season to give you yours," he said, turning to Leo and Dan. "It's up to you what you do with them, but I had them engraved!"

The multitude of guilt-stricken faces averted Jack's astonished glare.

As everyone stumbled forward to take their prize, Jack was shouting. "It ain't Denarii though, is it, bro…?" He reeled back on his heels.

"Catch!" Dan yelled, throwing a watch for his brothers. Jack caught it and quickly read the inscription on the back:

'Gifted to Jack Franconi, Circus Franconi, 1937'

"Had yours specially engraved, like it? Sell it, give it away. Give it to Faye – do what you want with it. In for a penny, what do ya reckon…?"

Jack returned the watch at Dan with such force and without warning. It struck him hard in the outer corner of his left eye, leaving a gash slowly welling up a trickle of blood.

"Keep it, you bastered!"

The men's eyes darted at each other. One of the older Joeys grabbed Jack's arm and pulled him away. He motioned to the rest anticipating Dan's reaction. Dan tensed as Jack kept striding forward. He grabbed Dan by both arms. One of the other stronger men positioned himself between the two brothers, and everyone looked towards Leo, who was now motoring over like a bull. Dan dropped his head and laughed, then exhaled slowly and dabbed the corner of his eye on the back of his hand.

"I'm alright, Leo," he said calmly.

Leo relaxed his grip on his brother and patted him reassuringly. As he glanced down at his new watch, Dan wriggled free and slowly stepped forward without taking his eyes off Jack. He bent down to retrieve the watch. As soon as his fingers felt the cold steel, the object became a weapon. His reaction utterly defies all laws of gravity and everyone's expectations. Being trained since childhood in the art of aerial aerobatics, Dan had inhuman agility and extreme strength; he swooped on Jack like a leopard, levitating from a crouching position, feet flinging out from beneath him as he launched through the air in an almost horizontal position, planting both feet firmly into his brother's chest. Dan's feet arrived just seconds before Jack's punch.

Their fight created a state of mayhem and forced all men to break ranks and begin a mass brawl. Jack was knocked backwards, left wide open; in an instant, Dan was upon him, thrusting the chain from the watch around his neck. It sunk effortlessly, deep into his flesh, forcing his body to go rigid. Dan stirred through wild, animalistic eyes as the veins in his hands bulged with the pressure he was exerting onto his brother's neck. Then jolted by the fading life in Jack's eyes, he let go and rolled off. He heard his own blood boiling and his heart beating in his ears; he tasted fear, both his and his twin brother's, who now lay blue and silent beneath him.

High Oakham Cottage 1937

Amy climbed out of bed and went downstairs. She was greeted by little Janey Price, delicate for her age. She was a bright blue-eyed sweet child with strawberry, silky fine hair that fluttered like cobwebs in the slightest breeze. Janey was so tiny, so polite and adorable. Her mother kept her neat and clean and taught her all the skills and graces she would need to one day serve in one of the big houses in the nearby city of Sheffield. Amy always wished she could take her home, keep her and dress her like a porcelain dolly. Janey's bright blue eyes flashed at Amy as she stroked kittens in a basket on the hearth and waited for milk.

"Janey! What a surprise. How long have you been here?"

"Mum's making cheese today."

"Yes, I know. Is that why your mummy sent you to order extra milk?"

"Do kittens like cheese?"

"Oh, yes, I am sure they do. In a few weeks and you can choose one to take home. Which one would you like?"

"Daddy said I can choose one all by myself." A broad smile wrinkled up her cute, perfect little nose, and she squeezed her large almond-shaped eyes closed. "I like this one because it is so soft." She pressed the kitten gently against her cheek and then placed it back among the litter. She picked up another tiny ball of fluff and stroked it before carefully placing it back. "And I like this one because it has tiny paws and a pink nose look, and this one has a whitetail. And this one because...Oh, I don't know." She giggled. "Must I wait two whole weeks? Can't I take one home today?"

"How would you manage to carry home a kitten and yourself all at the same time?"

"I'll come back tomorrow."

"Okay, but they are still too young to take away from their mother, and your mother needs you to help her make that Cheese. Think how upset the Circus

65

people will be if they don't get their Cheese in the morning. No doubt they'll come into the village once they have put up their tent."

Janey's large almond-shaped eyes lit up.

"Did you see them yesterday, Amy? Did you, the Clowns, the stripy horses, and the elephant!"

Amy gave the urn she was washing a quick shake and screwed the cap tighter. "What time did your mother say she was coming to collect the milk?"

"I've forgotten!"

"Zebras."

"What?"

"The stripy horses," Amy said, flicking a strand of stray hair from Janey's face, "They are called Zebras."

Janey cocked her head to one side and thought about it. She looked up wide-eyed as Amy placed the milk urn at her feet. "There we go. Let me see if you can pick it up?"

Janey grasped the urn handle with both hands, her tiny pale fingers changing a funny shade of blue as she heaved with all her strength.

"And it hasn't even got any milk in it yet." Amy laughed.

"We should wait for your mother to collect you. I didn't see the Circus arrive," she said as Janey returned to the kittens, "but I heard all about it."

She placed the urn on the table. Janey climbed onto a chair and tried to pick it up herself again but dropped it back down heavily.

"Come on." She took it from her. "Open the door; I'll fill this and take you home."

"Just let me say goodbye." Janey tucked her skirt behind her knees and crouched beside the basket of kittens.

"Oh, I don't want to leave them."

"You can visit them anytime you like."

Amy left her crouched beside the kittens awhile and went off to fill the urn with what small amount of milk she had, then returned a moment later to find her still stroking away.

"Amy!" "Come with me, lass. I need to get over t' fields –" A sudden gust of wind brought in a few stray leaves from outside.

Seeing Janey, Amy's Dad removed his cap and changed his tone. "Hello there, little missy!"

Janey rose quickly from the kittens and took Amy's hand.

66

"Taking one home with you?" the old man said, winking at Amy as he ducked through the cottage door.

"No, not today, Dad –" Amy shook her head, silently indicating for him to stop encouraging her.

"Don't listen to her; she's a bossy old boot, isn't that right, missy?" He winked. "And why not?" he dropped a brace of rabbits on the table.

He turned back to the door to close it, overbalanced and staggered slightly."

"It's barely ten o'clock Dad, you're already –"

"…Hey, missy!" he called out over his shoulder. Ignoring Amy, he staggered again, walked towards Janey, lifted her chin gently, and looked into her bright eyes.

"You take one home with you if you want one."

"Don't listen to him, Janey," Amy said, pushing her dad's hand away from the child. "Come on. Let's get you and that milk home before your mum wonders where you've got to."

With one hand firmly wrapped around a bottle, the old man slid slowly along the table, grasping at chairs for stability.

"Them there Gypos are in m' field!"

"Ahy Pop, I know. I'll go talk to them once I've dropped Janey home. She quickly removed the bottle from him.

"Alright, alright. Come on, Missy." The old man gave a courtly bow, took her hand, and hooked her arm over his. She reached out for Amy, who gave her a reassuring nod.

"Can you skip?" he asked.

"Yes," Janey giggled.

"Do you reckon you can skip faster than an old man?"

Janey giggled behind her hand again.

"Yes."

"Calling me an old man, are you? I'll show you who can skip the fastest."

The old man gave a skip towards the door. Amy placed the milk down and clapped.

"Aye? Not as drunk as you thought I was, am I? He skipped out of the door. Janey let go of Amy's hand and followed along behind him.

As soon as they got over the brow of the hill, they began seeing Circus people dotted about along the road, which ran between their land and the Price's, much to the delight of Janey, who was beside herself with excitement. She chattered as they wandered toward the Price's Farm at a snail's pace. From the moment they left the cottage to arriving, a good ten minutes along the lane, Janey had excitedly planned her entire visit to the Circus from start to finish.

Amy's father did not share the child's enthusiasm and was only too pleased when he saw the roof of the Price's barn on the brow of the hill. Exhausted and not too happy either, he saw that the Gypsy caravans had churned up the narrow lane, and he cursed when he realised that the village children had broken down a considerable length of dry stone walling to take shortcuts across the fields to get a better view of the strange animals and trailers scattered around in all directions, and what made it worse, for as far as he could see, they were still arriving in their droves.

The gate from the main road was open as they reached the Price's farm. The kitchen was lit by an inviting fire, and the barn door ajar had a warm light flooding out from within, bringing a great sense of relief. Janey turned and tried to take the urn from Amy. The weight of the old man and the milk urn had been unbearable. The old man hugged and kissed Janey gently before helping her to the barn with the milk. Amy watched as the child hopped and skipped the rest of the way to the house with excitement.

"See you tomorrow," Janey called to Amy, waving and skipping backwards. "I'll come to see the kittens as soon as I can!"

A moment later, the old man returned with great delight, waving one last time to Janey and her mother, Rebecca, who was now waving back from the kitchen door. He turned on his heels and began waving the milk money in the air, which embarrassed Amy, especially since his usual sideways waddle was more noticeable, and he was looking peaky, a combination of fresh air, booze and physical strain. Amy could tell it was all taking its toll and wondered if she'd get him home, let alone over the fields.

The Price's farm, once arable, now had only a few sheep and cows and the odd chicken. Since Mr Price (Gregory) returned home from the War in November of 1918 minus a left hand, it was inevitable that the land would fall fallow.

"I barely remember our land ever looking any different; green, lush and prolific as it used to be when Mum and my brother were alive," Amy whispered to her father. "It is all but a faded childhood memory now."

"I know." He agreed sternly. "Our land and theirs no longer reflect a desire for life, let alone its sustainability."

Amy was impressed. On occasion, there was the odd flash of her old father, who had once been a man of great respectability, but since the death of his wife and son, he was half the man he had ever been.

"If it wasn't for the small amount of livestock and a few fields of corn that we keep, this whole valley would be nothing more than moorland scrub."

"That's exactly why we should keep the Prices happy. We'll be alright as long as they keep renting a few acres seasonally."

Amy looked over the mass expanse and tried to imagine her mother strolling beneath the early evening moon. She gazed up at a violet streak across the sky— an icy bite could be felt upon the breeze. The sky seemed to spark a memory. Suddenly Amy remembered her mother chasing her down the hill with a big bright smile. She glanced down at her hand and tried to remember what her mother's hand felt like in hers. She could still hear her gentle voice telling stories of days gone by. She drew a fold of her shawl around her cheek and linked an arm with her father's. Nowadays, he just kicked his heels and took life easy. When he wasn't staring at the bottom of a bottle, memories of much the same filled his days too.

"Crumbling barns, broken down walls, and barren fields are not that important," Amy reassured him , then gave his arm a light squeeze. "We still have each other."

"That we do love, and as long as the Prices rent our land, we can still cherish its memories."

"Do you remember when the Circus last came to town, Dad?"

"They embraced this horizon annually at one time," he said, straightening his cap to make himself more presentable. "Yes, of course, I remember, but it was a few years ago; why?"

"I'm always happy to see the Prices work our land, especially as I know it's the one thing that mother would have wanted – an alliance with our neighbours." She said, "This lot...." pointing at the field ahead, full of caravans, carts and horses, "...they'll give us a bit of money for a day or two."

Amy and the old man came to a halt by the road. They were forced to wait for a pony and trap to be freed from the mud.

"Yes, they will, but do they need to churn the paths?"

"Hmm, I see what you mean."

"How's the milk cart meant to travel down to the cottage in the morning?"

"Maybe they'll buy produce," Amy said, trying to console him. "That will make up for it."

It was hard to decipher who they were supposed to be looking for when they reached the site, which appeared to be at the hub of the Franconi Enterprise. Amy was surprised at the ripple of excitement she felt in her stomach, like a child again.

"I haven't seen a Circus since I was young," she said with a little giggle. The excitement and anticipation of what the Circus had to hold were as thrilling to Amy in her thirties as it was when she was a child. The sweet, smoky aroma of campfires and Paraffin reached their noses a while before the lights from their campfires could be seen flickering in the distance. Dark-skinned and strange people ushered items in and out of caravans in a distant silence, busy, purposeful and bizarrely wrapped in their own world.

"It's a Mr Danielle Franconi you need to speak to." The old man said. "I made enquiries in the village." His brows furrowed, as they frequently did when he tried to focus through a drunken blur.

"I exchanged words with him at the Traveller's Rest earlier and told him I'd go over a few things before he set up camp. He reminded me that Mr Leo Franconi senior brought the Circus to our farm several times as a young man before you were born."

"Hmm, okay."

"You were just a little' un the last time they came; maybe five or six. The Franconis couldn't afford to pay, so we had a game in the Traveller's, and I won his old Showman's Traction Engine from him. He cleared his debt, and I never saw them again –"

"I was 10, actually."

"Ten, my, where's the time gone…?"

The old man's eyes scanned the landscape with the far-off look he often got when speaking of the past. He sighed, removed his cap and twisted it. "Wish I never laid hands on that damn machine –"

"Why?"

"Farm was lucrative in those days," he said, shaking the creases from his cap. "We made a good living, your mum and me."

Amy ruffled his snowy white hair before he replaced the cap back on his head and smiled. "Come on then…" she said. "You go first; I'll follow. Did they leave on good terms after losing the Engine?" Amy asked, sensing her father holding back; taking the lead, she turned to face the ensemble.

"Yeah, they were a good lot. Gypos are hard workers, you know? They help out on the farms, potato picking, ploughing, bailing, fruit picking, you name it."

The old man stumbled. Amy steadied him.

"Alright, alright… It's erm a Mr…?"

"Franconi, Dad. You said it was Leo Franconi?"

"No, no, that was the dad. It's Dan you need to speak to. He's the one… the one who is interested in the traction Engine."

"But you've always said we'd never part with it!"

"Not ever, but he's heard the stories. If he mentions it, tell him it's not for sale, nor is it up for collateral! I always said that if you find a good husband, there's at least 800 pounds worth of machinery for your dowry. It's not going to waste."

"How much!"

"Go, go and sort out this rabble. Whatever Dan says about that Engine, it's not for sale!"

"But, Dad, we can use that money. If he wants it, take the money and run."

"No, never mind that. It's yours when the time comes, it's not for sale, and that's that!"

Amy left her father leaning against the gate; she hoisted the hem of her dress over her boots and set out across the muddy field. A burly-looking man with a red face thundered towards her. Believing it to be that of Mr Franconi she held out a hand. He breezed by, nearly knocking her entirely off her feet. She spun around to see him do the same to her father, who was now swearing and throwing up a quivering fist in disgust. The sudden jolting vigour tired him, and he reached with both hands for the gate.

Amy's heart sank. Disappointed wasn't the word for how he made her feel. No matter how often she saw him in such a state, which seemed to become more frequent of late, she always felt disgusted and embarrassed.

"Hello!"

"Oh!" Amy spun around clumsily. "Hello!" Her mouth dropped open. She'd never seen a man so handsome.

"Farmer's err…wife?"

"Wife?" Amy laughed.

"Dan Franconi, pleased to meet you?" He took Amy's hand in his and shook it vigorously.

"No, daughter! Well, I'm Dad's erm –"

"Daughter?"

"Yeah, I am his –"

"Wife?" Dan laughed mockingly.

"Yeah, no, no, I'm his –"

Dan scratched his head and laughed again. "Daughter, yeah, you said, I get it!"

"Sorry. Erm, oh God…Pleased to meet you!"

"And your name…?"

"Oh yes—my name, Amy! It's Amy!" She took a breath, wiped her hand on her skirt and offered it out for him to shake a second time. "You must be Leo?"

"No, I'm Dan!" He laughed again. "Leo is my brother, who is here, somewhere," he said, looking over his shoulder at the troupe who were all busy going about their business behind him. "And my dad's name… he's no longer with us, Amy." He paused slightly as he said her name and seemed to look over her. "Now that's a lovely name."

She heaved her heavy sinking feet free of the mud and turned to face him with a pretty smile.

"Amy," Dan said again. A frown wrinkled slightly on his forehead as he took her hand in his and introduced himself again for the third time.

"Pleased to meet you, Amy." He laughed and blushed ever so slightly.

Amy pointed across the field, as her father raised a shaky hand.

"He's wondering… my dad, how long you were thinking of staying? He said you spoke earlier in the village but didn't state how long you were planning?"

"Oh, a while," Dan nodded. "If that's alright with you? He quickly wiped a trickle of blood from his eyebrow.

"We need to do repairs; it may take some time."

"Okay, yes, of course, yes, that's fine. Keep the place respectable and pay one week's rent in advance; those are the only rules. There's fresh spring water at the pump in the yard, and we have livestock, too, so there is no need to pay butcher prices in the village for meat for you or the animals. We've hay also in the barn, eggs, chicken, milk, butter, that kind of thing. No cheese, though."

"Cheese?"

"No, Rebecca does all that now. You'll need to go the Price's Farm for that. We have a little pact."

"Oh, I see. So, Rebecca is still around, then? Good."

"Oh, you know her, Rebecca? And Greg? They're in the house now, on the farm, they moved into the farm; we took the cottage recently. We did a swop, see. We decided to let them take the bigger property when their child was born. Dad and I were rattling around in the farmhouse; they needed more room, so –"

"A child? She's a young un now, you say?"

"Yes. You know the Prices well, then?"

"No, not really. We had a brief encounter when we were over in Bakewell some years ago. How old is the erm, the child?"

"Janey? I think she's about six, nearly seven maybe."

"Wow, time flies"

"Yes, it does." Amy shivered slightly and curled her shawl tighter around her shoulders. "It sure does."

"The Prices' farm is just over yonder. That's the place there. You can just about make out the chimney stack, see?"

"Milk, eggs, meat and water from the farm cottage and Cheese from there. Okay. I get it. We'll take a visit."

"Yes, please do; I'll let Rebecca know you'll be going over. I allow her to make Cheese for the locals. They have a child now and need the money, so, anyway –"

Amy felt she was rambling. Her voice faded.

Dan removed his cap and screwed it into a ball. He leaned in to look at Amy's face while examining her eyes. Her eyes trailed from his hands to his deep-set dark amber eyes that reflected his amusement and curiosity. He glanced over her shoulder and flicked up an eyebrow. "Your Dad?" he whispered. "Heard he has a Showman's Engine for sale? Is that true?"

"Yes, but it's not for sale." She thought about asking him to make her an offer just to find out how much he really wanted it.

"Oh, shame." He sighed. "I'd like to see it all the same –" Dan glanced up. As he raised his head, his brow furrowed in a puzzled expression. "Is your dad alright?"

Following his gaze, she turned. "Oh god…!"

"Yeah…?" A slight smile drew across his face.

"Oh, bloody hell, Mary, mother and Joseph –"

"He looks very?"

"Drunk? Yes, he is—always!"

"I was going to say familiar, but yes, he does look a bit pissed." Dan was really laughing loudly now.

The old man was attempting to aim his manhood at the wall for a discrete pee, but the rocking floor beneath his intoxicated feet was getting the better of him. By the time Amy reached the gate, he'd disappeared beneath the long grass.

"I'll help you take him home if you like?"

"Leave him there. He's no use to me at home."

"Like this a lot, is he?"

"Aye, most days."

Dan removed his jacket and dropped it gently over him. "Aye, remember this well."

Amy shot him a glance.

"My dad –" he drew a breath – "exactly the same. Brings back memories and not too pleasant ones."

Amy watched Dan and two other lads striding around in the mud rounding up horses, and just as she began to wonder how long it would take them, a horse was bridled, attached to the trap and heading towards her. The old man looked feeble in Dan's arms, though Amy felt no pity. Dan scooped him up like a mother would an injured child and, to save Amy from further embarrassment, said nothing more until they arrived at the cottage. Amy pushed open the door wide to allow them through.

"Alone?"

"Just me and Dad."

Dan laid the old man's lifeless body upon the bed as Amy hastily began removing his boots.

"No husband?"

"Nope." She winked and smiled ruefully. "If I stay here unwed for much longer, folks will start thinking I prefer cats, sheep and cows to men." Dan shot her a sideways glance, then laughed.

"I suppose people could say the same about me if they wanted. Perhaps cats and cattle are easier than your father, eh?" His voice was warm and amused.

"You're probably right; they are."

"You're a prize catch for any man, as far as I can see. Tell your father I'll call back when it's more convenient." He sighed.

He threw his cap on, turned towards the door, and then stopped, "Don't suppose I could have a quick look at that Engine?"

"Don't know what you've heard about it, but I was told Dad won it in a game of…?"

"– Poker, from my dad, Leo, yeah, that's what I heard from my old man. I'd love to see it?" He looked at the sleeping man: the image of his own father in a drunken slumber. "What am I thinking? I'll call back tomorrow."

"Your jacket…" The cottage was big enough for both Amy and her father, but the sudden thought of Dan leaving made it feel so much larger. Amy was filled with a dreadful sense of loneliness, an emptiness she had never experienced before.

Dan flung himself around to take the jacket, then stopped. "I'll call another time. Goodnight." Amy stood holding up his jacket. He pulled his cap down over one eye and turned towards the door.

"Would you like your jacket?"

"Nah, it will give me an excuse to call back first thing in the morning." He winked and laughed.

"Would you like a drink before you head back?" Amy wasn't nervous anymore, but suddenly he was.

His eyes quickly scanned the room and avoided looking at her. "As you like."

Without looking directly at her, his voice grew serious. "You'll regret this one day!"

"Oh?"

"Staying here with him, I mean?"

"Oh…"

"Ever considered doing anything else?"

Amy exhaled and lowered his eyes to the floor. "No, this farm is my life!"

"Because you haven't met the right man?"

The house was dark and quiet. The old man began snoring rhythmically. Smiling, Dan removed his cap and smoothed his hair. "Don't be left on the shelf. He can look after himself, you know."

Amy reddened. "I know… I'm sure he can."

"Don't know why you put up with it." Gesturing towards the old man, who has now curled around on the bed like a small child.

"A few years ago, my father was like yours. I had a girl; she lived around these parts, actually. I was going to marry her, but I left. I left because my old man had gotten so bad he wasn't running the business properly, and my brothers needed me; then death came to my father, so I lost him, but I also lost my fiancé."

"I understand; now you're alone."

"I should go. I've talked too much." His voice echoed in the silence, and Amy was sure she could feel him cringing inwardly.

"Feel like I've known you for years." he laughed and opened the door. "I'll be back for my Jacket tomorrow."

As he walked across the yard, Amy heard him say, "I'll sort out that advance rent in the morning."

Amy smiled as she watched him walk to his horse and trap.

Impertinence didn't annoy her as much as it would if it had come from someone in the village. Dan was direct, that was for sure, but she liked it. She had never experienced anyone like him before; he spoke frankly, but it was with respect and from somewhere with genuine care. And of course, she reminded herself, he was extremely handsome.

"Don't rush off! I'll show you the Engine!"

Dan stopped dead in his tracks and took off his cap. "What? Now? At this time of night? Are you sure? I can come back tomorrow? I am planning on returning to pay that rent, I can assure you."

"It's fine. Come on. Look at my dowry, it's worth a bob or two, so I understand."

Dan's eyes lit up. "Of course, it's a fine commodity to have."

Amy wanted to bite her lip, but somehow, this man had bewitched her and was able to extract information from her about her most profound secrets, secrets she would never expose to others. In her heart of hearts, she knew it was because he was the only man she had ever met who offered a minute of his time and showed her an ounce of compassion.

Fresh air breezing in from the open door made the old man stir from his drunken slumber; he threw the shawl from his shoulders, rolled over and fell back to sleep. Amy closed the door behind her and crossed the yard. She couldn't help thinking, what on earth am I doing? Why am I taking this strange man into the barn at night? How had I suddenly got such a notion into my head that this is a good idea or even allowed the conversation to continue as far as it has? The man is a Gypsy; they hardly hold the best reputation around these parts, for goodness sake.

"Dad said you might be interested in buying the Engine; he was adamant it's not for sale."

"Everything's for sale for the right price," Dan said, holding open the door for Amy as she lit the lantern and stepped inside the barn.

"I'm glad he hasn't sold it. It is one of the reasons why I am here, actually, if I am honest."

"One of the reasons? The other reason isn't the lady you left behind, by any chance, is it?"

"Yes, well, that is playing on my mind, but with the sound of things, she is no longer thinking on me, so –"

"Righto …" Amy had already put two and two together in her mind but said nothing.

"This is still here, if that is any consolation. At least you can take a look at it. The beast that it is." Amy allowed the barn doors to close behind her.

"Hope your dad doesn't wake up. He'll wonder what you're doing in the barn with me." Dan laughed.

"Let him wonder."

The traction Engine was partly covered by a thick dusty canvas sheet which Dan helped remove. His eyes flashed over it as though getting an eyeful of a naked woman. He turned and looked at Amy, nodding with a broad smile. He began tinkering with various levers and wheels.

"Oh yes, she's a beauty, alright!" he blinked. "I love her. What is it doing going to waste in here? What a shame! You know, you can put her to work in the fields, at least put her to some use."

Amy sensed his mind whirling. "It's perfect." I'll make you a perfect offer?"

Amy made a vague gesture as if showing it to an audience in the Circus. "Ta Da!"

Dan laughed, but it was forced and brief.

"I'm sorry, it's not for sale. I waiting for my Mr Right apparently."

Dan shot her a look and laughed for real this time.

"That's what Dad says!" She added, "It's my dowry, that's what he keeps telling me!"

Dan kind of ignored the comment and only half-smiled again. Amy could see he was still so attracted to the metal lady before his eyes that he had lost interest in anything she had to say.

"Definitely, not gonna sell her then?"

"Nope!"

"You've no idea what I've had to put up with to get here just to look at this thing. I heard about it from my old man, but I just had to come here to see her. Many men have talked about this Engine, you know? And my men think I'm crazy bringing them out here to the middle of nowhere; I didn't tell them I've come to see this. It's a good job they don't know since I'm going back empty-handed. Does it work?"

Amy shrugged. "As far as I know, it didn't break down or anything; it was just made redundant."

"Showman's Engine, isn't it? The stuff I can do with this?"

Amy began pulling the dust sheet back over the machine; it was heavy and full of dead spiders and cobwebs.

"She beautiful!" Dan said, helping her to lift the sheet over from the rear.

Amy didn't wish to prolong Dan's disappointment any longer, and dutiful to her dad's wishes, she reiterated that the machine was definitely not for sale. Dan followed her out of the barn.

"Shame, shame, she's just what I need."

He repositioned his cap and fastened his shirt button that had come undone. "Might even have to marry you myself if that's the only way I can get my hands on it." His laugh faded when he saw Amy's mouth drop open.

"Oh well," she said as they walked back over the yard. "They're built to last, those machines. It will likely still be here when I'm dead and gone. I give you my permission to take it for free; I won't be using it then, will I?"

"Well, if ever your old man changes his mind –"

Dan laughed, knocked up his cap and scratched his head. "Such a waste, and I'm not referring to the Engine." He stepped back to revere her shape from head to toe. His tone was changing too. There was a definite hint of genuine pity.

"You must want it bad if you consider a lifetime with me to get your hands on it."

Dan laughed. "Trust me, I'd prefer to get my hands on you than on that machine, but a man can dream. Phew, getting hot under the collar here. Let me leave you before I do something I might regret."

"Thank you for your help today with Dad." Amy stopped beside his horse and trap and extended a hand.

"Don't mention it. We're leaving in a week. Tell your dad I'll make him a reasonable offer, just in case he does change his mind. Ask him to have a think about it, will ya?"

"Thought you said you were staying longer?"

"Well, now I've seen the Engine, and there's no chance of getting my hands on her; plans have changed."

"I understand! Goodnight!" Inconsistencies, Amy thought, how she hated that. His impertinence and sleaze. She felt ashamed. How had she judged him a better man than he actually was?

"Gypsy," she mumbled under her breath as she watched him climb aboard the trap.

"Goodnight! Oh, lighting rigging, by the way, just in case you were wondering. Tell your father I'd use her for lighting up the Circus."

He was grinning and shaking his head as he shook the reins. Why Amy found herself still admiring his handsome smile again, she couldn't say, but she was angry. Why had she gone and shown him that damn Engine? She wanted to kick herself.

Amy waved him off. He was still smirking and shaking his head in disbelief as he cracked the reins one more time and set off with a powerful jerking motion. As Dan turned the trap in the yard, Amy stopped the foolish waving. She felt herself stooping beneath the cold night air and reminded herself that love would never find her, especially with that damn machine looming over her in the barn like a curse.

As she stepped back inside the cottage and slowly closed the door behind her, she was suddenly struck by a dreadful thought, how she would never know if a man was genuinely interested in her or the Engine. No man she had met so far had more to offer, and none were worthy of that machine.

She looked down at her father as he lay peacefully asleep.

"That damn machine is more of a rival than a dowry. I should have told Dan you'd sold it!"

She picked up Dan's coat, which had fallen from the chair and dropped it over the back. She lit a fire in the grate and instantly relaxed into her old familiar self. As she bolted the door, she leaned back against it and shook her head, still very annoyed with herself and feeling incredibly foolish. Especially with Dad still sprawled out as a reminder of how ridiculous they must both seem. He had no idea whatsoever the torment he put her through, the drinking was one thing, but that bloody Engine was going to be the worm that decayed any chance of her ever taking a bite from the apple of life.

A sudden knock at the door stirred the old man and made Amy jump. If she hadn't just waved Dan off, never in a million years would she have answered a knock like that at such a late hour. Without thinking, alerting her father or grabbing the hunting gun, foolishly, she opened the door.

"Appalling place this! May I come in?" A man was already removing his cap and had one booted foot over the threshold before she could get over the fact that it wasn't Dan. Once Dan was out of sight, Jacamo, his brother, who clearly must have been hidden behind the hedge, had crossed the yard and had begun thumping heavy upon the cottage door with both fists tightly clenched.

"Can I help you?"

"I'm with the Circus"

"Yeah, thought as much!"

"You're here for Dan's coat?"

"Dan? Dan's been here? No, I've come to ask about rent; what's he offered you?"

"Offered?"

"For the duration?"

"We haven't discussed a rate yet. Dan is returning tomorrow with one week's rent in advance, but we never discussed a rate."

Amy looked over at her father, allowing Jack to forcefully push the door against her.

"Dad, wake up!"

"He can't hear you. Look, he's dead to the world."

"Do you mind?" Amy tried to close the door on him.

"Let's do a deal then –"

"I'm sorry, it will be my father you need to speak to about that, and he is sleeping right now, as you can see."

Hearing the commotion, the old man shuffled about momentarily.

"He's not fit to talk business; look at him. He'll still be in that state tomorrow."

Amy wished for her father to wake up, but with Jack already inside now, glancing around the place, she knew he would be an embarrassment if he did wake up, so she left him sleeping. She pretended to turn her attention to the dwindling fire and began stoking the embers. She gripped the heavy iron poker firmly in her hand and measured its weight in her mind, ready to take a swipe at him on no uncertain terms but her own. Jack began making himself home, pulling up a chair and lighting a cigarette.

"So, how much do you want then?" he moved the chair nearer to her and stopped by the fire; leaning over, he practically whispered in her ear.

"Or could we come to some other arrangement?" He suddenly looked at the kittens, squirming uncomfortably in the heat from the fire; its white-hot glowing ambers radiated heat into the cool room.

Amy felt Jack eyeing her. She expanded her chest, stood up straight, sharply smoothed out the pleats in her dress, and then flashed the Iron bar at her side, revealing just enough of it for him to get the message.

His tone softened slightly.

"I deal with the finances for the Circus, I don't know what Dan's told you, but the financial side of things is my job, see?"

"Like I said, we did not discuss anything, so perhaps you should talk to him about that." Amy opened the door to the outside world and waved over the threshold. "Come back when my father's around. He'll deal with you tomorrow." She waited by the door, pushing it open a little further.

To Amy's relief, Jack rose to his feet. She leaned on the door to ensure it remained open until he was through it. Ignoring the gesture, he began wandering around the cottage, picking up oddments with no genuine interest. He stopped at the side of the bed where the old man lay snoring.

"Sounds like a train. Had a few, hasn't he?"

"Look, come back tomorrow with Dan, please."

"With Dan!" he laughed mockingly. "Listen! You don't deal with him; it's me you need to speak to just so you know. Let me get that straight; I'm the one who decides how much we pay!" He spoke loudly, slowly, deliberately sounding patronising.

"No good talking to Dan." He laughed again, this time to himself. "We ain't staying in this shit hole long anyway, so it'll be too much whatever he offers you."

Jack's tone was deliberately threatening now. Amy sighed. She's prayed to god every night that this type would never turn up on her doorstep, especially with the old man being the way he is. It was no secret in the village that he staggered home in the same state every night. Amy had always wondered how long it would take before someone followed him. She took a step forward and wielded the poker. It was heavier at arm's length than she had anticipated.

"I don't know who you are, but you're in my home. I'm not asking you to come back tomorrow; I'm telling you!" She flung open the door again. "Get out."

Jack threw up his hands. "Hey, hey, hey, no need to be like that. Just wanted to know how much you're charging for the site. I need to keep abreast of things, that's all."

"Get out!"

Jack shot a glance at the old man and then thundered forward. He stormed out, leaving the door open behind him.

Circus Franconi 1937

The setup had been taking longer lately, but the mud on the High Oakham Farm was something else. Rain pelted against mounds of stiff canvas laid out in 4 squares in the centre of the muddy field, ready for the setup of the smallest tent, the one used to showcase the animals. The smaller tent set the Circus apart from others, as most only carried one. What with a lack of funds, a shortage of personnel and equipment, in what would be described as the ordinarily smooth order of things, the small tent would typically have gone up hours ago, but Circus Franconi was experiencing its fair share of disasters of late, in Circus terms, setup was the least of their worries. Since arriving in Castleton, disruptions were fast becoming commonplace. Two shows had to be cancelled in the last stand due to a food poisoning incident, which affected the air suspension team, first, then two Joeys and a couple more little people. And then there was an incident when a few animals fell ill from some mysterious sickness, which freaked everyone out. The whole crew were growing suspicious of all sites. A rumour was going around that a visiting act had worn green to jinx the Circus. Green was no colour to wear in the Franconi Circus. It was just a no goer in most Circuses, but the Franconis did not even allow the colour upon the animal's vestige. No Franconi, nor any member of the Circus family could record any green garment worn by any act, but who could still blame the gossiping, what with one thing after another? Even Dan was beginning to get superstitious; after all, superstition ran deep in the Franconi Circus, as it did in any other Gypsy life. Everyone was on their guard, each one half-expecting an emergency or catastrophe to occur at any given moment, but nevertheless, against all odds, while Dan had been otherwise disposed over at the cottage admiring the Showman's Traction Engine, his crew, for all their faults and foibles, had used their initiative and set the King Pole in place for the larger tent. Dan could not believe his eyes when he returned to the site. It was a sight to behold, pulling up into that field and seeing it proudly standing like a totem pole. Following Jack's fracas earlier in the evening, he felt that the assembly of the poles in his absence was somehow a token of his governance.

The idea of setting up a game of poker with a rookie jeweller in some late-night tavern on the road was the best move he'd ever made and just the right time when he knew his crew were on the verge of staging a cue – a genius move, if he had to say so himself. How was it, he wondered, did he always seem to instinctively know? As he dismounted the horse-drawn wagon, Dan began to wonder how long his show of chest-thumping and retaliation against his brother and cronies would deflate the multicultural alpha male egos in the camp. The Italians were quickly inflated and volatile, specifically among the traveller community. Jack was right about one thing: watches wouldn't appease them for long.

Dan's fears were short-lived and soon subsided as he approached the camp; most of the Italians among them are family anyway, he thought, and no matter what happens, they could still pull together when faced with adversity, so why was he so worried? Then, he grew suspicious and wondered what the hell had happened in his absence. Why had they all pulled together while he wasn't there to get the King Pole up? Obviously, they were quite capable of operating that Circus like a well-oiled machine with or without him; it scared him a bit. A lump formed in his throat, if not a tear.

"You all waiting for me?" Dan said, creeping up on a small number of Albanian youths gathered by a wagon to share a smoke. Leo and a group of young Jossers had a fire going and listened to one of Leo's notorious jokes that would go on for weeks without ever reaching the punch line.

Leo was ripping the Albanian guys about being weak and feeble compared to Italians as he wound rope around his forearm. He threw his free arm around Dan's neck. "Thought you'd deserted us, bro?"

"Where were you?" A little guy furrowed up his brow and spat.

Leo was more than Dan's brother; he was his right-hand man. Their father had travelled to the UK from Italy shortly after the war. The boys were family, but to Dan, Leo was the only member of the Circus he could really trust above all others. One or two of the Jossers started to step forward awkwardly, eyes not meeting Dan's as they shuck his hand; a few stepped back, colour rising in their cheeks.

"Hey, cheers for the watch, boss," one said, gleaming down at his new shiny time piece.

"What are you ladies gossiping about anyhow?" Dan said, offering out cigarettes. "Ah, rumours." Leo laughed. "Some say we're deliberately seeking out bad sites to fold us." Leo leaned relaxed beside the carriage and coughed and laughed, smoke snorting from his nostrils. Dan laughed at him, glancing over at the rest of the men and wondering where Jack was; he shrugged and laughed again. "Why on earth would I do that?" He said. The young josser's eyes flickered around at each other.

"That's absurd! No truth in that, no logic in that at all."

Dan drew a long drag on his cigarette and blew out a curling blue haze into the ebony night sky, streaked with campfire smoke and paraffin fumes.

"If only you'd talk to me, ask me outright about rubbish like that." Dan tossed his cigarette, observing its tiny red tip fizz out in the damp grass.

He noticed the younger ones in the group looked more youthful than ever. He suddenly realised he'd been steadily losing more experienced performers to other Circuses and to the sure wages of coal mines and factories, and a few of the more notorious acts were lost years ago to the Military. Circus life had always been challenging, but it was getting harder, and they appeared to be collating more kids who were desperate to avoid starvation in their own countries, or the trappings and confinement of the coal mines and factories—and now, with another war looming, Dan didn't know how many more would leave.

"Good men came ten to the penny once," Dan said aloud.

Leo rolled his eyes. "But those days are gone, bro. Oh, Jack's gone, by the way." He added.

"Yeah? Oh well…" Dan gave a deep sigh and rose slowly from the side of the wagon.

"Took a handful of watches with him."

"What! How'd that happen?"

"Who knows...his sleight of hand."

"Weren't until you left that we all noticed."

"Must have gone through pockets." A small guy, a skilled equestrian, said, striding forward with a serious expression. Dan couldn't help but think that he'd take Jack out if he was bigger; shame he wasn't a taller lad.

"He didn't get them all, did he…?"

"Dunno" Leo said.

"He didn't take mine," A South Asian Mahout said, whirling the piece around his finger with its chain.

"We passed a lot of pubs on the way in; no doubt he's staring at the bottom of his fifteenth pint by now." Leo cracked his fingers and began moving off.

"How you feel, bro?" he asked, beckoning Dan away with his head.

Dan followed him. "It's two or three hours since my brush with Jack; my head's still buzzing." Dan confided in Leo.

"Ya getting old, lad. You always used to scrap with Jack like that when you were younger," he said, sniffing.

He thrust his hands deep into his pockets and began coughing. "Wouldn't be anything to do with the pretty girl you took home, would it?"

He winked and laughed between fits of coughs and wheezes.

"I'd already forgotten about Amy," Dan said. And that was the truth, but he hadn't forgotten about that Showman's Engine.

He wanted it, and he was gonna get it one way or another. He hadn't come all this way for nothing. He'd already cut back and creamed off the top of the takings for months and he wasn't going to leave empty-handed, especially since the crew were growing restless and gossiping like old hags.

"So," Dan said, changing the subject. "Reckon he'll be back tonight or tomorrow?"

"Putting a wager on?" Leo said, holding out his hand. Dan took it firmly.

"Yeah, go on then, what do you reckon…?"

"No, you first."

"Alright," Dan said with great conviction. "I reckon he'll be back tonight with his tail between his legs. Where's he gonna sleep, out there with the sheep? He'll be back tonight; he likes his warm bed next to Faye."

"Who wouldn't, hey?"

That comment made Dan slightly uncomfortable, but he let it slide; it was just brotherly banter.

"Then again," Dan joked, "maybe she won't even let him back in tonight, stinking of sheep, the old perv."

Leo laughed. "There's plenty of warm sheep in those hills," he indicated over with his head and laughed again."

"Nah, he'll be back tonight."

"Nope, tomorrow, with his tail between his legs, like you said." Leo put his hand out.

"Nah, reckon tonight." Dan slapped his brother's hand to seal the deal. "Go on then—2 shillings, 6 pence—tonight?"

"On the morro, I reckon. Alright, half-crown it is?"

"On the morro?"

"On the morrow!"

Dan nodded, "Okay, we'll see."

Leo's wife leaned out of their trailer, wiping her overworked hands on a spotless apron! A pool of warm lantern light shone at her feet. Dan envied his brother at that moment.

"Is it ready, m'amore?" Leo shouted.

"Aye," she said, waving to Dan. "Evening Dan, want a bite, love?" Her soft Irish lilt had a warming tone—inviting, motherly. It made Dan feel even more envious.

"Nay, Iggy love, need to get the tent up!"

"In the dark?"

"Yep."

"Since when?"

"Since tonight!"

"Oh, my lord! Go on then, that I'd like to see! Leo, hurry up; kids are starving!"

"Eat without me, lass…!"

Dan always smiled when he heard his Italian brother speak to his Irish wife with such a mixture of accents.

Leo slapped Dan hard on the shoulder and then clapped his hands. "Come on, lads, let's get this tent up!"

Usually, kids from the villages would come down to help, but those who'd followed down earlier to offer assistance had dispersed along with the setting sun, which had now slipped back over the distant hills. It was not usual for the tent to go up in the dark; it was too tricky and too dangerous.

"Typical," Leo said, looking around anxiously, "Where is that rompipalle Jacamo when you need him?"

"Man's full of lies and secrets," Dan said, "Don't trust him. We'll manage on our own; come on!"

Leo strode off. "I really dislike secrets…!" He said to himself and smiled.

"Me too," Dan said, overhearing his brother's comment. He watched Leo round up his best crew members.

"Secrets are too bloody hard to keep in your belly," Dan whispered into the darkness.

The following morning brought the rain with such velocity; travellers and their youngsters were out in force. Despite the bitterly cold wind and rain, they bustled around the camp, trying to prevent everything from blowing away or getting soaked. Keeping things as dry as possible was easy, but drying them out once wet was another matter. The Roustabouts formed teams. Armed with a sledgehammer a piece, they made ready to drive wooden stakes around the tent, waiting to peg it out while little people ran the circumference of the canvas to gain clearance around the sides. Leo and Dan had called in the fittest and most muscular men on the team to hoist the canvas. They achieved an excellent thirty foot at least the night before, which wasn't bad considering they had no help from the elephant. They gained height by using the bale ring method only, but darkness descended when they were ready for the final hoist, and all hands were on the pulleys. The darkness was so intense; it fell quick, and it fell black. When everyone unanimously decided to leave it until morning, the crew couldn't see their hands before their own faces.

With the high peaks and surrounding moors swallowing up a hint of moonlight, night fell like a blanket of black crushed velvet thrown over a lantern. It was nearly impossible to see the bale ring, let alone each other. A new precedent for the Circus and been set; never before had the tent been left hoisted to half-mast in the middle of the night, but like everything else of late, discipline was getting sloppy, manpower virtually down to nothing, and like the amateurs they were fast becoming, the disturbance with Jack and six inches of mud, made the task of putting up a tent near on impossible. The ensemble was tired and running on low morale, so pursuing the mission further was pointless. In the stark light of day, all that remained of the job was to heave the damn canvas another fifteen feet before securing it off.

Everyone ate early and then made ready. A team of the most unlikely crew were assembled and waiting beside the tent at sunrise. Each group of small men took up a quarter pole and waited. Their job was to go under the canvas and push them upright as the tent lifted slowly above them. Someone, somewhere outside the tent, as they methodically ran beneath the folds of canvas with their side poles, cried out. It was muffled but clear enough to know that someone was in agony. Immediately, everyone was alerted. For whatever reason, their time-old method just wasn't going to plan.

As Dan ran backwards, he saw one of the ropes used to hoist the bale ring drop, causing the ring to hang lopsided. He threw down the quarter pole and scrambled out from beneath the tent. When he found the abandoned rope, it was hanging, locked off solid. He tugged lightly upon it, immediately sensing slight slack at the top.

His eyes followed the rope skywards, his worst fear recognised, when he saw the bale ring wasn't just slightly lopsided but had tilted entirely on one side. It had slipped into a vertical position without warning, and then suddenly, the rope he was holding with his bare hands whipped through his palms. He grappled with it instinctively before calculating the best he could do was let go. Dan's strength alone wasn't enough to stop the rope from whipping upwards as it released its grip on the bale ring. Now dislodged, the whole structure became uneven and unsteady. The tent slowly flopped down on one side. Suddenly, a sheer force hit him from the side, knocking him off balance. A pair of strong arms and bare hands took up the rope from the rear and began heaving.

The Asian lad, the best Mahout Dan had ever known, yelled out at his elephant on the other side, and voices shouted, "Pull! Pull! Pull!" Then a voice beside Dan barked out commends. It wasn't a voice he recognised, not immediately. Throwing himself at the rope, he hung on to it with all his strength and held it until the guy by his side heaved his entire body weight upon the rope above his grip. Dan took up the rope above his grip and heaved down as he released his. Between them, they eventually got a rhythm going. Gradually the bale ring looked even from their side, and the structure began to regain some shape and form.

Dan sensed that the quarter pole he had thrown down was being put into position, and the tent stabilised. He dashed around the tent and took up an adjacent rope until the centre was back to a reasonable height. Little people ran beneath the folds of the canvas pushing up the remaining quarter poles. By the time Dan had completed the circumference of the entire structure, returning to the far side of the tent, he had found Jack and the others kneeling beside Leo-collapsed.

"He just coiled over," Stout said to Dan as he approached with a look of sheer horror on his face.

"He was heading up the Bale Ring when suddenly he just went."

Dan realised his best pal, the best Joey on the job, had tried to take on what would typically have been a more muscular, fitter man's job.

"I should have stopped him... I knew full well he hasn't been well."

Jack looked up at Dan.

"Jack! You're back! Thanks. Thanks for jumping in."

Dan removed his cap and knelt beside his brothers. "Leo? Hey, Leo! You alright, mate?"

Dan couldn't help thinking that Jack's wrongdoings from the previous day had suddenly been cancelled out by his own. Why had he allowed his brother to take on the most challenging job in the Circus? Jack and Dan clasped arm in arm and rose to their feet.

"We need a doctor."

Jack eyed his brother in a way only high trapeze artists understand; a shared mutual instant glance that speaks volumes in seconds; no apology needed, nor words spoken. All was forgiven.

"He's coming around! He's awake!" Little Stout's feet pattered around his best comrade excitedly.

"Thank god!" Jack said under his breath.

"Get off me, you load of puffs." Leo sat up slowly and looked up at his brothers, rubbing his forehead, "Oh, Jack's back! When did you get back?"

"Just now."

"You owe me, Danielle!"

Coins jingled in Dan's pocket as he dug deep and tossed a coin down at his brother. "Half-crown, you bugger!"

High Oakham Cottage 2020

A loud knock came at the door as the sun rose over the valley. Len, staggering down the narrow stairs, bounced off the sides of the whitewashed walls before crashing through the small door at the bottom and stumbling across the kitchen into the living room. In three mighty strides, he cleared the room, bumped his head on a low beam, and avoided the last one by ducking before flinging the door open. He shielded his eyes against the bright, fresh morning.

A car with 'Marlow & Brown Estates' emblazed on its sides was parked.

"Morning!" A female voice sounded lively and wide awake.

Len scowled, scratched his head and grunted. "Yeah?"

Holding out a slender hand, a woman stepped forward, smiling brightly. "Good morning!" She said again. "A little housewarming from the agency." She handed Len a neatly wrapped bunch of delicate flowers. "Sorry I missed you last night. I was passing just now, saw the car, and the gate was open, so I thought I'd drop in. You had better get those in water. I brought them over last night; they've been in the car. Well, glad you managed to get inside. How did you get inside, by the way? Thought you'd ended up staying in the village or something? Did you find a key hidden somewhere?"

Len shook his head. "Sorry, who are you?"

"Oh, I'm from the agency, for the house. I should have met you here last night. Sorry, you must be tired."

"We thought you'd dropped by last night and left the door unlocked?"

"No. I did drive over and waited a while. Quite a long time actually…but –"

"Did one of your staff members bring over wood and eggs?" he glanced down at the flowers.

"Wood?"

"Yeah, a basket of stuff."

"Firewood?" The woman laughed…

"Honey as well. With a little parcel tag on it."

The agent comically rolled her eyes. "That wasn't anything to do with us; I can assure you. We're lucky if we get a Christmas card from management."

"Must have been a neighbour or a mistaken amazon delivery," Len said, scratching his head. The agent laughed.

"Please, come in." Len stepped aside to allow her to enter.

"There's only me and Bilal in the office," she explained as she ducked beneath the low door lintel.

"I've no idea who could have let you in last night." She was still laughing as she stepped down the little step into the cottage and then stood upright, looking around with a quizzical look on her face.

"Unless, of course, it was someone from the village. Honestly though," The woman rubbed her chin thoughtfully, "There aren't any neighbours between us; well, apart from the brothers Grim." She made quote marks with her fingers and laughed at her own private joke.

"The Grim brothers live further up on this road on the left, but no one has anything to do with them—they're a little odd; into Gothic stuff. I don't mind a bit of Steam Punk myself – anyway, you'll learn about this place in your own time."

She paused for a breath, which Len was glad of, then looked about. "There's no one else around here, not for miles. I'm your closest neighbour. You met my husband—in the top field—Mark?"

"Ah, right, him with the tractor…yeah, nice fella, said something about storing his Engine in my barn?"

"Oh, that's right. It's been parked in there for years. Mark's a bit of a collector of Engines. He already has a few in our barns; what with the farm equipment and tractors, we had an arrangement with the Davenports who lived here; Mark agreed to maintain their hedges in return for storage space in their barn. Mark's been meaning to come over and clear it out, but he's been too busy."

"Okay," Len said quietly. The woman was exhausting him. There was nothing that he wanted to do more than close the door and go back to bed, but now she was standing in the middle of his living room.

"Like I said," she went on, "I did pass by last night and waited quite a while, but I had to get home for my little boy. Mark said he saw you arrive, so we were confused why you didn't turn up?"

She spun on her heels and pointed out through the open door and across the far-field, where a tiny loop of smoke drifted over trees. "That's our farm house, see? Smoke?"

"Saw that place on the way in. That's some house. In fact, it's more like a mansion?"

"Our manner house, we like to call it. Yes, it's quite a property."

A small face pressed against the car window.

"Oh, and that's our son, James, or Home James, as we call him. I'll be with you in a minute, pet! I've got to drop him off at school before nine, so –"

Len nodded and smiled at the child, who was looking restless.

"Strange," he said, his mind returning to the previous night. "Well, someone definitely greeted us here, let us in, told us about the kittens."

"Kittens…?"

"Yeah…" Len leaned around the door. "Them…"

The woman's expression grew weird, her mouth falling open. She was shaking her head vigorously. "Don't know anything about any kittens."

"Take a look –"

"Oh, can I show James?"

"Of course, bring him in."

The woman waved back to the child in the car, and Len watched from the door as she ran back up the path to get him.

Len stepped back to allow the woman and her son over the threshold and watched as they slowly approached the hearth hand in hand.

"Oh, they're not here," The woman said.

"What? Oh Georgia, my daughter must have taken them upstairs, sorry. They were right there last night –" Instinctively, he shouted at the ceiling. "Georgia, do you have the kittens?" Then, realising she must still be fast asleep, he suddenly wondered how weird it must appear—he stood in his pyjamas, holding a bunch of flowers, yelling up at the ceiling to some unseen person in the loft.

He toned down his manner quickly. "Excuse me," he said, calmly correcting himself. "I'll go ask my daughter; she's upstairs. When we arrived last night, they were on the hearth, right there."

Len scratched his head and turned to go upstairs, then stopped. "Sit down, sorry, please, take a seat." he pulled out chairs, closed the door, placed the flowers on the table and headed off upstairs.

The woman stood in the living room feeling quite bewildered. She held her briefcase nervously and her son's hand in the other. They both followed the sound of Len's heavy footsteps with their eyes as he thudded around above them. Then they raised their eyes to the ceiling again when he began shouting.

"Georgia! Where did you put the kittens?" Len peered inside the tiny, darkened bedroom. "You got them in here?"

Georgia sat up. "What?" she said, rubbing her eyes.

"Kittens? You got them in here?"

"No!"

"They're not downstairs."

"What?" Georgia climbed out of bed, slipped on a jumper and Converse and followed Len downstairs.

"Morning Georgia," the woman said brightly as Georgia stumbled down the last tiny step and landed awkwardly in the kitchen.

"Oh, hi…" Rubbing her eyes, Georgia made her way into the living where the two strangers stood staring at her.

All four stood beside the fireplace, staring down at the spot where a basket of kittens had supposedly been the previous night.

"Strange." Georgia said, pushing the empty basket with her foot, "I've not moved them."

"Well, I haven't!"

"Someone must have."

Everyone turned to glance at the door. Len looked at Georgia. "That visitor?"

"Last night?" Georgia pulled a weird face.

The estate agent gave a visible sigh of relief and looked suddenly elated. "I'm off the hook then for not being here last night, as I said." She laughed. "Whoever let you in clearly has something to do with this property; the previous owner perhaps? They must have left the door unlocked when they returned for the kittens."

"In the night?"

The agent was nodding vigorously, "Mystery over! Thank god! I was worried it might be squatters. If I'm honest, all those dangerous scenarios were going through my head."

"The last owner still has keys, then? But that's not right!" Len looked nervously about the room.

"Well, no, it isn't! Technically, I have the only bunch of keys for here." She began delving into her briefcase, then tugging a bunch of keys free, she pulls them out and hands them over to Len. "Not a huge bunch, but they are strung together with parcel tags. Here you go. Please sign here; thank you." She handed over a release form and a pen. "Did you lock up when you went to bed last night, Dad?"

Len dropped his glasses down over his nose and signed the document before handing the form and pen back to the woman. He looked down at the keys in his hands and read the tags.

The estate agent craned her head and looked at the door.

She laughed. "To be fair, I did hear your dad unlock the door with a key before he opened it for me just now."

"I did? Did I?"

"Hmm?"

"Weird."

"Well then…" The woman sighed then glanced at her watch. "I must go."

Everyone looked at the door, then down at the lock… "There isn't a key in this door!"

"Well, it was definitely unlocked yesterday when we arrived."

"Rebecca!" Georgia announced suddenly. "That woman who met us last night was called Rebecca." Georgia looked at the estate agent. "Do you know her?"

"What does she look like?" The estate agent turned to Len for the answer.

"I don't know; I didn't see her."

"I did," Georgia snapped. "Was she the previous owner?"

"No, the owners were called Mr and Mrs Davenport, William and Barbara. Mark has had dealings with them because of the storage thing, but I never met them. They never lived here. I can check with the office to see if this Rebecca is a relative. The Davenports bought this place years ago. Renovated it and let it from a distance, or so I gather. This Rebecca may be a relative of theirs, a daughter perhaps? No one's ever really lived in this house, not for years"

"Rebecca Price, she was called Rebecca Price."

The agent laughed. "Well, that's funny. Sure she was called Rebecca Price?"

"Yeah, she told me."

"How odd."

Len was rubbing his chin, glancing about. "Yep," he was saying. "She definitely had keys."

"As far as we know," the agent said, "we are supposed to be the only ones with keys, but if they don't hand them all to us, I guess it's up to you to change locks."

"She knew we were coming because she was waiting for us." Georgia pulled her sleeves over her hands and wrapped her arms around herself against the cold. "She said we were neighbours."

"Well, then she must be the one who came and took the kittens in the night; baskets of kittens don't just disappear like that," the agent said.

Georgia nodded.

"I do know the 'Prices'." The woman did that quote thing again with her fingers. "The only Prices in the village are infamous. You know, THE Prices? You must have heard the stories?"

"The ghost story? Kind of found something about that last night."

Len pulled the paper from his pyjama pocket. "I was reading it in bed."

"Oh, yes. I know that article. It's about the little girl, isn't it?"

"No, it's about the 'Ringmaster,' or something like that!" Georgia found herself doing the quote thing now. "About him who ended up living here from Eyam after the Plague."

"Oh, I'm referring to a different story. I don't know that one."

"There are more horror stories?"

"Oh god, no! Just stupid rumours."

"What little girl are you referring to?"

"Oh, never mind. I don't know any ghost stories. Rumours start-up when places stand empty for long periods. Bed and breakfasts love to add history to their properties or a ghost or two. Helps bring in trade…there's never any truth in them."

"Go on," Georgia said, folding her arms. "Tell us the story, you know…about the little girl."

The woman sighed. "Well, the history about the Prices is certainly true to some extent. I should know; I am one." She laughed and shook her head. "I'll explain another day. It's a long story…but the ghost stories are just silly— honestly, nothing to worry about. The place is old, so people just like to make things up. Oh, my goodness, look at the time. I've got to fly. We've owned most of the land around here for generations, you see, and the Prices are famous around these parts because of the 'disaster'." She quoted disaster with her fingers as she walked towards the door. The air quoting thing was starting to infuriate Georgia. "Ask anyone; they all know the story. I'll tell you about it when I have more time."

Len and Georgia stood, arms folded, unwittingly mirroring each other, like father, like daughter.

"Sorry about that young un," Len said suddenly to James, whose little face looked distraught.

"Aw, sorry little un," he said again as he ruffled his hair and led them both to the door. "Maybe next time when those kittens turn up again, we'll show them to you!"

The woman edged towards the door. "I'll ask Mark; he might know who this Rebecca is. But please get the locks changed just to be on the safe side. You can ask him about the Prices when he comes to see you about the Engine."

"What Engine?" Georgia, pretended not to know, looking from her father to the woman.

"My husband stored his traction Engine in your barn, but Mr Davenport died before Mark could get it back. Whoever took over the sale of the place changed the lock on the barn, so Mark couldn't get in." She turned to Len and nodded. "No doubt he'll come over to talk to you about it

later today. God, is that the time? Come on, James, we're running late!"

Len shook the woman's hand and walked her to the car.

"The name's Rebecca, by the way," she said smiling. She helped the boy into the car, closed the door. "Rebecca Price," she said laughing, "It wasn't me who left all those things last night, though, I can assure you of that."

Len watched as she drove away down the narrow drive.

High Hopes in High Oakham Cottage 2020

Len crossed the room carrying a tray with two plates of freshly cut
slices of homemade bread, poached eggs and two glasses of fresh milk.

"Curtesy of the Ms Rebecca Price, who came a-calling last night."

"Whoever she may be…host, or ghost."

Beaming from ear to ear, Len sat the tray down on the table put his hands on
his hips and stepped back to revere his handiwork. "Found cups in the cupboard."

Georgia looked up from her phone, peered over her shoulder at the steaming
mug, and then returned to her phone. The light slung low above them suddenly
flickered wildly before extinguishing completely. They both looked suspiciously
at each other and laughed.

"Lights have tripped again."

"I know, I know." Len got up from the table and went into the kitchen to re-
set the switch in the fuse box. "The place is a dump." He came back moments
later and paused indignantly by the kitchen door. "But, we have acre upon acre
of the greenest pastures, and every 53,760-square foot of it is ours."

Georgia scratched her chin and wondered if he had sneaked a quick drink. A
crow cawed outside somewhere off in the distance as though laughing
mockingly. With the lights restored, Georgia swiped the screen on the phone in
her hand, pulled her knees up to her chest, wrapped a throw over her shoulders
and gazed down at messages from old friends; inevitably, going off into her own
cyber world, Len accepted that was the end of the conversation and sat back
down at the table in silence.

The brilliant glow emanating from the palm of Georgia's hand seemed to
wash her youthful complexion in a blueish filter. Len noticed how long her
eyelashes were and how porcelain her skin was. She reminded him of her mother.
He drew a breath and hung his head. "What time is it?" He asked. Taking a sip
from the milk, he glanced away from the table, grimaced in disgust, and then
forced another mouth full in one gulp.

"Eight fifty." Shocked at her own response, Georgia looked up. "Ten to nine! Is that all! Feel like I've been up for hours. No wonder I'm knackered!"

"It was that bloody cockerel that woke me up early." Len drew his chair in closer to the table and collected together his cutlery.

"And her from the agency, what time did she turn up?"

"I was awake already when she came."

"Yeah, me too."

"I'd expect cockerels to wake you up in the country first thing in the morning, not women hammering on the door to offer you flowers; didn't expect that at the crack of dawn."

Georgia laughed. A spark of life between father and daughter returned. "Joys of country living, eh?" Len poked a fork into his eggs. Georgia watched as they popped and oozed. "We should find it," Georgia said. "Wring its damn neck."

"That cockerel? Yeah, I second that. Save us from having to shop for dinner today." Len pushed a fork full of dripping eggs into his mouth.

"We do need to go shopping, though?"

Len's eyes drifted to the light above him. "We need light bulbs." He put another fork full of egg in his mouth.

"Could just order them online."

Len scratched his nose, opened his wallet and counted the money.

"No, we'll find a shop. There's no internet; you won't get a signal." He put the wallet in his back pocket and picked up his knife. "I called that number from your phone last night, that builder?"

He tore away at the heavily crusted bread with his teeth. "Rang them when you were in bed." He indicated over his shoulder, "Had to stand over there to do it." He tucked his hair over one ear and pointed at the window with his fork. "That's the only place you can get reception."

He looked up at Georgia over his glasses as she examined the fresh milk, sniffed it, took a sip and heaved dramatically.

"Jesus Christ, Georgia! It's not that bad." Len hid a smile. "Fresh milk," he said, pretending not to notice her repulsion, "Tastes like shit."

They both laughed. "They're coming around 10:00."

"Who?"

"The builder, and he's bringing a plumber with him."

"Good!" Georgia looked around.

"I tried to open the barn," Len pointed over his shoulder with his fork. "I can't open that either."

"Is it safe?"

"The barn? Dunno, why? I tried to prize the door open but thought I might as well replace the lock instead of breaking the door down. Since everyone in the village seems to own keys to every door in this house, might as well get all the locks changed to be on the safe side."

"What's in there?"

"Apart from their Engine, I have no idea, won't find out until I get the door open."

"A steam Engine; who has a steam Engine in their barn? It's a bit random."

"I'm not sure what I think about someone just claiming the contents of our barn. We've not even been in there."

"Ask for proof of ownership."

"Indeed! Good idea. I'm not just gonna let someone waltz in and take it. We brought this lot on auction with all its lot!"

"People are weird here. This place is strange." Georgia said, pushing the eggs around on the plate with her fork. Her body seemed to relax and slump back momentarily in her chair. "I don't know why but... it feels."

"Horrible –" Len nodded and laughed – "like it's possibly the biggest mistake of our lives?" He looked up at the bulb as it began flickering again.

He waited for Georgia's response, watching her as she dipped bread into the bright yellow yolk. Cooked to perfection, the skin of the egg popped, yolk oozed slowly over the plate.

"I like it!" She smiled brightly at her father and then lifted a piece of yolky bread to her mouth. She took a bite and wiped her mouth on the back of her hand. "I do. I like it here. Do you?"

"It's a bit –"

"What?"

"Dunno, like you said, it's weird; I didn't think I would say that, but it is." Georgia looked around the room. "I do think it's haunted, though, do you?"

"Haunted, this house?"

"Yeah."

Smiling and shocked, Len nodded and began tucking into his eggs. "No, I don't think it's haunted. I think it is spooky that you've changed your mind about the place. It's like my grumpy daughter has been abducted in the night and strangely replaced by a nicer, more, friendly updated version."

"So, have you! You thought this place was the bee's knees yesterday; now it's a dump."

"Ah well, that's before I saw how much work needs doing and how much money needs spending, but hey, if you like it, it means we're not heading for the nearest 5-star hotel in town, so happy days!" Georgia laughed, missing her mouth with a fork full of egg.

"Happy days? I wouldn't go that far!"

"We'll go shopping after breakfast!"

"Cool!"

"You coming?"

"Hah, not sure. I might set up my studio and hang out here, if that's okay?"

"Well, someone has to stay here, let in the builder and the plumber. They'll need to be paid, and they've asked for cash. I'll leave a list of jobs that we need doing, and you can pass on the message."

"No problem. I'm glad the boiler's getting fixed; it's freezing and feels damp. It will ruin my equipment."

"It would if exposed to it over a long time, but hopefully, we'll get it fixed today." Len rubbed the back of his neck and scanned the room. He pushed a fork full of eggs into his mouth. Georgia watched as half of it fell back into his plate.

"Great, danger averted!"

"What you working on?" He asked her.

"I have a new client; she's cool. There's no deadline or anything, so there is no rush. She knows we've just moved house too, so –"

"Good. Did you hear that?" Len jumped up and rushed to the window.

"What?"

"Voices. What time is it?" He looked about the room for a clock. "There are two guys in the yard. It can't be the plumber not at this time, surely not?"

"I reckon it is." Georgia peered through the curtains.

She jumped up and opened the door.

"Is it the plumber?" Len asked, following her to the door.

"Can't tell. Could be. It is that van from yesterday? Well, it is 10 o'clock I suppose."

"Nah, can't be them; it's too early. It's not ten yet"

Georgia flung the door open a little wider and saw the van from the previous day parked out in the lane. A gush of frozen air whipped around their ankles.

"Yeah, it is them. Morning!" she shouted across the yard. Len turned and watched her step into the dampness with only PJs, untied Converse and a throw wrapped over her shoulders.

"Is it them?" Len called after her.

"Yes!" she said, walking over the yard, her laces dragging in the wet, growing wetter with every step she took in the gravel. Len watched her from the door. The two men stood vamping with their backs turned against them. One guy was trying to blow smoke rings in the air while the other was hunched over at the barn door, hammering something with his vaporiser hanging loosely from the corner of his mouth. The other guy seemed to be telling him what to do.

Georgia approached them. "Morning!" White breath drifted from her lungs and floated in the cold morning air.

The guy who was trying to blow smoke rings stopped and turned. "Morning!" He removed the vaporiser from his mouth. The guy hammering stopped, waved the hammer without looking up, and returned to work.

"What's he doing?" Len was saying from across the yard.

"Haven't a clue," Georgia whispered back.

The guy attempting to blow rings in the air with his vaporiser turned to face her with a huge bright smile.

He removed his cap.

"Did we wake you?" He scratched his head, put his cap back on, and strolled towards her. "Sorry, did we wake you?" he said again. He quickened his pace and stretched out a hand to greet her. "Hi, I'm Jake. Is he up?"

Georgia was thrown entirely off track by his question. "Hi, sorry, what?"

Doing a half turn back to the cottage, Jake laughed. "The guy who rang me last night. Your husband, is it? Is he around?"

"Indeed. I am! I'm here. I'm the one who rang you!"

Len's voice came strongly from behind Georgia. He peered over her rubbing his hands together. "Fancy a brew!"

Georgia laughed "He's not my husband."

Four people huddled together around the kitchen table that bitterly cold morning. The guy with the hammer had left his tools outside and was coughing and wheezing over a water basin. He asked for it before entering the house.

"Something to wash my hands in, Ma'am," he'd shouted from the doorstep before cleaning his muddy boots and shuffling his feet on the mat outside.

Georgia thought he was joking at first; calling her Ma'am, but he waited at the door for her to oblige him, which she thought was the strangest thing she'd ever heard someone say to her, and it was only when he waited at the door refusing to enter that she realised he wasn't joking at all, especially when he held out his hands before him like they were contaminated with Novichok poison.

Georgia invited him in several times and tried to direct him to the kitchen sink, but he refused repeatedly and remained by the door rigidly.

"He's a germ freak," Jake said, walking in. "Won't come in until he's washed his hands, and he won't wash his hands in the same place you wash your dishes."

"Okay then," Len said before disappearing into the kitchen to make tea. "Boiler's in here." He shouted to Jake.

Georgia followed Len into the kitchen and exchanged a secret laugh about the weirdos. She returned to the living room, smiling with a bowl of cold water and a clean towel. The other guy, who had introduced himself as Jake, was crouched on one knee beside the hearth and lit a fire before anyone noticed what he was doing. "You have a back boiler," he said. "You can get hot water from your fire." By the light of the tiny flame that now danced invitingly in the hearth, Georgia placed the bowl on the doorstep and watched as the other guy rolled up his sleeves and splashed his hands in the cold water.

"Sorry, it's cold. The boiler's out, but obviously, you know that." Georgia laughed and slightly blushed.

"It's okay. As long as there is a detergent, like soap or something, you don't need warm water; that's just for our comfort. Soap kills 99% of germs anyway."

Georgia rolled her eyes and looked for her dad, but he was still in the kitchen making tea.

"I see," Georgia said slowly. She so desperately wanted to close the door on him. As she stood freezing, waiting for him to finish, she couldn't help but notice he was wearing an old-style cravat and gingham chequered cotton shirt. His shirt sleeves were rolled over his elbows, and his shooting trousers, frayed, greyish-brown, which he wore high around his stomach, were held up by a black leather belt strap with a shiny, bright silver buckle in the form of a stag's head. Also, Jake was accustomed to wearing rough forest shooting trousers made of nylon, with an assortment of pockets, articulated knee patch pockets, and a high rear waist. He also wore a similar shirt and wax jacket. Jake was used to getting strange looks from the ladies and sensed Georgia's fascination with him was apparent. Blushing, he smiled, then turned and gave her a cheeky wink. Georgia was mortified and so embarrassed. She quickly turned her gaze away, then secretly smiled to herself. Well, he is fit, she was thinking, and now truly smitten, she kept feeling her cheeks warming up and wondered if he could tell that she liked him.

He could.

Gazing back at him several times, Georgia quickly decided that she didn't really care if he could tell that she liked him. Something was mesmerising about him, about them both. They were amusing, and lord knows, Georgia needed a giggle. She thought that Jake had hypnotic eyes. There was something about his eyes, glistening in a way Georgia never knew eyes could shine. He's bewitched me, she was thinking. She held the door open for the other guy, hoping he'd hurry up with his obsessive hand washing, and tried desperately to stop glancing back over her shoulder at Jake. He rose from the hearth, saying something about needing to sweep the chimney. Georgia turned a bright shade of red and giggled like a schoolgirl. Then he picked up the ashes he had scraped from beneath the grate into a carrier bag and took them outside, mumbling under his breath as he climbed over his brother. "Shift, Josh!" She heard him say.

Josh moved away from the door to allow his brother to get out. Len, unaware of the fatal attraction that was going on, was agreeing from the back of the room vigorously that the chimney needed sweeping, which made Georgia even more embarrassed. In fact, Georgia noticed Len was weirdly agreeing with everything Jake was saying. Len strode into the room carrying a tray of tea and toast. He sat down at the table and offered out the rounds of scorched bread, which no one touched.

"Wood ash it's great for raising the pH levels in your soil," Jake said when he returned.

"Come on, Josh. Let me pass." He strode over to the doorstep and over Josh's water bowl. "I've tipped the ashes around back. It'll help make a great herb garden." Everyone glanced out over the garden and fields beyond. "There's a storm brewing," Jake said.

"Boiler's through here," Len reminded him again, hoping Jake would follow him into the kitchen. A blast of fresh air coming in from outside made Georgia shiver.

"Josh, come on, mate. People are freezing in here."

The cold rush made the room smell damp, like mouldy wood and rotting carpets. She wondered if the others could smell it too. The room, illuminated only by the light of the fire, felt freezing now. Another gust of wind thrashed rain against the windows making the kitchen door slam shut. Each tiny pane of lead glass creaked in the frame, Georgia couldn't help thinking she was happy she wasn't alone with that noise. It made her feel uneasy. She saw her breath condense on the pane as she turned to look out at the rain.

"God, it's freezing," she said. Shivering, she drew the throw tighter around herself and got up to close the door, but Josh continued to wash his hands on the doorstep, not taking a hint. Everyone slowly began gravitating towards the fire with hands wrapped tightly around mugs of hot tea, which Len had poured from the pot. They all watched as he ran the last drop of tea into his own cup and then turned his attention to the tiny flames slowly beginning to spit and crackle around the wooden logs in the hearth. He thought of the strange woman who came the previous night, and even though no one could establish who she was, the logs she had provided were really coming in handy now.

Georgia sipped the last drop of tea from the bottom of her mug. There was a sense of familiarity in the room, as though everyone had been friends for years. Georgia knew Len felt it too and thought it might have been northern hospitality rubbing off them both.

"So," Len said again, "this boiler, then?"

He sat forward and slapped his hands on his knees. Another gust of wind threw more rain at the tiny window panes; the cottage seemed to shake from its foundation. Leaves blew in over the doorstep.

"I'm sure those hands are clean now, Josh, for God's sake, mate!" Jake rose and waited to take the bowl away from him.

"The boiler," Len announced again. "It's in the kitchen.'

Jake leaned in towards Georgia. He lifted a finger towards her face as though he'd seen a smudge he wanted to remove. She flinched. "You've got your dad's nose."

The other guy swished the water in the bowl loudly and coughed; he flashed a glance at Jake. Jake shot him a look in return. Josh smiled up at Jake as Jake snatched the bowl away from him.

"You're taking the piss now, you bugger," he whispered to Josh.

Len, now beaming with pride, winked at Georgia, took one last sip of tea and rose from his chair.

"Indeed, she does look like me. This boiler then?"

"Okay," Jake said, sighing. "Where is this boiler?" He winked at Georgia and smiled, making her heart melt into her tatty, wet Converse. "Josh, come on, mate, go and look at the boiler!"

Georgia, blushing, toyed with a tendril of her golden-brown hair. Her eyes fixed on the handsome guy as he moved steadily across the room carrying the water bowl.

Len leads him off into the kitchen.

"Ahy, there's a storm brewing alright," Josh announced, shaking his hands dry. Georgia jumped as his voice suddenly broke the uneasy silence in the room. She was glad that he stepped inside and closed the door behind him. He shook his hands some more and looked around. "So," Georgia said, handing him a towel.

"Thanks." He took it with his thumb and forefinger and let it hang like it was on fire.

"You don't like germs then?"

"Who does? I see another lady in your dad's life," Josh said.

Georgia was mesmerised by the weird way he was holding the towel. She shook her head. "What?"

Josh nodded over in the direction of the barn. Georgia followed his gaze but didn't know what he was talking about; she shrugged.

Jake appeared from the kitchen. "Get the tools out of the van, Josh. It needs pressurising and the radiators need bleeding."

"Yeah, mate; what's wrong with it?"

"Ya asking me?" Jake laughed.

Georgia, still perplexed, suddenly had an aha moment as the penny dropped. "Oh, I've no idea about my dad's love life; I don't ask."

Josh laughed as he walked into the kitchen. "I was talking about the Engine, you idiot. Does it work?"

"What's he been going on about?" Jake said to Georgia shaking his head and laughing. "He was talking about the Engine in the barn, apparently."

"Ah, the steam Engine. Yeah, we need to talk about that – Josh, tools!"

Josh came from the kitchen and went out to the van, leaving the door open to the elements again. Georgia jumped up and shut it behind him, and sat down.

"You've been in the barn, have you?" Len said, leaning against the kitchen door.

"Yeah, changed the lock. Oh, here's the new key."

"Great, thanks."

"So, you do everything then: locks, plumbing?"

"When times are hard, love," he said to Georgia taking a sip of tea.

"We do need everything done, don't we, Dad?"

"Ah, he's your dad; I thought this was your husband."

"Err No!"

"I'm a mechanic." Josh announced as the front door creaked open. He stood with a bag of tools that looked heavy, even in his strong arms.

"You're a mechanic, oh!" Len said, looking at Georgia, trying not to laugh.

Josh groaned. "Whatever." Sometimes, he had the habit of coming across as out of sync, but he was no idiot. He knew when he was being laughed at.

"It's a real beauty that Showman's you've got in the barn," Jake said, placing his cup down.

"Josh can get it going for you. It's worth a bob or two, you know?"

"Interesting, but apparently, it's not ours." Len looked over the rim of his glasses.

Jake picked up his tea, took a sip and placed it back down.

"No, well, you're not wrong there." He gave Josh a nod and shrugged. "We were going to talk to you about that."

"It's ours!" Josh blurted.

"Are you going to fix that boiler or what? You can't just blurt it out like that, Josh" Jake laughed and shook his head. "He's not wrong, though." He picked up his tea again and took a long drink. The silver stag's head buckle flashed in the firelight as Josh pulled his trousers high up over his waistline. "It's dark in there."

"Sorry, can't put the light on, "Georgia explained. "We have no bulbs."

Josh didn't respond; he just sat down at the table. Jake looked up from his tea, shook his head, picked up the bag of tools, and went into the kitchen. Almost immediately, the pipes around the house seemed to clang into life and began knocking loudly as hot water surged through them.

"Sounds like Jake's fixed the boiler?" Georgia said into the room.

Jake reappeared from the kitchen, wiping his hands on an old rag.

"We don't know what you've been told about that Engine, but it has a long history."

"Basically, it's ours!"

"Well, his and mine." Jake laughed at his brother's impromptu speech. "It was handed down to us, like, you know, in the family from our Great-grandparents and that. Like I said, it's a very long story."

"We've not even been in the barn, have we, Dad? So, we don't know what the fuss is about, but everyone seems to think they own it. We haven't even seen it yet."

"We said we can't allow anyone to take it without proof of ownership." Georgia looked toward her dad and nodded in agreement.

"In fact, that barn is probably full of all manner of things were don't know about."

"Antiques, hopefully!"

"We just don't know. Everyone seems to be claiming ownership of that Engine, though; we know that."

"Could be my inheritance, hey Dad?"

Len leaned over to ruffle Georgia's hair like she was a child.

"Radiators are working," he said. "You can have your bath now."

"Yeah, you heard that," she said, ducking beneath his hand.

"That old steam Engine must be worth something; that's why everyone seems to be coming out of the woodwork for it."

"It's not like that, mate, not for us, honestly. It's genuinely ours." Jake stood up and pressed his hands down flat on the table. "If you haven't seen it, I'll tell you exactly what it looks like, its build and boiler number, anything you want to know about it."

"All's I want to know if we sell it, will it keep him in luxury?" Georgia laughed into her cup. "Pay for his upkeep in the pensioner's home?" she smiled as she joked.

"You're not stopping with me forever," Len answered.

"Good, I'm glad."

"Well, I'm glad you said you want to keep me in luxury."

"Dad, anywhere is luxurious compared to this place."

"True, indeed, but you don't need to worry about me; I'll look after myself in the future when the time comes."

"You ought to visit that barn," Jake interjected. He was growing impatient. "It really does belong to us. I was with this woman, see, and we split up and…" he sighed. "Look, just take my word for it. Josh will get the machine working, and we'll come and collect it. The trouble is, she's got bloody got the documents."

Josh's eyebrows raised slightly; he shook his head and sniffed. "We need them papers, Jake."

"Aye, I know we do, mate."

"Well then, let me know when the papers turn up because if it isn't running, it ain't going anywhere fast, now is it?"

"No, guess not. But please, don't let Mark get his hands on it until I can prove it's mine."

"Find your papers, and we'll discuss it then…!" Len suddenly sounded serious.

Jake changed his tone and tried to sound punchy and light-hearted. He'd learned from his Roman heritage to always keep friends close and enemies closer. He walked across the room and placed a hand on the radiator. "Our astrologer can tell you what's going to happen to your dad, if you'd like to know." Looking down at Georgia, he winked again. Georgia thought the winking was beginning to get a little creepy now. He rolled down his sleeves and gave her a gentle, playful nudge. She smiled, then stared wide-eyed at Len with what appeared to be fear. She was flattered; she liked the attention but wasn't sure about the blatant flirting. It wasn't something she was used to.

"You know one?" Blushing, she felt heat rising in her cheeks. "I do believe in all that stuff."

"What, fortune-telling?" Len was shaking his head. "Codswallop!"

"Well, we run a Hamlet further up the road; we've been there about five years, anyway, we've got this fair coming up at the weekend; a vintage fair with a Steam Punk theme, well, a Victorian, Gypsy, bohemian kind of theme running through it. There'll be a fortune teller there if you're interested."

"Oh, really." Georgia's eyes shot to Len's, who she knew was thinking the same thing. Rebecca's words, Brothers Grim, suddenly came to mind.

"Sounds great."

"We saw something like that the other day, didn't we, G?"

"There's has been a few of them going around lately. Ours will be better, though."

"We saw an old Circus wagons and Steam Engines, but how does the Gypsy thing come into it?"

"Well, we're Gypsies, aren't we, Josh?"

"Except we don't live in caravans." Josh smiled and walked to the window.

Jake followed him with his eyes and nodded. "We have a few rare breeds on the farm now, don't we mate? And the café is already open to the public. In fact, we have a few lamas coming in for the weekend, which should be fun."

"…And local cattle breeders are showing their breeds."

"Yeah, it's a community thing, if you like that kind of thing?"

"There's going to be arts, crafts, street food…and—"

"Okay, Josh, they get the picture."

"It's slightly different from the other rallies that have been going on in the area lately."

"So, this fortune teller then, is she/he a traditional Gypsy in a real Gypsy caravan?'

Jake laughed and nodded.

"We saw it, didn't we, Dad?"

"In Bakewell? That's the one. I've booked her. She's been doing all the Christmas shows; I thought she'll look great on the Hamlet."

Josh stiffened and began tapping his thighs—thrashing them repeatedly.

"Yeah man," Jake said, imitating a stoned gangster wannabe.

"Course I booked them, bro. Said I would, didn't I?" He held his hand up for Josh to high five. "It was supposed to be a surprise for him. He loves all that traditional stuff. Let the cat out of the bag now, haven't I! I booked everything you wanted."

The thigh thrashing increased but then stopped abruptly. It warmed Jake's heart. He hadn't seen his brother react like that in a long time. As a child, he would often stiffen up, go wide-eyed, and start thigh thrashing whenever he heard the ice cream van or was told Santa was on his way. Josh just could not contain excitement like most others. The feeling associated with the emotion was more of a sickening, almost fearful experience. Any trip to the swimming pool, or cinema, Jake remembered, would be preceded by the onset of sickness, thigh thrashing and crying, but luckily, now, although it was still noticeable to Jake, no one else would recognise the panic and onset of Josh's deep-rooted 'messed up feelings,' as he used to call it. Jack knew his brother couldn't cope with the anxiety associated with overwhelming emotions such as excitement or fear. Josh's childish idiosyncrasies were still there to witness, but, thankfully, to a much lesser degree, so others didn't notice.

"Engines? And the travelling Circus?" Josh asked. He suddenly felt his stomach cramp up; he wanted to vomit. He raked his fingers through his hair and sighed. "Wow, man! That's great news."

"Yeah, I got them all. We'll go over it later."

"We'll come to it, won't we, Dad?" Georgia said.

"When is it?"

Len sat, arms folded, nodding "It'll be a nice day out, won't it, love?"

"It's this Saturday and Sunday. It's on for...." He looked up at his brother. Josh was walking in a random circle now. "...Two days," he said, sighing and hoping his brother would stop doing that.

"Over the bank holiday?" Josh's excitement and surprise were cute to see, Georgia thought.

"You've arranged it for two days over the bank holiday? Fucking hell, that's genius!"

"Josh, language!"

"Sorry."

"And so, this fortune teller, where does that come into it?" Georgia asked playfully.

"You'll be doing the telling, won't you, Josh?" To distract his brother from endless circle-walking, he threw a tea towel at him that had been hanging over the back of a chair.

"No, you will!" Josh caught the rag and began wringing it tightly.

Jake nodded and laughed. "Yeah, I'll be doing it. We really are Gypsies, you see, Josh and me. It's true; it's in the blood, apparently."

"In his blood, not mine."

"It's in yours too, mate."

"Are you psychic?" Georgia's fascination had been stirred now.

"Liz, from the fair, she does the psychic shit!" Josh blurted. He knew her from the village. He threw the tea towel back to Jake playfully and laughed when Jake placed it over his head. "Yeah, she's like…" with the rag wrapped around his head, he waved his hands over Georgia's. Taking her palm in his, he flattened it out in his hand and began examining the lines and creases which made up her past, present and future.

"I see a man, a tall, dark stranger. Coming all the way from –"

"Castleton!" Len laughed.

Josh shook his head, laughing at the spectacle his brother was making of himself.

Len and Georgia looked at each other and laughed. This facade's sheer spontaneity and randomness made it even more comical to watch.

Len rose from the table, tucked his vest into his trousers, shook his head and walked away, "Load of old codswallop."

"Well, I'd like to know." Georgia tormented Jake. "Who is this tall, dark stranger coming into my life from Castleton?"

Jake was still tracing lines in the palm of her hand with his finger when Josh leaned in to look closer.

"I see a tall stranger."

"Oh, yeah…?" Jake joked, "Where?"

"Stood right here. I'm taller and more handsome than you."

"Who'd have you?"

Len laughed as he knelt by the hearth to rake up the cinders in the fire, which had now burned down to just an odd spark beneath a pile of white ash and chard wood in the grate.

"I see him, dark, with green eyes." Josh looked into his brother's eyes. Jake pushed Georgia's hand up towards his brother's eyes.

"Look again!"

Josh leaned across the table to look closer. He took a long hard look into Jake's face, then glanced back at Georgia's palm. "Grey eyes!"

"Look again," Jake repeated.

"We're twins, you fool. How can my eyes be different from yours?"

"Ah, so you are twins! I thought so. I thought you looked so similar. Just that your beard makes you look –"

"– Older. I told him that," Josh said. "Makes you look older than me, Jake."

Josh and Jake laughed. Josh slapped his brother on the back again. "See, Jake, I said that. I told you. I said you looked older than me."

"I am older than you!"

"By 30 minutes."

Josh looked over and re-looked into Jake's eyes. "Okay, your eyes are bluer than mine… or greener?"

"They are the same as yours, you Wally. How can you not know?"

"I don't know. I never look at my eyes. I'm not as vain as you. I don't stand admiring myself in the mirror for hours like you."

"No, but you wash your hands ten million times daily." Josh waved him off.

"My eyes are blue, you idiot!"

"Okay, blue then!" Jake saw colour rising in Georgia's cheeks. "Here," Jake said to hide his own embarrassment. Growing red, he took Georgia's hand in his again. "I'll show you how it's really done!"

"Come on then," Josh said, moving away from the table; he took a small bottle of hand sanitiser from his pocket and began splatting it into his hands.

"See, what did I tell you? He's obsessed." Josh walked away, shaking his head. "Let's hear it then!"

Jake pulled his trousers higher up his waist and squared Georgia's hand out. "Hmmm, let me see."

Josh laughed and retired to warm against the fire. He turned to Len with a beaming smile, "Shall we have a look in that barn then?"

"What?"

"The barn."

"The Steam Engine, Dad," Georgia interjected without looking away from Jake. "He wants to look at the Engine."

Intrigued, Len took his coat from the back of the door and stretched his arms out until he burped loudly.

"Whistle if you need us."

"Dad, God!" Georgia laughed and shook her head as Len opened the door. She thought how gormless he looked. Always did when he was around other men; a kind of butch, more macho Len would surface in the presence of other men, and Georgia never knew why.

"Come on then m' old," he called from outside. "So, you reckon it's your Engine then?"

"We know it is, Len. She nicked it, that bitch Jake was going out with."

"Well, I don't know anything about that, so we'll just have to see who comes up with the paperwork first."

Georgia and Jake listened to Len and Josh's conversation a while longer.

Georgia tutted loudly. "Here comes the whiskey story," she said.

"The what?" Jake was still holding her hand. She gazed up at him, rolling her eyes, then looking back down at her palm, placed her other elbow on the table and supported her chin in her other hand.

"Did I tell you when I was a student at University," she said mockingly…

"Did I tell you?" They heard Len say. They both laughed. "When I was a student at University," Len continued. "I once distilled m' own whisky in a barn up in Scotland."

"Told you!" Georgia said, laughing.

Georgia sensed that Jake was looking at her when the two men's voices trailed off, and their boots crunching in the gravel could no longer be heard.

"He did it the old-fashioned way, no chilling; real whiskey, no colouring, just pure oils and alcohol."

"Sounds like bloody good whiskey to me," Jake laughed.

Josh, so focused on looking at the Engine, paid no attention to what he was hearing about Len's whiskey, and Len didn't notice that Josh wasn't listening. When Len stopped and turned to let Josh into the barn

he saw Josh was already inside examining the boiler on the Showman's Engine. Josh stood back, lifted the collar on his coat and began thrashing his thighs with the palm of his hands. "Yeah, it's ours. Knew it was!"

"I've forgotten the jargon for all this," Jake said to Georgia.

Playfully, Georgia hit him.

"Let's have a look then." Jake moved nearer and pretended to trace the creases in her palm again.

Georgia felt excitement deep inside, a sexual excitement that she was sure he could sense.

"That's interesting."

"What?"

"This dark fella, he's Italian, blue-eyed, like me. Yep, it's definitely me."

"Oh, give over," Georgia pulled her hand away. "Stop it."

"Wish it was me."

Georgia stopped laughing and hung her head. She felt suddenly foolish.

"What's wrong? I'm only joking. What is it?"

"Nothing!"

"Here, let me look again!" He lifted her hand, held it closed between his hands, and looked at her with a seriousness that he hadn't done before. "Could it be me?" he asked quietly. "I'm only joking!"

"Stop teasing!"

He stroked her face, lifted her hand to his lips, and gently kissed her fingertips. "I'm only joking, mate. Right, I'm off." He stood up and pulled his jeans down slightly. "Let me go and check out this Engine then…You coming?"

There was a knock on the door. At first, Georgia wasn't sure if she imagined it. They both laughed. "Saved by the door," Georgia said, rising to her feet.

She flattened her hair and went to answer it. "Can I speak to your father?"

Mark stood agitated at the door, nervously raking his fingers through his hair. "I've come about the Engine."

"He's in the barn?"

"Oh, is he? Good!" He turned on his heels and walked over the yard towards the barn.

Jake shouted something over Georgia's shoulder. He rose from his chair and came to stand behind her at the door. Shocked to see him, Mark hurriedly walked back towards the cottage, "Jake! What are you doing here?"

"You saw the van. You knew I was here! I'm here on business; what's it to do with you?"

Jake placed his hand on Georgia's shoulder and pressed himself against her in a protective manner.

Len and Josh appeared from within the mist creeping across the yard. Their boots crunching in the gravel stopped.

"Dad!"

"Who is it, Georgia?" Georgia ran to him.

Len clasped her shoulders tightly.

"What's wrong?"

"It's Mark, Rebecca's husband. He wants to talk to you about the Engine. I think there's going to be a fight."

Jake pushed past Mark and went to join his brother and Len.

"It is definitely our Engine, Jake," Josh said quietly. Everyone stood in silence. "I don't think so," Mark said.

"Look, I don't know what's going on between you boys, but that Engine is on my property, and possession is nine-tenths of the law from where I'm standing. So, for now, I'm locking it up. It's like I told the boy's mate." He turned to Mark. "If you come up with the papers to prove it's yours, I'll let you take it. Until then, I think you should all forget about it."

High Oakham Cottage 1937

Despite red, watery eyes, a facial feature Amy had become accustomed to seeing, her father was washed, shaved, fresh-faced and smiling. He'd led the horse and trap from the stable and crossed the yard to pick up the milk urn from her.

"Wait, love, I'll get that!"

The horse breathed white plumes into the moist air. Amy thought it was always a good sign to see her father up and about, so to see him walking in a straight line at such an unearthly hour was an excellent sight to behold. The old man took the milk urn from her, "Ready?"

Amy laughed. "Do I look ready?"

"You look beautiful to me." He hoisted the milk onto the trap. "Go get ready, then."

Amy went inside to change. She tried on several dresses before returning with a curtsy at the door. She pirouetted girlishly; the old man gave a nod of approval.

"Let down your hair."

"Why?

"Amy, my dearest, God made you beautiful, but the most of it he spent on your lovely hair."

"Why, thank you, father."

He took her hand and helped her up onto the trap.

"Do you know why God put all your beauty into your hair?" he asked, shouldering her weight as she climbed aboard.

"No, why?"

"He had to ensure your face didn't outshine your handsome father's."

He framed his face with his hands and laughed.

Amy sat, smoothed out her skirts, removed the ribbon and shook down her hair. "Satisfied?"

The old man affectionately flipped the horse's mane, patted him firmly, and climbed onto the trap. He sat heavily beside her, causing the wood frame to creek and dip beneath his weight. The horse jutted forward.

"Hey," he whispered, beckoning her closer. The cap he was wearing was slightly askew and slipped backwards. "What do you reckon?" he nudged her annoyingly with his elbow, "Reckon I'll finally get rid of you?"

"Price's farm first." Amy reminded him.

The old man took hold of the horse's reins and doubled them around his fist.

"Meat for t' lions?" Amy enquired before he gave his final tug on the reins.

"Yep, got it. There's a Circus full of good, hardworking lads here. We could be in with a chance."

"Eggs?" She asked.

Amy's Dad ignored her, added a few choice comments under his breath about having a nagging woman beneath his feet, and gave her a few more elbow jabs before Amy, being the perfect lady, returned a few choice words of her own in retaliation. She gave him a playful thump on his arm before he finally succumbed to the demands of the excited horse, who could hardly keep still any longer. The horse sprang into action, heading across the forecourt towards the lane beyond.

"We've got everything," The old man finally said as he turned the trap towards the hill.

"So, what do you reckon?"

"Freshwater…?"

"Oh, for goodness sake." The old man sighed. "Women!"

The sun was breaking through. Under the horse's hooves, warm glittering rays of early morning sunshine evaporated the ice causing misty sprays of muddy water to stain the hem of Amy's skirt. Over distant fields, rain and dew gave way to gentle sweeping mists. The old man pushed his cap up over his ears.

"Why?" Amy asked, finally.

"What?" Pretending to be surprised by her question.

"Why, why are you so keen to marry me off?"

Well, there might just be a lovely gentleman among this lot who'll take a fancy to you. And why not? You can't stay with your old man forever."

"So, you want me to meet an old Josser and run off with the Circus? Every father's dream, I'm sure!"

"You don't have to run off. There's plenty of work around here."

Anyone who knew the old man knew he would exchange gossip and a drink with anyone who favoured him with a nod. When Amy was a child, she enjoyed listening to his tall tales. She hoped he would leave the drink alone today and grace her with the father she was once proud of. They rode towards the Price's farm in silence for a while.

"When you were a waif," the old man said suddenly, "This Circus, the Franconi Circus set up, right there," he pointed to the sight in the distance. The grass had been cut, raked into neat lines and awaiting collection,

"Then you were born, I lost your mother, and then as if that wasn't enough, we lost your brother in the War."

Silence fell again. Amy gave a sigh and looked out over the ancient hedgerow, bursting with bloom. She thought about why it always led to the same conversation; how they had lost everything when she was born.

"I lost them too, Dad."

"I know."

"But it's all in the past now."

The old man patted his daughter's leg and drew the trap into the Price's Farm.

"Amy! Amy!" Janey ran across the yard followed by her little Jack Russell, which yapped annoyingly at the lathered horse, who skidded to a halt, spraying the dog with mud.

"Where are you going?"

"To the Circus."

"Shh, don't tell her that." The old man was exhausted at the mere thought of taking her with them.

"Oh, can I come, Amy, please, please!"

The old man gave Amy a glare with a look of annoyance. "Ask your mother." Amy looked at her father with a wry smile.

Mrs Price appeared around the side of the farmhouse carrying a basket of eggs. "They're still laying loads!"

"Morning, Rebecca. Mine too," Amy said.

"Can I go, please? Please, can I go?"

"Go where?" Rebecca asked, looking at Amy enquiringly.

"The Circus."

"No! Absolutely not!"

"Oh, please. Why Mummy? Please, Amy!"

"I don't want her over there, mixing with that lot."

"Okay. Mummy said no, Janey, sorry."

"But Mummy, please, please. Why can't I go? Oh, please, Mummy!"

Mr Price, hearing the commotion appeared from the barn. "Morning!"

"Morning, Mr Price."

"What's wrong with her now? What is she after this time?"

"She wants to go to the Circus with Amy. They're taking over supplies."

"Why can't she go? Get her out from beneath our bloody feet for ten minutes. Go on, get off. Feed her to the lions and give us all day off, will ya!"

"Greg! Don't say that!"

"I'm only joking; they know I am."

Rebecca checked for approval from Amy with a questioning frown. "Just don't tell anyone she is from this farm. I don't want them coming around here. Keep her with you. Hold Amy's hand and do not speak to anyone, you hear!" She pulled Janey close to wipe her face clean on her apron. "Go on then, but your chores will await you!"

"I'll do them, Mummy, promise!" She ran over to her dog and squeezed it tightly, turning its yap into a muffled choke.

Rebecca Price carefully placed the few eggs she had on the trap next to Amy's and a bundle of neatly wrapped cheese. "I was going to take them over, but since you are going…I'll take the same price as you're charging."

Before lifting Janey onto the trap, she walked away to collect the items the old man had paid her for. Then before leading the horse into a U-turn around the farmyard, she dropped a demijohn of Mead on Amy's knee, stood back and waved as they set off up the hill towards the campsite.

As soon as the trap pulled into the field, hungry children, affectionately called Gypos by the old man, were upon them. A slender blonde girl rounded them back up and sent them off to do chores.

"Here, let me help you," she said, taking the demijohn of Mead from Amy's lap. Danielle Franconi poked his head out from a caravan grinning from ear to ear.

"Hello there, morning."

"Morning," The old man replied, cheeks all a-flush from the wind. He removed his cap. "Thank you for the, erm."

"Yesterday? Forget it. Amy, good morning!" Taking her hand, he helped her down from the trap.

"Please come in, come in." He waved towards a hand-painted and crafted bow top caravan.

The old man hurled Amy a distinctive nod of approval as he stepped aside to let her climb into the caravan.

Discretely, she nudged him and shrugged off his insinuation.

Lined wall to wall with hand-built beds, a large three quarter and two singles cleverly doubled as seats, giving the illusion of space and additional deceiving depth and width that wasn't apparent from the outside. The flooring, made of a worn dark oak, polished to the highest degree, shone and looked exceptionally clean. At the far end of the van, a pot-bellied stove warmly demonstrated its efficiency in burning logs. Amy could feel the heat immediately on her frozen cheeks. She had always wondered what the interior of a Romany Caravan looked like and was pleasantly surprised. She smoothed her hand over the lush upholstery and stared in awe at a beautiful Italian style hard-wood cabinet that appeared to house crystal glasses, expensive crockery and silver utensils.

Everything was immaculate, modern compared to the High Oakham Cottage amenities, and beautifully preserved and maintained.

"It's perfect," she said, almost to herself. Dan closed the door behind him and began bustling about until he eventually sat with a tray of

steaming china cups sat on delicate saucers.

"Amy allowed me to look over the Engine," Dan admitted to Len with a smile, albeit with a slight apology behind it.

The old man shrugged and sat back.

"Impressive piece of machinery that!" Dan said, handing out the cups.

The old man sniffed and looked up, "Yes, it is."

He raised a distinct eyebrow at Amy. She read his thoughts immediately, A million things he could have said about you, yet he chooses to waste his words on praising an Engine!

Reaching out with a trembling hand to take the steaming cup from Dan, he gave a long sigh. "I'm keeping it for my Amy; I suppose she told you that?"

"Yes, she said?" Dan shot Amy a look that she pretended not to notice. "I'd take it off your hands, put it to good use if you ever decide to get rid of it."

Janey tugged on Amy's arm. "Can I go see the animals?"

Amy shushed her. "Not yet, dear."

"You couldn't afford it, son, I'm sure."

Amy looked around the caravan and widened her eyes at him. She wanted to say there's a fair few pence worth in this outfit—horses, animals, wagons, expensive Italian furniture; where was he looking.

"I'd willingly let it go, but with all due respect, you'd be looking in the region of £800–900, and I was hoping that Amy's husband, whoever he may turn out to be, might put it to use around our own land. After all, that's what it's there for!"

"Mmm, that and much more. It's a Showman's, built for road use and can generate electricity. But, if Amy is thrown in too, isn't that just a bonus?" The two men laughed. The old man laughed louder, making Amy feel humiliated. They both laughed again, and Dan winked at her, but she didn't find it amusing. Why would she?

"Not quite that way around, son, but yes, the whole package is priceless, as you can understand."

"Of course, sorry, Amy. Just joking!"

The word package was hanging in Amy's thoughts. She felt like a commodity, and her father's odd humour wasn't helping.

"Mr Franconi. Mr Franconi, sir!" The caravan door swung open and let in a freezing rush of air that reeked of smoke, paraffin and manure."

A stout young fella struggling up the steps bounced in breathless. He hobbled further forward. Everyone looked down at his filthy boots covered in horse shit.

"Boots off, man!"

"Oh, sorry!" They all watched as he began unlacing his boots.

"Just step back out," Dan said. "Tell me from the door."

Politely, the man stepped back outside. "Sorry." He removed his cap.

The old man and Amy looked down at their boots and then at each other.

"You need to move this horse and trap because we can't get past with the rigging."

Dan gave him a shrewd look. "And you couldn't do that?

The old man jumped up. "Sorry, fella, that's me. I'll shift it."

"No," Dan spoke patiently.

Janey sniffed the air. "I can smell the stripy horses, Amy!"

"Zebras, Janey!"

"Wanna see them?" Dan said, holding out a hand. "I'll show you. Come on."
The old man was upon his feet. He placed his hand behind Janey's tiny neck and led her out of the caravan; Amy, looking for somewhere safe to leave her cup, suddenly felt Dan's hand takes hers. "You too, come on!" Janey shot her a look,

eyes widening as she looked down at Dan's hand holding Amy's. Beaming, she jumped down from the caravan missing all three steps. Dan took their cups from them and placed them on the steps of the van. "You don't need them."

"Lions, Janey…oooooOOOOOooooo!" The old man taunted.

"Oh yes," Dan joked, "That's where we take naughty kids first. Especially when the lions are hungry."

Amy felt Janey's hand creep around hers. The smell of smoke and manure was much more pungent now.

Another pair of little people stood beside the trap, looking quite annoyed, but didn't say anything or even glance up. Instead, they just hastened back to lift rigging and cabling. Dan climbed onto the trap; the old man set the horse off with a slap on its rear, then turned to beckon Amy and Janey after them.

Over the din of working Jossers and roustabouts who were whistling and shouting and weathered faced women yelling at children and children with rosy, red cheeks, pressing in all directions laughing and screaming, Amy tried to listen to Dan explaining the origins of all the strange and beautiful animals they had in the show. With great pleasure, Dan explained the where's and what fors, what they were useful for, where they had acquired them and how much they needed looking after.

Amy noticed horses roaming freely in the field alongside zebras, camels and llamas. A few other strange-looking animals were tied to wagons, but she dared not ask what they were. Janey and Amy flattened themselves against the side of the tent as an Asian boy leading his lumbering elephant into another field passed by with a bright smile.

After they had walked the circumference of the tent and returned to the entrance, Dan reversed a canvas flap and held it open. "Come in," he said, nodding towards the mysterious darkness.

"Get in," repeated Janey, pushing Amy through from behind. Deceiving the eye, once inside, the tent's dimensions appeared to grow, expand and extend upwards and outwards in all directions. Shimmering silk drapes at the auditorium's far end drew everyone's attention. Glancing up into the big top, Amy grew dizzy. Men were hanging from ropes and swings, carefully assembling rigging, ropes, nets, pullies and lamps. Dan's attention returned to the matter of the Traction Engine.

"You're not likely to reconsider selling the Engine then, Mr –"

"– Harley," the old man responded.

He pointed up at the rigging above. "Electricity, you see. I could light this whole place a treat and haul gear – a Traction Engine is what we need – what the business needs, if I am honest. And the only way we can achieve that is by using your Engine." Dan tramped off into the centre of the ring. The old man followed, glancing upwards at the rigging as he went, listening to Dan discussing the many uses for the Traction Engine in the Circus.

"It is something not many have done yet in England, you see. We wouldn't be the first, but it would help us put on one hell of a show." Amy couldn't help but notice excitement glistening in his eyes.

"Amy, I'm scared," Janey whispered, her hand grappling under Amy's bag that hung over one shoulder as she tried to find hers. For years Amy had longed to hold her mother's hand in the same way. Feeling the gentle tenderness of Janey's tiny warm palm brought comfort to Amy too. In an instant, a rare memory came flooding back, of a time when she remembers doing the same thing with her mother, doing just this, holding hands in probably the same place, and at the same Circus, years earlier.

"I'm cold." Janey shivered slightly. Amy wrapped her arm around her. "I'm hungry!" she said, looking up with tired, tearful eyes. The novelty of the Circus had worn off. The child grew restless and bored as the old man whittled on and on. A grey, short-haired puppy with sharp blue eyes and a black tail suddenly came trotting out from behind the silk curtains, chewing and shaking a boot hanging from its teeth.

"Okay, we'll leave now," Amy told Janey.

"No, not yet –" Janey scooped up the puppy and began prising the boot from its mouth.

A familiar voice came from behind the curtain. "Mac, you little…!"

The man who had presented himself as Jack Franconi the previous night at High Oakham Cottage appeared before them, one boot on and one boot off. "There you are… Oh, hello," he smiled at Amy and winked at Janey. "Well, hello again!" he reached out a welcoming hand, and Amy took it reluctantly. Jack patted Janey on the head. No matter how pleasant his smile, Amy thought she had seen quite the opposite persona the previous night. Not wishing to give him the time of day, she discretely moved Janey away and pulled her close.

"Can we start over?" he said, offering a hand for the second time. "I must have come over a bit of a…well, I was rude last night and drunk, sorry. No excuse, I know, but –"

Amy didn't reply or even allow him to shake her hand again. She turned away, picked up Janey's hand and tried to coax her away from the puppy.

"See, you've made a new friend," Jack said, stepping closer to remove the boot from the animal's mouth. He crouched down to stroke the pup. "He gets into trouble and chews things he shouldn't!"

Janey giggled.

Amy glanced around anxiously, looking for her father, hoping he'd walk over and offer support. He was still deep in conversation with Dan, now discussing the Engine in more intricate detail, or so she assumed; neither was concerned for her safety against the very creepy man.

"Look, sorry about last night," Jack said again; he seemed to whisper, making him sound creepier. "We were all tired, grouchy, you know? We'd been travelling for days—it has that effect."

Amy wondered if he thought he sounded convincing. He didn't. There was an unctuous tone in his voice. He sounded amused with himself and cocky, he certainly wasn't managing to align her sympathy with him.

She nodded.

"Dan thought it was his responsibility securing the site; crossed wires, you know how it is? You were caught in the crossfire last night, I'm afraid. Sorry about that!"

"Apology accepted," Amy lied, she looked around for Janey, who was running around after the puppy, giggling; the puppy appeared to be enjoying the fun.

"Amy!" Dad waved her over.

"Yes, Dad." She didn't hesitate to run over and join the men in the centre of the ring. It was all the excuse she needed to get away from Jack.

"This is Leo, the poor man collapsed yesterday, and he still hasn't seen a doctor. Can you believe that?" The old man was so concerned that Amy had to question where it was coming from.

"I said he ought to see Dr Smyth; what do you think? You'll take him, won't you love?"

"Sorry to hear that! Yes, of course, I will!"

"It's just m' chest!" He said, thumping his chest firmly with his fist.

Amy nodded, but her concern was for Janey.

"Excuse me." She gave Leo's arm a reassuring squeeze and left him standing in the centre of the tent, looking bewildered as she turned and walked away.

"Janey! Where's Janey?"

Walking the internal circumference of the tent, looking for a way out, it suddenly dawned on her, as she headed outside, that Jack Franconi was also nowhere to be seen.

Stopping in her tracks, she turned towards her father, hoping that he'd sense her concern from afar, without her shouting at him, but he didn't. Then she saw Jack slipping out through a side exit with Janey plodding beside him, holding his hand.

"Janey! No!"

Janey hesitated between the folds of the canvas.

"I'll come back," she shouted excitedly and waved before disappearing outside, clenching the wriggling puppy awkwardly.

Since Leo had joined the old man and Dan, their conversation was now on repeat for his benefit. Amy heard the odd word about mechanics reverberating around the canvas, but by all accounts, it seemed there was a bit of competition as they each tried to establish who knew more about Traction Engines. It seemed Leo was winning. He knew more and enjoyed impressing the men with his knowledge between coughs.

They all paused momentarily to offer Amy a glance when she called her father for the third time. Then Leo shook the old man's hand, which signalled the end of the conversation. Amy waited, but then the men returned to the conversation again, and the old man began discussing how he'd once ploughed fields using the Engine and acknowledged the great benefit the machine would provide to the Circus.

"Priceless, priceless… a piece of machinery like that in this trade." The old man saw Amy watching them, gave her a nod, and then restored his attention to the men and their interest in his dormant treasure. Failing to sense her urgency, Amy stormed outside alone.

Amy's search for Janey leads her around row upon row of caravans, down the side of animal trailers and into the open field. The place was a maze, lined with hay bales, washing lines, guide ropes and narrow lanes; a frantic mess of straw, Circus paraphernalia and mud. She scurried around the backs of caravans and carriages again, peering through windows, unintentionally gaining a sense of Romany life, like a fly on the wall, spying in on their strange existence, poles apart from that of her own, if not, more sheltered existence.

Amy was beginning to sense the troupes' solidarity and their strong family bonds, something she had never experienced or ever could, and even though the land beneath her feet was by birth hers, she felt outcast, alien, trapped between their world, one she was not privy to, and her own, which now seemed miles away.

Parched, anxious and drenched in a cold sweat, Amy stopped running and leaned against the side of a caravan. Struck by a hot, dizzy breathlessness, she wiped her parched lips on the sleeve of her dress. The dryness in the back of her throat and lungs was choking. Anxiety was getting the better of her, too; awful scenarios were playing out in her mind; visions of things unimaginable that could be happening to poor little Janey. Then, the most horrid thought sprang to mind, if Jack was repulsive and disgusting, she should probably be just as worried about the rest of his strange, street urchin, vagabond friends, and be equally as concerned about them.

How could she have let this happen? How could a good Christian woman allow a strange man, who she knew capable of such aggression, to tempt the child away from her in that way; and he had used the oldest method in the book. Why hadn't she stopped him when she had a chance? Wracked with guilt and worry, she failed to notice, between the narrow rows of caravans, a figure in white hedging towards her, half-hidden by the haze of her burning tears, the golden glow of the early sun, trapped between the sides of the caravans, bouncing off the sides like mirrors. The figure, a woman, spoke softly.

"Remove yourself from my caravan, please." Suddenly, Amy was the criminal. She didn't dare refuse; she moved away respectfully. The voice was female with an Irish twinge, gentle yet assertive.

"Can I help ya?" Her voice grew louder, stronger as she moved closer. "This part is private, not for public use."

Amy raised a hand to protest. "I'm sorry. I'm looking for a child."

"A child?"

Amy managed to speak between erratic heartbeats. "She's with Franconi, erm…Jack?"

"Jack?"

"Do you know him?"

"Ahy. What's his business with your little girl?" She sounded surprised.

"He's taken her –" Amy suddenly regretted her tone because it sounded like she was suspicious, if not even accusing. "He's taken Janey." She didn't care how accusing she sounded now.

"Taken her! What do you mean, he's taken her?"

"To see lions," She shook her head and smiled. "I think, maybe…I am just panicking."

Without a word, the woman turned away briskly and walked off. "What's she called, this girl of yours?" Faye weaved through the avenues.

"Janey!" Amy said, trotting along behind her.

"The lions are kept behind here." She stopped, glanced back and pointed. "Your little girl's here, fine and dandy, as far as I can see!"

There was a wooden structure, billboard-sized, parked beside the tent. As the two women approached and peered around it, they saw a tiny foot swinging, one sock rolled down to the ankle, and one grazed knee bleeding, behind which a sleeping lion lay undisturbed and still, its soft ginger fur protruding in clumps through rusty iron bars. Janey sat on the truck's tailboard, watching Jack Franconi as he held her foot upon his knee. He was wiping the dirt from the bleeding wound with a handkerchief. Janey quietly swung her other leg and hummed gently to the puppy she held on her lap.

She turned on occasion to touch the ginger fur through the bars. The women in white did not share Amy's anxiety.

"Looks like there's been an accident." She walked over to Janey, ruffled her wispy blonde hair and walked away, leaving Amy alone with her mind racing with irrational thoughts and feelings of embarrassment.

"The sunshine's low in the sky; it's that time of year, blinding, isn't it?" Jack said, shielding his eyes as he looked up and saw her squinting through the haze.

Jack tucked the blood-stained handkerchief away in a back pocket and spat, "So, it's still like that?" Amy didn't answer; she couldn't. She pulled Janey away from him and stood her on to her feet.

"Where are we going, Amy?" Janey stammered as Amy dragged her away.

"Home!"

*

It was around tea time when Amy dropped Janey off at the Prices' on route to Dr Smyth's with the increasingly sick; Leo sat beside her, shivering with fever.

Though she didn't even know Leo, she grew more concerned about him. It hadn't been a pleasant ride back, having to listen to his coughing and wheezing. It seemed to Amy that he was getting worse. And now she was responsible for his safety, too, thanks to her father. As he had pointed out earlier, the man looked increasingly sick, and the ride to the village hadn't helped any. His eyes, bloodshot and heavy, were slowly closing as his head nodded with the motion of the horse's trotting hooves. His skin was pale and clammy, and each gulp of air followed a fit of coughing, leaving him straining to breathe.

Amy was relieved to finally knock on Dr Smyth's green door, the one on the end row of cottages, which sat at the edge of the village. They waited for the Doctor's home help to answer. She would always be there, ready to respond, no matter what time of day. She led them through the front room into the back, where Dr Smyth was sitting in a haze of pipe smoke beside a blazing fire. Sucking on a pipe and reading a manuscript, he rose to greet them.

"Ah, come in. Come in."

Leo removed his cap, ducked beneath the tiny doorway and edged into the room. Amy followed, greeting the Doctor with a nod.

"Evening Amy."

Evening, Doctor."

"How's your father?"

"Well, Doctor, thank you."

"Good, Good. Now, what can I do for you both?"

Leo glanced over at Amy. She gave another courteous nod and left him to answer for himself. "I'll wait outside."

"It's my chest, Doctor." Amy heard him say as she closed the door behind her.

"I see. Fancy a tot of the good old stuff?" Doctor Smyth said as he reached for a beautifully carved crystal decanter. "You look like a man who needs one!"

"Never did me any harm, Sir, thank you."

Amy heard glasses chinking as she sat beside the closed door and waited.

Dr Smyth was notorious for sharing a glass of something substantial with his patience. Often, he attended his appointments slightly worse for it, but he was a good man, caring and well respected.

The Doctor's home help made Amy welcome with a cup of tea. She sat in the silent room listening to the clock tick, thinking how Dan had offered to escort Leo, but she was glad she had refused because the Circus had a show to put on, and this being the first night, would be the most important one and therefore allow them the means to pay their rent and tab that was slowly beginning to increase.

"Bed rest and a tot of ya' best brandy, that's the best remedy for bronchitis, young fella." The Doctor appeared, ducking through the door with the Leo following, still sipping on his glass. Leo rolled his eyes at Amy.

"Bed rest?' He laughed. "Well, now there'll be plenty of time for that when I'm 6ft under, Doc." His laughter followed a fit of coughing and more croaky wheezing.

"Aw, you're not quite there yet," The Doctor wrapped a bottle of fluid in brown paper, looked at Amy and winked.

"That'll sort him. He'll live to see another day with that concoction and a bit of TLC." Leo flushed, not from the misconception that Amy would be administering the TLC but from the room's warmth and the brandy.

He looked better for it, Amy thought as she rose, smoothed out her skirt and made to leave. Due to the home help's loose tongue, she knew there would soon be some speculation in the village about her relationship with Leo, but there had been the same speculation about hers and the Doctor's for years. Leo hung back to settle his fees with the woman.

Amy had never bothered herself with such tittle-tattle, so it didn't worry her too much as she said goodnight and closed the door behind her. The Doctor stood by and watched the transaction from the warmth of the hearth. He swilled the last dregs of Brandy around his glass before tipping it back.

"Thank you," Leo said, as he too closed the door behind him and ran to catch up with Amy. "That was very kind of you, er –"

"Amy," she reminded him.

"Very kind, thank you."

"Hope you feel better."

"Not sure what's in this," he said, holding up the bottle wrapped in brown paper, "but if it is anything as good as that, Brandy, I'll be fine in no time."

They both laughed, crossed the road and made their way down the alley to the rear of the Inn. Hearing them coming, the Inn's stable lad prepared the horse and trap. Amy reached into her purse to pay his fee, but Leo clenched his hand over hers. "I'll settle it," he said with determination; she retied the ribbon and slipped it back into the pocket of her dress.

The night air was freezing, moist and misty; lamps burning in the Inn windows penetrated the grey, brownish fog gently rising from the distant grass on the village green. Lights from nearby lamps tinged the air with a warm tangerine glow, and soot from the many smoking chimneys around the square sweetened the early evening air. Amy threw the corner of a shawl she used for outings over one shoulder, climbed aboard the trap, took up the reins and set off into the dark foreboding peaks that circumference the village-like sentinels on guard in the shadows.

As they reached the narrow point of the village where the streets are squeezed out of existence to make way for the vastness of the Derbyshire Hills, Leo asked her a question through another fit of wheezy coughing,

"Pardon?"

"I said, coming to see the show later?"

"I might do. Well, actually…" Amy drew a deep breath and thought a moment, dark thoughts of what might be waiting for her back home. The question led her attention into the depth of the night. Struck by a sudden sickening suspicion, Amy wondered if her father had an ulterior motive, sending her, un-chaperoned out into the night, to escort a stranger, albeit a decent man, to visit the Doctor. Had he used the opportunity to allow her the pleasure of meeting a lovely young man, or he'd been so desperate for a drink that he couldn't wait to see the back of her? After all, her father had been sober for the best part of the day; he was starting to show signs of desperation.

"Not sure, might do," she said finally.

"Good, hope so!" he replied, nodding towards the distant hill where smoke rose from the many campfires.

"You will follow the doctor's orders, I hope?"

"What? Sleep?" Leo laughed.

"Yes, take yourself straight off to bed?"

Leo turned his head towards the darkness again. "No, rest is not for the wicked," he mumbled.

Amy cracked the reins. The horse stepped up its pace.

"Dan won't let you lift a finger after your episode yesterday, I'm sure."

Leo laughed again and coughed.

"He'll want me at work as soon as I get back; there's no time for illness in the Circus. The show must go on, you know the saying."

"Not a kind man to work for then?"

"Work for?" Leo looked surprised.

Amy was beginning to think they were talking about different people.

"No one works for Dan." The man burst into another fit of coughing.

"You okay?" She gave him a gentle pat on the back. Spluttering into his handkerchief, he finally nodded. "He'll be the death of us all." He caught his breath and tucked his handkerchief away.

"Why?"

Leo shook his head again and shrugged.

"And Jack, what about him?" Surely, she hadn't misjudged him?

"Jack, he's not a bad lad."

"Jack isn't a bad lad?" Amy found her mouth still gaping. She shut it quickly.

"He's trying to get the better of Dan, but it ain't gonna happen. We're all rooting for him, but he hasn't got it in him. He's too soft."

"Sorry. What's that? Jack is too soft?" Amy's mouth dropped open again. She shot him a look of bewilderment.

"Ahy, soft in the head, I mean" He threw up his hand. He made Amy jump. "Look," he said, pointing. "Fox! Sly bleeder."

"Oh yeah, very sly. Foxes get into everything." She agreed. "They get at least half a dozen eggs a week from my coop. It is falling apart, mind, so that doesn't help."

"I'll have a look at it for you."

"That's kind of you. When you feel better, of course, "It's the least I can do for all your help; the name's Leo, by the way." He turned to face the darkness again, then turned back towards her and offered his hand.

Amy smiled. She knew his name. "I remember, Leo" she repeated after him. "Pleased to meet you, Leo. I'm Amy!"

He laughed."Ahy, I know."

*

The lamp was on in the High Oakham Cottage window when Amy eventually turned into the yard. The door opened, and the old man's proud, straight silhouette filled the pool of light. He's still awake. Always a good sign, she thought.

"Hey, how did you get on?" he shouted from the doorstep.

"Good, good," she said, climbing down from the trap.

"How is he?" He asked, crossing the yard.

"Doctor Smyth sorted him out."

"Ahy! Knew he would."

The old man led the horse to the stable as Amy followed behind. They bedded the horse down together and returned to the house. There was a smell of cooking drifting from the cottage as they walked back over the yard.

"Smells lovely," Amy said, stepping inside. A bubbling pan of broth filled the room with a warm, welcoming aroma. Amy stirred the pan. "Dad! What a surprise. How lovely!" She threw off her damp shawl and placed it over the back of a chair to dry by the fire.

"Yes, well, don't make a fuss. Sit down." The old man brought the bubbling pan to the table. They sat together, split the only piece of hard, stale bread they had between them and ate in silence. The old man dipped his bread into the broth with a trembling hand, spilling globules of it down his shirt.

Amy pretended not to notice. "How are you feeling?" She asked.

"Tired. You?"

"Cold! Have you not had a drink then? …"

"No, not a drop!"

"Good, that's good!"

They ate more in silence. Amy waited for him to speak. He said none of his tormenting comments as she had expected, no jibes or probing about Leo or sarcasm; instead, the old man remained silent throughout the meal and hunched over his plate like someone was about to snatch it away from him. As she watched him huddled over his dinner, Amy became aware of how he was struggling to leave the drink alone. Recognising the difficulty that the old man faced for the first time made her appreciate the abnormality of their lives. She knew it was hard, but she was proud of him for trying, if only for one day. He began scanning the room, eyes searching for money, perhaps a drop of something. Amy was sure that there was neither money nor booze in the house but could see the drink was calling his name.

"Let's go out!"

"What? Now? Where?" He swung around to look at the clock.

"To the Circus," she said, pushing her chair back away from the table and brushing crumbs from her skirt.

"No, no…"

"Come on! Besides, Leo invited me."

"He did?"

"He invited both of us!"

"Did he?" His eyes shot up from his plate. "That bloke? He invited us?"

"Yes."

"Aw well, then."

"He's married, so don't think you've gotten rid of me just yet."

The old man raised a weak, trembling hand to his chin and rubbed it. "He invited us, did he? Hmm, now there's a thing."

Amy nodded, let down her hair and shook her head. "I'll let my hair down for you. I can't go alone, now can I?"

"'Course not, love." The old man shrugged," 'Course not." He leaned back on his creaking chair. "Going like that?"

"No!" She jumped up. "I'm going to change." She rushed to her room, slipped on the only semi-decent dress in the closet; a green fern one with white flecks woven through the soft wool, a lace collar, and white cuffs, then returned to the table and gave one of her customary curtsies. "Lady Green sleeves!" the old man was upon his feet, clearing the table and raring to go. He turned, looked up and down at his daughter and gave her a toothless, beaming grin.

The Greatest Show 1937

The old man drew the trap onto the grass verge, released the horse and led him into the field. Finding a quiet space at the rear of the tent, between a trailer and the canvas, they secured the horse to the fence, though the area looked very different in the dark. The air was thick with fumes from fires and oil lamps, and the sheer excitement made the atmosphere around the colossal tent feel just positively charged. Despite the bracing cold and freezing rain, the grounds around the Circus were crawling with folks, mostly locals, a few faces Amy didn't recognise.

"We'll leave him here," the old man said.

"Do you think he'll be okay?" Amy patted the horse's mane.

"Aye. It's sheltered." The old man wrapped the reins over the fence and gave it a firm yank. He gave a furtive glance around the field and shrugged. "Hope so," he whispered, "You never know with Gypsies."

"Ain't that the truth!" They both hopped over ropes that led under the canvas.

"I'd recognise him a mile off." The old man said, "If anyone tried to walk off with him, they'd know about it with his temperament."

As they began walking around the circumference of the tent, the old man stopped to look back at the horse. "They wouldn't get very far with him, Dad," Amy said, trying to reassure him.

"Nah, if anyone tried to steal him, everyone around these parts would recognise our Raisin."

"Ahy, Dad, they would."

One thing always preceded the Circus: their reputation for thievery and horses were at the top of the list of things they were notorious for stealing. Their favourite trick was to paint stolen horses in boot polish to disguise them or paint their whiskers to make them appear younger when trying to sell them on.

Children ran in all directions as they edged around the vast canvas palace. A small boy dancing beneath a bobbing balloon, purchased by his dad from the dark-haired lady at the entrance, stepped backwards beneath the old man's feet, who was now more preoccupied with straightening out his wiry hair, failed to notice.

"Watch where you're going, son."

"Hey, come on, move along." The balloon seller snapped in a rich deep Irish accent. Amy recognised her instantly.

"Hello."

"I'm Faye," she said with a quick curtsy. "Good to see you both. Glad you could make it," she said, taking another guinea from the boy's father. She patted the child firmly on the head and returned the man's change.

"Make sure you pay attention in there, young un," she said, smiling down at the child. The boy's tiny rain-drenched face beamed back at her with excitement. "I'm gonna be asking you questions when you come out!"

His expression froze momentarily. "Go on in, will ya? You'll be catchin' your death. You too," she said, turning to Amy and the old man. "Get yourselves inside."

The old man dug deep in his pockets for the entrance fee. "Aw, get on wi' ee'. And you can go in too!" she whispered to the frozen child, who had frozen to the spot with fear. He glanced back at his father and dashed in beneath the canvas flap without a second thought for him. The father nodded at the Irish balloon seller, removed his cap and scurried in after his child.

"Thanks," Amy said eagerly, edging forward towards the warmth of the glowing lanterns inside.

"No problem," she said with a wink. "Enjoy!"

Once inside, the charged atmosphere sent a tingling nerve down Amy's spine, and she was sure her heart would miss beats. Her father hesitated, looking about in awe. "Come on, Dad," she said, taking his cold hand in hers. "Let's sit over there." She helped him remove his coat and sat him down. She removed hers too, gathered it into a loose bundle, tossed back her hair, flattened the seat of her dress and sat down. From the corner of her eye, she saw a gentleman jump the bails of straw that formed the outer ring that ran the perimeter of the round performance arena. He leapt between a crowd of children, threw himself at her feet and handed her a rose. She smelt it delicately and wondered where he'd found it so early in the season. There was no fragrance. Dan laughed. Realising it was a fake rose, Amy blushed with embarrassment. The old man rose from his chair.

"Dan!" he said, surprised.

"Don't get up!" Dan said, climbing back to his feet. He clenched the old man's hand in a warm, welcoming shake. "Please, take a seat. I have to go. Lovely to see you both."

Leaping back over the hay bales, he stopped suddenly and flipped his body around in a running, twisting motion.

"Glad you came, Amy!" he called back, laughing.

Amy and the old man laughed and nodded like small children; Amy realised how silly they must look. Feeling exceptionally foolish, she slid back slightly in her seat and covered her face with one hand. "Oh, my God." She whispered to her father. The crowd around the perimeter of the Circus grew thicker. As they sat, realising how early they were, they waited patiently for the show to begin. Amy began growing cold from her feet upwards until she was shivering. She stood up to put her coat back on and scanned the vast soft palace, looking around at the excited faces of children and families, all waiting, just like them, with nervous anticipation.

"Toffee Apple?" She said suddenly, spotting everyone enjoying theirs. "Want one, Dad?"

"With my teeth? No, thanks."

"I won't be too long." She scanned the circumference of the tent. "Are you sure you don't want one?"

"Nope. Hurry; it might start soon."

Strolling around the narrow corridor between the stalls and the ring, Amy searched for the Toffee Apple vendor, her eyes scanning the walls of the grand palace, which were waving and dipping in the wind. Lit dimly by oil lamps casting long dark shadows that arched over the convex ceiling, the smell of sweet toffee apples added an air of magic, awe and wonder to the whole atmosphere. A moment later, the heavy velvet curtain at the rear of the circle parted and flung open in a sweeping motion to the sounds of blaring trumpets and horns that vibrated in Amy's chest. Her stomach leapt into her mouth, and her heart missed a beat.

In an explosion of noise, confetti and ribbons, a beautiful bronzed girl dressed in white, riding bareback on a Stallion, swept in. As she galloped past, her feathery, silvery plume wafted in the cold night air. Amy turned to look for her father, wanting to share her excitement with him but caught sight of a man waving angrily in the shadows behind the stalls. She recognised him instantly. It was Jack Franconi in some form of dispute with another, who she couldn't make out. The horse galloped past again, so close that it left a trail of cold air in its wake. As the horse reared up on its back legs and pirouetted around in a circular motion, Amy realised the bareback rider was Faye, the balloon seller standing by the door. She bore down on the animal's hindquarters with her heels and threw up a free arm to a screaming crowd. Her face, now illuminated, was painted in a greasy cream foundation, her eyes heavily outlined in black briefly glanced down. Amy was sure Faye had recognised her, but then the flash of her thick red lipstick smile turned up towards the roaring crowds, and she was gone.

There was something eerily disturbing about the greasy paint mask she wore; Amy couldn't help thinking as she joined the queue to purchase her Toffee Apple. The crowds were going mad now, cheering and whistling. Faye had opened the show with elegance and great skill. Those who looked on either wanted to be her or be with her.

Amy looked back for Jack, but he had moved into the shadows. The other man, who she assumed had been talking to him, had moved out from behind a stack of seats into full view. Amy strained her body to see who Jack was talking to and realised it was Dan.

Dan seemed to be waving his hands, then straightening his attire; he was just about to run into the centre of the ring when Jack grabbed his arm and pulled him back.

Leo appeared from nowhere and twisted a tight grip on Dan's arm, looking seething. "We don't need any more trouble." She thought he said. Amy purchased her apple from the slender blonde girl she'd seen earlier that day and began to make her way back to her seat. Just as she reached the length of space that opened out into neat rows of seating, she realised she could see what was happening beneath the stalls much clearer.

"Don't get involved." The old man said, nudging her leg with his. "It's not your business."

"Dad!"

"I got worried about you."

"I'm fine. Let's sit here," Amy said, returning her attention to the show.

The old man glanced over his shoulder to see Jack walking away from Dan and Leo. He could not resist taking another peek. Shocked to see the fracas was still going on between Leo and Dan. The old man cocked his head, intrigued to find out where the argument was leading. Amy crunched down on her Toffee

Apple and watched in awe as Faye leapt upon her Stallion's back; then, with precision balancing, rose straight up, standing, flinging open her arms to the roaring crowd as the horse continued gallop at full speed around the ring.

"This Circus needs her right now. Listen to them!" Dan said.

The old man wondered who Dan was referring to?

"I know her better than he does. She is all we have. She is the life of the show!" Dan was pleading, flattening his hands on his brother's inflated chest. "Please don't let her go!"

Leo shouted, pushing Dan back away from him. "What she does with her life has nothing to do with you!"

Dan took a step nearer, "Please, Leo, don't let her do this."

"She is our brother's wife! This has nothing to do with us. It's up to her what she decides to do!"

"I can't believe you're letting her do this."

"If our brother wants a family with his wife ...." He laughed. "It's got nowt to do with you or me, bro. Get back in that ring!"

"I'm telling you…," Dan said as he walked away. "It's Jack who wants to leave, not her. And that's his way of controlling me, controlling us!"

Leo said, pointing back towards the ring. "Just get back out there."

Dan waved his hand as though in some derogative gesture. Leo flew at him without warning, but somehow Dan got in the first punch, splitting the corner of Leo's mouth wide open. "You bastard!" Leo said, climbing to his feet and wiping the blood from his lip.

Amy saw her father looking over his shoulder and turned to see what he was looking at.

"Hey, hey!" Jack was shouting as he raced over and threw himself between the two brothers, tearing them apart. He pushed them both into the shadows, out of view of the crowds.

"What's going on?" Amy asked her father.

"Seems to be a fight."

"Oh!"

The old man looked about, wondering if anyone else could see what was happening behind them.

"The show behind us is far more interesting than the one in the ring." He whispered to Amy.

Amy looked to see if anyone else knew, but all eyes focused upon Faye and her beautifully skilled horse.

"Leo's trying to gain back his breath." The old man said quietly.

"He's supposed to be resting."

Dan stared into Jack's eyes. "We can't afford for you to leave mio fratello, not now!"

Leo was saying nothing more. He pushed Dan back gently. "There's never problems, only solutions," he said calmly. "And this problem has nothing to do with you, bro!"

"But he has to understand; this is not the time to leave. You understand, bro, tell him!"

Leo looked at Dan as he wiped more trickles of blood from his split lip.

"Make them both understand, Leo."

"Take yourself out of the equation, Dan," Leo answered. He stormed off, leaping over bales before disappearing through the curtain and out of sight.

Jack turned to his brother and threw his hands up. "What the hell was that about? I don't understand how my life has anything to do with you; that's crazy, man!"

Dan shrugged and walked away. "Ask Faye if she wants to leave" he shouted over his shoulder. "Go on! Ask her!"

Behind the curtain, Dan, shaking and sweating, punched the air in anger. Then as the crowds bayed at Faye on horseback beyond the curtain, Dan ran out, pulled Faye's galloping horse to a halt, leapt on its back and sped around the ring with Faye holding on loosely with one arm around his waist."

"Where the feck have y' been?" she whispered in his ear. "Thought you were never coming."

The curtain whipped open again as the Circus rose with a roar. Leo, arms raised, soaked in the energy and atmosphere as he yelled out to the crowds:

"Good evening, ladies and gentlemen, girls and boys. This evening, we extend a warm welcome to you all. Please put your hands together to welcome 'Bhengra', our gorgeous dancers from Asia."

Tiggy-Bob-Down 2020

Driving towards the village of Castleton, it soon became apparent that something was happening in the village; a fair, a festival or some music event, something that required loads of road traffic police swarming everywhere. Georgia and Len grew closer; a police officer pointed them off the road. Georgia pressed her face up against the windscreen. "What's going on? Where's he pointing to?"

"It's a she," Len said, peering over the steering wheel. Stood in the centre of the white line, the policewoman redirecting cars, pointing them off the road to some alternative route. As each vehicle inched towards her, Len noticed they were indicating, then swinging a left. Len grabbed his seatbelt, threw it on, wound down his window, and stuck his head out.

"What's happening, officer? Can I not go into the village?"

"Not with the car, not today."

"Why?"

"Festival day. Look, can you please go park up along Peak Hill Road?"

"It's a mile away from the village."

"Move along, please."

Eventually, having parked and walked an extra twenty minutes back towards the village, Len and Georgia found the local amenities somewhat disappointing. Partly because most of the tiny Victorian shops, resembling a set from a Charles Dickens novel, lined the one single road running directly through the centre of the village, were adorable to look at but useless for purchasing essentials like bread, and milk and light bulbs. They were very annoyingly crammed with tourists, cyclists and dog walkers. They'd descended upon the tiny village of Castleton on this particular day because, apparently, according to a soggy pamphlet Georgia picked up off the pavement, it was one of the few places in Britain still to celebrate the time-old pagan tradition and ritual of Ostara.

"There will be a real white horse lead precession if we haven't missed it."

"What's that about then?"

"It dates back years. It's something to do with the equinox."

"Ah, equinox derives its name from the Latin term "eqi" which means "equal" and "nox" which means "night".

"It says here, according to the astronomical calendar, there are two equinoxes each year."

"That's right, March and September when the day and night are approximately 12 hours each everywhere on Earth."

"Well, it says; many cultures worldwide celebrate the whole day as the March equinox. However, this equinox celebration occurs at a specific time when the Sun crosses the celestial equator from south to north. It says its true origins are not fully understood, but in Castleton, it appears to align with the famous Franconi Circus disaster. It didn't even happen here in Castleton, but the story was thought to have started somewhere near Castleton."

"Is that, right?"

"Symbolically, the burning of the Ringmaster represents rebirth and purity, like an ancient fertility rite. Look, there's a photo." She held out the pamphlet for Len to see.

"Right, purity, in Derbyshire, that's questionable."

Georgia continued reading without comment, "It's similar to the Harvest Festival, isn't it? This celebration begins with garlands made of cut flowers prepared on the day by villagers before being placed on the head of their 'Ringmaster'."

"Ringmaster? Who is this Ringmaster?"

"I think it is a variation of the May Queen and Harvest Festival. The Ringmaster is paraded around town on horseback with a fully laden cart, and the audience shout to him – ladies and gentlemen, boys and girls, roll in, roll up, take a pew and leave your troubles behind you!' The Ringmaster, dressed extravagantly, asks for money from the audience.

Once crowned with green foliage, he makes a speech before the show and festivities begin."

"Right."

"It says that only children are allowed to lead the procession. I don't know why that is."

"Yeah, well, there's Morris Dancers here; I've just seen them. They look like big kids prancing around anyway, so –"

Len stopped talking and stepped off the pavement to allow a very ignorant couple with an over-excited bull terrier to pass. They were hurrying without regard for anyone who may be in their path. Before they nearly took his legs out from beneath him, Len manages to leap out of the way.

"It denotes the end of the Circus here in Derbyshire and the beginning of the huge fire that took place over in Nottinghamshire." Georgia was still reading.

"Oh, the joys." Len, scowling at the couple as they hurried along as though they hadn't even seen him.

Suddenly, there was a surge of bodies, a whole wave of people pushing along the tiny road, taking the curve towards them like a stampede of banshees.

"Hey-up," Len laughed mockingly in the area's local dialect. "Here he cuums, all gadizened t'owd Ringmaster!"

Georgia slowly pieced together what her father had said and laughed. "Where?" she said looking around. "Where is he, the Ringmaster, all dressed up?"

Amid the mayhem, young girls in pink-white dresses and one small boy in a traditional Clown costume appeared, sprinkling the road beneath their slippered feet with tiny paper rose petals from woven baskets clenched in tight fists as though their lives depended on it. They scattered their colourful petals with deliberation and concentration, making Georgia smile. Occasionally, their steps changed in unison, as one of them would suddenly remember the routine they were supposed to be performing; but the petal sprinkling had taken priority as they all trotted along, trying not to look over at proud parents, whose phones were flashing from a safe distance so not to put them off.

Georgia watched as the crowd melted back from the road. Close behind the children, a beautiful white Stallion trotted along elegantly, tossing its silver-white mane gracefully in the air, showboating for all those gathered in awe to see the procession. The fantastic beast appeared unencumbered by neither crowd nor commotion as its handler, a man with a pale white painted face, long spikey white hair—a very cheap nylon wig, Georgia suspected—in a Ringmaster's costume that draped over the horse's hindquarters, waving down at people below him, like a royal visitor in town. Georgia looked at Len and laughed. "It's a man!"

Georgia thought the man enjoyed his role too much for his age.

The crowds waved back and followed as the procession weaved to the square. It turned out that it was not so much a square but rather a broader bend in the road that housed a stone monument. Georgia suspected it would double as an epitaph in November; nevertheless, for now, it marked the place where the Ringmaster would later be crowned. The coronation space was precisely where Georgia and Len had no intention of going, but since they had no option but to inch along with the crowd, they were delighted to find a way of escape finally.

Len and Georgia broke ranks and scuttled quickly down a back street that somehow led to the main road.

"Right," Len breathed. "Shops!"

They discovered the few shops they could get into now but didn't sell anything other than Blue John: the semi-precious stone, so-called because of its distinctive colour, but they offered a little refuge from the mayhem outside.

"They've got that stone in everything."

"Indeed, and in every shape possible." Len laughed. "It's expensive too."

Peering in a shop window to examine the prices of the semi-precious stone, she agreed. The stone had been fashioned into various shapes and placed in many forms of cheap-looking silver jewellery. It sparkled in every shop window and cafe beneath led light displays from floor to ceiling. Exasperated, Len and Georgia found out that even though the roads were empty, there were still queues inside the tiny shops; women mainly, whose bored to tears partners, husbands and children shuffled along behind them like zombies.

As ladies gaped through windows at glass cabinets displaying the locally mined mineral, beloved other halves were secretly looking for the nearest pub. Georgia again pulled the pamphlet from her coat pocket and read it to Len as they pushed through the queues.

"Apparently," she was yelling over his shoulder, "Blue John helps stimulate and sustain good health… and mental and spiritual well-being!"

"Well then, that covers it all, doesn't it—job lot? Powerful stuff!"

Georgia began scanning the endless signs in shop windows as they inched along in the crowds again. Len stopped suddenly to allow a woman with a pushchair to come out from a cafe backwards. Georgia read the menu in the window while they waited. "Blue John, Bakewell Tart, Cream tea and scones… as well as silver medallions and rings—shall we?"

"Shall we, what?"

"Go in?"

"Are you mad? Not a chance. We might never get out again."

Georgia thought the mysterious blue rock was fascinating. Information about it was in abundance. It was everywhere. You could even read about it while indulging in a chocolate pancake.

Len shook his head, waiting for a flustered woman with a pushchair to manoeuvre herself backwards out of the cafe.

"Here, love," he said, "let me help." He held the door open for her as she freed herself, then left him holding it for several others, who were sick of waiting to get out behind her.

While spotting space on the pavement, Georgia ran and stood in it while waiting for Len to play doorman. He caught up with her eventually, shaking his head in disbelief.

"It's madness, madness, I tell ya."

They set off again, and Len marched away at breakneck speed, determined not to get caught up again.

In an attempt to imitate the local dialect, Georgia shouts to Len over his shoulder, "That blue stuff in them there hills was found 150 years ago."

"Oh yeah?"

"Or so it says here..." Georgia pushed the pamphlet at him. She paused to flip it around, "Look; apparently, the Blue John's rare mineral vein was found in Derbyshire's Peak District."

Len moved an inch or two along the pavement. He stopped again when the mass of bodies before him suddenly squeezed at a bottleneck.

"But it is only obtainable from here, beneath Treak Cliff Hill, in Castleton." Georgia bumped into Len's back.

"Well, yeah. We know that! ..."

Georgia laughed. "Sorry. Looks like Blue John is all they have in this place. Do you know, it purifies the soul?" Georgia glances around at the high Peaks that dominated the horizon. "It also restructures and eliminates all negative energies and vibes in the overall torso."

"In the what?"

"Oh, I don't know; we just need light bulbs."

Georgia and Len squeezed into the doorway of a shop that looked more like a grocery store than a gift shop.

"There's no Blue John in here," Georgia shouted as Len was just about to set off again.

On a mission, he spun on heels and stopped dead. "A shop! A real shop?"

"Well, there's candles, dragons and angels." Georgia pushed her head inside briefly "...but there's normal stuff here like bread and milk."

"Y-e-s!"

There were no energy drinks, magazines or nail polish remover; Georgia immediately noticed when she stepped inside. And no light bulbs anywhere either. Georgia kept a wary gaze on Len as he paid for something he thought was necessary. She scooped up a carrier bag and smirked as Len dropped playing cards into the bag without paying for them.

"Nothing else worth buying in here?" she asked him.

He winked. "No!"

The bright blue and red name 'Tesco' branded across the carrier bag amused Georgia. "I wish it was Tesco."

"In Castleton? I bet they wish it was Tesco." Len looked at the bag, laughed, and then spotted a few light bulbs on the bottom rack beneath envelopes. He let the weight in the bag fall from the counter and hurried to look. The trip to the shop hadn't been as easy as hoped, but at least they obtained ten bayonet bulbs, so the whole horrendous experience had been worth it. He paid for them, dropped them in the bag and sighed as he turned to look at the door.

"We've got to go back out into that lot."

"And walk another 20 minutes to the car."

"Stay positive," the shop assistant laughed as she gazed at their disgruntled faces.

Len nodded over to the shop assistant. "Do you have any tourist information? For young people," He added, looking at Georgia. He winked at her and watched the colour rise in her cheeks.

"I was hoping to do some sightseeing this weekend. Maybe take a trip down some of the caves nearby, but the crowds and the traffic."

"I know," the woman shrugged and smiled.

"...And now it's raining!"

Len looked out of the window between the Blue John and glass displays. Above the crowd mulling around, the sky beyond was almost black.

His shoulders slumped. Georgia looked from Len to the shop assistant and back again. Len's slate-blue eyes regarded the assistant shrewdly.

The assistant moved around the counter, "I know," she said sympathetically. She pointed out a rack displaying leaflets, various scenic postcards and maps.

Encouraged, Len dropped the shopping bags and began sifting through leaflets and brochures for something of interest. He sensed Georgia taking an interest too. Eventually, she moved closer, drawn by a postcard of a strange-looking man, dressed in black, face like a Clown, which seemed to be jumping out from the card in an almost 3D print.

"Looks like that Dickens character."

"Which one, Fagin?" Len was straining his neck to see.

"Yeah, him." Georgia tilted the picture for Len to see, "Look!"

"Yeah, it is a bit like him."

"He does, doesn't he?" The shop assistant agreed as she looked to see what they were referring to. "Except his face is painted like a Clown, not in the traditional sense."

Georgia looked closer. She nodded and agreed with the shop assistant, "More like that character from the DC Comics."

"Joker?" The shop assistant offered.

The three of them nodded, then stood in silence studying every detail—the blue veins sliding down its white complexion looked like viscose veins, and black ooze appeared to be dribbling from the corners of its mouth.

The shop assistant chewed down on her pen and leaned in to look closer. "He's disgusting," she said finally.

Georgia straightened the photo card and looked at it again. "Creepy."

"Yeah," the shop assistant said, pulling her glasses down from her head to peer closer.

"Who is it supposed to be?" Len asked.

"He's local folklore, known as the Ringmaster."

"Not him again."

"Most places around here have the Ten O'clock Horses, Castleton has him." She took the card from Georgia and inspected the back.

Len shrugged. "I don't recall reading anything about him, and I like folklore. Fascinating, isn't it, Georgia?"

Georgia raised an eyebrow. "Profoundly unsettling."

"He's part of this folk festival today."

"He's the May Queen?" Len and Georgia spouted at the same time, then laughed.

"No! BBC Radio did a story on him this morning; didn't you hear it?"

"No!" Len said. "We missed it."

"I think if you get online, you can re-listen to it. The Villagers will be celebrating him tonight at the bonfire. First, there's a procession that's has already passed; it's just manic around here—not that I'm complaining, it's great for business, but later there'll be a lantern procession in his honour."

"The Ringmaster, eh, so what's the story behind it?" Len moved over to look at the card over the shop assistant's shoulder.

The assistant handed the card back to Georgia, who pushed it back into the rack and thrust her hands in her pockets as though wiping him away from her flesh.

"He does a jig and plays with the children."

Georgia and Len glanced up at each other but refrained from commenting.

"He chases them around."

More eyebrow lifting from Georgia to Len, but he pretends not to see her.

"They play that game, 'Tiggy Bob Down.' Did you play it when you were a kid?"

"In the playground with other kids. I wouldn't want to play it with him." Georgia laughed to herself.

"If you get tagged, you're out, that kind of thing?"

"Yeah, I know it," Len said.

"Just a bit of fun for the kids, you know?"

"Fun? Being chased by him?'

Len laughed loudly and nodded in agreement.

"They get sweets for joining in.

"Oh well then!"

"Georgia!" Len wished she'd stop commenting. He nudged her.

"Nothing like a bit of stranger danger," she whispered to him.

"Well, when you say like that, it does sound a bit weird."

"Weird, do you reckon?"

"Only in Castleton!" Len said, laughing. He moved on to a book about local bird sanctuaries.

"Aw, well. You know that song—'Girls and boys come out to play, leave your supper and leave you tea'?"

"Yes, it's creepy as hell."

"Well, they sing a song similar to that until someone tigs him back. Once he is tagged and caught by the kids, they get to burn an effigy of a him-a bit like Guy Fawkes."

"Hmm, and folks come from miles around to do that?"

"Not much else to do around these parts then, I'm guessing?"

Georgia laughed mockingly, though secretly she thought it sounded cool; a bit Halloween-ish.

"Aww, you should hang around for it. It's fun." The shopkeeper walked back around the counter. "Or, if you want to see the fireworks come down t' village tonight around 7:30. You'll enjoy that."

To Ride an Engine or Two 2020

When Len steps out of the shop with a carrier bag in each hand, his mouth falls open. He pulls Georgia towards him. She gazes up. "Ooo!..."

"Fuck's sake! Steam Engines, great! We'll be here all day" Len sighs and places the heavy bags down. Two steam Engines travelling parallel to each other, separated by a little under two meters, leave hardly any space between them and the pavement. Len nods down to indicate their proximity to the edge. "Careful," he says, reaching to move Georgia out of the way slightly.

"Think we can make a run for it?" Georgia shouts over the noise.

Len pulls her a little closer to him. "No, get back! Move out of the way!" Before Georgia can convince him otherwise, Len grabs her by the elbow and pulls her towards him. "Don't be stupid!" He pushes her again as though she is still not out of danger. "We'll never get out of here at this rate." Len raises his voice over the thundering noise and dramatic industrial Edwardian music emanating from the lumbering beasts. Len sees the shopkeeper peering over the open sign behind the window. She smiles and nods at the spectacle; shrugging his shoulders, he leans against the shop door.

The Engines dramatically and explosively inch by with music blurting as an entourage of weird, beautiful characters following behind, conjure images in Len's mind of clockwork worlds, sky ships and Galactic battles raging in giant floating cities. Len stares in a shocked silence before mumbling again, "For fuck's sake."

Both Georgia and Len remain pinned to the shop door, squeezed together like sardines in a can. The tiny porch has polished floor designed in a blockwork of black and white mosaic tiles, which remind Georgia of humbugs. They wait for the Engines to slowly edge past. Inch by inch moving at a snail's pace along the main road, which leads out of the village towards Hope. Silently they watch as pedestrians scatter in all directions as the heavy metal monsters lead the procession of Neo-Victorian Steampunks, marching in a huddled group, all dressed to kill; each another's audience within the now smoky and grimy aesthetic space once recognisable as the sleepy village of Castleton. The ensemble, Victorianesque and Edwardian in theme, are clothed to the nines in an array of tight corsets, long dresses, feathered hats and leather; men in suits, top hats, long straight coats, high leather boots, gloves, and goggles; dreaming, it would seem, of being in touch with some dystopian reality with Castleton as the most unlikely backdrop.

"Is this a post-Brexit thing or an anti-war march or something?"

"Indeed, it's a manifestation of some political or religious crisis."

"You think?"

"Either that or –" Len glances down at a man's black Leather 3 1/4-inch platform Gothic-punk boots, with six straps wrapped around each boot flapping as he clogs by – "too much material abundance, leading to a lifestyle boredom." He laughs. "Oh my God, the Tories have a lot to answer for. They've completely deprived the masses of a meaningful existence; why else would people feel the need to cast themselves in such weird roles and go around parading like this? Unless of course, it's a new sexual fantasy trend or something?"

No daughter ever wishes to hear their father even remotely allude to sexual fantasy, let alone discuss what he perceives as being one. Georgia wishes she never asked.

"Or…" Len offers, taking off his glasses to wipe away the fine film of rain that is beginning to form a mist over the lenses; Georgia cringes in expectation. He sniffs up a droplet of rain as it clings to the tip of his nose. "…They're just simply searching for a deeper meaning to their existence." He pushing his glasses back up his nose, then stares up and down at Castleton's answer to Gomez and Morticia as they breezed past almost as silently as you would have expected the actual characters to have done. Georgia notices an aroma, a mixture of cat wee and tobacco, which she instantly associates with the sweet, pungent smell of weed, trailing off behind them.

Georgia and Len look at stared other wide-eyes. "Or, maybe they're all just stoned!" Len noded in agreement and laughed, "That would explain a lot."

Georgia, suddenly notices a character slinking towards her in a tight, black one-piece; resembling the anti-heroine, Catwoman, who, Georgia always suspected, was attempting to demonstrate a utilitarian moral philosophy.

Imagining herself dressed in such a way, she glances down at her over the knee polyester high heeled boots then smiles at the woman as she breezes past smelling of Lenor and Chanel Coco.

Suddenly, she became aware that someone is watching her. She turns , looking up at the cabin of the Traction Engine beside her.

"Oh, you've got to be joking!' She blinks through the smoke and shakes Len's arm. "Look, it's him!" Len instantly looks back to where Georgia is pointing. There is a pause as Georgia waits for the penny to drop.

"Oh, yeah…" Len says finally. "Martin?"

"Mark!" She corrects him.

"Hello there!" Len begins shouting and waving. "Can he hear me?"

"I sincerely hope not!" Georgia rolls her eyes

Mark is standing at a funny angle, looking over the edge of the cabin. There's a strange, pressurised, intense ambience surrounding him, like a mad scientist working late at night in a lab on some highly volatile concoction that is likely to explode at any given moment.

"He's like that man –"

"Who?"

"From The Time Machine."

"Oh, yeah, him!"

"I can't remember his name." Although she had actually read that book umpteen times, she never identified his name.

"The protagonist?" Len said, laughing. He was nodding in agreement.

"Yeah, in the original 1895 version.

"He never had a name,"

The Engines were right beside them now. Steam and smoke pothering over them. What a strange sight to behold, she thought.

"This is so random, is this still in Castleton 2020?"

Len was waving frantically now at Mark, whose odd Victorianesque silhouette seemed to fit in brilliantly, especially since he was wearing an exceptionally tall hat with googles sat around the crown and a peacock feather flapping inelegantly in the wind. Georgia could see he was also wearing a Steampunk vintage court coat, with long sleeves, stiff stand-up collar, and velvety black and white stripy trousers through the steam and smog. Georgia shuddered. Amidst all the madness, chaos and mayhem, she thought he resembled the Child Catcher from the movie Chitty-Chitty-Bang-Bang. Then he spoke.

"Hello th-e-r-e!" he shouted in the oddest voice, elongating the 'e-r-e,' which to Georgia seemed to reaffirm her suspicions; he is weirdly partaking in some 'Child Catcher' character role.

She laughs to herself. She would never have believed Mark, farmer Jo, would be into something like this, the ordinary man from next door. A creepy grin seems to spread across his face when looking in Georgia's direction. His eyes wideneding, and his facial expression changing to one of a malicious child contemplating all manner of naughtiness. Even the ruggedness of his well-weathered leather complexion seemed to fit perfectly in the role; Georgia saw him in a different light as his face shone orange in the Engine's firry glow.

She turns away, pretending not to notice. Len, still waving frantically, looking as giddy as the rest of the crowd, and there is a lot of signalling and signing between them. Len reciprocates with his version of hand signals, which takes over the conversation entirely but means absolutely nothing. As Mark frownd, flummoxed, he leans further over to make his presence known to her. Georgia is getting tired of it. "Come on, Dad, let's go."

"He's trying to say something to you," Len said, convinced his ridiculous signalling is communicating all sorts to the man.

Mark suddenly reaches over the cabin at the last minute, throws open his arms, and waves them up. "Come on! Come on! Get in! Jump on!"

Embarrassed, Georgia looks away, pretending not to see him. Len is up, laughing like a child and waving at Georgia, "Climb aboard! Hurry up!"

"For God's sake, Dad!" Georgia grabs the bags he has left behind in the shop's doorway, reaching up to her father, she take the bags from her and hauls her inside. Both Mark and Len pulls her in like a sack of potatoes. There is hardly enough room on board, but they squeeze her between them. The shopping she held in both hands spilts out beneath their feet. Len kicks it into a tight space beneath the seat. Mark lunges forward, standing upright, offering up his place for her to sit.

Len's conversation with Mark focuses on the workings of the Engine, its piston capacity, its age, model and use of Tannin.

"It forms a thin resistant film to prevent corrosion in the boiler," she heard Mark explaining.

"Indeed, indeed," Len agrees like he already knew. His eyes fixed, feasting and drooling over the machine like a child in a sweet shop.

A rush of moist air suddenly slaps Georgia in the face, washing off her creatively applied foundation to replace it with grease, oil and grime. She quickly searches her pockets and thankfully finds an old tissue squeezed into the back pocket of her Jeans. She wipes away the sludge and looks at it on the tissue. It's not dissimilar to what I have already caked all over my face, she thinks, rubbing more beige-orange and brown sludge off with the tissue.

"Even if an Engine isn't in service, it still benefits from a dose of Tannin," Mark was still going on.

"Don't we all," Georgia thought as she gazed out at the shop windows, awash with glittery Blue John, silver and tiny golden-bright lights. With the wind blowing through her hair, she had a slight sense of freedom, but as the Traction Engine crawled by shop windows, reflections told a different story, unlike the glamorous one she had in her head. The wind blew more slush on her face. At that moment, she dreamed of lying on golden sands on a warm and remote tropical beach. The cold embrace of the season reminded her more of what she was missing. Wishful Summer thoughts drifted through her mind like a sea breeze through palm leaves. She wiped her face again as another spray woke her from her daydream.

"This model…" Mark's voice droned on, "It's what we call –"

Georgia was listening now but wasn't paying attention; after the following ten minutes of secretly thinking, am I about to fucking die? To her surprise, she found she was now immensely enjoying the ride.

What made her feel good was looking out at the sea of weird characters following the procession, like excited children running and laughing beside the Ice-cream van, worshipping at the edge of the pavement, waiting for it to stop and yield its wares. As the Engine parade inched slowly by, the crowd's presence gave her a sense of camaraderie. Men, women and children all ages waving up, faces beaming with joy. Then, she clocked Len smiling from ear to ear, enjoying every second. Even the music now sounded amazing, dramatically growing in intensity, making her feel like she could "traverse the whole God damn!"

Len looked down at her. "What…What did you say?"

"Oh, nothing, just thinking out loud."

Len returned to his conversation with Mark.

In her mind, Georgia was now marching like a warrior with a troupe of Goths, heading down Castleton High Street on a mission to save the Planet from the tyrant that could well be Trump or worst, Vladimir Putin. Then a ridiculous thought sprung to mind 'Hmm, Putin is capable of Nuking the whole Planet, but Trump's deterrent would be to build a 24,901 mile wall around the Erath. She gave a small laugh as a gust of wind and rain thundered through the machine, making her sway and danced suddenly. Like a fairground ride, jutting from one side to the other, Georgia caught her balance, folded her arms, tossed back her hair and breathed in, inhaling carbon emissions like it was the latest craze. She felt every grind and thrust of the Engine's pistons surging through her and thought how powerful and sexy it made her feel. The dynamism was war-like, Trojan. She could be the Boudicca of the Steampunk World right now. With the elevation provided by the Engine, she felt giant. Turning to Len, who was now in his element, Georgia could tell he loved it.

They stopped dead, then set off again with a jerk. Mark's mop of straw-like hair, protruding from beneath his ridiculously tall hat, was taking every direction as he heaved on the wheel, first one way then back the other. He hauled the mass of metal in an easterly direction before slowly bringing them all to an abrupt end in a water-logged car park at the Travellers Inn. Georgia felt an enormous sense of disappointment suddenly wash over her.

"What an anti-climax!" She shouted to Len.

"That was great fun, wasn't it?" He said.

She watched Mark switch off, pulling levers and killing the Engine, which confirmed the ride was well and truly over. She began climbing down from the cabin and stood bewildered as Len followed her.

"What the hell just happened?" Georgia said, laughing.

"Yes, indeed, that was great fun!"

"Who knew?"

They had both been dropped off and left ankle-deep in puddles of brick-red sludge in the overflowing car park. They waited and watched as Mark prepared to load the Engine onto a recovery truck poised ready to haul it off to its owner in some unknown location in the Derbyshire countryside somewhere.

A leather-gloved hand waved through the steam as the second Engine crawled into the car park.

"Are they stopping here too?" Georgia asked Mark.

The machine began manoeuvring into its rightful place for collection.

"This is the end of the road, I'm afraid."

Most of the crowd disbursed; some continued their walk longer, while others bolted into the pub out of the rain. A small group of die-hard enthusiasts gathered around the Engines, taking photos and firing a barrage of questions.

"Steam Heads," Mark joked.

"They want selfies in their get-up for Facebook," Georgia whispered to Len.

"Indeed. It's not something you see every day."

"Guess not."

"That one belongs to the Brothers Grimm. They live near you." Mark leaned in towards Georgia a little closer and pointed with his cane. "You've met them already, haven't you?"

Georgia and Len admired the machine from a distance. "They're twins."

"Ah, yes, we know…Good lads, did a couple of jobs over at our place."

"Idiots, pair of them." Mark sneered. He pointed with his cane. "Especially that one. He's the weirdest of the two, Joshua. Must admit, he's a genius with Engines though; there's nothing he doesn't know about them."

Georgia and Len watched as Josh worked on mounting the Engine on the pick-up truck.

"You've got to watch the other one, though."

"Oh?"

"Jake will snatch that Engine right from under your nose if you're not careful. I'll come and take it before he gets his hands on it." Mark removed his gloves and rubbed the brass top on his cane.

Georgia looked at Len, then up and down at Mark; his hat and cane truly resembled the Child Catcher. She couldn't take him seriously and could not stop thinking about the fact.

"Everyone has him working for them. He works practically for nowt, that's why. He's putting professionals like me out of business. Pair of twats!"

"Well, people can sometimes be facile."

"And disposable."

Georgia glared at Len; he shrugged and said, "Well, a little competition in business can do us all good when it comes down to it. It's whatever's best for the consumer in the end."

Mark nodded, but Georgia noticed his eyes narrowing and his broad grin melted slowly down his face.

Everyone turned to watch Joshua from afar as he worked to get the Engine on the truck. The driver jumped down from the cabin, followed by a plume of vapour; tucking his vaporiser into his shirt pocket, he hooked up the Engine, face forward, threaded it onto the trailer, and waited until Josh very slowly guided the machine up and on. Once secured within the constraints of the trailer, the beast let out its last puffs and pops before slowly cooling off.

"Where you off to?" Mark said, turning his attention to his trucker, who had mounted his Engine without help or direction from him. He inched first in, then back out and was about to go again when Len stepped in to offer assistance. He threw up a thumb and yelled, "Okay, go! Go on, mate!"

Once Mark's truck driver had the Engine were in alignment, he mounted the beast up the trailor, climbed down from his cabin, pulled his trousers up over his hanging gut and gave Len a thumbs up. "Thanks Pal!"

"Home!" Georgia said, answering Mark's question finally. "We're going home now. Thanks for getting us out of the village. It was manic."

"Wasn't it!" Mark laughed.

They all stood waiting for the truck to carry Mark's Engine away from the car park and onto the main road.

Len laughed, suddenly and turned to Georgia. "We only popped out to buy bulbs." He lifted the shopping bags to refer to them. "We didn't mean to get caught up in all that mayhem."

"Mayhem! It was crazy, wasn't it?" Georgia laughed. "And God knows where our car is?"

Len was looking around dramatically. "Where is the car, G?"

"It's over there." Georgia pointed out.

"Well, I'm off for a pint," Mark, ignoring a barrage of questions from eager, enthusiastic Steam Heads who had gathered beneath the pub porch for a smoke, walked through them, parting them with his cane as though they were sheep. Georgia looked over at Josh, who was now climbing into the truck's passenger side. There was laughter and banter taking place between them. Mark returned and shouted suddenly from the door. "Wanna come and meet the Mrs?"

"Let's not, Dad; we've got stuff to do."

"Ahy, we'll grab some lunch," Len shouted back. "Fancy lunch, Georgia? Make a day of it?"

"I'm having lunch with the Mrs Join us if you want? Becky would love to see you both."

"No, no, no, let's go home, Dad."

Mark continued to hold the door open. Len was already making his way over, so she had no choice but to follow.

Breathing heavily, Len took the highly polished brass handle and pushed the door open, allowing Georgia through. The warmth, smell and noise from within sounded inviting, but it filled Georgia with dread, not for herself but for Len. Looking at Georgia with one eyebrow raised, she didn't need to say anything; Len knew she was annoyed.

"We won't stay long," he whispered.

"Promise?"

Len knew she was referring to a private conversation only two days previous. He had sworn, yet again, never to step foot in a public house.

"We have a deal," she reminded him as she stepped over the threshold. And indeed, Len knew what he had promised. His promise to her had clinched the deal five months previously when he finally convinced her to move from her childhood town of London to his childhood town of Castleton. 'I'll never step foot in a public house ever again.' They were his very words.

Yet strangely, since arriving in the village, Len's yarning for civilisation had been far worse than Georgia's; moving to the country had been a bit of a culture shock for them both, but more so for Len. Georgia was settling in okay, however, surprising, Len wasn't. The persistent rain hadn't helped, and while Georgia had work to keep herself occupied; sitting at the computer, doing pretty much the same in Castleton as she did in London, was easy for her; Len, on the other hand, had been pacing the tiny rooms, consistently moaning and asking Georgia to join him on a walk: walk to the shops, walk in the woods, walk to the village. He was driving her mad, and she secretly wondered if he just needed an excuse to go to the pub. He didn't usually crave civilisation and human interaction, nor did he ever ask for a tantalising conversation, which he had been repeating since the move from London.

When in London, Len was happier with his head in a book or tinkering with electronics in the shed. Georgia refused to feel not an ounce of sympathy. She knew there wasn't much for him to do in the cottage, especially with it raining constantly, but it had been his choice to move to the sticks, so she was determined to make him stick to his promise; after all, he was a recovering alcoholic.

"How do I know you're not just going to go to the pub for a drink?" she had asked.

"If I do pop to the local, it's just to meet people—to meet our neighbours."

"Why would you go to the pub and leave me at home?"

"Who said you should stay home? Come with me."

"No, I can't go to the pub with my dad; it's weird. People will think I'm some freak."

"Will they? Why?"

"Why? Because it's not the same for guys—going with their sons to the pub is normal, but going with your daughter, unless it's to eat, looks wrong."

"Well, go on your own then."

"That's even worse! Girls can't just walk into a strange pub alone!"

"Why not...?"

"Why not? Because it's not proper. It just isn't right."

"I don't get the youth of today! Okay, I guess you're right. It isn't the same for girls, but there's nothing wrong in going to the pub with your dad."

Georgia recognised the look of contemplation on his face. That raised eyebrow, furrowed forehead and a little crease running from his hairline to the bridge of his nose.

"So, now you're in the pub, after three years. How does it feel?" Georgia whispered as they stood among the crowd in the Traveller's Rest, waiting to be served.

Len nodded at Georgia. "Are we okay doing this?" He pulled a face and looked at her sheepishly.

"Not really. I'm not happy about it." Len reminded her of a naughty child looking to its mother as he reached for a lollipop in the sweet shop, having just been told he couldn't have one.

Len began rubbing his hands together as they inched closer to the bar. Then the crowd eventually parted to allow him through. Eyebrows lifted, eyes sparkling, he turned to her,

"What do you want, darling?"

"Becky's over there," Mark interjected, pointing to his smiling wife and overexcited son, bobbing up and down with a crayon in each hand. Sat beneath the pretty lead glass window in the far corner, Becky waved and indicated the spare seats around her. She began moving coats and bags.

Georgia looked back at Len, "Food! We want food, Dad, just food, no alcoholic drinks, make it two cokes—two!"

As Len returned to the bar to place his order, Mark had already ordered. He handed Len a swift pint. Georgia widened her eyes at her father and took it from him. "I'll have that!"

Len nodded in agreement. "I'm not drinking, Mark, thanks."

"What!"

"I'm not drinking because –"

"He's on the wagon." Georgia jumped in. She took a sip from the lager. "Thanks, though."

Half listening, Mark just laughed. "Aren't we all, love?"

Not wishing to appear rude, Georgia pretended to be distracted, her eyes fixed on something across the room, secretly wondering if Jake was in there amongst the Steampunk fanatics, but she doubted it very much.

She heard Mark's laughter growing louder with each sip of ale.

"…And…" she heard him say, "I thought I'd got it bad having a nagging wife, but, I tell you something, if my son ever starts trying to tell me what to do… fuck me… I'd have to kill him!"

There was a long chorus of laughter from the hoodlum holding up the bar. Len glanced at Georgia when he suddenly found himself holding another pint. Just as Georgia had reached the end of her tether and felt like screaming, she spotted Jake. Her heart leapt into her mouth. She wished her best friend was there, so she could blurt it out and say, "That's that guy I was telling you about; he's gorgeous!" But she had to contain her excitement and pretend disinterest. Also, at that point, she no longer cared if Len drank the damn pint or not. But then that feeling was brief. Suddenly, she realised she was staring at Jake. She slid away behind Len and admired him from afar. He wore a faded denim jacket over some grey hoodie, which she thought looked cool. He jumped up from his chair and hurried outside, a pint of something in one hand and a phone clamped to his ear.

"Of cause, mate…" she heard him saying. "I'll get Josh to pick it up. Yep, no probs, mate, see ya, yeah, see ya later, man."

Georgia thought he'd looked over to her briefly before pushing the door open and disappearing outside. Her heart kick-started again as he slipped out. Sighing, she knew he hadn't seen her at all, and even if he had, he probably wouldn't remember who she was.

She played his actions over in her mind. Did he see her? Did he look at her? Then she resigned herself to not being seen, as the telephone conversation he was having with someone seemed intense. He was hurrying outside for a better signal or, more likely, for more privacy. She found herself wondering who he must be talking to?

"There you go," turning, Len thrust a glass of coke under her nose. "Why don't you sit down, love? Leave that pint; you don't have to drink it, you know."

Georgia glanced over at Rebecca; she'd made space and looked over eagerly, waiting for them to join her. James had escaped from his chair and bounced with excitement from one stool to the other. He appeared delighted to crawl over everyone's legs like an escaped animal. His mother, reaching out to stop him, failed miserably. Georgia's heart sank a little at having to sit with them, but then realised she could at least see the car park from there and maybe, with any luck, might catch sight of Jake.

"Hi, love! You alright?" Rebecca moved her handbag from the table and tucked it away beside her. Georgia placed the coke and the pint on the table, dropped her jacket in the allotted spot prepared for her, smiled and sat.

"Hi, yeah, not bad, thanks. You?"

"Yes, thank you. Enjoying your new house?"

Georgia thought it quicker to nod and took a quick sip from the coke.

"Settling in, alright?"

Conscious of seeming awkward, she knew she had to speak to this woman and be polite. She said deliberately guarded and with a forced friendly smile, "Yes, we're loving the place, thank you."

To her astonishment, Georgia could see Jake from the window. He was still on the phone outside, watching as his brother, who was now evidently washing his hands in the pint of water that Jake had just given him. Georgia smiled, remembering how Josh would not enter her house until he thoroughly cleaned his hands. Jake wasn't looking amused. He turned, walked away from sight a few times, and then wandered back. Georgia sprained her neck, trying to keep an eye on him. She knew that if he took just one more step to the right, he'd be out of her line of vision again. Then, from the corner of her eye, Georgia saw that Mark, who had joined a group of the local lads at the bar, reaching over to offer Len another pint of lager. She waited with bated breath to see if he would take it. He did, flashing her a look of guilt. Georgia looked away quickly, pretending not to notice. Len took a long sip from the lager and joined the banter as loudly as the others. Georgia knew Len was thoroughly enjoying himself. He looked comfortable and happy, happier than he had looked in months. It appeared to Georgia that he felt like he'd been a punter at the Traveller's Rest for years.

"Have you met your new neighbours yet?" Rebecca asked, glancing out at the brothers. Georgia was bought swiftly back into the room. "What? Sorry? What did you say?"

James had begun crawling over her knees, purring like a kitten. Georgia moved her drinks further over the table, just in case.

"I said, have you met any of your neighbours yet?"

"...I err ..." Georgia could see Jake slowly walking out of view. She scratched her head, trying hard not to look out again.

Rebecca nodded her head in Jake's direction. "The brothers, you've met them then, I take it?"

"Oh!" Georgia scratched her head again awkwardly. "Oh, yeah, once, both of them...they fixed a few things at the cottage; the locks, remember?"

"Oh? Ah, good! Very wise. That was a mystery." Rebecca was smiling but looked pissed off.

"Have you been up to the Hamlet? Sounds lovely; there are craft shops up there now and a cafe?

"We haven't been yet, but we're planning on going at the weekend for the Vintage Fair thing...?" She glanced out over the car park casually.

Rebecca cleared her throat. Eyes narrowing with knowingness, she nervously began rotating the bracelet on her arm.

"Yeah?" She sat up, cleared her throat again and looked over Georgia's head at Mark, whose laughter had become so loud now that it wasn't hard to know exactly where he was in the room; even Georgia felt embarrassed to be with him.

Rebecca flicked her hair casually over one shoulder, took a sip from her Prosecco and smiled down at James. Georgia slid a beer mat beneath her coke and took another a sip. James kicked her hard in the thigh as she was about to return the glass down. It hurt. She moved away slightly and smiled down at the child. He kicked again with the heel of his shoe, digging into the top of Georgia's leg. Georgia tried to remove the child's foot gently.

"He loves kittens," Rebecca said. "Plays kitty-cats all the time...Loves um." She leaned over and tapped her son's foot lovingly. "Sit up, love, come on. You're hurting Georgia."

Georgia smiled, felt embarrassed and wanted to thump the child hard. Instead, she gazed casually out the window and over the car park. Rebecca twisted a tendril of hair around her finger and followed Georgia's gaze.

Jake had gone; only Josh was still in full view, splashing his hands with water from the glass and scrubbing them like they were on fire. Just as Jake came back into view, Rebecca took another sip of Prosecco and followed Georgia's line of vision again. Rebecca sensed Georgia's growing agitation and interest in Jake. She glanced at Mark and wondered if he knew that Jake was coming back inside. A second later, Georgia took a casual sip of coke and another glance outside, confirming that Josh was still washing his hands, but Jake had gone.

She sighed and looked at Rebecca, who appeared to be looking at someone. She seemed lost in thought. Glancing over her shoulder to see who Rebecca was looking at, Georgia released Rebecca was staring at Jake. He had returned and was now standing at the bar. Both Georgia and Rebecca exchanged an awkward smile, casually returning their attention to the view outside. Georgia picked up her phone to hide her embarrassment. She began scrolling through social media apps while Rebecca, feeling awkward, leaned over to retrieve her handbag. She tucked a tendril of hair over one ear and brushed the rest of her hair with a small comb from her bag.

"James, get up off the floor, come on."

Mark walked up to the table, looking pissed off. He placed another glass of Prosecco before his wife and went to the bar. "Seen who's here." Rebecca ignored his gesture.

"Get up, James!" She moved the Prosecco away from the excited James and smiled. "Thanks, love."

Irritated, Mark snapped at the child. "James, behave, listen to your mum, get up!" James' hair was all over his red, sweaty face when he emerged from beneath the table. He stared around the room. "Mummy, look, it's Daddy." James was pointing off somewhere and was just about to run off when Mark grabbed him by the wrist and made him sit down.

Len came over from the bar and placed his lager on the table, eyes flashing at Georgia as he sat. She said nothing, just took one look at the pint of lager and rose from the table.

"Car keys!" She clicked her fingers impatiently.

"Why?"

"I'll go fetch it."

"Now? But I've ordered food."

"I'll be back before it arrives."

"Do you even know where it's parked?" Len pulled keys from his coat pocket and handed them over.

"I took a screenshot; I know where it is. I'll map it."

"Okay then."

Georgia sensed Rebecca nudging Mark and felt judged by her, but what did they know. Len was getting the message, he knew his daughter was angry; the reason why wasn't something she could share with strangers.

"Aw, she's pissed off with you, Len!" Mark blurted. "You've gone and done it now, mate!"

Rebecca took a double-take at her husband and nudged him – "What! She's got Len on the wagon." He laughed loudly. Rebecca wasn't amused, so she didn't question it further.

Georgia forced a smile, "I won't be too long," she said to Rebecca, who shrugged and offered a weak smile before dropping her head to smooth out invisible creases in her jeans.

"Okay," she said, forcing a smile. When she looked up a second time to see Georgia still stood there, she gave another weak smile and looked at her as if to say, still here? Georgia gave Len a look that only he would comprehend, shook her head, spun on her heels and practically ran from the table. The humiliation was almost unbearable. Finally reaching a sufficient distance, she gave a huge sigh and felt her shoulders drop. She was relieved to have escaped Mark, his wife, his god-awful child, and that lying scumbag of a father; who, incidentally, she couldn't believe was drinking again. He was back to his old ways after the first opportunity had presented itself.

Jake looked up from his empty pint as Georgia walked by the bar. He was still waiting to be served and watching the door for his brother. Instinctively, she smiled at him and nodded, albeit very self-consciously, but judging by the lack of his response, it was clear; she convinced herself very quickly, that he hadn't even seen her, let alone recognised her.

– But he did....

"What are you doing here?" A dark, lush masculine voice came from behind her as she leaned against the heavy oak door to push it open. A strong hand raised above her head to take the weight. "Allow me."

"Oh, thanks."

The demi-god himself stood so close to her that she could almost feel the heat radiating from his muscular, solid body; she noticed he smelled amazing. Georgia went into a strange paused mode for what seemed an eternity until Jake laughed. "Are you going in or out?" He pushed on the door to open it a little further.

Georgia snapped back to Earth, "Out, thanks. The door closed slowly behind them as they ended up outside, huddled beneath the narrow wooden trellis that doubled as a porch. Jake picked a flower from the plant that climbed over it. "Clematis," he said, placing it in Georgia's hair. "It's a gorgeous flower."

Unbelievably, Josh was still there, wiping his hands frantically. He tucked a handkerchief into his back pocket and looked up.

"Are you coming in or not?" Jake snapped at him. Georgia wondered if Josh had ever slept with a woman. She doubted it. He looked younger than Jake up close, slimmer, fitter, though not that much different—same eyes, same shadow-beard a day or two old. He had a broad, strong jawline, and cute lips with a childish pout, like that of a petulant child. His eyes flashed past her like she wasn't even there.

"Didn't you buy me one?" he said, looking at Jake's empty pint glass. Georgia noticed Josh didn't look at Jake either.

"An hour ago, mate. I drank it! This one is my third!"

Jake laughed and shook his head. "Amazing," he said, "I always seem to know what he's talking about, even though he is so out of context and random. Are you saying hi to Georgia, or what? You do remember her, don't you?"

Josh shrugged like he didn't care, then nodded at her, eyes neglecting to connect with hers. He stared at the floor momentarily where she stood. It seemed to take so much of his strength; Georgia felt sorry for him. Feeling his pain, she spoke to fill the pause.

"Alright, Josh?"

Josh nodded, then brushed between them headfirst and lunged for the door. As he reached the curl of the brass handle, sensing its cold beneath his hand, flinched back again.

"Okay then?" Jake laughed. Georgia sensed a slight embarrassment in his tone. "Hypersensitivity, yet another of Josh's idiosyncrasies." Jake shook his head and laughed again.

Josh turned, looking in Jake's general direction. Jake waited for him to say something else, but he didn't. Growing impatient, Josh leaned upon the door with his shoulder to push his way inside.

"See ya then, Josh!" Jake laughed. "Wait a minute, hey Josh? Hang on, bro." He grabbed out at his brother, just managing to snag the back of his coat. Josh turned, looking annoyed. He scratched his head vigorously; now half in and half out of the building, he cringed beneath the noise from the public house behind him. It was thundering through his brain like a train; the sweet smell of booze and bar food was more sensory overload then he could handle. His stomach did a summersault. Holding the position by the door just a second longer, he snapped, "What!"

The pressure was proving too much; the traffic was thunderous, the elements harsh; combining the two – the public house and the world beyond was causing his head to feel like it was about to explode. He needed a calm place, a space which was either one or the other. Josh went inside leaving the door to close under its own weight.

"Did you see if big Al's coat was in the car?" Jake shouted.

"No!" Josh's voice trailed off as the door slammed shut.

"Don't bother; I'll go check," Jake said to himself; then, to hide his embarrassment, he turned to Georgia to finish what he was saying, even though she didn't know who he was talking about.

"– Big Al," he said. "Has left his coat in the car and his wallet is in his pocket. He took the Traction Engine back on the low loader for Josh."

"Oh, I saw that."

"Crap, I don't know where the car's parked either" He spun on the spot.

"Mine's here," Georgia said, whipping her phone out and scrolling through images. She found the photo of the street where Len parked earlier. "Maybe yours is there too."

"Could be. Al, drove in with Josh this morning, and I brought the low loader down. I heard this car park was full this morning."

"It was. The police were guiding everyone off the main road and making them park here." She waved up to her phone slightly. Instinctively, they both set off walking over to the car park. "Let me see that again, where did the police sent everyone?"

Georgia scrolled her phone to the image she had stored.

Jake leaned over her shoulder and stretched the screen out between his thumb and finger. "Town's End Road, I know it."

He pulled his jacket together and thrust his hands into his pockets. "It's freezing, isn't it?" Georgia said. She was shivering but had left the pub without her coat, and there was no way she would go back in for it. Shrinking her body against the coldness, Georgia suddenly felt small beside Jake. This guy has got to be six foot ten, she was thinking and wondered if he knew how nervous she felt. Feeling more self-conscious than ever, she thought she would say something stupid or trip up or something so she clamped up. Even shivering felt ridiculous. She tried to stop herself from doing that, then decided if she contemplated having a cigarette or something instead, it would hide that she was freezing and feeling ridiculously self-conscious. She studied her reflection in a shop window. Do I look cold? She wondered. I do not want to look like an infant, a cold, shivering child next to him. Why is everyone taller than me? I'm tiny, skinny, ridiculously white, and so inarticulate. Georgia's anxiety was running away with itself. I'm not ladylike one bit. Why did I go and wear these boyish Converse again? They make me look so small and childish. Her face flashed up in a darkened shop window, and she looked again. I'm not that bad looking, not good looking either, but this guy is just fucking gorgeous, though. Oh God, I look scruffy! Forget it; she consoled herself. There's absolutely no way he's even remotely interested in me anyway. Check your watch like you've got to be somewhere else. No, not the watch, the phone, it makes you look popular. I'll check my phone. The phone is fine; recheck it. "Have you lost something?" Jake's black curls wafted beneath the cap he was wearing.

"No, have you?" Jake didn't answer; he just laughed and shook his head.

"I mean, do you have a cigarette?"

"I don't smoke. I vape sometimes, but not often. But you look like you need one." 'Oh no. I don't. I don't smoke either."

Jake looked confused. He glanced back abruptly over his shoulder and ran over the road without warning. Georgia jogged after him. He sprang up onto the pavement and pointed off up a steep hill. "It's up here. It's a good walk, twenty minutes at least." He turned back to see where Georgia was. "You alright?" Jake's strides were twice hers. Georgia was just about struggling to keep up. I've put him off me, she was thinking. He can't wait to get away from me. She rechecked her phone and shook her head, fuck him. "You keep checking your phone. Do you need to be somewhere?"

"I'm supposed to be having lunch with Dad. He's just ordered food." "Right. So –" Jake slowed down a bit for her to catch up. "Now you've seen the famous Castleton parade then?"

"Yeah, it was er… mad."

Jake laughed loudly and began striding over the road again, his pace now covering three of hers. Georgia felt even more childish trotting along beside him. "Saw you hitched a ride!

"On that Traction Engine?"

"Yeah, with Mark Price, good old Mark Price."

"Oh God, you saw me?"

"Yeah, it looked like you loved it and your dad was enjoying himself."

"He just told us to jump on."

Jake threw his head back and laughed. "Mark did?"

"Seems like he was angry with you when he came over the other day. Do you know him well?"

"Wish I didn't. Why is it when that man says jump, everyone jumps; in your case, you did quite literally!"

Georgia looked up sheepishly, "What do you mean?"

"Aw," Jake scratched his beard. "He's just that kind of guy, you know."

"I must confess, I did love it!"

"Did you!" Jake laughed with a kind of surprise. "Great…" he laughed again. "Love it!"

"Your brother, he drove one of the other Engines."

"Josh did, yeah. He loves all that kind of stuff." He shook his head and smiled. "You've gotta love him for it. He's been working on Big Al's Engine; the guy who left his coat in our car, so Al asked him to drive it in the rally today, check it out, have a listen to it."

Georgia speeded up a touch to catch up with him again.

"It's what he does best, my brother. It's his t'ing man." Jake said laughing. He checked the road over his shoulder again before striding over. "So, you're into all that Victorian vintage Steampunk stuff then?"

"I wasn't, but that was cool today. I might be a convert."

"A Steamhead eh? Like our Josh? He spends hours doing up old Engines. You should hang out with him."

Jake suddenly turned a sharp left, nearly taking Georgia out.

"Oops, sorry."

Georgia just managed to dodge a road sign indicating a 20% gradient in a red triangle which was splattered with pellet indentations.

"He travels all over the world."

"Does he?" Georgia was trotting beside him, struggling to breathe as the hill inclined.

"Don't be surprised. I know Josh seems, well, a bit weird, but he is autistic."

"Ah, right."

"He's amazing at fixing up old machines and things. He got accepted into the Army, passed all the examines, and it looks like they're taking joining him up as an Engineer." There was an unmistakable gleam of pride in his eyes. "Well, he was going in the Army until he got a phone call the other night; some American guy called him up. Said he wants him to go to America to work on an Engine. He collects um', this American, he has an Engine on the highest train track in the world, between China and Tibet."

"Really?"

Nodding, Jake laughed. "He only wants to pay our Josh thousands to go work with him."

"In Tibet? What about the Coronavirus?"

"Debateable, isn't it? This dude wants to fly Josh out to the States, then to China, then onto Tibet to pick up this old rust bucket, then drive it back to Doncaster."

"Doncaster! In the UK?"

"Overland, like, yeah. It's mad, isn't it?"

"What...!" Georgia was totally out of breath now.

"Sounds a little unsteady to me, this dude, but hey, if the price is right!"

"God, quite a trip though, eh?"

"It's weird, isn't it, how people with money seem to develop out of control obsessive hobbies and go to great lengths to get what they want. But he wants to pay Josh more money for one trip than he 'll earn for in a year in the army, so go figure. It's all part of the fun, I guess. Apparently, Josh was saying, there's about 30% less oxygen where this Engine is. You can't breathe without a canister of air."

"Altitude sickness? I know the feeling right now!" Georgia lifted her hand, covered her eyes, and then wiped her forehead. "Phew."

"You alright?"

"Yeah, just knackered."

"You'd be great in the Himalayas!"

She coughed. "I'm out of breath now, and this is only 20% incline!"

"You'd be useless in Tibet."

They both burst out laughing. Jake slowed down noticeably and waited for her to catch her breath.

"30% less oxygen, hey?" Georgia shook her head and stopped again to catch her breath. "Sorry, seems I can't walk and talk at the same time. 30% less oxygen, bloody hell, imagine that!"

Jake took his hand out of his pocket and put it through the crook of Georgia's arm. She glanced up at him. Smiling down, he looked at her strangely, as though he was seeing her for the first time. She wondered what he was thinking. He brushed her hair aside. The dampness of the rain in the wind had given her a fresh glow, making her complexion shine in the pale afternoon light.

"Your cheeks are shimmering, flushing rosy pink like my mums used to."

A Range Rover came growling up the hill behind them. Startled, they separated slightly, making it awkward to recompose. Georgia blushed.

"So…" Jake said, linking arms with her again. "It's not your fault you're so knackered, you know?" They began sauntering up the hill.

"No?"

"There's 30% more carbon monoxide up here now; thanks to that Engines rally today, they've choked up the place."

Georgia laughed and nodded. "Ah, that is true." She swallowed hard, caught her breath and nodded again. "That's the problem, you see."

"I reckon…" Jake said, pulling her closer towards him, pressing her hard against his side; he hung his arm over her shoulder; she felt the warmth of his chest. "You don't do much walking, do you?" She felt his fingertip briefly brush the back of her hand.

"No."

The chilly gloom unexpectedly seemed to take on a new freshness. Suddenly, Georgia felt alive, awake, happy and excited.

"I spend most of my days sitting at computers working; that's the problem." She sighed and smiled up at him. "If I am honest, I spend most of my life sitting at my computer."

"Well then, for the sake of your health, and since we're now neighbours, we'd better get you outdoors more. Get you climbing up some of these hills." Georgia followed his gaze towards Mam Tor that loomed ahead in the distance.

"There's really no excuse when you live out here; there's no shortage of hills and green spaces on your doorstep."

"Sounds err…"

"Like a good idea?"

"No, painful!"

Jake laughed, "Good. You're up for it then!"

"So, Josh, has he agreed to go to Tibet?"

"Tibet, with the crazy American dude; I dunno, he wants to go, but he might end up just going in the Army. He wants me to go to the US in his place if he does decide to join the Army."

Georgia glanced at him. "I haven't travelled in, fucking, years. Are you going?"

"I'm tempted."

"Can you do his job?"

"In theory …and there's always Zoom."

Georgia had a horrible feeling, just her bloody luck, to go and meet someone who was contemplating a trip to America and Tibet. She was worried that he might never come back.

"What are you doing with the one in your barn? You know it's a Showman's Road Loco you have stored away in there."

"I know. Well, alls I do know is that it's some old Engine."

"Some old Engine!" He laughed. "Have you not been in the barn to look at it?"

"No, I haven't."

"It's amazing. You'd love it."

"I haven't even been in the barn, period. Is that bad?"

"Yeah, really bad; if you love Engines as much as Josh and I do, trust me, you'd love it. Josh would do anything to get that machine back in the family."

Nodding, Georgia smiled and considered what he had just said, then the penny dropped. "… back in the family?"

"Aw, it's a long story; it belonged to my great-grandad. I have a photo of him with my Great-grandmother; they're stood with it when they were about twenty years old. It was shiny and new looking then – an Enoch Farrar 1925 Majestic."

"I thought it was called a Burrell or something?"

"I can tell you the original colours on this thing if you want to know. It must have been gorgeous back in the day. It's green and gold now, and the reg, it's WT 2255. It was made—"

"Sounds like you know everything about it…?"

"That's because I do! It was passed down from my grandad to my dad and then to us. It was made in Yorkshire, Doncaster. Honestly, you have an amazing piece of kit in there."

"So, why is it in our barn and not yours?"

"I made the mistake of leaving it in my Girlfriend's barn; then we split up."

"Sounds complicated."

"You could say that, yeah, until I can find a way of getting my hands on the documents, to prove it's outs, it's a waste of time me even going on about it."

"Hope you find them."

"Oh, I know where they are… Hey, look at you; you're speeding up a bit."

"I still can't breathe, though." Jake's arm was getting heavy, but Georgia didn't mind. "So, how come your great-grandad had a Steam Engine?"

"He said they bought it originally for hauling fair rides across the UK, but he never used it. It's a road Engine ; great for haulage but also it generates electricity to power lights and fair rides."

"Sounds like you're passionate about it."

"Let Josh take a look at it. He'll tell you what state it's in and get it up and running again."

"Mark said—"

"As soon as I hear that name, I smell bullshit. I didn't want to say anything when he turned up at yours the other day. I swear to God-anyway, Josh said it's our Engine, same reg and everything, but we can't prove that he stole it."

"Who, Mark has?"

"Not exactly stolen, like, but, I said, it's complicated, let's just say that, he was crafty, and I shouldn't have left it where I did, so it's my fault."

Georgia pulled her phone out. It was ringing silently in her pocket.

"It's my dad."

Jake nodded and took a few steps away.

"Dad, yes. Okay, I'll be there in a minute…" she slipped the phone away. "Food's arrived. He's waiting for me."

Jake smiled.

"That's my car."

"Right, I passed mine ages ago."

"Oh really!"

"Just wanted to make sure you found yours first."

"Aw, that's sweet, thanks. Want a lift back down?"

"Nah, I'll walk."

"Right. Well, thanks."

"When are we going on that walk then?" Jake smiled when Georgia's face lit up. "If you're still up for it?"

"Absolutely. Can't wait." The car beeped as she opened the door with the fob on her key ring.

"Tomorrow then? Or, is that too soon?"

"No, no, that's great."

"Pick you up around 12-ish?" He pulled her gently towards him. Georgia's heart stopped. No longer breathing, she found herself gazing up into his watery blue eyes.

He kissed her hesitantly on the forehead, then laughed, blushing a little, as though he'd gone all shy. Suddenly he leaned in harder, pressing her against the side of the car—her legs went weak; she closed her eyes and stretched up to him slightly in anticipation of another kiss. Then to her amazement, he opened the driver's side of the car and laughed. "Your chariot awaits, my lady."

Georgia glanced up at him and blinked. "Oh! Right! Thanks!" Just as she was about to climb into the car, she stopped, turned and threw herself into his arms. For her, it was the kiss of the century, long, passionate, ravishing, and when it was over, they both wiped the rain from their drenched faces and laughed.

"Wow!" he said breathlessly, leaning over her to open the car door. "God knows what I'd have done with you if you had carried on kissing me like that… You'd better go!"

She was breathless and shaking; all she could do was nod as she climbed into the car.

"See you tomorrow then?" He said, closing the door.

She nodded again, put on her seatbelt and watched as he walked back down the hill towards his car, hands in his pockets, black curls, now drenched with rain, blowing in the wind, like Adonis, she thought. She decided there and then she was totally in love. She switched on the Engine and free-wheeled passing him at 30mph. She wanted to wave but thought it was cooler not to. She watched as he faded out of view in the rear-view mirror. Once she pulled out onto the main road at the bottom of the hill, she turned the radio up full blast and screamed, "A-m-a-z-i-n-g! Oh my God, Yes!"

The Reunion 1937

It was a bright day, with blue sky, fresh wind, and a touch of frost on the trees giving everyone a skip in their stride.

"Well, in layman's terms," Dan was deliberately being patronising to his brothers, Leo and Jack, "there are four different parts in a Steam Engine, yeah: the boiler full of water, the fire, that's the hot bit that heats it up, and the cylinder and piston—which is like a bicycle pump. Steam from the boiler is piped into the cylinder, causing the piston to move first one way then the other."

"That's not what I meant," Jack said, pulling at his end of the robe, trying to free it from the tangled mess it was coiled up inside. "I said, what makes this particular Engine more special? Why did we have to come here for that one?"

Dan followed behind his brother as they stretched out a rope from the rigging and began untangling the length between them.

"He just meant he doesn't know why that machine is so important?

You bring us out here, no consultation, no explanation."

Leo stood up, shook his head and put his hands on his hips, "Why?"

"Well, if you must know, this Engine just happens to be the Engine! You know, the one Dad lost.?"

"What!" Jack was just not having any more of it… "Who cares about that? That was his loss, not ours?"

Dan nodded. "It was our loss, bro; we were the ones who missed out on that opportunity. We could have been the first in the UK to light up a Circus with electric lamps!"

"Yeah, so…?" Jack pulled at the heavy rope aggressively.

Leo sighed. "We don't really care, bro… It's all in the past."

"Um, well, imagine, if Dad hadn't gone and gambled that damn Showman's Engine away… we'd also probably have been the first in the UK to run fair rides… It would have been a game-changer."

"Yeah, well, it's too late!"

"Antoinette Concello! You know her?"

Leo stopped what he was doing, "One of those flying Concellos?"

"Yeah,' course we know of her; why?" Jack looked up at Leo. "What has she got to do with us?"

Leo shrugged.

"She was the greatest woman flyer of all time!" Dan said, straightening up. He took his cap off, ran his fingers through his hair and put it back on.

"Ahy, the only woman to complete a triple, so what?"

"She's famed for completing three full somersaults between leaving the bar and being caught by the catcher… in live shows."

"Faye does that all the time in rehearsal…!"

"Yeah, she does, but it's dangerous…too risky."

"Faye doesn't think so. You're the one who stops her from doing it…!"

"I wouldn't want her doing it, especially not in our shows with me and you catching her."

"So, what's your point?"

"Antoinette did it in every show!"

"And…?"

"So, she pushed boundaries—went beyond her limits…and that Lion trainer, Isaac Van whatever –"

"Amburgh, the American?"

"Yeah, him, reputedly, he was the first man to stick his head into a lion's mouth."

"Leo does that when he's prating about," Jack said, slapping his brother's shoulder.

"Only when I've had a few," Leo said, pushing his brother back in retaliation and laughing.

"The Americans bought their act to England and performed for Queen Victoria …and us; we've achieved zero notoriety."

"We've got more than most, and we've lasted longer than most."

"We have elephants, Clowns…and …what more do you want?"

"They're merely pegs on which to hang a Circus, you know how the saying goes… We need more, bro. Where's the passion, the drive, the ambition…?"

"So, what are you asking? You want Faye to start triple somersaulting because I'm telling you now, you don't pay her nowhere near enough!"

"Look, Jack, I'm not arguing; I'm just saying, we've lost our drive... We need to start breaking some boundaries."

"Bro, you break them all the fucking time."

Leo crouched down and pulled at a knot in the rope until it wore loose. He shook his head, removed his cap, wiped the sweat from his brow, raked up his fringe and sat back on his heels. "So, what do you want, bro?" he asked without looking up.

"I'm not forbidding Jack to have kids,"

Jacked laughed. "Here we fucking go again."

"Listen, that is not what I mean. This is what I tried to tell you the other night before you cracked Leo in the mouth."

"I'll do it again if you fucking start –"

"The other night, I just wanted to say...I need...we need more time, yeah? If we're all gonna live off this place a few more years, avoid getting drafted, and –"

"No one's going in the Army."

"That's not what I mean, listen, will ya! I think we all need to put the sparkle back into our shows until I can get my hands on that Showman's; we could all just put in a bit more effort."

Leo stepped to one side, allowing Jack to wind up the rope over his shoulder. "What we can't do with that Engine isn't worth thinking about. We wouldn't be doing this job, that's for sure—just forget about your electric lamps, fair rides... we can't afford a machine like that, and they aren't selling it in a hurry either."

"Can't believe they've got a beautiful Engine like that just going to dust in a barn. Let's see if we can find one in Manchester or Sheffield—one that Leo can do up?"

"Good point."

"Oh aye...like I've got time to do that. Hey, who's that?" The brothers turned to follow Jack's gaze across the field. "She's waving. She's shouting you, Dan."

"Who?" Dan turned and looked again.

"It's that little' un who came here with your bit on the side."

Rebecca Price stood by the gate with little Janey by her side. Dan rose to his feet, crossed his arms, and then mumbled to himself as he ran over the field to greet her.

"I'll leave you to it, then, Leo," Jack said, dropping the rope coil into his brother's arms. "If he's buggered off, I ain't hanging about." Slapping his brother on the back, he walked off grinning. He turned a few times to laugh and nod in Dan's direction. Leo nodded back and laughed as he carried the rope inside the tent.

The habit of taking an afternoon snooze originated in Italy; the age-old custom of shutting shop mid-afternoon and reopening in the early evening when the sun was less intense suited the Circus's way of life. It was mid-afternoon; true to the Franconi tradition, mid-afternoon meant only one thing—siesta. With early morning starts, long gruelling journeys and late-night shows, the practice of siesta was even more appealing in the UK, where the weather was always cold, so the habit stuck.

When arriving at the caravan, Jack realised how late it was to find Faye curled up, sleeping by the stove.

"Jack, is that you?"

He closed the door behind him. "Dan has a visitor."

"Who?" She yawned.

"No idea, some woman and that kid."

Sitting, she pulled herself up to peer from the window. "Who? What kid?"

"Remember the little girl who fell? Amy from the farm caming looking for her?"

"I do recognise that kid. Who is that with her, her mother?"

"I don't know, but she came to find Dan."

"Oh?"

Dan threw his arms around Rebecca. "I didn't think you'd come here."

"I spoke to Amy, she said you'd been asking about me. I just couldn't leave it like that." She looked down at Janey and offered up the child's hand.

"This is…" she took a deep breath and pulled Janey forward slightly for him to see, "… Janey…" leaning in a little closer, she whispered, "… She's yours… she's your daughter."

Dan stepped back, took a sharp breath and slapped a hand to his forehead.

"Wha…!"

As the penny dropped, he let both arms fall heavily by his side and stood motionless, perplexed. His eyes scanned the child from head to toe in silence, studying her every detail.

"Are you sure?" he said quietly. Janey nodded. "But, you didn't say…you never said… No one told me."

"Why would they? No one knows."

"Not even…er… well, I hear you're married now…?"

"He doesn't know. Greg thinks she's his."

"Oh! Shit!"

Rebecca sighed, "Yeah, well… you never came back and… Greg did so in December 1931, as a matter of fact. We got married."

"Jesus…you didn't…you actually didn't tell him you were pregnant?"

"No. Greg helped my father on the farm, as you know. And the truth is… I needed him."

"Oh, so you just."

"Married him, yes! Why you are so shocked!"

"…But you hated Greg; you loathed him; said he was a dirty old man!"

"What else was I supposed to do?"

"He was always leeching around you… that's what you said, you found him annoying and… I wanted to knock him out!"

"Umm, and that's exactly why it was so easy for me…to… you know…as far as he is concerned…my child…well, she's his …no questions asked. And it's different now. He love me and he love the children."

"But I'm here now… I'm back… I came back for you."

"You've come back for that damn Engine, I've heard."

"That's not true… I knew there was a Showman's, one that might be going cheap, but the truth is…I wanted to see you!"

"So, you thought you'd kill two birds with one stone?"

"You should have told me… why didn't you tell me?"

"How could I? I Didn't even know where you were for the best part of the pregnancy. I waited…and I had no choice when you didn't come back. I didn't know where to find you… and you lied! You promised you were coming back…but you didn't!"

"But I'm here now, so."

"Six years late, nearly seven! A lot has happened in all that time, Dan."

Rebecca looked thoughtful. She looked up and down at his battered, albeit hand-made Italian boots and the frayed elbow of his jumper. His rolled-up cuffs and torn trousers.

"Look, Janey," Rebecca said, kissing her daughter's cheek. "There's the stripy horse you wanted to see… go look, don't get too close … Keep your distance."

"It's a Zebra, Mummy…!"

"Yes, dear, I know, Zebra!"

Janey was gone, running across the field without looking back.

"Shouldn't we go after her?" Dan said, sidling up to Rebecca and hooking his little finger through hers discretely.

She pulled her hand away and thrust it in her pocket.

"Too late, Danielle! Please, don't." She watched her child as she ran down the slope towards the gate where the Zebras was tied. "You and I were just."

"…a mistake?"

"You know I thought more of you than that."

"I can't stand being apart from you any longer; that's why I came back."

"But it was over before it began, wasn't it?"

"You mean the Circus came to town, and I was just…."

"Do not turn this around on me—how dare you! I was infatuated with you. You know I was, and I stupidly thought you loved me! I thought you'd come back and marry me like you promised! I waited, but I had to marry someone before it started to show… I had no choice!" Her voice trailed off. She pulled a handkerchief from her pocket and wrung it around her finger.

"So, how long did you wait…?"

"I slept with him straight away…soon after I found out. I knew I'd never see you again…I just knew you were never coming back. Getting with Greg was easy, the way he used to be around me…a few drinks and…well, I didn't enjoy it…I was ashamed …but needs must be for self-preservation and all that! What else was I supposed to do?"

"Why didn't you try to find me…let me know…?"

"I knew you were never coming back…turns out I was right; you didn't."

"So, how long did you wait… before you married him?"

"Is that all you can say… Six months! Is that long enough! When I was six months pregnant, Greg stood by me and said he'd do the right thing. He thought it was his. I wasn't showing too much so – when the child was born, she arrived spot on by his calculations, give or take, so there were never any questions asked… He's been a good man, really. And we have another baby called Jacob! He's a little terror, but Janey loves him… I think myself lucky to have Greg… He must never know—ever!"

"Where is he, this… Greg?"

"Away, RAF. Pays well, better than any work he can get around here. He's testing a new plane at the moment, the Blenheim Light Bomber. I probably shouldn't be telling you this. He's a supervisor"

"How long is he away for?"

"He gets home often… or as much as he can. He's due back today as a matter of fact, which is why I thought I'd tell you. I won't get another chance once he's back."

"Okay…" Danielle stretched. He rubbed his chin and felt abruptly sick.

"I'm glad you came back to Castleton, I thought you had the right to know …I wanted you to know everything."

"Do you need anything? Money, you alright for money?"

"I don't want anything from you. We don't need anything… I just wanted you to know, that's all. All I ask is that you never turn up, never come around asking questions, or bother Janey in any way… We never existed to you—do y' understand? I just wanted to clear my conscience with you and hope you can do the same."

Dan had not anticipated any problems in his mind. Finding Rebecca would be the most challenging part, but winning her back would be easy. How wrong he was. How foolish of him to believe she'd still be waiting for him. His instant reaction was anger and rejection. He felt rage. The last thing he had wanted or expected was to be turned away by this woman. He had imagined her sitting by the window burning a flame for him for nearly ten years, with wishful eyes watching, waiting for his return…

After all the heart aching misery he'd endured while trying to work his way back to her, he never expected this would be the outcome.

Rebecca, giving a small gesture with her shoulder, nudged him gently. "Okay? Daniel?" Dan could not bring himself to look at her. "Janey! Come on, we're going!" Before Dan could react, Rebecca walked away hand in hand with Janey. The child turned and waved; Rebecca stopped to coax her along. She lifted her head and smiled. "What will you do, Dan?"

An angry flush came to his face. "Same as I have been doing all my life…Trapeze!"

"I remember those muscles," she laughs. "God, I loved those muscles…and no safety net, phew."

Dan looked aghast at her.

"You took me around the back of that Village Hall in Castleton, remember?"

"I do."

"It was a bright day, blue sky, fresh wind... Cherry pink blossom petals around our feet, freezing cold...just like today."

"I'm sorry it had to end the way it did."

"Me too, another girl, another town, another time... you'll be fine, Dan. Oh, I forgot to give you this."

Dan stood there nodding, waiting. She took his hand.

"Here, I believe it belongs to your mother ...?"

Dan's mouth fell open.

"Yes, thought you'd forgotten about it."

"I didn't."

"Don't be so un-gifting next time; consider giving it to someone you really intend to marry, okay."

Dan glanced down at the sparkling brooch in his hand. Rebecca turned, staring ahead and walked away.

"Here, give it to Janey; something to remember me by"

"You just don't get it, do you? You're dead to me now."

"Aw come on, don't say that!"

"You'll be fine Dan; men like you always are!"

Feeding the Devil 2020

"Shit! Ouch! Shit!" Georgia tossed another dead match on the smouldering logs and sucked her stinging finger. "It's so cold, and I'm sick of this weather. Why does it constantly rain in Derbyshire? It's red hot in London!"

"Here, let me do it!" Len crouched down beside the hearth.

He lit a piece of paper, tucked it beneath the kindling, then leaned a shovel against the fireplace, spread a sheet of newspaper over it, leaned back on his heels, and waited for the steady flame to spread out behind the paper. After waiting a moment or two for the kindling to ignite, he quickly removed the shovel and newspaper. He disappeared into the kitchen and reappeared moments later with a bag of sugar.

"Oh well," he said, digging his hand in the sugar, "Sorry, mum, I'm feeding the devil, but who cares as long as we get warm."

Len tossed a generous handful of sugar into the fire, placed the shovel and newspaper back then stood back to watch as it burst furiously into high angry flames that licked at the back of the newspaper, scorching it an old brown colour before the edges of the burn patches sparkled with red sparks that quickly turned into flaming black holes.

"Ooh, Bear Grylls in d' ouse?" Georgia said, walking over to watch what was going on. "Can't believe we have to do this every time we need hot water!"

"I'll call that Jake fella; get him back out."

"No need, I'll be seeing him tomorrow. He's coming here to pick me up. I'll ask him to take a look at it."

"Well, well, well. I wondered where you'd gotten. Seemed to take you a heck of a long time to find that car."

"Well, it did, actually. I just happened to walk up from the Traveller's with Jake."

"And…?"

"And, what? He offered to show me around Castleton tomorrow, that's all."

"Good, then you can show him around our boiler, get him to fix it properly this time."

"What did you mean; feeding the devil?"

"My mother died before you were born, anyway, to answer your question..."

"So, what was your Granny's name again?"

"Amy, you've seen photos. You look just like her, delicate, pretty, dark. She was born around here somewhere."

"So, what's this about the devil feeding, then?"

"Well, if you'd stop interrupting, I'll tell you. Your Great-grandmother Amy hated fires and wouldn't even light one in the house. She believed fire evoked evil, the devil. And, if you ever fed the devil, oh my god, she'd go mad. And by that, she meant throwing food on the fire; she'd go crackers! In her later years, she would only use electric fires and the electric rings on the cooker, and she was terrified of doing that too. She had a real fear of fire; pyrophoric is the correct term. She somehow thought the devil was connected with it."

"Why?"

"Don't know; I know in her later years she became very religious; maybe that had something to do with it, but she truly believed if you threw food on the fire, you were somehow inviting the devil into your home.

She used to say, 'Once you've fed him, you'll never get rid of him.'"

Georgia moved closer to the blaze, reaching out the palms of her hands towards the glow from behind the newspaper. "I don't care," she said, rubbing her hands together. "He can come as often as he likes as long as we get hot water."

Once the paper had drawn up enough oxygen through the flue, and the warm glow of the fire increased behind it; an amber light began turning into tiny red scorched marks that spread slowly in no particular direction. Len took the poker, tapped the paper down into the fire, and watched it disintegrate into white papery ash that floated around in the grate like snow; it landed slowly and gently over the kindling until Len dropped a heavy log into the flames causing sparks to fly.

When satisfied that the fire had taken hold, he rose to his feet and disappeared into the kitchen. Sitting by the fire for the first time, its warmth gave Georgia a homely feeling. She moved in closer, sat on the rug and began scrolling through her phone.

Another Nightmare 2020

Amy stood beside the fire, looking down on Georgia. "Put it out! Don't sleep. Don't let the baby will die?"

"Georgia. Georgia!"

"Eh! What!"

"Go to bed, love!" Len stood looking down at her tapping her lightly with his foot. "Come on, you'll catch your death." He turned away, then turned back and studied her face. "You having nightmares again?"

Georgia looked up. "Hmm? Eh? Say again?"

"I said, you having another one of your nightmares?"

She sounded half asleep. "Hmm, yeah. How did you know?"

"You were shouting in your sleep. You're doing it a lot lately."

"Am I?

The rain had subsided by the time Georgia went to bed. She pulled back the quilt, crawled beneath it and peered out of the window. Set against the early evening sky, the dark khaki greens of the landscape distorted through the tiny lead panes, glistening periodically beneath the ominous glow of moonlight that broke through the thick blanket of cloud.

The dark horizon had become a band of infinite blackness blurring the space between land and sky. The horizon looked bruised, mauve-purple, as though the day's constant rain had battered it to an inch of its existence. Georgia drew the curtains together and tucked them behind the radiator, then slipping off the bed, she moved a jumper to one side with her barefoot. She had lost her phone after finding earphones slung over the mirror earlier. Eventually, she found the phone and bent down to retrieve the silver square that lay face down on the carpet. Then fumbling with the earphones, trying to get them to fit snuggly in her ears, she scrolled the menu to make a song selection. Suddenly, a strange sensation crept over her. She straightened and looked around. "Hello?" she said into the room with consternation. Before the storm had blackened the skies, she had washed the bed linen and managed to dry it outside before the rain came. The light flickered, but she had gotten used to that. She noticed an aroma, like chard, burnt wood and paraffin. It hung heavy and was intermittent. Wondering if perhaps one of the farms on the southern tip of the town had had a fire, she lifted the quilt to her face and breathed in the delicate fragrance of Apple Blossom fabric softener. Sometimes when the wind turns, it brings that very same smell over the hills from neighbouring farms; an awful rancid smell of burning tyres, plastic and all sorts; whatever it was seemed to have suddenly dissipated.

She let the quilt drop and sat staring at her bare feet, nodding to the music in her ears. The coloured gel painted on her toes was a bright, metallic yellow with a rhinestone embedded into each big toe. She liked it when she had first had it done but now thought it looked disgusting. As she considered where on earth she would find a boutique out in the sticks to remove the god-awful polish, an overwhelming sense of sadness suddenly crept over her. She felt lost and homesick. It's the void, she told herself in a Scooby-doo narrative voice in her head. Have I just become one of the lost and lonely souls who, according to that stupid newspaper article, pass through High Oakham Cottage, never to be seen again.

She whipped out the earphones and glanced around. Everything was quiet and still. She made a tutting noise with her tongue, sat back on the bed and turned her attention to the phone in her hand. The music playing from a playlist she collated months ago shifted her spirit slightly and temporarily took her back to London; memories of her time living in the city sifted her emotions from sadness to a shiver of excitement. Inspired, she sent a quick text to an old friend and waited for him to reply.

"Hey, Pipsqueak! What are you doing next weekend? Fancy coming to Derbyshire?" As she threw down the phone, an overwhelming wave of home-sickness came crashing upon her again; nostalgia descended. The tune playing in her ears made her think back to all the clubs where she and Pipsqueak had danced till dawn. The feeling associated with the song momentarily glossed over the surface of her memories, making any sense of reality somehow warp into a whole new realm.

She closed her eyes and saw an image of some club in Mayfair—sparkly and glitzy. Slowly the memory turned grey and smoky, like a black and white photo taken in the sixties. The sound of sirens, racing cabs, and endless rows of street lights, shops, bars, and restaurants slowly faded to an image of a field with grass blowing in the wind. Campfires and babbling brooks wash over the city scene, like the transition of an old silent movie flickering before her eyes. Then the smell of burning ascended in the room again. The smoke carried upon a light breeze, with the tinkling of laughter filling the air. She sensed the warmth of a summer's day upon her cheeks; all the feelings associated with the memory drifted down upon her like layers of multi-coloured tissue. The Cottage stood in the distance, looking, as it does now, though different somehow. Suddenly, as if from nowhere, a screaming inferno of flames engulfed the whole mise-en-scene. Georgia tried to run but couldn't—poised on the edge of the nightmare, she was half-awake trying to shout out, knowing she was engulfed by a dream but was trapped within it…

"Georgia! Wake up!"

"Eh!"

"I told you to go to bed hours ago. Go on, go to bed!" Len stood looking down at her tapping her lightly with his foot. "Come on, love, you'll catch your death." He turned away, then turned back and studied her face. "You having nightmares again?"

Georgia looked up. "Hmm? Eh? Say again?"

"I said, you having nightmares again?" She sounded half asleep. "Hmm…"

Georgia climbed the stairs to bed, entered her bedroom and snatched the earphones from her ears. She stood bolt upright and remained perfectly still, holding her breath in the silence, acutely aware that something indescribable was in the room. Though there was nothing visible, she felt whatever it was, it was trying to communicate.

That familiar sense of loss returned again. It was becoming a familiar feeling now, but somehow appeared to be adopting an intelligence of its own, as though trying to manifest; import itself into the room. In a cold, clammy blindness, Amy ran towards the door. The door slammed shut, barricading her inside. She began clawing at the handle, grabbing and fumbling to open it, but it was useless. All sense of logic was telling her that she was fine and that her father was only downstairs and would probably be able to hear her panicking, but she could no more escape the panic within herself than she could the bolted door. All sense of self-awareness had gone; new emotions engulfed her. Amy knew they were the feelings experienced by whatever was in the room with her. She heaved her body around to face the room. Then voices began to whisper in her ear; a woman's above all others, as clear as a bell. Others spoke in indecipherable languages, both male and female muffled and angry, almost inhuman. "My baby! I want my baby; I want my child!"

"Georgia! Wake up…"

"Eh! What!"

"Go to bed!" Len stood looking down at her tapping her lightly with his foot. "Come on, love, you'll catch your death." He turned away, then turned back and studied her face. "Nightmare again?"

Georgia looked up. "Oh my God, yes!"

"Go to bed!"

Georgia rose to her feet as Len switched on the TV and complained about the signal again. The curtains began to ripple gently. An aeroplane hummed in the distance, and nature's sound carried in through the open window. Georgia slammed it shut with both hands. She backed away, her reflection crawling slowly up into view in the half-transparent glass. Darkness shone back against the blackness in the glass panes behind her reflection. Then slowly, the landscape's greens, browns, blues and blacks and the night sky beyond came back into view. Georgia stared a moment longer at her reflection, stretched her arms above her body, and observed her lithe form in the window. Never before had she felt so grateful for every inch of her magnificence.

"Thank God," she whispered, "I'm fine. I'm fine!"

Giving a little laugh and fearing nothing more, she lifted her hands to the glass and relaxed, then dropped her arms heavily by her side. Slowly the

door to the kitchen creaked open, allowing the warm light from the crack in the door to illuminate the shadiest corners of the room. A sudden sense of normality returned and the sound of Boris Johnson's voice on the 10 o'clock news brought Georgia back to earth.

"Good evening, the Corona Virus is the biggest threat this country has faced for decades!"

Georgia was sent laughing into the kitchen. Len looked up over the rim of his glasses, mouth gaping, wondering what had gotten into her.

"Do you want a cuppa, Dad?" Moments later, she appeared at the kitchen door with two hot steaming mugs of tea. Just as normality returned, and the history of High Oakham Cottage had been sent packing back into the walls from where it had tried to escape, a weather bulletin on TV blurted out, "Storm Goliath to hit East Midlands tomorrow."

Another Great Show 1937

Peering over a sea of heads and shoulders, Amy sat ringside, staring in awe at colourful dancers as they somersaulted out into the arena. Suddenly, catching site of Leo disappearing between the curtains, she found herself following him with her eyes. She was distracted now, intrigued to know what he was doing, her eyes fixed on what was going on backstage. She peeped between a fold in the heavy crushed velvet curtains; she saw Leo reading off a clipboard. Several performers appeared, hurrying around him, each deep in thought, some chatting, others speedily throwing off garments and swapping them haphazardly. Soon clothing lay around like there had been a frenzied sale in a rag shop. Amy watched through the tiny gap as Leo sat heavily and rested his chin in his hand, waiting for his next act to get their act together. He peered at the dancers who were now pirouetting around in the ring, creating hypnotic formations with waving, rolling ribbons and scarves. Their elegant performance brought them between Amy and Leo's focal point, obscuring Amy's view of Leo at that moment and momentarily drawing her attention away from him.

When the dancers swooned off in opposite directions, Amy glanced up to find Leo had gone; then she caught sight of him again bundling all the garments of loose clothing into a chest. He straightened, then adjusted his own apparel and ran out into the ring, much to the disappointment of the crowd, who were still howling at the glamorous dancers. Men rose to their feet wolf-whistling as their children waved frantically by their side at the glorious ladies gracefully making their exit ringside left.

The new act bounded in with an explosion of Handstands, Back Handsprings, Whip Backs, Back Flip and Ariel Cartwheels. Suddenly, remembering Leo, Amy found herself wondering where he was. Then, spotting an opportunity to glimpse through the space in the curtain again, she saw him clearly, sifting through the chest of clothes and removing items from pockets, bags, and purses. Then, with the dancers starting to make their way around the tent, he quickly closed the chest and sat on it. Amy, looked at her father, he looked puzzled. He nudged her softly. "Stop being nosey. It has nothing to do with you, not your concern!" When Amy dared look again, Leo seemed to be talking to someone, a dance member smiling and laughing at his jokes. Then, he took up some brass or woodwind instrument and began gesturing rudely with it, holding it suggestively in his hand. Amy sat back and shook her head in disgust, looking only occasionally to see if she could still see him; she eventually forgot about him and allowed the evening's entertainment to progress.

Later in the evening, the young blonde Indian boy on his bejewelled elephant certainly took centre stage. When the elephant act finished, Leo re-appeared in the centre circle, knocking a few Clown's heads together, both of them, plump, unstable on their stumpy legs, and dressed in matching attire, whose job and skill it seemed was to demonstrate that they had a head full of nothing and a heightened sense of hysteria. While other more sophisticated acts prepared backstage, Leo tossed the third Clown into a barrel and rode upon it. Amy shot a look at her father. They both shrugged and laughed out loud. They laughed so much that they hardly noticed Leo sending the Clowns off with a kick up their rear end. They'd sneaked out beneath the curtain several times and flung foam pies at unsuspecting audience members.

"Whoop!" They shouted, "Here goes another one!" Then the crafty Clowns crept up behind the supposedly unsuspecting Leo and bombarded him with pies.
"

"Hey! Where did they go?" Leo was shouting to screaming children, who were now crying out commands as he dodged the rogue Clowns.

"Thank you, ladies and gentlemen, girls and boys, don't forget to tell your friends about us. And before you go, we will be bringing out a few of our wonderful animals so that you can come down here and take a look—oh, no, you don't –" Leo shouted suddenly, as a cheeky Clown hit him square on in the face. "Why, you little!" The Clown took one in the face too as Leo ran after him wiping foam from his eyes.

"Goodnight and God bless!" he shouted before disappearing beneath the drapes. Dad and Amy were still laughing as people began leaving. The old man wiped away a tear and put on his cap. As everyone began to rise to their feet and slowly began to exit the bellowing tent to the soft melody of a solo horn, a swing drifted gently down from the rigging into the centre of the arena. Holding hands, Dan, Faye and Jack followed each other to the chime of cheers, horse whistles and stomping feet. People, including Amy and her father, stopped in their tracks to clap and quickly returned to their seats. They sat abruptly for the encore. Faye waving and pirouetting elegantly, sat upon the swing as Dan and Jack began pushing her gently back and forth between them. She waved as she swung softly between the two.

Illuminated by several lamps, her oily lips shone blood red, and the many heavy layers of facepaint made her appear Egyptian, like Queen Cleopatra, which somehow projected the theatricality of her whole existence and made Amy question the life she was leading. It was intriguing, mysterious, if not somewhat eerie.

Once the swing had built up momentum, it rose into the rigging. Dan and Jack each climbed upon the sides of the swing, riding one foot on and one-off until it reached a good thirty feet above the centre circle. Swinging back and forth high above craning necks, Dan gracefully stepped off the swing onto a platform at the side of the rigging; simultaneously, Jack did the same at the opposite side. In two graceful movements, Faye fell back into a hanging position. She continued to swing while dangling from bent knee, upside down, arms spread and hair loosely trailing beneath her; she turned thus back and forth to a chorus of oohs and aahs. Dan mumbled to her words of encouragement and commands, which Faye appeared to obey. She reached up for the bar between her knees and gently manoeuvred herself into a free-falling position, hanging on literally by teeth tightly clenching a purpose-made mouthpiece. Faye placed her neck through a hoop attached to it and continued to swing gracefully by gritted teeth, until now hanging from the back of her head and neck, while still spinning first one way then back the other with her arms folded neatly over her body. For increased dynamics, she twisted and spun harder, faster. The crowd below exploded, hoorays and hurrahs. Dan's muffled calls, more frequent now, became a little louder. Amy found his command of Faye erotic and sexy, but she also felt jealous. Dan suddenly pulled the swing in by another rope as she continued to spin from the arch of her neck. Jack reached to pull her in on the opposite side as the swing swung his way. Her arms now outstretched, like a spinning star, waiting for the men to pull her in, she missed the vital connection point.

There was a rise of Ooo from the crowd, then silence as Dan made a second grab for her when she swung his way. Jack glanced over at Dan. He gazed back, eyes dark and wide. He gave a reassuring nod as Faye continued to swing, turn and spin first one way and then the other. She reached out again to Jack and failed to connect a second time. Quickly, Faye grabbed at the hoop behind the arch of her neck and pulled her body weight off the noose. She then tried to gracefully free herself of the loop and shift her body weight back up to the bar. Jack yelled out a command as she came back his way. Dan pulled her in with his rope. Her body arched upright as she released the hoop and hoisted herself back into a seated position to the audience's relief below. Then in one swift movement, Faye stood upright on the swing and threw open her arms. As she turned, her slipper strap broke, and she tripped slightly. The crowd cheered as she swung towards Dan and prepared to step off.

Dan caught her before she'd even realised that she was falling. He lifted her gently towards him like a child's doll, softly placing her tiny form safely on the narrow platform beside him, and held her there until she was steady. She grasped his shoulder and leaned upon him while throwing up a theatrical arm for effect. Jack watched from the opposite side, looking and feeling awkward, while Dan held his wife in his arms.

Jack began yelling to the couple, then, nodding down at the faces below, started clapping and cheering. The audience responded by clapping and whistling back. Dan and Faye stared briefly at each other, then she looked away. Dan threw the swing over to Jack's side. Catching it, he called across to his brother. Dan released his grip from around Faye's waist and waved down at the adoring crowds below. Jack leapt from his platform and did a double somersault before returning to his ledge and allowing the swing to return to Dan.

Dan took up the swing bar and leapt off the platform, curving and arching his body like a furiously swinging pendulum swinging back and forth; hanging from his knees, he reached out for Jack. Their connection is swift, decisive and precise, allowing Jack to leap from a standing position off the platform and fling back and forth above the circle suspended by the good grace of Dan's firm grip and his faith in God.

"There's no safety net!" Amy gasped. Her dad didn't care. His eyes were fixed on the two men.

The audience fell silent as Dan suddenly let go of Jack. He somersaulted twice in mid-air in one full circular swoop and caught his brother's firm grip again; wrists interlocked like vices as the two swung back to the platform, where Jack was deposited swiftly and gracefully.

Dan, remaining upon the swing, heaved his body backwards, arching back for speed; he suddenly somersaulted four times before regaining his grasp upon the swing. Jack yelled; Faye gave a stifled cry and then yelled at the crowds, encouraging them to offer their appreciation.

Then as the crowd's cries slowly died down, Dan leapt upon his platform, threw up his arms for one last round of applause then returned upon the swing to bring down Faye and Jack, gently lowering from the heavens above while the swing continued to slide backwards and forwards with all three upon it, down into the centre of the ring to tremendous applause. They each closed their eyes and absorbed the energy. When the audience's cheers faded along with the illumination of the heavens above, Amy saw Leo standing beside the ring, shaking his head and clapping. As people began rising from the seats they had been sitting on the edge of all night, Leo ran out to join the trio, shook Dan's hand, and hugged Faye.

As promised, animals of all descriptions began appearing in the ring, led by a procession of performers, Jossers and Clowns. Chattering children made an orderly queue with parents waiting to marvel at the wonder of the beautiful yet strange creatures in the ring. Amy wrapped her coat over her shoulders and waited for her dad to knot his scarf and put his cap back on. Only as they started to make their way out behind the crowds did they see Dan striding towards them, still dressed in tight pants and vest, thick leather straps around his wrists and soft white fabric shoes, designed for the high wire and trapeze. He was wiping chalk from his hands on a towel and beads of sweat from his brow. His face, still flushed, was shining in the paraffin lamplight.

"Are you not staying to see the animals?"

"No, it's late."

"Did you enjoy the show?"

Dad intervened, shaking his chalked hand. "Great show, lad! Yes, we enjoyed it, didn't we, Amy?"

"Good. Don't rush off; join me for a cuppa!"

Dad looked at Amy. "Shall we?"

"It's late, Dad."

"You know what, son, I'd love one. And Amy would…?"

"No, Dad, thanks, it just too late."

"Great. We'll go out this way." Before Amy could protest further, Dan had already set off, leading them towards the back of the tent.

They'd just about made it halfway around the circumference of the seats when Amy spotted Rebecca Price leading an excited Janey into the ring. Jack was waiting, arms outstretched. "Dad, excuse me…" she said, leaving his arm.

"Amy, where you going, love?"

"Won't be too long. Back in a minute!" Amy didn't get far when a sudden soft Irish voice sounded near.

"Keep bumping into each other, don't we?" Faye said, tapping Amy on the shoulder.

"Hello" Amy looked down at her tiny frame. She nodded over at Dan.

"Well?" Faye asked inquisitively; she, too, looked up and down at Amy, then smiled. "Was it you who came over earlier to see Dan? Are you his old flame?"

"Old flame, me? No!" Amy offered abruptly. "Never met him before this week."

Dan heard and came over, leaving the old man leaning on his walking stick laughing; he put his arm around Faye. "Barking up the wrong tree there, Faye!" Amy sensed he was slightly embarrassed. He laughed again. "I'm putting the kettle on, joining us?"

"Dan, I'm starving!" Faye said, linking her arm through his. She pulled him close, placed her hand on his muscular chest and spoke into his ear. "Is it true? You've bought us here for an old flame? Or is it for an old Engine?" She turned slightly and looked up and down at Amy.

"Come on…" Dan laughed awkwardly. "You've got all that mixed up in your tiny little head. No, no truth in any of that at all." He raised his voice a touch for Amy to hear. "Why don't you come and join us for a cuppa." His voice faded suddenly when his eyes met Rebecca's across the ring.

Faye followed his gaze and smiled.

"I reckon you need something a bit stronger than tea tonight, Dan, especially after that performance, a triple; who were you trying to impress?" She glanced between the two women, threw back her head and laughed. Dan moved away from her allowing her arm to drop from his. Faye sprung off, took the reins of three ponies and began leading them in single file. She smiled and nodded at the old man as she passed him at the circle's edge, then shouted at Dan. "T'anks for the invite, but three is already a crowd!" Turning to face the group as they stood huddled in the centre of the Ring, Faye looked Amy and Rebecca up and down again and laughed. She did a kind of running skip and mounted one of the ponies before leading them off to where adorning fans, men mainly waited to greet her.

Faye yelled back at Dan over the crowd, "Hey Danny boy! Don't let any of that green rub off on you!"

Dan shot Amy a sideways look. Faye laughed loudly.

"Lovely green dress brings out the colour of your eyes," Dan said, taking Amy by the arm.

More concerned for Rebecca and Janey than any flirtatious woman, who seemed a tad bit jealous of her, Amy waved at Janey, sitting in Jack's arms.

"Excuse me, Dan," she said, patting Dan's shoulder, "Just seen the Prices' Do you mind? I'm just going to pop over to say hello! Dad, I won't be long."

The old man tutted silently as he walked closer, "Alright, love," he said, watching her weaving her way through the crowd. Once Amy was through the sea of bodies, she thought of nothing but getting the child away from Jack Franconi. To prevent them from getting separated again, she grabbed the child's leg just as Jack was about to lift her high upon his shoulders. "Here, I'll take her," Amy said, lifting the child down. She held her hand tightly in hers.

Janey began pulling away. "Stop!" Amy pulled her closer.

"Amy, hello!" Rebecca was surprised and looked somewhat bewildered. "Jack was about to show Janey the animals and said he had a present for her. He remembered her from the other afternoon when you brought her to see the animals?"

"Yeah, bet he does."

The child was clearly very excited to go with Jack and, unable to contain her anger at Amy's intervention. "Let go!"

"Mrs Price, I was just about to go have tea with Danielle Franconi; why don't you join us?"

Rebecca flushed a little and grew agitated. Hearing Dan's name mentioned, she felt herself shaking with concealed anger. She took Janey's hand. Amy felt her tug her child away from her. "Look, Janey, elephant!" Rebecca said, lifting the child into her arms. She held her up for Jack to take. He instantly swept her up in his arms.

"Didn't know you were here, Amy!" Mrs Price forced a smile. "This man, Jack, he's really quite lovely. Like I said, he kindly offered to show Janey the animals, so-."

"I understand," Amy said.

"You've met already, I hear?"

"Yes, we are acquainted. I'd like to buy Janey a toffee apple if that is okay with you?" Amy said, opening up her arms to Janey.

"I want to see the elephant!" Janey insisted. She flashed a look at her mother. Jack lifted her up higher onto his shoulder again.

"Oh, she'd like that." Mrs Price looked up adoringly at her blonde-haired baby. "But, I think she'd like to see the elephant with Jack, thanks. Perhaps after, she'd like that, wouldn't you, Janey, a toffee apple after you've seen the elephant with Jack?"

Jack turned and smiled. "Sounds good," he said. He looked directly at Amy. "I'll take her for a toffee apple; I'll take you both." He smirked mockingly at Amy and laughed.

"Where's your wife, Jack?" Amy asked.

Jack's response was rebuffed by Mrs Price. "Oh, your dad's here. He looks…?"

"Sober, yes, he is!"

Jack looked over at Dan, standing in deep conversation with the old man, waiting for her to return.

"Shall we go see this elephant then…?" Jack said, moving off with Janey.

Amy saw Leo and gave him a wave. Jack waved to him too and laughed mockingly.

"Can I stroke the elephant, Jack?" Janey asked, kicking her heels hard into his chest.

"Careful, Janey!" Mrs Price said, gripping her daughter's striking heels. "That's rude!" Even Amy is shocked by the child's behaviour and thinks Jack brings out the worst in her.

Jack placed Janey down on the ground and took her by the hand. "Come on then!" He left Amy and Rebecca standing as he led the child over to the young Indian lad, allowing Janey to pat the animal's trunk.

"Aw, I love Jack…I mean, he seems like a lovely man. Aw, look, Janey really seems to like him!"

"Do you mind? I will be honest; I don't care if I'm honest," she said, correcting herself. "I only met that man briefly… for the first time the other night. He came to the cottage yelling and threatening me… something about me ripping him off."

"Really, why?"

"Your guess is as good as mine," she said. "He was drunk…and angry about the rent I was charging, but then he apologised for interfering with Dan's negotiations."

"Dan!"

Amy stopped briefly, then continued. "He said Dan deals with the business side of things, but sometimes their wires get crossed."

"Strange. I'm sorry, but I don't know what you mean…?"

"Put it this way, I saw a side to that man that was far from nice or lovely. And as if that wasn't bad enough, he took Janey off when I bought her here without even asking me."

Rebecca smiled as though to herself, then nodded. "I understand."

"I was terrified." Amy sighed. "Watch him!"

"Where did he take her?"

"Oh, I don't know; to see the lions. It was very inappropriate if you know what I mean?"

"Of course. Did Dan see her too?"

"Dan? No. Well, yes, he did. He was lovely, kind as always."

"Well, I'm sure Jack had no ill intent with my daughter."

"But he had no business taking her without my consent. I had to chase around all over the fields looking for her!"

"Mmm, yes, I can see how that must have worried you. You're absolutely right," Rebecca said. "I will keep my eye on him." She smiled. "But he's fine…honestly."

Faye suddenly prised her head between Amy and Rebecca. "Don't believe her…" she taunted. "Devil in disguise that one; got a real nice behind, though, don't ya t'ink!"

Both Rebecca and Amy jumped. They hadn't even been aware she was there. "Ah, he's harmless enough. You know, it is a Circus; entertaining the kids is what we do!"

When Amy and Rebecca turned to face her, Faye had already spun on her heels and was heading out of the tent, arms tightly folded around Leo's neck. The women watched, mouths gaping, as she left the tent with Leo giggling and singing like children at the top of their voices.

"That woman, she's like –"

"Lice," Rebecca said. "Just when you think you've got rid of her, she re-appears."

"Yeah…I know what you mean"

Rebecca tossed her thick plait over one shoulder disapprovingly.

"Just had the pleasure of meeting my wife?" Jack asked, returning a beaming Janey to her mother. "Shall we go get toffee apples then?"

If Dan Can 1937

Amy woke about 7:30-ish and went downstairs. She knew what time it was because the cockerel had been waking earlier, adjusting to the brighter mornings. Amy heard hammering in the backfield. And since the old man was fast asleep, she also knew because his boots were by the door, and she could hear him snoring. She slipped on shoes, grabbed an overcoat off the clothes horse, and then slipped out to see where the noise was coming from.

Dan and Leo stood by the hencoop. Dan stood smoking with his back turned against her, and Leo bent over hammering.

"Morning!" she shouted across the yard; a blast of white breath drifted from her lungs and floated in the cold morning air.

"Morning!" Leo stopped hammering momentarily and waved the hammer. He turned and removed his cap.

Amy waved back.

"Sorry, did we wake you!" Dan said, walking towards her. "Is he up yet?"

"You've got to be joking!" Doing a half turn back to the cottage, Amy stopped and pulled the overcoat tighter around her midriff. "No, he's fast asleep."

"Nay, I am up, lass!" said a voice behind her. The old man peering over Amy's shoulder stood in the door with a mug of something hot. "Fancy a brew!"

Four people sat around that kitchen table that bitterly cold morning. Leo, still coughing and wheezing, washed his hands in a pale of water on the kitchen table, and Dan took it upon himself to take out the ashes and tip them out back where it looked as though Amy might grow herbs and veg, then went back inside, lit a fire in the hearth and sat to watch the tiny flames slowly lick at the kindle beneath the freshly cut logs. Rising slowly to his feet, he stretched and turned to Amy, trailing his finger down her nose.

"You've got your dad's nose; do you know that?"

Leo swished the water in the pail loudly, flashed Dan a smirk and coughed deliberately. He shot him another glance over his shoulder as he leaned over the table to find something to wipe his hands on. Amy blushed and toyed with a tendril of hair. The old man smiled at her.

The two men, Leo and Dan, were both falling for the girl, but neither told the other. "We've done a few bits and bats around the barn," Leo said to impress her. Leo, "Oh, I forgot. I prepared a broth meal. It's on the trap,"

"Oh, thank you!" Amy looked surprised.

Dan laughed and shook his head.

"A small gesture for going out in all that rain." He ran out and returned moments later with a dish. "Just to show my appreciation for your help, like," he said, carefully placing the dish beside the sink. Dan laughed again. "It is the least I can do," Leo said, glancing at Dan. Dan had suspicions about Leo's true motives but kept his thoughts to himself. On the other hand, Leo had noticed a twinkle in Dan's eye every time he spoke Amy's name.

Dan wrapped his hands around his empty cup. "Glad you came to the show last night."

"It was a good show," The old man interjected. He slurped his tea loudly.

"Thank you for the invite again," Amy said, looking at Leo with a warm smile. Dan felt a pang of jealousy.

"Come anytime. It's the least we can do for putting up with us."

Leo lit a cigarette.

"How are you feeling?" Amy seemed genuinely concerned.

"Right as rain, much better." He picked a stray piece of baccy from his lips.

"Not rested much, though, have you?"

"You really ought not to have bothered." Dan chimed in. "He never listens anyway."

"And it's a bloody good job I don't because I'd be dead by now if I did."

"Well, you're still here now," Amy laughed. "Dr Smyth's Brandy didn't finish you off then?"

"Ney, it didn't." He laughed. "…that's true. Now there's one doctor's door I'll be knocking on again."

Leo shook his hands dry and took a drink from his tea. "This is a bloody good brew."

"He has a natural mistrust of doctors," Dan said.

"Because they tell you to stop all the things you love."

"He thinks harping on about his ill health makes him weak."

Amy discretely pointed over at her father with her thumb. "He's the same," she whispered.

"We took a crafty look at that Engine," Leo confessed, still looking around for something to dry his hands on.

The old man looked up so fast that he nearly choked on his tea.

"Ya talking to me?"

"Aye!" Leo laughed. "I'm talking about that beaut you've got in the barn."

"Oh, right, the Engine?" Leo looked at Dan and winked.

"You've been in the barn, have you?" The old man asked sternly.

"How else could I look at it? You did tell me to drop by and let you know what I thought…."

The old man scratched his head. "So, what are your thoughts…?"

"Great. A magnificent piece of machinery—a real beauty. You're sitting on a fortune there."

Amy jumped up and offered him a rag. "Thanks!"

"Yes, we know, but it's a sleeping beauty for now until Amy finds her Prince charming."

"And do we have Pprince charming on the horizon?"

"No!" Her voice was soft with embarrassment.

"Not even over that distant hill?" He said, nodding in the direction of the site.

Leo looked over at Dan.

Amy shrugged.

"…The only hill she sees the other side of is the same one she looks at everyday." The old man pointed to the window, and everyone turned to gaze out. "– And that's too close t' river. It is more likely to be the river that sweeps Amy off her feet when it bursts the bank again."

"Well, those hills do stretch out further than Castleton. Someone will carry you off to broaden your horizon one day. If you let them."

"I'll drink to that," the old man said, lifting his tea.

"See these flames?" Leo said, giving Amy a gentle nudge.

"Hmm, what?"

"There's an old trick Gypsies use –" He took up the iron poker beside the hearth and probed the smouldering logs. Flames began flicking up the chimney. Leo's eyes lit up with amusement. "We've travelled the globe doing this—telling fortunes—been travelling since we were born. Ain't that right, Dan?"

"Yeah, you have, with your wife and kids!"

"Yeah, well, I was just saying, we've learnt a trick or two about fortune telling, haven't we?"

"Have you," Dan said, pulling out a chair to sit on.

The old man laughed. "Does it tell you that old Engine isn't going home with you?"

Everyone forced a laugh. The old man had got them sussed.

Dan looked down at his hands, wondering where Leo would take the conversation.

"Somethings are passed on in Gypsy bloodlines, like green eyes or double jointedness."

"You mean double chins like yours."

"If I've got it, you have it."

My mother and hers before her were all able to read the fire. That was their vessel to show them beyond."

Amy nodded. Her eyes looked very wide. Leo was getting turned on by the way she was looking at him. He wanted to lean over her and kiss her.

"I know travellers have a reputation for being able to do things like that, don't they?"

Dan sighed and looked up. He twisted one corner of his mouth and raised both eyebrows. "See into the future? Is that where this is going?"

"It's true, Dan, tell her! What Gypsy doesn't have a fortune teller in the family?" Leo winked at Dan.

"What about Faye?" Dan narrowed his eyes at his brother.

"Oh, that old Irish woman?"

"Can she read the future," Amy asked.

Both Dan and Leo glanced up sharpish, looked at each other and laughed.

Leo shrugged. "I hope not! Don't want her knowing where we are all the time."

"No way, we'd never hear the end of it… she doesn't tell the future; she dictates it."

Dan looked at Leo and watched as he burst out laughing. "True, true."

Dan leaned his head back and closed his eyes. There was some truth in that, at least.

"Well, if you've got a moment," Leo asked. Amy looked up at him. "If you're not too scared to see your future. We can stop?"

Amy raised her delicate eyebrows inquisitively.

"Do you want to know?" The old man asked, shaking his head.

"No, not entirely, but I'm intrigued."

"Come on then," Leo said, crouching to face the fire. He stirred it up again with the poker and watched the flames roar up the chimney leaving tiny little amber sparks in the soot.

"Give her the poker," Dan nodded over. "The woman is supposed to hold the poker, not the man." He gave a wry smile, and Leo pretended not to notice.

Instead, he smiled a taut, sort of half-smile, as though he wanted to laugh but was controlling it.

"The poker is always better in the woman's hand," he laughed.

"Put it in the fire, love," Dan said, curling his lip at his brother. "Get it nice and hot."

"Interesting." The old man blurted. "When you've done, I've got to be getting on."

Leo held his hand tightly over Amy's as she gripped the poker in her hand and pushed it into the dancing flames. "You've got to do this with your hand, the left one, because it's nearer the heart," he said. "Now, lift the log over…roll it, that's it, so the red-hot side is facing us." Amy leaned in closer.

"The idea is to see what is written in the red-hot ambers beneath the logs."

Amy looked down again.

"Now, we can see if there is anything dancing in the embers."

She didn't look convinced. "Can you see anything?"

Leo grinned. "It's nice and warm."

Amy looked down into the scorching embers. Leo leaned over the top of her. The heat from the fire was making his mouth dry. She looked up at him, eyes wide, lips pursed. He could see down her dress from where he was standing a little. Her pert pale breasts looked soft and inviting. Leo made a show of looking into the fire again.

"Oh, no, I'm not pleased about that."

"What?"

"You're waving goodbye –" He cleared his throat. Amy looked up at him breathing hard. "I see a soldier outside here… he's knocking on the door."

"Do I open it? Do I?" Her face looked red and hot.

"I don't know." Leo caught a glimpse of a little bead of sweat running down between her breasts.

The old man rose from the table, tucked his vest into his trousers and, shaking his head, went outside. "Load of old codswallop," he said, closing the door behind him.

Amy smiled over her shoulder at Dan.

Dan flicked a glance at her and smiled back. He felt the colour rising in his cheeks.

"Here, Amy," he said, surprised at his own feelings of jealousy. He held out his hand, and as she took it, he pulled her away from Leo. "Come over here. I'll read your palm."

"Read my palm? Okay."

Leo laughed.

"Bugger off; you've done enough damage already."

"Right…" Leo said, straightening up. He lit a cigarette.

Dan sat Amy down at the table. "I'll show you how it's done!"

"Come on then," Leo said, leaning against the fireplace. "Let's hear it!"

Dan squared Amy's hand out into his. "Let's see!"

"Well, while you're doing that," Leo said, "I'll look at that beaut' in the barn, cool down a bit."

Dan knew what he was insinuating. He waited until Leo had left.

"Sorry about my brother. He's a joker." Dan breathed out heavily and sighed. "I've forgotten the jargon for all this."

"So, you have actually done this before?"

"Of course, I've done it before… like Leo said, Gypsies just have it in their blood, but, to be honest, all my dreams came true right now." He kissed the back of her hand. "I don't need to look into the future. I know exactly what I want…this." He kissed her hand again.

Amy pulled her hand free. "So," Dan said. "You want to head for greener, newer pastures?… Why don't we take a walk up that hill to my caravan? Get to know each other better…?"

"Is that what you say to all the girls when you travel from town to town?"

"No, that would be exhausting. I've only ever said that to you. And I'm saying it now because I might never get the chance again."

"God almighty, you don't waste time, do you…you nearly had me convinced…" she laughed. "I'm sure this is all part of your grand scheme."

203

"Grand scheme? Grand schemes just come to nothing, costing a fortune and going up in flames along with all the promises and dreams. I don't believe in grand schemes."

"And the Traction Engine?"

"Oh, that! Well, let's see." he looked into the palm of her hand again. "Okay…" he began trailing a crease in the palm of her hand again. "It's running smoothly in the field outside here."

"So, I must have found my Prince charming then?"

"Well, you've not flogged it to me…and I haven't run off somewhere exotic with it."

"I should sell it and run off somewhere exotic!"

"Like where?"

"Italy?"

"God no, why there? Why go there when you can have your dark Italian right here now?"

She laughed. "So, whose is this lucky person then?"

"The one who gets me!"

She hit him jokingly.

"The one who gets lumbered with you, you mean!" She hit him again.

"Well, let's see if it will happen then, shall we? Dan hutches his chair nearer, pretending to trace the creases in her palm again.

"That's interesting!"

"What!"

"A tall, dark stranger is knocking on your door; Leo was right about that."

"But Leo said it was a soldier."

"Blue-eyed soldier, yep, it's definitely… me!"

"Oh, give over. You're not a soldier."

Not yet, but you never know. All this talk of another war."

Amy laughed, pulling her hand away.

"Could it be me that carries you off to greener pastures, up that hill to my caravan?"

Amy blushed.

"I am serious!"

"I was afraid of that."

Amy stopped laughing and hung her head.

"What's wrong?"

"Nothing!"

"What is it?"

"You're being cruel!"

"Cruel! I'm not. I do mean, I would like to spend more time with you…Here, let me look again!" Dan lifted her hand, held it close to his chest, and looked her square in the eyes. "It could be me," he repeated. "If you'd have me!"

"Maybe…"

There was a knock; they both looked up and burst out laughing.

"Saved by the door," Amy said, rising to her feet.

Dan straightened up and picked up the empty mug, cupping it in his hands as though drinking from it. He wasn't sure why he had done that but wanted to make his hands look busy. Amy straightened her hair and then opened the door.

"Can I see your dad?"

Dan didn't recognise the voice, not straight away.

"Greg!" Amy said, surprised. "God, it's good to see you!"

Dan breathed under his breath, "Fucking hell"

Amy stretched up and kissed Greg on the cheek. "You're home!"

"For now."

"Come in, come in! Rebecca and Janey must be so pleased you're home." she stood back and waved him over the threshold.

Greg came in smiling.

"It's good to be back…" removing his cap, his voice floated down to the floor when he saw Dan.

"This is…"

"Yeah, I know who that is?"

Dan rose to his feet and offered out a hand.

"That's not necessary," Greg turned to Amy. "I'm not stopping… I just wanted to speak to your dad about the err…Engine? Said I'd call around when I got back. I've only got a few hours, so…I was passing."

"Okay, he's in the barn, Greg. He's looking at it now, as a matter of fact, if you'd like to go over." He turned and went outside.

Leo and the old man were right on cue. Closing the barn, the old man turned and waved casually when he saw Greg. Dan followed Amy outside and stood by the door. Once Amy saw Greg had located the old man, she turned to go back inside. Smiling at Dan before closing the door, she whispered to him, "Maybe."

Dan thrust both hands into his pockets, spun on his heels, and waited for Leo, pleased with himself. Leo flicked up a nervous glance.

"What's going on?" he whispered. "Is that him?"

"Yep."

"What's he doing here…?"

"Dunno. Come to talk to the old man about the Engine."

"Fucking hell…!"

"I know…"

The old man waved. "Be with you in a minute, boys."

"Does he know?"

"Know about what?"

"You know, the kid…?"

"What kid?"

"You know… Rebecca's little un?"

"Nothing's going on, Leo. Don't know what you're talking about."

"Aw, come on, bro. We know…we all know."

"About what? What is there to know?"

"We all saw Rebecca… and we all remember her. We're not daft. Thought all that had blown over."

"It has…ended years ago.'

"But then she turns up, looking to see you with a little un."

"And…!"

"We can all do the sums, you know. And why else would you bring us out here if it wasn't to see Rebecca…and that kid."

"I don't know anything about that kid, I assure you!"

"Jack spotted it straight away…he said she's your spitting double."

Dan looked down at the floor and sighed.

"And she has Dad's eyes."

"Aw, shut up, Leo. He's the fucking Dad, that fucking Greg!"

"That kid could even be Jack's."

"Now, what are you saying…?"

"She was Jack's bit on the side that whole summer. She was coming around the Circus going off with him, remember, then suddenly, she was with you…and now this kid looks exactly like a Franconi! Come on, man!

I wasn't born yesterday."

"Well, whatever happened, we were all kids, and she was putting it about."

"Well, there you go. The lass has made a life for herself anyway; it's as simple as that. That kid isn't mine, and she's definitely not Jack's." Leo said nothing more, just shook his head and looked disgusted. There was a long pause as they waited for the old man and Greg to come from the barn. Leo broke the silence. "I wonder what's going on?" Rage was boiling in Dan. Far too much had been said already. He spoke in a strange tone, making Leo look around suspiciously. "I've fucking had enough of this."

Leo grabbed his arm and turned him around. "Where you going, man. Come on, let's go!" Leo quickly opened the cottage door and shouted in. "Tell your dad we'll drop by tomorrow, Amy."

Amy appeared at the door. "I'll tell him!" Dan doffed his cap. They left.

Amy's Decision 1937

"Have you made your mind up yet?" the old man clattered in through the door and dropped a bucket full of potatoes on the table. Wiping his brow, he sat to unlace his muddy boots.

"What... oh hello daughter, how are you daughter...?" Amy laughed and turned back to the boiling pot on the stove.

"Heard all about it in the Traveller's; thanks for telling me!"

"News sure travels fast in this village. Anyway, there's nothing to tell. In so many words, Dan only hinted at the idea, and I haven't accepted, so..."

The old man rose from his chair and took her hand, "Why not, love? You like him, don't you?"

"I'm going to say no, Dad."

The old man sighed, scratched his nose, sat back at the table, and removed his boots. "Because?" He asked finally, throwing the boots under the table. "Because? Because of that machine of yours!"

"What! Why? What's that got to do with it?"

"I barely know this man, Dad!"

"So, get to know him then. He seems to really like you!"

Amy felt herself becoming emotional; her voice had risen to a pitch. "I also know he really likes that damn Engine. He is a traveller by nature; what's to stop him getting his hands on that then buggering off!"

"The man's in business, Amy. You've seen the crowds flocking to his shows. He's doing alright with or without that Engine."

"It's not me he's interested in, though, is it? In the right hands, that thing's worth a fortune. Just sell it, or, I don't know, hire the damn thing out or something. You know what hurts me the most, Dad...why you never sold it in the first place! Why didn't you ever put it to some use for us... gave us a better chance?"

The old man sighed, "Ahy lass, I know," Raising to pour water from the jug, he sat again. "It doesn't make sense, I know…but… it's your mum."

"Mum? She's dead; she's been dead a long time!"

The old man fell silent; his shoulders slumped as he sat back with the water jug in hand. He seemed to shrink into his chair somehow; then his head bowed as he placed his hands on his knees and sighed again. "I'm doing what I know she'd want." Amy waited for him to continue.

He took another long hard sigh and appeared to shrink further into himself.

"Oh, come on!" Amy said finally. "Whatever that damn thing means to you is your business."

"No, lass, you're right; I have been selfish." He straightened back up again as though he had more wind in his sails. "I've been holding on to it for you." He paused as though his words were stuck in the back of his throat. "I could never bear to operate it. I'm bloody terrified of the damn thing. Didn't want to sell it because of its worth, but didn't want to use it again either!"

"Why didn't you just rent it out then?"

"It's cursed! That damn machine is cursed, and I'm scared of it!" His voice tapered off to a mumble. "It scares me to bloody death."

"What do you mean it scares you? Why?"

"I lost my nerve since your mum died. She wasn't ill, Amy. I know you think she died because she got ill. She didn't…I killed her. I killed your mum! It was my fault! I killed her with that fucking machine."

Amy fell back against the stove, shocked. She stared at him with her mouth open. Finally, she gasped. "I don't understand."

Dad took a long breath. "I was driving…" he said, glancing out of the window at nothing. He was nodding in the direction of the lane outside,

"– Along the bottom lane," he added, finally choking back tears.

"Your mother was with me; we'd been bailing all day. It had been a long hot summer's day. She saw you in the yard when we returned home and jumped down. She was afraid you'd try to run out and be knocked over. I don't know how it happened, but her skirts got caught in the damn thing and –" He cupped his face in his hands and rubbed his eyes.

"Oh my God, Dad!" Amy felt a rush of cold shivers run to her feet.

"That was it," he continued through floods of tears. "By the time I'd shut it down…" he said, gulping back the tide of guilt. "I'd gone over her." He composed himself a little and looked up at Amy shaking. "She died very quickly.

Doctor Smyth said your mum might lose a leg at worst, thought She'd pull through, but she never did…she didn't even wake up. She never came around. She was unconscious, and she never came around."

"Why didn't you tell me about this? No one ever told me, not ever! The whole town kept this from me? All this time?"

"You were too young, Amy. Just a baby. It wasn't anyone's place to tell you, and I couldn't even bear to tell you the truth."

"The Prices, do they know?"

The old man shook his head. "No," he wiped tears quickly and looked up. "It happened before they arrived. They don't know!"

They sat in silence.

"Get rid of it!" Amy said, finally rising to her feet. She snatched up the pail by the hearth and headed to the door. "Do you hear? Get rid of it! I don't want anything to do with that disgusting thing! Oh, and lose the guilt; it wasn't your fault!" Amy stood at the door gazing out over the yard. "I've always hated that machine; I knew there was something evil about it! You're right about one thing, it is cursed!"

"Ever since that Engine came into our lives, things went wrong."

"Give to the Prices then; increase the yield percentage and let them work your land with it."

Fresh spring air breezed around her ankles as Amy stepped outside. An overwhelming aroma and notes of nature's seasonal death greeted her like a delicate wave of saturated earth, decaying foliage and decomposing life; remnants of the long winter past still hung in the air. Amy suddenly felt optimistic; like the new emerald buds in the trees, there was a promise of new life. Suddenly the dark horizon appeared to present a way out of a sea of doom and gloom. Somewhere beckoned beyond the Peaks were new possibilities waiting to happen. Finally, she had awoken from the nightmare her father had been dwelling in for years. Before she closed the door, the old man looked up, his eyes wide and watery.

"I will talk to Greg tomorrow," he said. "He's already expressed an interest, being an Engineer and all; he said he'd love to get his hands on the Engine and put it to good use."

"Yes, I'm sure he's the best person for it. He's certainly the most deserving. He'll know what to do with it."

"Amy?" Amy stopped and turned. Her father rose from the table "I am sorry!"

"Don't be. It's all in the past."

"I should have told you sooner."

"Yes, you should have, but I forgive you. Now let's put the past behind us and move on."

Amy closed the door behind her, strode across the yard, threw the pail under the pump with a loud clatter, and began pumping. The well was reluctant to release its freezing element from its depth. Eventually, a rush of clear freshwater filled the pail, and with its contents sploshing against her skirt, she strode back across the yard, opened the door, slammed it behind her and smiled.

"I'm going to say yes!"

The old man rose, took her hand in his and shook it warmly. "Good lass, I am happy for you, Amy!"

"Does it still work, that bloody Engine?" The excitement in Amy's voice alerted the old man to the urgency of getting rid of it as quickly as possible.

He sat at the table, wiping his peppery white whiskers on the red handkerchief Amy had bought in the Christmas market. He finished wiping away years of stress and anguish from his face and tucked the handkerchief into his top pocket.

"Aye," he said finally. "The last time I turned it over, it was still working."

"Then take it tonight!"

"Tonight!" The old man looked puzzled. "Why tonight?"

"If Dan wants me, he'll want me without that damn machine."

"Dan's a good man, Amy; he'll be back for you, you'll see.'

"What if he doesn't come back? What if he thinks I have rejected him?"

"He's a man with means; take your chance, go to him—say yes before it's too late."

Amy forced a weak smile. "I can't go chasing after him."

The old man's eyes flashed around the room as he slowly began rising to his feet, chair scrapping against the flagstones. With both hands on the table, he gradually straightened himself and sniffed. "This calls for a drink."

"No, Dad, it doesn't!"

"Never said I was gonna have one, just said it called for one. I'll get over to the Prices; let Greg know he can take the Engine tomorrow, and I'll drop you off at the site."

"At this hour!"

"What we got to lose!"

"No, no, you go. Go tell Greg the news, and I'll see Dan in the morning, I promise, I will."

"If you wish."

Restless in High Oakham 1937

Amy lay in bed, not daring to close her eyes for fear of seeing the same image repeatedly playing in her mind. The vision of her beautiful young mother being dragged beneath the Traction Engine. It was all she could think about. She couldn't sleep and guessed she never would again. As she lay, staring up at the ceiling, listening to the restless animals in the barn, a wisp of breath hung in the air, lit by of pool of silvery moonlight flooding in through the window. Even the cows had been restless all evening, as though they too were distressed by discovering her late mother's actual demise.

Amy sat up and peered out of the window. She wondered if the cold was causing the cows to be restless. It was freezing; even beneath an extra layer, she was shivering. It had been a really long night. Her father still had not returned from the Prices'; he'd been gone a few hours. Frost had formed on every inch of the landscape; a thin layer lay, like a dusting of refined sugar lay over fields, trees and fences. The odd whip of hazy cloud hung motionlessly in the sky, surrounded by a sprinkle of stars. Amy watched them a while, slowly drifting by the moon. She tried to muster the energy to get up and go tend to the animals; she knew if they too were refusing to be taken by the veil of sleep, no one else would sleep either.

She climbed out of bed, slipped into her working boots, tiptoed downstairs, took a coat from the back door and crept outside. The barn door was slightly ajar. There was a cigarette butt on the floor. She had already visited twice since tea; even her dad had been out twice before going off to the Prices, but she didn't recall the cigarette. On her third visit, she noticed one of the kittens had gone, probably a fox, sadly, but sometimes it was inevitable – nothing craftier than a hungry fox. Amy hoped it wasn't the kitten Janey had set her heart on, or she'd never hear the end of it.

Amy lit the lamp she always kept beside the door, looked down at its warm glow and swung it upwards to see if any more cigarettes were lying around. Leo and Jake had been in and out of the barn a few times over the past few days, tinkering around, fixing things, helping the old man, that kind of thing; perhaps it was one of theirs, she would ask next time she saw them—whenever that would be. Her heart sank; she hoped she would see Dan just one last time so she could give him her answer and accept his offer of marriage.

With lantern held high, Amy wandered through the barn and checked all the animals. Old Raisin seemed happy enough in his paddock, the goats

were fine, and the few sheep they had seemed happily bedded. Only the two heifers and their calves were fidgety and grew even more, when Amy disturbed them with her lamp. One of the older heifers showed

signs of stress, lowing and wandering as if looking for her calf.

Amy noticed the whites of the cow's eyes flashing with a wild expression; her ears flickered and twitched. Amy continued to walk the circumference of the traction Engine and around the rear of the building. Walking through the milking parlour, she was glad she had tucked the cows away in that part of the barn; it had improved their lactation tremendously. The air was fresher, and the morning sun rose through the large dusty window at the rear. Amy searched beneath the large sheet of tarpaulin covering the Traction Engine, half expecting to find a fox lurking there, but found nothing. Upon returning to the front of the Traction Engine, she caught sight of another cigarette butt on the ground. Picking it up, Amy dropped it in her coat pocket. She was puzzled and angry. Her father would never smoke down there, especially not near the Engine or the cows.

Returning to the parlour, the stressed heifer was licking the other cow, then tried to mount her, obviously displaying signs of coming into season. Amy had been expecting this, so she was satisfied that the old girl was ready for her last attempt at motherhood. She patted the cow's rear before leaving her to settle. Over the years, Amy had developed a good understanding of her ladies. They were intelligent and showed emotion like children. For this reason, she had been keen on housing them in a system that met their needs. Now assured, Amy left them all to their business and returned to the front of the barn.

Before leaving, she ensured the kitten, Janey's favourite, was there. It was, muzzling against its mother's tummy.

Closing the barn, she heard heavily segged boots crunching over the cobbles in the yard behind her. She turned to see Dan walking beneath a plume of smoke. Of all the charm in his mannerisms and in his handsome, rugged good looks and solid masculine features, the way he wore his cap cocked on one side, pulled down over one eye, made her grow weak at the knees. He was smiling from ear to ear with a look that melted her heart.

"Hey, you! What are you doing out here at this time of night?"

"Good evening! I could ask you the same question," she said, laughing.

"Evening you! Come here." He took his coat off and wrapped it around her. "It's freezing!" Dan was shivering now as he took her by the arms, kissed her forehead and wrapped his freezing cold hands over her face. She looked up into his eyes. Amy was shivering uncontrollably by this time and wanted to do nothing more but run back to bed.

"Get inside," he said, leading towards the house.

"No!" She wrenched herself away.

"Why?" Worry flashed in his peaceful eyes. "What's wrong?"

Her stomach clenched into knots. She had never wanted anyone more than she wanted Dan right now. She felt her eyes stinging and realised she was fighting back the tears. "Why are you here?" She asked, looking away into the fields beyond the yard.

"What do you mean, why am I here… Isn't that obvious?"

"Not really, not to me."

"I needed to see you."

"I wanted to see you..."

"So, does that mean you'll give me your answer?"

"I don't know what it means…because I don't understand why you are interested in me."

Dan laughed slightly and shook his head, confused…Their eyes were locked.

"Plain Jane with drab looks and an empty purse…that's me. I live a simple life." Amy whispered.

"You're going to say no to me, aren't you?" Dan released her and stepped back. "How many times have you broken men's hearts this way?"

"Never," Amy said, completely shocked by his response. "It's just… I'm a farmer's daughter; I muck out cows, scrub floors, and my hands are rough." She threw her hands to her face… "I'm pale, knackered—for want of a better word, and have no prospects—look at me. I'm hardly…."

"Hardly what? …I love what I see."

"As I stand before you, this is all you're ever gonna get—this is me …at my best, no glamour, no skills—I don't even own lipstick or rouge, nor am I pretty. I don't own posh frocks or pearls…and I'm certainly not like…."

"Like what?"

She paused, suddenly embarrassed by her outburst, and rushed to the barn. Following, Dan grabbed her by the wrist and threw her around to face him. "Talk to me! Who, who are you not like, Amy?" Amy thought of Faye but could not—dare not mention her name. She saw how he had held her tightly in his arms as Faye wrapped herself around him like an enchanted snake, her slender body enveloping his. How she paraded in delicately embroidered silks and soft veils, with her shimmering olive complexion adorned with jewels and precious stones, Amy knew there was no comparison. She envied Faye and wished she could be her, and even though Faye was the wife of another man, Amy knew there was something between them that was so profound and untamed; she wondered why Dan was suddenly interested in her when he was so obviously in love with Faye?

Amy looked back at the dark mass, which lurked at the back of the barn, sleeping like a beast in its lair. Amy hated it, and she hated that Dan wanted the damn thing more than anything in the world. Unlike Faye, she knew she had something, the one thing he wished for, the one thing Faye could not offer—the Showman's Traction Engine.

"I'm not like, Faye," She said, whispering in the darkness.

"No, you're not! And thank God for that! That's why I love you."

They both stopped as the word 'love' fell from his lips to the ground like an anvil.

"I've seen how she looks at you, Dan, and you at her."

"She's my brother's wife, Amy!"

"I know that, but yet… I've seen you together."

"We work … and live together. We're family, close family –"

"She's in love with you!"

"You shouldn't start foul gossip; it destroys lives. Fucking hell, where did this come from! Why did you have to say that?"

The accusation angered him; he was furious. He stormed out. Amy bolted out after him. "Sorry. I'm sorry, Daniel, forgive me, please…!" Dan stopped and turned, taking Amy by surprise.

"Faye encouraged me to come to you tonight," he said. "Oh, what's the fucking point?"

"What, what did Faye say. Tell me what she said, please?"

"She said, you're the best thing to happen to me…Oh, and Jack…by the way? Let's not forget what you said about him to Rebecca at the Show tonight;

216

he's not creepy. He might be to you, but he's my brother and Faye's husband. The only creepy thing about him is that he tries too hard...too hard to please everyone..., especially me! Fuck knows, he's a

good man, he's just a bit... I don't know... misguided and misunderstood sometimes... but he's good here!" He slapped his chest hard. "Do you know why he took that child 'off' as you put it... oh yeah, Faye heard you say that too. She heard everything. Jack took Janey away from you so he could get to know her because she's mine. She my child! Janey is my kid! Jack knew that!"

"What?"

"Yeah, my brother is a better man, a far better man than me! He knew straight away—just shows you what sort of a man I am."

"Janey?...Janey is yours? No, that can't be true. She's Greg's baby; everyone knows that! She can't be yours."

"Jack knew it as soon as he saw her. He always knows everything about me, even before I know myself... It's a twin thing, I guess. No one need ever know, by the way!"

"Greg doesn't know?"

"Please, don't – don't, whatever you do, don't tell him."

"I won't. I don't understand."

"He thinks she's his."

"Why have you told me?"

"I don't want secrets between us... Does it affect the way you feel about me—about us?"

Amy shrugged, made no reply, shook her head, walked unsteadily to the hay beside the milking parlour, and sat, shocked.

"Jack wants a family with his wife. Faye said she wanted to see me start a family too... she said she liked you." He threw up his arms and laughed ironically, "That's why I'm here...! Forget it!" He started striding out of the barn. Amy ran out after him.

"I am sorry, Dan, I am – I was jealous, afraid...."

He stopped abruptly and spun to face her – "Well, don't be... You've no idea what a huge commitment it is to have family and children in the Circus. It's hard; it's a tough life, so most people give in. I was always scared of commitment, and probably I stayed here for so long because I thought you'd be that woman who would be strong enough for a life with me...."

Amy put out her hand, and Dan hesitated. "No, it's no good, it's impossible. I'll only hurt you," he said, turning to leave. "You'll resent me in the end...They all do!"

"No, Dan, please, please, don't go!" Amy cried after him. "You're right; I don't know you or your family... and I was wrong to judge—please, please come back."

Dan headed towards the main gate and out along the old bridle path.

Amy ran after him, her feet falling aimlessly in the mud along the dirt track. She eventually caught up with him. He was standing in the hedgerow blowing smoke rings into the dark, silky blackness. Ignoring Amy, he first turned his back and leaned over the fence to watch the flag above the Circus flap gently in the breeze. She walked slowly towards him, placing her arms through his; she held him tightly around his waist. Turning towards her, she rested her head on his chest.

"Do you know the funny thing?" he asked quietly. "...I thought you were different."

After a long pause, he gave her a reassuring hug and tutted loudly. She felt his fingers caressing her hair like he had done with Faye. His touch felt safe and warm.

"Do you want to tell me what that was really about?" he asked, looking down at her. She felt like a child in his arms.

Glancing up, she couldn't form words; she was too emotional and embarrassed.

"Shall I tell you?" he tossed his cigarette into the field. Amy lifted her head and looked up at him. "I'll spice it up a bit for you, shall I? You, my dear –" he said, tapping her gently on the nose mockingly, "...are afraid." Amy was puzzled. "You are... You think that you're too good for me."

Amy looked up sharply. "No, that is not true!"

"Don't be afraid to brag about it," he laughed. "You are!" Amy stood gaping. "There must be something special about you; otherwise," he laughed "...you wouldn't have gotten me to fall in love with you."

Amy smiled. "Well," he gazed across the sea of dark fields into the shadow of the pine forest beyond. "There's definitely something special about you because I've never fallen in love before... not like this...I know I'm in love because I would give up the Circus to have a family with you today, if you wanted me to!"

He leaned in and kissed her softly on the head. He broke off, wrapped her coat tighter around her. "Tell your dad to get rid of that damn Traction Engine, will ya? Coz that's what's really bothering you!"

Amy stepped back. "I'm not stupid," he said, pulling her back towards him and leaning her head against his chest. "Tell him to sell the damn thing, give it away, burn it—I don't care...smash it up—whatever, just make sure it's gone before I get back."

"But... I thought you might stay. So, you are leaving?"

"Yeah, I have to go. You know I'm going to Nottingham tomorrow, you knew that, but when I get back, I'm gonna marry you."

"You're going to Nottingham tomorrow?"

"Yes, of course...with the others..." he laughed. "Did you hear what I said...?

"I heard..."

"Well...? Will you...marry me?" Amy was silent for a while. Dan felt her turn away and stare off into the shadows. "I'll be back, I promise!" He bent slightly to kiss her. He felt her eyelashes flutter against his chin. "You've got to marry me now... I've told you my darkest secrets... I'd have to kill you if you didn't." He gave a little laugh.

"I won't tell a soul." Amy laughed and threw her arms around him.

"Sell that damn Engine, yeah?"

"What about us...our future."

Dan laughed. "I don't care... do what you like...I love you..." he bent to kiss her again.

"But, Dad has told the Prices they can have it now."

Dan shrugged. "So? Good!"

"Are you sure? ... It's going to the Prices. Does that bother you?"

"No ... okay, yeah, fuck it—it does a bit... I'm glad your dad is offloading it... I'd prefer if it didn't go to Greg of all people... but, hey... you'll never trust me. You'll never be sure if I'm genuine until it's gone, so...whatever." He gave a long sigh. "Greg wins again, but I got the best girl in the end...The Showman would make our life easier, but I know what you women are like. If it's still there when I return, you'll throw that damn machine in my face every time we have a row. It's not worth it, trust me... I'd sooner have a peaceful life than an easier one."

Amy smiled and huddled herself deeper into him.

"Come on, you're freezing. I can feel you shaking." He squeezed her hard in his arms and rocked her back and forth. "Here, I nearly forgot." He reached into his pocket and pulled something wrapped in a delicately embroidered handkerchief.

"This is for you… It's the reason I came tonight. I wanted you to have it."

"It was my mother's, diamonds and sapphires, or so I'm told. That brooch has been in the family for years."

Amy unravelled the tiny bundle and tried to examine it under the moon's light. Clasped in a trembling hand, she began pinning it to her nightdress. "It's beautiful. No one has ever given me anything so beautiful before. I'm going to miss you," she said.

He began kissing her forehead gently, her cheek and neck.

"Shit," he pushed her away gently. "You have to go; look at you. You'll catch your death, and I must walk you back now and do all these goodbyes again?"

"Do me a favour," Amy said. "Just turn around and go…It won't take me long to run back down the lane."

"Alone…?"

Amy tried to hold him once more, but he held her off. "Go. Just go! I love you!"

When Amy closed the door, and peered through the cottage window, rays of gold and yellow light had begun appearing over the grey-purple horizon bringing with it a brand-new day.

The old man had fallen asleep, waiting, or so it would seem, for Amy to return. She gently lay a shawl upon him and warmed a small pan of cider on the stove; then, sitting beside the fire to summarise the day's event, she watched the dying embers flicker and fade. Amy removed the brooch Dan had given her to examine and admire it. She smiled and kissed it. It could only be perceived as his valid declaration of love for her.

The intricate and beautifully designed pale ice crystals sparkled in the firelight. They were formed into two interlinked Venetian masks; Arlecchino and Brighella. Flashes of blue sapphire and ruby-coloured flowers at its centre, as bright as the real things, flickered like tiny flames against a red and black enamel. A stamp on the back revealed the charming piece of mosaic jewellery on a miniature scale was indeed the work of Ugo Correani—his depiction of Venetian Melodrama Masks is world-renowned. The primary aspect of Arlecchino was his physical agility, acrobatics and elasticity. They were the attributes an audience expected to see in his performance, though various troupes and actors would alter his behaviour to suit their style, personal preferences, or a particular scenario they attempted to portray. Typically, he was cast as the servant of an Innamorato or Vecchio.

Much to the detriment of his master's plans, Arlecchino would often have a love interest in Colombina—his lust for her only superseded by his desire for food and fear of his master. At the antithesis of his nature was his masked partner and older brother, Brighella, the more vindictive, comedic, money-grabbing and villainous one of the two, portrayed by his inveterate schemes driven by a preternatural lust and greed.

Brighella's costume consisted of a loosely fitted, white smock and pants with green trim and a battachio or slapstick, which he used to significant effect. His green half-mask displayed his nature aptly with unctuous look of lechery and wantonness.

As Amy clipped the brooch to her nightdress and ran her finger around the edge of its repeating pattern, she thought about Rebecca, Dan, and their love child. Then, her father's admission about the death of her mother came flooding back like a tsunami—of all the most distressing information she could have ever had received had been given to her most matter-of-factly, she hadn't even taken any of its ramifications on board—how should such information affect her? How should she respond to such news? As she sat in stunned silence with her eyes half-closed, Amy felt her chest growing tighter like she could no longer breathe, let alone comprehend how she was supposed to react.

She glanced down at her pale, freckled hands and thought of Faye. She swallowed a little pride, not to mention some common sense and pushed away from her initial gut feelings. Dan's acknowledgement that the Traction Engine could never allow them to be truly happy resonated with her on a deeper level. He was pleased to take her with or without the dowry. She, in time, would learn to let go of everything that had gone before…let the past be past, and the future unfolds into a reality that God and God alone intended. Life for Amy was finally worth living.

Thick as Thieves 1937

Dan found the caravan door ajar as he climbed the steps, knocked and pushed it open. "Faye, Jack back yet?

Faye was sat by the light of a lantern sewing; she seemed happy to see him. She looked up with a smile. "No! Thought he was with you… Come in." Dan climbed the remaining step, and she placed the garment she was sewing in the basket beside her and closed the lid. "Sit down," she said, rubbing her hand over the seat beside her. "Jack said he was going to the village and would call in at the cottage on his way back to settle the bill and pick up supplies." She rose to pour a drink from a decanter on the side. "I was just there earlier; I didn't see him. Forget it." Dan turned to leave. "Dan, wait. You two argued again?"

She'd know. She was like Jack; she always knew more about Dan than he did himself. "What do you think?"

"I did tell him to leave everything up to you.

"Well, looks like he didn't. Don't know why he returned to the cottage when he knows Amy hates him."

"Despite what she thinks, what all of them think," Faye said, putting her glass down and sitting down again, "Jack said this has been a good site."

"Did he say that? Did he really?"

"…and you met Amy, so, yeah, it's not been too bad. Good on y' for sticking to your guns!"

"Yeah, it's not been bad, has it?" He turned to leave.

"You know, she's okay, Amy. I like her…I do!" Faye gave a warm smile. "Come in," she said with a laugh. Obligingly, Dan removed his cap and stepped in over the threshold. "I hate to say it, but I don't think I've ever seen you look so…happy and in love. You're literally glowing. And, yes, you have better business judgment than our Jack."

"What's that got to do with anything?"

"Well, even I'm amazed at this place, never thought we'd do well here." She was moving over so he could sit beside her.

"Just goes to show," he said. "You never can tell."

"So, did you ask the girl?"

"I did!"

"And?"

"What else is she going to say? I'm gorgeous; how can she resist."

"She's not said yes yet, has she?

"No." Dan laughed and flushed a bit. "but she will."

Faye's eyes widened; it was like a light had gone on, her skin glowed, and she sighed then laughed. She placed a delicate hand on his arm and squeezed it gently. "She's making you work for it?"

Dan stretched and looked at his watch. As he did so, he moved away.

"Have a drink?"

"No, ta. I'm gonna catch a bit of sleep before we push off. Give me a shout when Jack gets back, will ya!"

"Will do."

Dan began dismounting the steps, Faye following, held the door open over his shoulder. "Hey!" she shouted as he began striding over bales of hay and guide ropes. "You're not thinking of going to Nottingham tomorrow morning?"

Dan looked up at the tent and nodded, "Early, yeah!" He suddenly caught her approving eye roaming over him.

"You're as bad as each other, you know?"

"Who, me and Jack?" Dan said, moving back towards the van. "Why's that?" He placed a foot on the bottom step and leaned on one knee.

"You say one thing; he says another. Can't you just put your heads together and get along?"

Dan looked at his watch again and, wanting to sound genuine, smiled at her, "I'd like to, Faye," he sighed, "In fact, I'd love us to get on, he is my twin brother, for fucks sake, but it's complicated."

Dan enjoyed scoring points and thought he could score a few more now, even maybe win a bit of sympathy from his ex-girlfriend.

"Is it Dan? Is it really that complicated…?"

"It is. Jack never forgave me… over you."

Looking up at her, he saw her eyes narrow and this look of sympathy he was hoping for grew to anger. She sighed and frowned. "What the fucking hell are you talking about? I mean, what the fuck are you actually saying? Am I supposed to feel bad about that?"

"What? What, no! God! What is it with you girls tonight?" He smiled at her and gave a little laugh. "I'm just saying… it's true."

She appeared to be trying to out-stare him now and then finally shook her head in disbelief.

"It's true," he said, again laughing.

"That was a long time ago, Dan, water under the bridge."

"For you, for me, but not Jack."

"For all of us, come on –"

Faye was going back inside the caravan and was closing the door in a way that suggested Dan follow before it shut.

"The past has nothing to do with it…" she said, leaning on the cupboard, arms folded and hair shimmering in the lamplight. "You have your ideas; Jack has his. You're like two horses pulling one cart in different directions."

"A lion and kitten, you mean?"

Faye placed a hand on his cheek. He saw that twinkle of approval in her eye again; he'd won-he knew he could.

"So, what's Danny boy's next move…?" she asked, tossing back her dark, golden-brown hair. She looked lonely and concerned, Dan thought. They smiled at each other.

Suddenly, a man's voice echoed behind Dan. He played the dummy, jumped down from the top step, and Faye took a step back. Leo skipped up the steps behind Dan and pushed past him into the van, forcing Faye to move further inside and making the van dip beneath his weight. He held open the door with his foot letting in a blast of the cold night air.

"Coming in or what, man?" he said to Dan.

Wrapping up in his scarf and sitting down at the back of the van, Dan stretched and yawned.

Faye had sat opposite Dan, long silky legs crossed, arms folded across her chest, which pushed her soft breasts up slightly. Dan had no idea whether he was looking for some action, wanted to see how far he could go with her, or whether he just had a fucking death wish, but his eyes lay upon those breasts a moment too long, and she knew it. He followed Leo with his eyes and watched him sit down, but those breasts were calling his name in the warm lantern light. Faye was now sprawled across the soft furnishings she'd lovingly stitched by her own hand for Jack.

"Dan!"

"What!" He jumped.

"Alright, bro?" Leo said, lighting a cigarette, smiling. He knew his brother too well. "Looks like you've had a few or seen a ghost!" he said, looking at Faye. "What's up with you two? Where's Jack?"

Faye and Dan jumped; their bodies jerked apart, even though they weren't near.

"He's gone off somewhere, again!" Faye said, rising to her feet.

Dan sat back, amused.

"Not again? What's it over this time? Have you been to find him? Shall I go?"

"No, don't go, Leo. I hope he's falls in a ditch." Faye looked at Dan. She reached into the cupboard, took out a bottle of JW Whisky and began pouring it into a couple of glasses, then reached for a third and poured herself one.

"I'm sick of him. I'm sick of this, every time…" Faye took a sip from the bottle and wiped her lips. "Every time he falls out with you or Dan, he takes off… like a child!"

Dan didn't respond or react. He was good at that; he didn't even let his eyes wander in her direction. He was getting better at that too.

"I'll find him," Leo said, rising to leave.

"Don't!" Faye said, handing him the glass of JW's. "You're always looking out for these two. You're not responsible for them. They are two grown-up men."

"Leo, he's like our dad. Always has been since Dad died."

Leo laughed and sat down beside Dan and crossed his great tattooed arms. "Can't you two agree to disagree for once?"

"That's what I said." Faye handed Dan the Jonny Walker.

He took it, knocked it back and shook his head. "Never, it's never that simple…"

"He'll be back when he's ready!" Faye said, examining her glass and taking small sips.

Dan sucked in through his teeth. "There's nothing us two can't say to each other that either one won't take the wrong way! I'll just apologise… again…and he'll forgive me… again…."

"And he'll come back when he's had a skin full," Leo said.

"Again!" Faye and Dan rang out at the same time and laughed.

"Like a married couple, these boys!" Faye said, gazing into Dan's eyes.

Leo laughed. "Oh yeah…?"

"Sorry."

"Don't apologise, Dan; you've done nothing wrong." Faye was smiling playfully at him over another sip of the good stuff.

Dan grinned. "I'll say cheers to that!"

Leo tutted. "Don't say anything to him tonight; leave him until tomorrow; you'll only end up scrapping."

"I mean, what is the argument anyway…?" Dan sneered and held his glass. Faye topped it up from where she was sitting.

"I thought our mum and dad did a good enough job of bringing us up; where did it go wrong between you two?" Leo held out his glass for a refill.

"I suppose, what started off as a kid's thing—a kind of jealousy never really left Jack. He always said I was mum's favourite, and since Mum was a gorger, I was always the gorger, and he thought I took after her… in his mind…like…."

"Yeah, but we all have the same mum. And Dad brought us up the same way, not that it was something I noticed as a kid."

"So, your mother, she wasn't a Gypsy then, by blood?"

"No." The two boys resounded simultaneously.

"Not by blood, but she was in soul," Dan said.

"Gypsy is as Gypsy does!"

"She spent forty years on the road with Dad; if that doesn't make her Gypsy, lass, then I don't know what does!"

"Well, she was a good woman, a really good woman."

Faye poured the last dregs of whisky into Dan's glass, then reached up on the cupboard for another bottle." As she stretched, the thick black skirt she was wearing rode up her legs; Dan feasted his eyes on her long honey-skinned thighs, silky, soft and lovely. He thought, wow, what have I been missing. He waited for one more inch to rise…

Leo turned to see what Dan was staring at and saw her struggling to reach. "Here, I'll get that!"

"T'anks."

He grinned down at Dan. Dan bowed his head. Leo whipped off the cap seal, leaned over, and poured more Jonny Walker into his brother's glass. Faye hitched down her top and skirt and sat down. "You know Leo, you've always seemed older than Dan and Jack," Faye said, her Irish lilt growing thicker with each sip of Walkers.

Dan nodded.

"He looks older an' all."

"You do, especially with that beard."

Leo yawned and poured himself another JW. "So, you reckon it's a bit of jealousy then?"

"Over Mum …I suppose, could be on Jack's part."

"Sounds like that to me," Leo said.

Faye grimaced. "Do you reckon?"

Dan shook his head, "Well, Dad did approach me now and then, asking me to be nicer to Jack, be nice to your brother. I never knew what I'd done wrong to him."

"What did you say…to your dad?"

"Well, I'd tell him that I'd not done anything to him, but it seems Jack would be telling him all these things about what I'd supposed to have done…I don't know; I always thought he was just jealous…."

"As kids are," Leo said, looking out behind the net curtain into the cramped field.

"…and who could blame him." Dan laughed. "I mean, look at me… I'm a god!" Dan laughed again, shaking his head again.

"Na, you're a twat! … It's just…."

"What?"

"I don't know. You did the wire a lot; that was your thing. As a kid, Jack was more theatrical."

"Better with those horses." Dan raised his glass at Leo, sighed and sat up straight.

Leo took it upon himself to pour another JW.

"So, now what?" Faye looked at the two brothers and raised her glass.

Dan looked at his brother; his hard face seemed to be growing softer, melting with every sip, and he knew their life story was giving him an excuse to linger longer and who could blame him. The whiskey was making Dan's lips loose, and Leo felt right at home with the bottle resting now between his legs. Dan had a story to tell and wanted nothing more than to share it with those he loved and trusted.

"Well," Dan said, leaning in. "It was like this... Jack wanted to copy me, remember Leo? He always wanted to impress Dad; I don't know why... If I worked out on weights, he'd want the weights at the same time; if I was on the rope, he'd say he was there first ... that sort of thing...."

"Like brothers do," Faye said, raising her glass again at Dan.

Leo got up and rotated his shoulder "...but he loved ya...."

Faye sank back into the cushion she was leaning on; she seemed contemplative, eyeing Dan, listening intently with a warm gaze.

Dan stopped, took a deep breath and knocked back another shot of whisky. He felt his heart beating because he could feel Faye's interest in him rising. He shook his head.

"I don't know," he said finally, trying to sober up. "Kids stuff, innit!"

Leo looked at his watch. It was the same fob watch that Dan had handed out to everyone, only to find most of them had been swiped soon after. Dan looked at the watch in Leo's hand and tried to focus. He couldn't remember if his brother complained of his being stolen or not.

"Yours turned up then...?"

"Eh...the watch? Hmm, never lost mine...."

"I still haven't asked Jack about those watches."

"What about them?" Faye said. "Sumthin' wrong wit' them?"

"Never mind," Dan drunkenly scratched his head and sat back down; Leo just pursed his lips and shook his head.

"Maybe I've had more Shandies than I'd thought, but in this light, bro, you look more like Jack than you do me." Leo repositioned himself in his chair and hung his head over. "What do y' reckon, Faye?"

"I always thought that... Yeah, hmm, interesting, two of a kind, I'd say."

Dan was indignant. "No way. No chance!"

"Tell ya what...I reckon the reason why you two fight so much it's because you're so alike."

"As in nature? Or just physically? I disagree!"

"Sometimes, both...but in looks especially. When you're both made up as Brighella. I can't tell y' apart sometimes."

"No, me neither." Leo smiled.

"No way!"

"I'll show ya." Faye jumped up and began going through tins of face paints. "You know what Jack looks like when he's made up, yeah?" Procuring a few pots and sponges in her hand, she threw a leg over Dan's lap and sat over him.

"I'll show you just how much you look like him when you're both made up… This is how I do Jack's slap."

Dan wanted to jump up, but as his hands fell around her warm naked thighs, he sank beneath her and relaxed. He had the urge to penetrate her right there and then. She was in the proper position; it was taking all his strength not to. He squirmed out of range. "This feels familiar, like old times."

"Shush, will ya!"

Dan tried to thrust up jokingly, but she was heavy, and the drink weighed down upon him even more than she did.

"I'm knackered.'

"Never stopped you before," Faye whispered into his ear.

"Yes, well, I might have been a clumsy adolescent back then, but that was 15 years ago …" He tried again to thrust up but couldn't move even if he really wanted to.

Leo put his glass down and sat up. "Are ya gonna do me…?"

"Give us another glass," Dan said, reaching out to Leo as Faye began applying make-up.

"We're going to Nottingham Fair… can't wait," Faye said. She slapped Dan's leg. "Sit still!"

Dan smiled. "That's my girl."

"Give me a shout early tomorrow, will you," Leo said, slapping his hands together and rubbing Faye's hair affectionately.

He loved her too, and she knew it.

"We'll set out about six-ish, or we could go at dawn, what do you reckon?"

"What! You're joking, right?" Faye protested.

"No. If we jump at dawn, I'll have an excuse to leave Jack behind."

"Oh, yeah, I'm sure he'll be happy about that?"

Faye levelled her eyes with Dan's. "Jack told everyone we're setting off Thursday, you know?"

Dan shrugged, "Well…I thought I'd agreed on it with him…at any rate, we're moving out tomorrow regardless."

Leo turned to Faye. "The big I am, again!"

"Well, I don't know...." Faye looked down. Her breasts were inches from Dan's face. He took a long look down, then levelled his eyes with hers again.

"Thought you'd got a spot of courting to do before we leave anyway," Faye looked down at her breasts, then up at Dan's face and smiled.

"Well, I wouldn't mind...."

"With your new girl...!"

Leo gave Dan his glass back and tipped his drink at him.

"Oh aye, the new love interest, how is that going for ya?" He was joking but sounded annoyed.

Dan had one girl practically begging for it and one waiting for him in the wings. He knocked back a shot without letting it hit the sides.

"He's had his fun," Leo said.

Faye leaned over to pick up her glass, rolled her finger around the rim, and laughed. "And now he's going to leave, isn't that right, Daniel?"

Leo shook his head, "In the true Daniel Franconi style?"

"Not this time bro." Dan said, looking directly at Faye, directing his answer at her knowingly, as she ignored his attempt to spite her.

"I'm serious about this one... I told ya I was. I like Amy. You told me she was good for me, Faye...remember?"

"I wasn't joking. I really like Amy...." Faye said.

"Do you now?" Leo poured another glass, took a long drink and laughed.

"Ahy an' pigs will fly an all," Faye said between sips of whisky. She put the glass back down and continued plying the grease paint on Dan's face.

Dan frowned deeply and shook his head in earnest. "It's true. I've already shorted it." He looked her square in the face. "I did tell you."

"Shorted... Don't you mean sorted...." She laughed.

"Like you need her approval," Leo said.

"Or yours?" Faye sighed, burping slightly. "So," she leaned back again. "There really is more to it then?"

"Of course, it's called a traction Engine." Leo laughed into his glass.

He curled up his lip. "Look at him... You know damn well he has something up his sleeve."

"What's this? What Engine...?" Faye sat up slightly, tucked her hair over one ear, and turned Dan's face to hers.

Dan smiled and shrugged. "I promised I'd return for her, gave her mum's brooch and told her!"

Leo shook his head and laughed. "Didn't you do that with the other lass? Just comes easy to you, mate, don't it…?"

"What's this?" Faye said again.

"He's just after getting his hands on a Showman's Traction Engine—aren't you? Can't say I don't blame him!" Leo glanced at Faye and nodded at Dan. "He's a schemer, this one, you know that?"

"What? What's all this about? What Engine…?" Faye began climbing off Dan's lap.

"Don't listen to him, Faye. It's not true." Dan hutched himself beneath her, trying to find where he felt at home.

"On the farm, right, where that lass is, Amy." Leo sat up and began explaining. "They've got this Showman's Traction Engine."

"A Showman's." Dan lifted his glass. "Thank you very much!"

"I hear you, brother!" Leo clinked his glass against Dan's. "You should see it, Faye. It's in poor working order, like, but…."

"Is it?"

"Ahy! It is now!"

"What do you mean it is now?"

"Well. It's not been maintained." Leo said, laughing.

"You been tinkering with it, haven't you?"

"Of course, I have! The old man said it was in perfect working order, and he was right, so I took care of it."

"What do you mean, you took care of it?"

"While you've been otherwise disposed tinkering with the lass, I've been tinkering with the Engine. Been down a few times in the night after the shows, if you must know."

"Why? You didn't need to do that… What were you thinking?"

"I was gonna nip over tomorrow night, ask him to turn it over and when he sees it's not working. I'll offer to take it off his hands."

"Why? You didn't need to get involved. Why didn't you talk to me or say anything to me?"

"If you'd have had a better look at it bro, you would have known. I would have told you, but you never asked."

"That's because it is none of your business."

"Well, it needs the bolts that retain the water gauge replaced; some of them are wasted, and there are a few missing now, dangerous if you get my drift…Also, it now has a leaking tube somewhere…no idea where….” Leo shrugged and laughed mockingly. “Oh, there’s a bit of waste on the water tank. It will wheeze, but it will work. It’s got more wheeze than me now.”

“Leo, why? Why have you done that?”

“When you try to buy it, I’ll point out all these faults, and you never know, could get it highly reduced.”

“Could he tell where the leaks are coming from without looking at it?”

“No, I’ve not made it that obvious. I’ve only made minor faults, nothing that can’t be put back right. It could do with some caulking. It would remedy it immediately, but the old man is not to know that.”

“What does it look like?”

“Needs a lick of paint, but it is a beauty, Faye; you’d love it, wouldn’t she, Dan? I can’t believe it wasting away in that barn; apparently, old man’s waiting for t’ young lass to get married. He’s keeping it for her dowry, or so he told me.” He turned to Dan and clinked his glass on his. “Thank you kindly, Sir!”

Dan shrugged and rolled his eyes.

“…Imagine!” Leo and Faye exchanged a look. “It’s worth a bloody fortune; get in there, my son!” Leo grabbed his brother’s arm and sneezed it.

Faye laughed, “Dan, is this true?” She laughed and attempted to tickle him; she climbed back over his lap and sat.

“Well, that’s got nothing to do with us; we’re both…. I like her; just put it that way. I wouldn’t do that to her, use her like that! I really like her. I’m not interested anymore, I was, but not anymore.”

Faye and Leo burst out laughing again. “You referring to the girl or the Engine?”

“…Both!” Leo blurted.

Dan glanced up, looking serious. “You need to get over there tonight and fix it. They’re giving the machine to their tenants tomorrow.”

Leo and Faye’s voices sang out in harmony, “What! No!”

“Are you joking? I’ve been going down there every night working on that damn Engine for you. After all the work, I’ve done on it! My wife thinks I’ve got another woman. Had to hide a few times; Amy thought she had foxes or something prowling around. She came out with her shotgun a few times.”

Faye threw her hands up. “But, Dan, this is your last chance at getting your hands on it. I don’t understand why you’d let it go…?”

Leo looked up at Faye and tugged on her sleeve. "Tell him! Tell him to get his hands on it before I take up the deal. I tell you what, I wouldn't half get in there if I wasn't married!"

"You're married!" Faye rang out.

"And so are you, but it doesn't stop you fooling around with him!"

"It's not like that!" Dan sniffed and sat up, lifting Faye as he did so.

Leo grinned and rolled his eyes. "Shut up, of course, it is!"

Blood rose in Dan's cheeks.

"You don't have to feel guilty, bro," he said quietly, "I'd do it. I would; I'd marry her. I'd marry her and her fecking Dad if it meant I could get my hands on that farm and that machine. No one would blame you…!"

Dan shook his head and laughed.

"Go on." Leo poured himself another JW. "Marry her, why not, you bastard." He tried to sound like he was joking, but he wasn't.

"Well, tough shit, he's not going to marry her …" Faye looked theatrically upset. "I'm marrying her!"

Leo was rolling with laughter now. "With or without that Engine?"

Leo clasped one hand over his glass and pulled Faye down beside him from Dan's lap. He leaned over to whisper something in her ear. She grinned and nodded.

Dan could see the crotch of her knickers now. "So now we have secrets, okay." He glanced out of the window.

Still, in deep whispered conversation, Faye and Leo began giggling and seemed to come to some agreement. Dan glanced at his fob watch.

Faye stood up, grinning, hands on his hips. "Shall we?" she said to Leo, pouring yet another JW and nodding.

"What?" Dan asked, shaking his head; Faye was beautiful; he couldn't help but stare at her again, couldn't take his eyes off her body. "Is it hot in here," he said. "Can't feel my fucking legs all of a sudden!"

"Yeah, right," Leo said, lifting his glass and eyeing Faye's rear.

She stood over Dan again, legs astride his, her skirt riding further up over her knees. Dan was of that age; what could he say? Girls were even more attractive to him if they showed interest in him; indeed, Faye was.

"What, what do you want?" Dan asked.

Leo was laughing, laying back, bottle in hand now, thoroughly enjoying whatever little game he'd instigated. He was sloshed—they all were.

Very amused, he said, "Go on then, Faye!" Giggling, Faye shaking down her long golden-brown hair, straddled Dan's lap further until she sat with her crotch on his.

"Come on then, Leo, where are you?"

Leo stood up, causing the van to dip. "What's going on...?" Dan laughed. "What's all this!"

Leo leaned in, thrust an arm across Dan's chest, and pinned him back. Faye sniggered quietly.

"Haw! Come on, that's enough now," Dan said.

Leo snorted derisively. "You're being taken hostage!" he said.

"Oh ahy, is that what this is? Take advantage of your drunken brother-in-law." Dan finally put his hands all over those silky, soft thighs again.

"You're being taken hostage," Faye said, laughing. "Amy ain't getting you until she hands that Engine over to us. She gets you; we get the Engine."

"Fair deal," Dan said. "But what makes you so sure she'll part with her Engine for me?"

"Mmm, good point," Faye said soberly, climbing off. Leo rolled off too, securing the whisky bottle in two hands. Faye flopped down beside Dan. He threw his arm over her head and looked at her; she was obliterated.

"It's none of my business," she said, rolling over and placing her arm over Dan's head. She looked rather attractive now laid like that. "...but, what the hell are you thinking, Daniel?"

"What?"

"I know I told you to settle down, but marrying a lass for an Engine, I don't care how much money it's worth; it's not forced to make you happy."

"I realise that; that's why I told her to get rid of it, take it out of the equation. Remind me to jot it down, just in case I forget."

Faye curved herself around and laid her long legs over Dan's lap. "Wouldn't you'd be better marrying a Gypsy lass, like me, with our ways..."

Dan stroked her leg. He felt he was taking advantage of her now, but who wouldn't.

"He doesn't want any lass, him," Leo blurted.

Dan had almost forgotten his brother was there. He pushed Faye's leg down and sat up.

"Gypsy lass or no... he just wants that Engine." Leo was serious now. He looked into the neck of the bottle and then took a long gulp.

Dan took the bottle from him. "I honestly don't care anymore about that bloody Engine. I love her, I do!"

"Well, since you've put it that way!" Faye said, annoyed. "Someone's gonna get their hands on it; it might as well be you!" Faye put her head on Dan's shoulder. They sat and said nothing for a long moment.

Dan looked in the mirror on the wall opposite and stretched. He then turned to look at the soft furnishings, which seemed to be moving up and down. "Jesus, what have you done to me?" He sighed.

"Me? Nothing!" she reached for her glass of JW, saluted Dan with it, took a delicate sip, then laughed and quickly wiped a drip from her chin before laughing again.

Dan thought about Jack and suddenly felt a surge of guilt.

"Told you," Faye said. "That Amy is good for you, brother-in-law!' She rubbed her blurring eyes and sat up slightly. "Now, you really look like Jack!" She squinted an eye and studied his face. "Look!" She handed him a compact mirror. "See!"

"Marriage can be good business," Leo said with a sober grunt. He sat up, passing his glass from one hand to the other, then pulled out a loose cushion from behind him. "That Engine could make us all a fortune." He leaned on the pillow and punched it slightly as though it annoyed him.

"Exactly! That was the idea," Dan said. "Now you see what my intention was? You what?" he said, suddenly remembering what Faye had said moments before. "You think I look like him? Do you mean Jack or Leo? It's why I bought us here," he said, returning his attention to Leo and changing the subject again. "...Initially anyway! The plan was to get Dad's Engine back...I thought I'd surprise you all! Thought you'd be pleased...And, of course, I had that other pressing matter to deal with."

"Aw, fuck that! You mean Rebecca?" Leo said, throwing the cushion clumsily onto the opposite seat before flopping back again.

"What...? What pressing matter?" Faye laid her legs over Dan's knees again. She leaned into him... "Why not just buy the Engine off Amy, then fuck her off like you do all the girls...You never get attached anyway!" She whispered in his ear. "Fuck her and fuck her off...Gypsy style...!"

"Remember, that lass, Faye...?" Leo butted in. "The one he went out with when we were here six years ago...?"

"Faye doesn't remember her."

"Rebecca, yes, I do! I saw you with her the other day!"

Dan sighed. "Shut up, Leo."

"He's a Daddy… to that little kid of hers…you know, the little girl running here with Jack."

"You deflowered Rebecca, got her preggies and fucked her off? Jack said you did that, but I didn't believe him. So, it's true?"

"It wasn't like that!"

"Oh well, if you hadn't done that back then, I wouldn't be with Jack now, would I? So, what do I care…?" Faye sighed deeply in thought and then let out a long, drawn-out yawn. I was 14."

"Fourteen! Is that all?"

"I'm only twenty now, Dan. I think you forget. I'm younger than you lot."

Dan was embarrassed. "Another one of my awkward adolescent moments. What can I say. I can't help being around girls who'd screw me at the drop of a hat… Anyway, it comes with the job, you know that!"

"So, what does she want you to do about it?"

"Nothing."

"Nothing! Thank fuck for that!" Leo raised the bottle and saluted. "Only Dan falls in shit and comes up smelling of roses! But I don't think you mean that!" Leo said, suddenly very serious.

Dan was nodding down at the floor. "No…I don't, not really." He sighed. "I was going to ask her to marry me." He suddenly looked worried and glanced up at Faye sheepishly. "I didn't even know about the kid, honestly!"

Faye sat up. "You are kidding!" She nearly choked.

"I was going to buy that Engine, marry Rebecca…and I had it all planned. Fuck it, give me another fucking drink. Then we were going to go on our merry little way with the Engine—go off to do the Fair and make a fortune with our Circus lit up like a fucking Christmas tree!"

"Right…That was the dream." Faye laughed. "Something like that, yeah." Faye sloshed more whiskey into Dan's glass and licked it off her fingers. "Oops!"

Dan licked her fingers, clasped his glass and stared into it as though lost for words. "I did think a lot of her, you know, Rebecca. But, hey… she's married now! If anyone asks, that baby isn't mine, Leo! You've got that wrong, mate. She's not my kid; I told you that before!"

"Right." Faye laughed again.

"And, I don't want the damn Engine anymore, just for the record! Amy is a great lass; I will prove it to her. I want to show her I am a man of my word… I've made too many stupid mistakes. It's about time I put things right in my life. I want to settle down… have a woman about the place, like you, Leo…and our Jack…" he glanced up at Faye and winked.

Faye nodded and smiled at him warmly. She flicked her hair over one shoulder and placed her hand on Dan's arm. "That's very sweet, but you haven't known her longer than two weeks, Dan."

"Love at first sight, man, what can I say."

Faye sighed and squeezed his arm, "You really like her then?"

"Ahy, I do."

"And Jack…?"

"Jack?" Hearing Faye mention Jack's name made Dan go cold and sober. He shifted uncomfortably, "What about him?"

"Can he manage without you?"

"Can you?"

Faye stood up and stared at him dumbfounded. She narrowed her eyes but said nothing.

"You picked the best out of us," Dan shrugged. "You should know if you can cope without me or not!"

Leo suddenly jumped up laughing, wagging a finger in the air, "Don't you two start now. Come on, Dan, think we've outstayed our welcome."

Dan got up slowly; Leo pulled him to his feet, checked his fob watch and stretched. "We're definitely off tomorrow then?"

"Yeah!"

He threw open the door and stuck his head outside. "It's throwing it down!"

Faye stopped Dan dead in his tracks. "You know what Jack's like without you."

Leo said, "We're definitely off tomorrow then?"

Dan moved Faye to one side. "Ahy, I do, but he's not my problem. Yes, we're jumping tomorrow!" He shouted at Leo as he started to leave. "…tomorrow…"

"Tonight, it is then!" Leo shouted back before staggering off. He left the door open behind him. A brisk gust of cold air and rain swept in the smells of animals and grass from the fields beyond.

Faye closed the door. "Jack'll be gone for hours."

"Ahy, I know. I'm knackered." Dan didn't want to go but knew he had to get out of there. "We've a long haul ahead; better get some rest…." He went to knock back the last dregs of whisky in his glass and missed his mouth, spilling it all down him.

"Are you sure you want to go after all this rain?"

"It's Fair time; of course, I want to go. I want to go now!"

"Do me a favour?"

"What?"

"In Nottingham…"

"What?"

"Keep your eye on Jack."

"Why?"

"You know, just in case."

"In case of what?" Dan sat back down again before he threw up. He felt sick. He stretching his legs out.

Faye looked embarrassed. "You know."

Puzzled, Dan scratched his stubbly chin and then stared at the white grease paint on his hand.

"In case he starts his old tricks…you know what he's like—with the lads."

Dan sighed, "What are you on about now?" But of course, he knew. He knew as well as Faye what Jack was like on Fair days. It was an unspoken knowledge that Jack seemed to like hanging around with young lads…

"He just likes to impress the young Jossers, makes him feel…important…I don't know."

Faye rolled her eyes but said nothing. "You don't understand," she said quietly.

"I don't understand what?"

Faye was clearly growing irritable. "If he starts again."

"Starts what…?"

"I don't like it. I've seen Jack touching them…!"

"Oh, come on, Faye. What are you saying now?"

"You know… it's more than showing off…!"

Dan got up to leave again. "I'm definitely going this time." He made his way down the van to the door, tucking his shirt into his trousers. He was getting a nasty hangover. "You know what your husband wants, don't you?"

"What?"

"A family." As he opened the door, a blast of night air bit into his bones. It was later than he thought.

"What's the point when we're on the road? Come back in—have another drink."

"No, ta. I've had enough—more than enough." He watched as she bit her lip. "Jack's ready to commit like—with family—the lot. He said he wanted to leave the Circus, so you could have a baby."

"He just wants to tie me down, you mean!"

"I don't think so; he told me it was what you wanted and that you'd agree it was time; that's what he told me."

Faye folded her arms, laughed, grunted, and looked over him into the darkness beyond.

"You are in love with him, aren't you?"

"Yeah." She looked puzzled. "Why would you even ask?"

"Well then, it's pretty obvious; why would he lie to me…!"

"Why, because he knows I don't want kids—not yet anyway. But it wouldn't be any of your business anyway if I did."

"So, you have talked about it with him? He does know how you feel because sometimes."

"Sometimes? Sometimes what? Come back inside and close the door; it's freezing."

"It's not always obvious… to the rest of us."

"Rest of who?"

"Leo, me…"

"Isn't it?"

"Come on, you know what you're like…."

"No, I don't." She was smiling now and licking her lips.

"Like that! That's what you're like… see!" Dan laughed and shook his head. "That's why Jack wants you to have his kids."

"What?"

"You're a big flirt…!" He took her by the waist, kissed her forehead and pushed her away. "Goodnight, Faye."

She smiled, stepped down from the caravan and took his hand. There was a moment between them, not as man and woman in love, or a couple about to tear up a marriage and a family, but as friends, very old friends—close friends.

"What happened here last night with our Jack and that Rebecca...So, Jack knew the kid was yours?"

"Yeah, guess so. Your husband guessed; I don't how. Why?"

"She walks about with that little un' like no one can remember her... but we do. We all remember her!"

"Rebecca? Oh, come on... what's that got to do with anything? She just wanted to bring her kid to see the Circus. Like any mother. Don't read anything into it. It's all in the past."

"It plays on my mind, Daniel! I worry about it!"

"Well, don't! It's not your concern."

"What if her baby isn't yours, but Jack's...?"

Dan's mouth fell open. "You boys look so alike; all of you do.

You're triplets; of course, you are all similar."

"I'm pretty sure the child is mine, but it doesn't really matter because she's married now to Greg, and wrongly or rightly, he thinks the child is his, so...."

Faye sighed. "Logically, I do know that. And I do think the little girl is yours because –"

Dan waited for her to finish...

"It's just that... you know what he's like around Fair time—you know how he gets with the young boys."

"Look..." Dan offered his most sincere response; she'd have seen right through anything less. "What happened with Jack and Rebecca all those moons ago was a genuine mistake, Faye. He'd had too much to drink, and I can vouch for that; I was there; even I thought she was into me. She had us both fooled. It could have easily been me who took her to bed that night, and she told me nothing happened between them because Jack couldn't... he was too drunk. Anyway, he didn't, they didn't...that kid is mine, Faye, honest. It all happened before we were together, so I don't know why you are so worried about it... And she ended up with me, so...forget it, like I said, water under the bridge."

"But she has spoken to him. She's been back, Dan! I saw them talking in private."

"I know, I saw them too, but trust me, she is not interested in him. Like I said, she's married now, got young ones, and we won't be seeing her again after tomorrow."

"But she was throwing it about, and even the villagers said she deserved what she got."

"Villagers…?"

"A women in the village said Rebecca got pregnant… and then managed to trick that Greg or whatever he's called into marrying her…"

"Wait a minute; so you knew – everyone knows?"

"I just asked if anyone knew her, then the woman in the shop said yes. She told me what I've told you."

"Why did you ask?"

"She's been hanging around Jack, what was I supposed to do!"

"Great, so what if he finds out, this Greg?"

"…Like you said, water under the bridge; he is married to her, so it's not our problem anymore, right?"

"People in small villages like to gossip, especially about the Circus and people like us."

"Exactly. Good job, you left her and came after me!" Faye laughed.

"You weren't that instrumental in getting me away from her, don't flatter yourself. Anyway, Faye; think back, you had both Jack and me eating out of your hand at that time and the better man won…."

"It doesn't stop him running after boys, though, does it…?"

"Faye, enough. Don't talk like that!"

"Stop covering up for him," she said, laughing again. "You know it as much as I do… That's typical of you two, always falling out then moving the blame onto others. How many times have we jumped because of him? We've had villagers chasing us… young men nursing broken hearts because of him… fathers wanting to get their hands on our men…and if that is isn't enough, we've been accused of stealing horses, bad gambling debts and father's chasing us because of their shafted daughters, thanks to you! … It's a wonder I'm not grey!"

"None of us are perfect, that's for sure—that's life on the road, eh! Anyway, you've got to stop talking about Jack, Faye… He's not like that anymore."

"Oh, he is! He changes his sexual preferences more than he changes his shirt."

"He won't do it again!"

Faye looked away for a moment taking in the dark distant peaks.

"We've been forced to jump because of me a time or two, remember?"

"Well, I know we have. You've broken hearts too"

"Well then!"

"We both sounded tired." She stood, arms crossed, shaking her head.

"…But this thing with Rebecca's little un'." She whispered. "Why did Jack take her off to parade her around like that?"

Dan shook his head. "I don't know…to get back at me, maybe?"

"He's not that much of a cold-hearted bastard."

"He's not a pervert either."

Faye looked at Dan weirdly. "Well, think about it. He hardly touches me. I was just another object he wanted to take from you… We all know he prefers boys."

"Shh, fucking hell Faye. This is your husband you're talking about—my brother!"

"It's true! You know it is."

"He's no faggot… he's an idiot, misunderstood—but not a fucking pervert."

"Dan!"

"That's what you're insinuating. And what sort of wife are you if you think like that of him yet purport to love him like you say you do!"

"You presumptuous bastard!" she snapped. "Your role in all this is what's perverse."

"My role…in what…!"

"In this, us—this Circus—our lives! Who the fuck are you to judge me?"

"Who's judging? Hold on a minute. I'm not judging anyone!"

"You don't know how I feel…you live in this Circus with your head in the clouds. You think everyone's fine as long as you're running the show… we are all just puppets under your control!"

"I don't control anything. I wish I did! We are all on the same side here. I've made choices for this business for everyone's benefit. I'm just a representative here. You must be happy with my choices, or you'd have walked. In any case, let's not distance ourselves too far from the past. I stepped in over my dying father and supposedly wiser brothers to save this sinking ship when I could have stayed here and married Rebecca!"

Dan got the impression Faye would have taken him out if she'd been a man half his size.

"Yes, I know," she said, squaring up to him. "I also know this business has made a monster of you… and Jack!"

"Monster, me?"

"You pretend to ignore the environment you created. You're demeaning to the boys, Jack and Leo! Both of them. Who were you to tell Jack and Leo how to run their business? Leo never says anything, but his river runs deep. One day, Dan, he will open his mouth, and you will feel his wrath."

"I don't mean to be controlling."

"Well, you are. You've no idea what you do to those boys. How you make them feel, especially Jack!"

"I thought I was helping him…helping you!"

"I'm not your responsibility anymore, Dan."

"No, and neither is Jack!"

"I love him…"

"I do!"

"Ahy, I know; I never said you didn't!" Faye scratched her back and gave a sigh. "Look, forget it."

"Yeah, let's, I'm going."

"Good…"

"I'm sorry."

"Yeah… me too."

Dan turned and raised a hand. "We okay…?"

"Yes, I'm sorry." Faye shook Dan's hand.

"I am."

As she turned to climb the steps back into the caravan, Dan's chest expanded; he felt he was about to burst. "See, these are the devils you possess," He ached to take her. Quickly looking around, no one watching, he grabbed her by the wrist.

"What!" she said, her eyes wide. Dan lurched for her, taking her in his arms; she didn't resist. As he pulled her close, he felt her heart beating and her whole body shaking.

"No! Fucking hell, Faye, what am I doing? Sorry, I'm so sorry –"

"Don't be," she whispered, pulling him back towards her. "I should never have left you!"

"What are we doing?" He pulled away. "Stop. This is madness."

"I love you," she said, tears streaming down her face. "I don't want Jack's babies." She ran back inside the caravan and closed the door.

Dan thumped the wagon's side with all the crazed emotion of a mad man. There was nothing he could do to undo what had just happened. Dan knew he had no feelings of love for her, just that age-old urge to take from Jack what he could never have… and he could never resist the desire to screw over his brothers, especially Jack. Thumping the side of the wagon again, he shouted. "What the fuck is wrong with me!"

He'd barely gotten two metres away from the van when Jack stepped out into the light flooding from the tiny windows. He leaned against a wagon, and a face peering out of the nearby window snapped the curtains closed as Jack's fist smacked the glass.

"Mind your own fucking business!"

Disputes between Jack and Dan were no headline news. Dan's mind flashed back to their father, hands in pockets, cap pulled down over one eye. Now Jack, more a man than he was, stood before him. He hated Dan with every fibre of his being. As a kid, he hated him; somewhere deep, there was always raw jealousy that neither of them could ever confront nor learn to cope with. Dan didn't know how long he'd been there, but Jack was smirking and nodding. He smelled of ale and tobacco.

"You bastard," he said quietly, calmly.

Acting as though nothing had happened, Dan slapped his brother's shoulder.

"Jack, you're back?" Dan tried not to show emotion. He wasn't sure how much his brother had seen or heard anyway.

Jack pushed his brother away. "Go near her again, and I'll fucking kill you!"

Wheels in Motion 1937

Her voice shrieking with excitement, Janey ran in, leaving the door open. "Amy…Amy…!" She tore off her hat and coat and dropped them on the kitchen floor. Amy glanced down where the wet garments lay on the Derbyshire Stone. "I'm taking my kitten home!" Janey looked happy and puffed. Amy sighed, rose from the chair where she'd been most of the afternoon sewing, leaned over and kissed Janey's forehead. Now she knew about Dan; she was sure she could see him in almost everything the child did.

"Where's Dad?" she said, picking up the coat and hat. She glanced over the top of Janey and out through the open door behind her. The river at the bottom of the yard was lapping over the banking. The soft pinks in the wool, greens, taupe accents and rather exquisite metallic silver thread that ran through the fine cable stitch shone in the light from the fire.

"What is he doing out there?"

Janey's almond-shaped eyes lit up. "I'm taking my kitten home!"

Amy nuzzled the hat to her face to feel the soft natural hand-woven fibres upon her cheek. She thought of Rebecca's love for the child and knew that every ounce of it had been lovingly crafted into every stitch to keep her favourite daughter warm and dry.

Amy shook her head and laughed. She had grown quite attached to the child over the past few months and now felt she needed to watch out for her on Dan's behalf, and Janey seemed to have taken a particular liking to both her and father. Of her own volition, Janey had also recently started to call the old man Grandpops, which both Amy and Rebecca thought was hilarious and very cute, but no one other than Dan and Amy knew of the irony in the situation. If they were to marry as planned in the winter, the old man would genuinely become her Granpops.

Rebecca had laughed when she heard her daughter say Grandpops for the first time. For a moment, Amy thought Rebecca knew that she was aware that

Janey was, in fact, Dan's child. Rebecca thought her little secret was safe. Amy and the old man would spend hours of an evening talking about the joy the child was bringing into their lives of late; Amy wanted nothing more than to tell him that Janey was Dan's daughter but thought it unfair and unnecessary, so she let sleeping dogs lie.

The old man suddenly breezed in. "Have you seen that river?" he said, removing his coat and shaking it all over the floor. "By Christ, never have I seen rain like this in all my years!"

"It's a curse; it came with the Circus," Janey said in an offhanded way. Guessing she'd heard her parents commenting to that effect, the old man and Amy glanced at each other and smiled.

"Well, they're leaving tonight," Amy assured her, "so let's hope they take the rain with them."

"Can I go get Bluebell now?"

"Who?" The old man teased.

"My kitten…my kitten!"

Amy stirred the stew on the stove and watched Janey as she began running annoyingly around the table.

"Can I? Can I? Please, please, please."

"Oh, for goodness sake…Dad!"

"Alright!" he snapped. "I called in at the Prices –" He gestured annoyingly over at Janey.

"I'd never have guessed."

They both smiled. Nodding over at the wildly excited child who was now crawling beneath the table, looking, she said, for the kittens.

"…and you acquired company…and at this time of night. Why isn't she in bed?" Amy said, wiping her hands on her apron.

"She refused to go to bed. I offered them the Engine, and they have accepted—snatched my hand off, as a matter of fact." The old man looked at her across the kitchen as though seeking approval.

Amy spun around and grinned. "You're kidding? Sit down, Janey, for Pete's sake. You know it's way past your bedtime!" Instantly, silence fell around the room. The child crawled out from beneath the table and found a chair to sit on. Amy sat beside her and brushed dirt from her white dress. Annoyed at being reprimanded, Janey dropped her chin into her hands and screwed up her little face. Amy pulled her chair forward a little towards hers, placed her hands on hers, then, looking skywards, gave a little sigh and squeezed the child's hands gently.

"She wanted to come... couldn't wait to take the kitten home!" the old man said.

"Well, let her have it then, for goodness sake—in fact," Amy said, turning back to the Janey—"You can take them all...how about that!"

Janey looked up, surprised and worried all at the same time. "But..."

"Shh!" Amy said, pressing a finger to her lips. "... We'll talk about it in a minute; just let me listen to what Grandpop has to say, then we'll discuss the kittens, okay? So..." she said, turning to her father. "...What exactly did you say to the Prices?"

"They want it. I've leased it to them!"

"Of course, why wouldn't they?"

The old man smiled broadly. "They agreed on the rate!"

"Are you sure? Are you sure this is what you want, Dad?"

"Ahy, should have done it years ago!" The old man bit his lip, looking down at his hands.

"We're doing the right thing, aren't we?"

The old man clasped his hands together and leaned forward on his elbows over the table. He lowered his voice, "The sooner we do this, the better it will be."

Amy nodded her head and shrugged. "If you're sure. If you're absolutely sure...?"

"Ahy!" The old man laughed and stood up straight. "I am. I'm definitely sure."

Amy threw her arms around her father and held him close. "Thank you, Dad! Thank you!"

"You said I could go home."

Amy and the old man separated and laughed. "Please do." Amy looked at her father and laughed again.

The old man snatched up his dripping cap, shook it, and sighed. Amy could almost see the relief wash over him.

"Why didn't I do this years ago...?" He frowned and put his cap back on.

"Don't want to get anyone's hopes up, though, not just yet, just in case the Engine isn't working. It used to run fine."

"Oh, by the way," Amy said, reaching to the mantle over the hearth. "I found these out in the barn last night."

Amy scrapped up the cigarette butts from the mantle she collected from the barn and dropped them in her father's hand. "Not yours, I hope?"

"No, not smoked in months... I can't afford to; they're not my brand anyway. I don't know anyone who smokes these around here. You found them in the barn, you say?"

"Near the Engine. The animals have been so restless lately. I thought perhaps...Oh, never mind."

The old man examined the cigarettes in his hand. "Nothing to do with me"

"Good, thought you were sneaking around in there to –"

"– Drink?" the old man said, annoyed.

"Maybe they're Dan's or his brother's. They must have smoked in there when they were fixing up the chicken coop."

"Dan doesn't smoke these either."

"Dunno love." He dropped them back in her hand.

"Come on! Let's go!"

"We're going now!" Janey said as she stood up and looked about for her coat.

"Okay, okay, missy. Go get your kittens then. I'll give that big old Engine a turnover. Get it fired up and ready for your dad?"

Amy began dressing the child, buttoning up the coat, now dried beside the fire, up to her chin and popped the hat on her head.

"I've not got a good feeling about this!" The old man said, stopping suddenly by the door. He took the child by the hand. "Say night, night to Amy."

"Night, night Amy."

"Good girl. Look after those kittens, alright?"

"I will, I will...."

"Piggy promise?"

"Piggy promise, forever and ever!"

"Good." Amy curled her little finger around the child's tiny digit to seal the deal and laughed. "You'll be fine with it, Dad. Of course, you're anxious about using the Engine, but it will be fine; you'll see!"

The old man's shoulders dropped as he let out a long sigh and looked back down at his hands again."

"What's up?"

248

He turned over his palms and examined them. "I'm dreading the thought of hearing the damn thing running again."

"Well, this is different this time, Dad," Amy said. "You'll be getting it out of our lives…and no one need ever know about the accident…And as far as Dan's concerned, we've sold it already, so…if that makes you feel better."

"It does; you've no idea!"

Amy leaned over and kissed him. Feeling very smug with himself, the old man neatly parted his grey feathery hair in the frameless art deco mirror that hung slightly askew beside the door. His reflection distorted in the bevelled scalloped edges.

"Come on then, Janey, let's get off before we need a boat to sail out of the yard."

"Coat!" Amy shouted to the old man as she tossed it over to him. He put it on and again took Janey by the hand to lead her out. Amy couldn't help thinking how cute they both were.

"Don't get into mischief together," she said, smiling as she watched the old man fasten up his coat and pull Janey's hat down over her eyes for fun. She tore it off.

"Put your hat back on; it's raining!"

Amy was worried about Janey in the same way she worried about her father. She feared for him constantly—concerned he would catch his death of cold, worried he'd strain himself or fall. The old man took the hat from her and led Janey out of the door. Placing Janey's hat back on her head, he gave Amy one last glance, winked and pulled the door behind him. "Don't let anyone in!" he called before shutting the door. "Not a soul!"

"Make sure you take all the kittens," Amy called. "Or we will never hear the end of it." She looked through the window and watched as her father waved back and gave the nod. He knew his daughter worried about him.

Leo's Advice 1937

Leo staggered out from behind his caravan as Jack stormed by. Still holding the bottle of whiskey he had taken from Faye's, he took a gulp, cheeks bulging, swallowed hard and breathed out heavily.

"Hoy! Where you off to?" Jack stopped and turned.

Leo stepped forward from the shadows and offered him the bottle of whiskey.

"Where have you been, you daft bastard? What's with the getup? We knocked off hours ago." Leo laughed. "It's true; you look like Dan with the slap on. Dan is wearing slap tonight. Your Misses made him up, just so she could compare you and him, like…We were saying tonight that you both look exactly the same when you're made-up…!"

Jack snatched the whiskey from Leo's hand, examined the bottle, took a long hard gulp and swallowed it back in one. He cleared his throat.

"So, you were in there with Faye… and Dan?"

Leo sounded exhausted, "I, I, was…and…Dan… was…" he wobbled and sniffed.

"I saw you in there. All of you!"

"Nah, we were waiting for you." Leo studied the bottle in his hand and took in another long gulp. "We've had a few, bro… you know… you know how mad it gets?"

"Did he fuck her?"

"What!"

"Dan, did he…?"

"Hell no! It's just Dan and Faye, bro. You know how they are? They go back, man…thick as thieves, bro…been that way for years, you know how it is…before you and her were married, like…?" Leo didn't know what else to say. He looked at his brother, trying to focus through blurred vision he closed one eye. He shut up. Leo was secretly seething with jealously; he always got jealous of Dan and Faye, just as much as Jack did, if not more.

He sighed loudly. "If you feel like that, why don't you go and sort out Dan's lass? Then you'll be equal."

"Who? Amy?"

"Go on! Get in there before Dan does. Get all this out of your system; That's what I'd do if I was you."

Jack thought a moment and sniffed.

Leo laughed. "Let Dan think he's getting a clean ashtray…It would piss him right off…bring him down a peg or two."

Jack snatched the bottle from Leo. "Thanks!"

"Nah, it's yours anyway."

At that moment, the wagon door opened, and Izzy stuck her head out. "Thought it was you two out here. Nothing wrong, is there?"

"No… aw, no love… we've just had a few, is all…Why should there be anything wrong?"

She paused at the door and then slipped back inside.

Leo slapped Jack's shoulder. "Look sharp," he whispered. "We're jumping tomorrow… Go and give Dan's girl one for me!"

The Clown is in Town 1937

Amy hoped her father's impromptu visit with Janey around suppertime would be the last visit of the day, but as the Circus prepared to leave for Nottingham, a few of the travellers began calling down to the farm to compile supplies for their fifteen-hour journey: feed for animals, milk and clean water from the well. As Amy busied herself out in the storage sheds all evening collecting supplies for red-faced, wiry-haired children, who had pelted down the hill in the rain from the Circus at the very last minute for much-needed supplies, all she could think about was Dan. She looked at the brooch he had given her. It was all Amy had left to remember him by. The tarnished 18-carat piece, albeit beautiful, was old, but as it shone and twinkled in the lamplight, she was reminded of their conversation beneath the stars, mainly on the topic of his intentions of returning after the season to make her his bride; a conversation she just could not put to rest. The discussion was still running over in her mind. The more she thought about it, the more she was surer about her feelings for him. It had been somewhat of a whirlwind romance, but now as the dust settled, she was surprised at her own sense of loss and loneliness without him. She knew now, more than ever before, that she loved him. If only she had told him when she had the chance, if only she had said yes. So wrapped in her thoughts of Dan and coupled with the bombshell her father had dropped that very same evening about the Engine, she hadn't paid too much attention to whether her father had, in fact, taken Janey's kittens home with Janey at all, or if he was still in the barn. She wondered if perhaps they'd returned to the cottage or were still at the Prices. She didn't much care at that point either, when she returned to the fire's warmth in the cottage and found no one there. She was too exhausted to question their whereabouts any further. She wrapped herself in a shawl, took refuge beside the fire and prayed that Dan would call to say goodbye one last time before leaving for Nottingham. While she waited and wondered, she sank into a deep sleep, the warmth of the fire penetrating aching limbs and heart.

"Amy, the pail!" The old man shook an empty bucket at her. "…Take it to the stream."

There was something about sewing by the fire when the sound of the rain bouncing off the cobbles outside in the yard made sleeping deeper and dreams more vivid and real.

"Don't spill it," he said, wiping sweat from his brow, his pinched features seeming to harden, his expression growing more sinister in the light of the fire. From a dark height somewhere above, Amy saw him drop, like a lead weight, then swing back and forth—back and forth. His head snapped back, and his body swayed like a pendulum. As she rose, picked up the pale and gazed up at him, he tried to tell her something. His eyes, steely and wide, stared down upon her. She sensed his sorrow—a pang of deep, heartfelt guilt and loss. His brow furrowed, then changed. Now masked in the white paint of a Clown, the furrowed lines creased, cracked and flaked and crumbled like snow to the ground. He was grinning; his tarnished teeth flashed spikes of yellowish-brown.

"Don't let anyone in!" he said softly, "…not a soul. Where are your brains, child?"

Amy awoke in a pool of sweat.

"Evening!"

She realised this word was absolute, present, and in the room. She thought that she instantly recognised its distinct raspy tone, giving her cause to imagine a slimy toad, which she'd become accustomed to associating with Jack Franconi.

She thought, the toad is here, as she sat upright, then turning to see where the voice was coming from, she had a shock. "Oh! God!" She jumped to her feet and groaned loudly. She threw the shawl over her head. A man dressed in full Clown costume and face paint was shouting into the room from the door he had opened fully. He was striding in with muddy boots without an invitation. Amy's heart sank. Of all the people in the world, this creepy Clown was the one she had not wished to see, this night or any other. She didn't like Clowns at the best of times and hadn't really taken a liking as a child. They'd always given her the creeps.

"I need supplies, a few eggs, meat if you have any?"

"It's very late, Jack." She laughed nervously.

The Franconi Clown smiled. "I'm not Jack; it's me."

Amy stepped back as he took further strides into the room uninvited. His breathless voice seemed notably high and emotional. He was now so close she could smell the Circus on him, the dampness, the paraffin, menagerie, and the smoke. She couldn't help but wonder why, in his tiny warped head, her relationship with Dan Franconi suddenly somehow made it okay for him to just turn up at her home uninvited.

"Oh, you're not Jack? You could have fooled me. Has Dan sent you?"

"No!"

Amy didn't ever remember making a conscious effort to speak to any of the Clowns on a sociable level, nor on any occasion had she invited them to the farm during unsociable hours; how had he got the audacity to turn up demanding supplies at the drop of a hat?

"Okay, okay." Sighing, she rubbed her eyes. "It's fine," she said, naturally lying. She pulled her shawl from her head and let it drop to her shoulders, secured it with the brooch Dan had given her earlier, tidied her hair quickly and rose from her chair to deal with the stranger in the room.

"I'm coming," she said again drowsily. She laughed, despite her heavy heart and, still reeling from the weird dream that she had just experienced, forced a smile.

"Oh, how cute," she said, turning to see the man dressed in full Clown attire. "Come with me to the barn, Jack"

"Oh, the best offer I've had all night," he said, giving a slight cough. Amy thought he sounded like Leo for a fleeting second, but then was sure he would have said so if it was him.

Trying to lead the man back outside, she hoped he wouldn't need to get settled in the cottage. As she passed him in the doorway, she saw sweat oozing from him profusely. The aroma of horses, mould, cigarettes and booze seemed to worsen the closer she got to him.

A bead of sweat, mixed with rain, dripped slowly from a piece of fine hair hanging like a stalactite beneath the orange wig at the centre of his forehead.

"Been running?"

"Are you alone…?" The man's eyes seemed to dart around. His voice, still breathless, dropped to a lower tone. He cocked his head on one side and eyed her up and down. "Any chance of looking at that Engine?"

"Oh, it is you, Jack. I thought it was" Amy clasped her hands angelically and smiled; nothing would give her more pleasure than to deliver the news.

"No, I'm not Jack!"

"Oh! Okay, well, my father sold the Engine tonight."

The man's naturally cracked, dry lips slowly broke into a wide toothy grin that spread over the exaggeratedly painted red ones. "Has he sold it to Dan, by any chance?"

To Amy's astonishment, she stepped back slightly. "No, not to Dan."

"Great!" He looked pretty smug.

"No, we've sold it to Greg Price to use on his farm."

With his evil-looking, painted face, the man grinned again either through politeness, which Amy doubted very much, or because he wasn't really that interested in the Engine in the first place. "Not sold it to Dan, then?" He was moving to one side as though allowing Amy to pass, suddenly pushing between her and the door. "You know, I've never seen you up close, not close enough to look at you properly. I hear Dan's taken quite a shine to you. He's proposed, hasn't he? Did you say yes?"

"No, he didn't, and no, I haven't. Jack, come on, are you sure that's not you?" She places a hand upon his chest and pushes him back slightly with a playful smile. "I am not joking, Jack; we haven't sold the Engine to Dan!"

The man brushed against her and began walking her back into the room in a passive-aggressive manner. Amy wondered how he had the nerve to behave in this manner. Then reciprocating with the same passive-aggressive energy, she stepped around him and opened the door. Shocked to see the night sky, even darker than ever, she realised she had slept longer than she had thought. It was still raining heavily too.

"Please, after you, Jack," she said, forcing another smile.

"I'm not fucking Jack, alright!"

"Okay, sorry, please…after you." Leaving the door ajar, Amy lit a lantern and waited for him to go outside, but he didn't take the hint. He began roaming around the room in the half-light.

"Satisfied?" she said. "Not much to see." She lit another lamp and held it high for him to take. "Here…"

"You're a good un," he said, taking the lamp from her and moving around slowly. He turned to her with a broad grin and gave a long, drawn-out sigh. "It's no good me lying to you. I'll tell you straight out, shall I?"

"What?" She sighed heavily, placed the lamp down and folded her arms.

"I don't like seeing good people getting ripped off or lied to; God knows it's happened to me plenty."

Amy couldn't be bothered with him anymore. She was tired and just simply at the end of her tether now. She was beginning to hate him more than ever. She was confused by his statement and no longer had the energy to question him further. Scowling, she huddled herself into her shawl, shivered and closed the door again. "Look, do you want these supplies or not? They're out in the shed if you do!"

The man started biting his nails and seemed to stare at her sideways. "Dan's being a bastard to you," he said bluntly. He gave another one of his half smirks. "You've no idea, have you?" He continued to bite his nails. "Dan's only has eyes for that Engine of yours. If you've gone and sold it from under him, he'll probably just fuck you off now; lose interest in you altogether."

"Good, then there's no love lost."

Amy shook her head and laughed. "You've got it all wrong. Talk to your boss; he'll put you straight."

Of course, in the back of her mind, Amy knew perhaps he was trying to tell her something, the truth maybe, but he was the last person she wanted to hear it from, especially since she didn't know him and he seemed to be deriving so much pleasure from it.

Instantly, her mind questioned how she should respond—holding a defensive stance was her immediate reaction; for self-preservation, dignity and pride, naturally, she dismissed him.

"Don't be ridiculous."

She had a niggling worry in her mind that perhaps the only one sounding ridiculous was her.

"He's not bothered about you, girl." Swinging the lantern, the Clown studied her; the paraffin-fuelled flame flickered inside. "Don't care about anyone but himself; that's just Dan." He put the lantern back down.

"Look," Amy sighed. "You'd better just go. Dan might come. He could walk in here any minute. You don't want him to hear you talking like that."

The man laughed. "Do you know where he is… right now? You've no idea, have you?"

Amy didn't answer.

"He's with her! He's with Faye! Right now, as we speak! He has been there all night. Had his hands all over her! That's how much he cares about you! Imagine, my own brother fucking Faye! Can you believe that?"

"So, Jack, I thought it was you!"

"I'm not fucking Jack, alright! Shut up, you stupid bitch…what do you know anyway…?"

Amy froze; her jaw dropped. He began patting his palm against his forehead. His lower lip quivered a moment. He took a cigarette packet from his deep colourful trousers and lit one.

Amy rushed to the door and flung it open wide.

"Whoever you are, Jack or whoever, I think you've overstayed your welcome. I want you gone!"

The Clown smirked again and waited a moment, surveying the yard through the rain before finally closing the door and stepping away. Amy watched as his hand reached for the latch; he held it firmly, then paused. "Sorry, Amy…"

"It's okay," she said, feeling a massive relief to see him leaving.

"This is what it's like living with him, our brother. I'm just trying to help you!"

"I understand."

"Do you? I don't think you do." He took a step outside, his eyes narrowing in thought. "Or maybe you did know; did you?" He turned around to look back at her, then, in one stride, was back in the room again. "I bet everyone knows what my brothers are doing behind my back; everyone but me."

"Jesus," Amy mumbled. "Like what? I'm sorry. I am sorry you feel that way. I'm hurt too?"

"So, do you believe me?" He said, laughing. "I can't believe someone believes me for once. There's a first time for everything. It isn't the first time Dan and Faye have hurt someone. They've hurt me plenty."

Reluctantly, Amy circled around him. She thought about making a run for it but had nowhere to run to.

"Bet you thought Dan was perfect. They all do! All this talk about getting married. I'm so sorry he pulled the wool over your eyes."

Amy just shrugged and chewed on her lower lip. She wasn't entirely convinced whether there was any truth in anything he was saying, but it didn't stop her from feeling ridiculous.

"There's no way he'd ever marry you!"

Amy laughed nervously.

"You're a Gorger, see!"

"Don't know what you're calling me now, sorry…." She laughed again. She didn't have a clue what he was talking about. "By Gorger, I assume you mean not a Gypsy?"

Tears were welling up through his anger.

"Dan, he's like me; too fucking set in his ways… our ways!" He slapped his chest in a tribal manner and leaned in closer. "We stick to our own kind, see… our traditions."

The non-Gypsy in Amy felt segregated. "I believe you," she said.

"We all trusted him, my brother…and her…. "He sighed. "I think she loved me once, and I was like you; I believed everything she said."

Amy raised an eyebrow, not convinced and very nearly said, I doubt it. but managed to bite her tongue.

"I didn't want to admit it either!"

"Admit what…?"

"Like I said, it's been going on years between those two, Dan and Faye."

To preserve any faith Amy had left in Dan, she reached for the brooch he had given her.

"That's my mother's, that is." The Clown said, taking a sudden lurch forward to examine it more closely; then he laughed. "Is that what he gave you? One of his bribes! Oh my God, it is! That's just so Dan." He shook his head and laughed. "So typical of him."

"Do you want it back?" she said, quickly removing it.

He scoffed. "No, keep it; Mum was a Gorger like you." He burst out laughing and shook his head. "That's so typical," he said again. "Can't believe he gave you that. Rebecca only gave that back to him yesterday. Oh, he works fucking fast!"

Rolling now with laughter, he doubled over and clasped his knees. "I'm sorry, oh my God," he said through fits of hysteria. "I shouldn't laugh, but that is so fucking funny!" He looked up at Amy's face and tried to stop laughing. "It's not your fault…I can't believe he gave you that!"

He burst out laughed again, repeating himself, rambling over and over about how she was being easily bribed, just like the rest of them. Amy lost track. He wasn't making much sense. Feeling childish and naive, she stood before him while he continued to mock her until gasping and panting, he eventually stopped and wiped tears from his cheeks. The white face paint he was covered in was now streaked with black-blue tear-lines. He swallowed hard and looked up.

"Tell you what, I've not laughed like that in years."

"Alright, that's it! You need to leave…!"

"Sorry, I'm sorry!" He threw up his hands in a gesture of apology and nodded. "You're right, that was rude of me. Let's pretend I never mentioned it. Let's start over …can we just start again?"

Amy gave a look of surprise but thought it probably looked fake because nothing Jack had ever said surprised her, and she didn't know Leo well enough to read him.

"Dan doesn't care about anyone, women especially. He bribes everyone to get what he wants.'

Amy was perplexed. She wondered again if there was a hint of reality in anything he said; she forced herself to think better of Dan. He had always seemed genuine.

"Is this a lie to hurt Dan?"

"No, honestly, they're all like that… especially him and Faye. I can cope with them, see, because they're family to me…I can't put up with them, but the thought of losing her, especially to him. Let's just say, I know this sounds crazy, but let's just say I act like I don't see what's going on because it makes my life easier. If we lose Dan, we lose Faye; we just can't let that happen. Simple as that… It's complicated."

Then straightening again, he rubbed his chin, looked directly at Amy, and winked. "Can you keep your mouth shut?"

She nodded.

"How about we make it fair…you and me…between us?"

"What exactly are you asking?"

He shrugged and lifted an eyebrow. "Well, you're an attractive girl… they'd never need to know if we, you know…went to the bedroom right now. We can carry on like they do, as though nothing has happened afterwards, but; we'd know. Wouldn't that make you feel better – empowered! …It would help me!"

Amy had no idea how they had suddenly started talking about sex—having sex…together.

"No…that won't resolve anything!"

"Sounds mad, I know, but it's not… think about it. Faye's only with us because of Dan, see; so, I ought to be grateful that I've got her in my life at all… and, well, now and then I do get a good fondle of her—she loves it, and it keeps me going for weeks… And you, well you don't know how lucky you are to be with him, so –"

"Look… come on…what are you going on about, really?"

"It will work –"

"Just leave, now!"

The Franconi Clown began hammering his forehead with the heel of his hand. He took a long draw of the cigarette and dropped it on the floor. Amy watched as the tip fizzled out on the damp stone. She recognised the brand from the ones she had found in the barn.

"For my peace of mind…and yours, we should just have it off."

"I don't know how you think that will resolve your problems with Faye or Dan; it can only worsen things."

"Dan doesn't love her!"

"No, he doesn't. Not like that, he told me."

"So, you have discussed it with him?"

"Ask them. Have you ever spoken to Dan or Faye about how you feel?"

"There's no point; they'll deny it, say they're only fooling about. And Faye always says she loves all of us. But I know she stays with all of us so she can keep close to him. That's what she wants…to be near Dan."

Amy sighed and shook her head.

"Oh, it's Faye; you just don't know her! Dan is a God in her eyes; she'll do anything for him—I mean anything!"

Amy shook her head again in disbelief. "This is just insane, honestly. You're not thinking straight. Go talk to your brothers."

"Mad? Am I? Well, you know you've questioned it yourself. You've just said so… Oh, forget it… it doesn't matter… that's just how it is. You'll learn!"

Amy must have been animating her thoughts, pulling a face or shaking her head because he suddenly went crazy.

"Stop shaking your head, you fucking bitch. You're doing the same thing!"

"How do you mean…? I'm not involved, don't bring me into it… You've got to understand, this…this game you're playing… it's between you and Faye, not me and Dan."

Clamping his ears, he looked down at his feet.

Amy clapped her hands hard and laughed. Big mistake, she knew immediately, but it was the only thing she could do to stop herself from crying right there in front of him.

Suddenly, he grabbed hold of her shirt and pulled her so close to him she could feel the heat of his breath on her face. He tried to ruffle the top garments over her head like he was undressing a wriggling child.

"I've seen courage like yours before," he said, moving in tighter.

Amy struggled to keep her blouse down around her waist. She put her arms over his and held his wrists, trying to keep his hands away from hers. Saying nothing, she could barely speak with the effort of maintaining a force against his.

"Dan's girls are just…so…fucking…" he broke off momentarily to remove her hand from his wrist. She squeezed her eyes shut. "…easy… you fucking gorger bitch!"

He was laughing now through gritted teeth, like her struggle against him was entertaining.

"You're…fucking strong. You've got fight in you. I like it."

Amy was fighting with everything she had. She yanked a hand free and reached for the latch of the door. Sensing her urge to run, he swung her around and slammed her against the door. "Where do you think you're going…!" Laughing, he lifted her arms above her head and held her pressed beneath him. "Do it…come on… what's wrong with you?"

"No…No…Get…off…?"

His body pressed against hers, their eyes locked as she struggled beneath him. He had an animalistic glare, lips apart, moist and drooling slightly. His eyes glazed, staring into hers. They fell from her eyes to fixate on her breasts, exposed through a rip in her blouse. Amy tore her hands free and folded her arms across her chest, but he threw up her arms again, pinning them against the door at head height. She felt his cold, dry, cracked lips pressing and scratching against the front of her neck.

"Dan gets whatever he wants…now it's my turn."

Amy was shaking her head in disagreement.

"Come on…come on, you bitch…we deserve this…!"

"No!" Amy screamed. "Faye wouldn't want you to do this. Stop it. Let go of me… let me go! I'll tell her! I'll tell Dan!"

Changing the subject seemed the only way Amy could think of distracting him. "Good idea." He laughed. He seemed to get more excited with Amy's interaction. "Do that!" Momentarily, his arms relaxed slightly, letting her arms fall beside her. "Go on then, tell them both. I don't fucking care; that's the point, you stupid bitch."

Amy tried to slide away beneath him. His hand dropped lightly on her waist, "Okay, okay…" he said, panting and wheezing. "I tell you what," he began coughing. "You talk to them after…tell them what it was like with me, and I'll tell Dan how good it was with you!"

Amy made her move and quickly ducked out from beneath him. He grabbed her by the hips, clawed at her skirt until he caught a tight hold, heaved her back towards him, and slammed her against the door again. Amy pulled away with every ounce of strength, stirring something ugly in him. He flashed his eyes over her. She could tell the man wasn't backing down. Holding her beneath the weight of his entire body, he pressed against her, pinning her to the door, then reached out with one hand to turn the key in the lock.

"Jack, no, no… please!" Amy began stammering in a last attempt to persuade him to stop. "Faye, she loves you! Please, don't do this." She was crying, petrified.

"I'm not Jack!"

He slapped a clammy hand across her mouth. She tasted dirt and the saltiness of his soiled skin. The flat of his hand pressed against her nose, forcing her to gag. She thrashed her head from side to side, gasping for breath. Then she felt his groin pressing against hers. Not able to manoeuvre, either way, he began kissing her face, neck and bare shoulders. She felt his sweat stinging her flesh as her knees began to buckle beneath his weight. Fighting to stay upright, their bodies locked in a very physical tug of war. They both began to slide slowly down the door together. Pushing himself ever closer to her, he fumbled to lift her skirt. He drew a bent knee high up between her legs. Using his whole body to hold her against the door. Exhaustion got the better of her. She could no longer stay on her feet or keep their bodies apart. He held her close for what seemed like a lifetime before stretching a free hand to pull at the crotch of her pants, then sliding to rest upon the cold stone floor; they lay in silence in the light from the fire.

Amy found bursts of energy to squirm beneath him as his hands roamed beneath her skirt. Grasping at her underclothes, his nails scratching her thighs and stomach. Amy mumbled words to him to make him stop, but he wasn't listening. He began tearing at her blouse with the other hand, his knee constantly rising between her legs, pushing them further apart. "No, please, no!"

She screamed into his chest as his fingers found the elastic of her underwear again. Then he entered her. She heard him groaning into her ear, "Good girl!"

His muscular body was not working with his brain. He was clumsy. He had to strain to keep himself inside her. "Hold still!" he choked and coughed. As she cried, he clawed at her hair, yanking back her head and biting into the side of her face. She screamed as he breathed three long grunts and thrust himself hard against her—half in and half out; she heard him sigh, then felt his body rise and fall. She knew it was over. His heart was pounding as he prized himself away, rolled off and pushed her to one side. Staggering, the man got to his feet and reached for the door; there was an almighty explosion outside that shook the very foundations of the building. With very little oxygen in her lungs, Amy felt herself fainting and fading, then everything went black.

Two Days, Two Nights 1937

Amy snapped awake. Sharp, agonising pains throughout her body and flashes of violence against her were playing out before her eyes as if she was still in the moment. It was cold. She was confused and exposed. Crawling across the floor, she pulled herself up against a chair and took stock of her surroundings. The front door was wide open; beyond was nothing but darkness. The wind howled around the cottage as she paused to listen to the rain outside. She could hear the stream over the fields thundering as though it was outside the door. Glancing out, she couldn't believe her eyes when she saw the river's dark, murky water was indeed rushing past the cottage door, lapping over the door step and trickling into the room. The yard outside was cut off from the lane and under at least three-four feet of water, gushing down from the high peaks where the stream usually ran idly.

Amy feared for her father and thought of Janey; she wondered if they had been caught in the raging flood outside. She called out into the darkness and waited for voices to respond. After a moment of hesitation, halfway over the top field where the road cut through the land, she saw two faint lamplights flickering and swaying in the distance; they caught her eye swinging rhythmically. It took her a moment to focus through the rain, but she eventually saw two people hurrying towards the cottage. They were women wrapped tightly in headscarves and mackintoshes. Amy reached the door and waited for them to get closer. They began to wave and shout when they saw her standing in the doorway. Sensing urgency, Amy lifted her torn skirt and hurried out through the water towards them.

"Please, this way." She called, pointing in the direction of the lane. "Help! Please! Help me!" She waded through more water and strode over pieces of tin, metal sheets, and debris, which she assumed had been washed up by the storm. She wanted to head them off away from the turbulent water and slippery embankment that stretched out before them.

"Hello!" She shouted.

"No need to be formal, lass." one of the women replied, puffing and panting as she neared the embankment's edge. "It's only us."

"We can't get over," the other woman shouted… "It's me, Rebecca! I've bought milk, eggs and a few sticks of wood." Amy recognised her instantly. She edged closer to the embankment. "Is Janey with you?"

"No, she left with Dad. They were coming to yours with the kittens!"

"Amy, we came over yesterday and the day before; what's happened? Your door has been ajar all this time. We can't get across. Are you all okay?" Amy felt confused, emotional and suddenly vulnerable but couldn't explain why. She didn't understand what Rebecca was asking…

"I…I… don't know."

Sensing the distress in Amy's voice, Rebecca took another step dangerously towards the embankment's edge.

"Don't cry, please, Amy, just try to remember; when was the last time you saw my daughter?"

"I told you—all I know is that Dad was taking her home…."

Rebecca's voice was sterner now. "We'll get over to you in the morning. We need to search the place. No one has seen our little girl in days; you were the last to have seen her!"

"Days?" Amy was even more confused. "What do you mean, days…?"

The two women glanced at each other. "We need to know where Janey is. Could she still be with your father, in the barn perhaps—what with all this water?"

"No, I told you, they left… There's no one here, honestly!" A vision of roaming hands grabbing at her body, ice-cold and painful, flashed before her eyes. She began trembling. Her mind felt tired and messy.

"Someone was here, I think, but –"

"Yes, yes, who? Who was there?"

"I knew it! Didn't I tell you, Rebecca?" The other woman began ranting and tugging at Rebecca's arm. "Come on, let's go call for help. We need to get over there right now—search the place…She knows something!"

"That's not true!"

"Look!" The woman shouted over the raging waters. "I don't know what game you're playing at, but one of those boys from that Circus was seen running from here two days ago…Who was it? One of those damn Gypsies? He was running like the clappers from here, apparently!" Rebecca was snarling now.

"Running as though hell had him… face all painted!"

"Was it Jack, or Dan? Amy, come on, tell me, who was it… Leo…?"

"I can't explain… I don't remember!"

"Something has happened to Janey, Amy! I think Dan has taken her! You must know if that is true! We've been shouting at you for days. Where have you been? Why didn't you respond? You must know something?"

"Of course, she knows; she's covering up for them, can't you tell?"

"Janey was here with you. None of us has seen her since! Did Dan come here? Did he take Janey?"

"No, no, he didn't!"

The other woman muscled forward. "If she isn't with this Dan person, or you, or your father, where the hell is she, eh? Eh! She's been missing for two days!"

"Two days? I've lost two entire days? I'm so confused. I don't even know where my dad is… Where's my dad? Have you seen him? He was supposed to be taking Janey home to you."

Amy's interrogation threw both women off completely.

"What the hell are you talking about—where's your dad? He left my house with my daughter and never brought her back!" Elevated to a sonic pitch, Rebecca's scream rattled through Amy's brain.

"Arrrgh… I'm going to kill you…!" Rebecca suddenly lunged toward Amy. She ran down the embankment and out into the water. "I'll tear you limb from limb if you don't tell me! Where's my fucking daughter?"

Amy didn't respond immediately; she froze with shock and disbelief for several seconds before reacting. She ran towards Rebecca, to the water's edge, without considering what might lie beneath.

"I'm sorry, Rebecca! I am. I'm sorry!"

Leaving the embankment, Amy fell and slid in mud into the darkness below, scrambling to her feet and stumbled out over rocks and reeds. When she emerged again, she was gasping for air, trying desperately to grab hold of something to keep from drowning. Then, she began wading deeper and deeper into the water's icy depth until the riverbed fell away beneath her feet. Rebecca heard Amy's faint cry further down the river through her bated breath. She stretched out her arms into the darkness, desperately hoping to save her, and saw her floating down the river.

Suddenly, Amy got to her feet again, saw Rebecca being swept behind her and reached out for her. Just as their fingertips met, Amy lost her footing again and was taken instantly by the riptide.

The other woman, who stood on the bank, was screaming for Rebecca to turn back but then suddenly disappeared beneath a surge of water flooding down from the peaks. No one saw where she had gone, she just simply disappeared. Amy felt her body being forced sideways by a wave, fighting to keep herself alive, she grasped out at branches and grass along the river bank. Suddenly, Rebecca shot up before her, mouth wide, gasping for breath, her hands thrashing widely. Amy tried to reach out to her but couldn't. She saw her body wash downstream, twisting and beating uncontrollably against rocks and trees. The water took Amy too, within its thunderous, dark, vice-like grip, until she crashed against something hard. She heard a crack and then felt her whole body grow limp.

*

"Janey's missing," Amy awoke to the words repeating over and over in her mind. Morning mist illuminated the mud and dirt where she lay. Though she could still feel the motion of the water, she realised she was on dry land. Squinting against a wash of colourless light that penetrated a thick, silent creeping fog, she rolled over onto her stomach and drew in a breath. The cold fresh air hitting the back of her throat made her cough. River water spewed from her lungs and ran down her nose as she tried climb to her knees. She began heaving and throwing up water and grit. The farm and the whole valley had disappeared under a torrent of dark murky water. She barely recognised where she was. She told herself that she had very little time and needed to get warm and dry. Logically, she knew she had to prepare for those who were coming for her. In a strange calm manner, she scrambled to her feet. Even if at worst, she thought, if they find Janey dead, they could no longer blame her, her father or Dan. They would understand; they would know that Janey had probably drowned like the rest had done. Once back inside the cottage, Amy pushed back the lace curtain in the window, wiped a circular patch to clear the moisture on the glass and peered out. She removed her wet clothes, dropping at her feet on the floor and stepping over them. She slipped on a night dress and went back outside. The floodwater had begun to subside over the cobbles in the yard. Pieces of steel and other debris strewn around was caught up in deep mounds of sludge that were starting to reveal themselves like razor blades. It didn't take long to recognise that the pieces of metal were parts of the Engine. She swung open the door and waded across the water to retrieve the first piece she came across. Wiping mud from its surface, she lay it flat in her hands. Blood drained from her face as she crouched to pick up another fragment. This time, instantly recognising the piece; a bent square plate of metal torn away from a side panel on the Engine's flank with the word Showman's embossed into the steel, along with a serial number reinforced the knowledge and reaffirmed her worst nightmare. Frantic with fear, she looked around and screamed. "Dad!" She staggered slightly and stared down at the piece of twisted, torn metal in her hand. Each flash in her mind came with a memory segment; revealing snippets of information, like grainy frames of a silent movie. Her brain tried to piece together a narrative from the broken fragments of information that she had seemingly buried deep within her subconscious, a story that she should never repeat to anyone-ever.

Amy could see a face in her mind's eye, one she knew well, but suddenly it appeared different, unfamiliar. It was smeared strangely in a streaky white greasy mess, like a whitewashed wall covered in a thick, oily blue substance. Grease paint plastered over stubble and dye bleeding into the eyes and down the Clown's cheeks into the creases of his nose and mouth made her shudder at the mere thought of it. The monstrous image of the Clown in her mind appeared so clearly now, she felt she could almost touch him. She closed her eyes, trying to picture the man before her; his face was the face of a Franconi, grinning with yellowing-stained teeth. Something was clawing away at the back of her mind. She knew this man had done something – something horrendous, but her mind was blocking the memory of it. It would not allow the information to reveal itself before her. She began associating feelings with the vague memory of the man, emotions she could not interpret or place into context. Something vital was missing from the puzzle, and Amy couldn't put her finger on it. Closing her eyes again, she tried to recall the night when her father and Janey went to the barn, allowing any thought to wash over her like an ocean wave, hoping something, no matter how insignificant, might stick. Then an idea came crashing over her; the Franconi had told her that Dan was only interested in getting his hands on the Engine. He had also said that Dan didn't love her and never had. This she remembered specifically now because it had hurt her so cruelly. Those words were still painful to think about; they cut so deep that she could still recall how it felt; the shock, the humiliation, and the embarrassment. She could still hear him talking in low sarcastic tones and remembered thinking that night; if the Franconi triplet, whoever he may have been, had said those words purely out of spite or for revenge or simply to hurt her, he had chosen them well. Suddenly, glancing down at the metal in her hand, she wondered; was he capable of doing this much damage to spite his brother, Dan; but why?

Questions began to formulate. Had the Franconi gone to the barn while Dad and Janey were in there? Had her father tried to protect his property, or worse, had he been killed in the process of trying?

A memory suddenly hit home like a tidal wave. There was a loud noise. Amy remembered a kind of explosion, a gunshot. She could still hear it ringing in her ears as its memory rattled through her brain. Amy found herself running to the barn. As she ran barefoot through the mud and water over the courtyard, more visions, noises, and smells flooded her senses. She remembered feeling a physical blast as she lay on the floor in the cottage; the windows, the doors and even the solid stone floor had shaken violently, but why?

She tore back the barn doors and held them open against the wind, looking for anything to use for protection. Spotting a good-sized stone in the mud beside the door, she dug it out with her fingers and grasped it firmly in her hand. Stepping inside the darkness, Amy let the door slam closed behind her. She held her place by the door, ready to swing or launch at anything that moved.

Alone in the darkness, the face of the Franconi brother began haunting her now, every inch of it; evil, demon-like, grinning fiercely and boldly before her, laughing and taunting. Amy grabbed a pitchfork that she knew was always leaning against the wall and, with it tightly clenched in her free hand, held it out before her ready to strike.

She was shaking and, like a child in the darkness with a head full of nightmares and nonsense, stepped bravely forward, shouting, "Dad! Janey!" Her first instinct was to look for the kittens, see if they had been taken or not. There was a lantern on the bench with matches. She put down her weapons and tried to light them but couldn't. Her hands were too wet and cold, and they wouldn't stop shaking. Then, suddenly, somewhere within the darkness, she heard a rustling sound. She turned and saw a sudden movement in the corner of her eye. A gust of wind slammed the barn door behind her again, making her jump. As the door rattled against the wooden structure, she dropped the lantern and hurried to pick it up. Reaching inside, tiny warm bundles of bony fluff huddled together were squirming, soft and warm. Bending down, she saw the basket of kittens by the stable.

Oily Rags, Steam and Kittens 1937

The old man and Janey stared down at the basket of kittens. "Poor beggars, they'll drown here if that river continues to swell. I've never seen rain like it, Janey." Janey lifted a kitten from the cradle of its mother's warm breast and looked up at the old man, heartbroken. "Don't let them drown, Grandpops."

"Are you sure you want to take them all?" The old man laughed. "They'll be fine; you needn't be concerned." He reached down and ruffled her hair. Janey rubbed her cheek against the kitten's tiny paw and nodded. The old man stood a long moment looking out over the yard, watching the rain come down, while Janey cuddled each bungle of fluff. Martha stood beside him. She pushed her arm through his, smiled warmly and laid her head upon his shoulder. Together they watched in silence as the rain danced across the cobbles outside. A gust of howling wind whipped the rain sideways, bringing the old man back to reality; he took a deep breath, blocked the distant memory of his late wife, Martha, from his mind and returned to his work. "Right," he said, looking around for his tools. "Let's see if I can get this old machine started up for you, shall we? It is finally time to put the past behind us and move on." The old man exhaled purposefully, strode towards the traction Engine and pulled off its ancient shroud. As he set about stoking up the furnace with coal, bits of paper, old timber, oily rags and just about anything he could lay his hands on, Janey sat peacefully beside the basket of purring kittens. She stroked the mother tenderly, who, by all accounts, was enjoying a much-deserved moment of attention. After maybe an hour or so of filling up the water tank and stoking up the fire, he finally rose nervously and glanced around the barn. A look of concern rippled across his face."Janey? Where are you? Janey!" he shouted again. Slowly Janey appeared from the paddock, strolled over, pulled a kitten from the litter and sat cross-legged beside the basket. She smiled at the old man and casually smelled the kitten she was holding before rising to her feet and walking over to him. "What, Grandpop?" "Good girl!" The old man said. "Nothing, dear, just stay where I can see you, please." "Okay, Grandpops." Wiping his hands on a rag, the old man jumped down from the Engine and lifted Janey into his arms. He seated her in the cabin. "There," he said, settling her comfortably on the seat beside him. "It's warmer here. Let's start her up, shall we?" As he stoked up the fire in the furnace and topped up the water in the boiler, the warmth rose up Janey's cold legs. She pulled her skirt over her knees and placed the kitten in the cradle of her thighs. "Don't move, Janey. Stay where you are." The old man reminded her, her restlessness putting him on edge. "It won't take long," he assured her. "This old steam Engine's capable of putting out enough power to drive a 500-watt generator, so all the Circus folk around here are keen to get their hands on it." Janey listened and watched as he continued to stoke up the furnace and build pressure in the old boiler. The red glow from the blazing fire turned her snow-white dress a tinge of ochre yellow. "Just think, Janey," he said, "when your neighbours run out of mantles for their gas lamps or oil, your dad will have power from this thing to light up your whole house. And just the exhaust alone can give you enough heat to warm your barn right through the winter. Imagine that." The old man laughed and then questioned why he'd not found the courage to do it before for his own benefit. Aw, well, he told himself, better to benefit from the profit of the beast than risk been beaten by it. Now there could never be another accident. He sighed heavily. "Just imagine," he said to Janey as he continued to twist knobs, pull levers and feed the devil within the burning coals. "Your mum, she'll be heating her hot water for her cooking, your dad will be grinding his own wheat, all these things and more he can do with this old machine." He rose slowly, wiping his hands again. "This beauty will change your life, lass—just you wait and see!" The old man jumped down from the Engine, threw open the barn doors, placed bricks against them and climbed back upon the machine. He began turning the flywheel clockwise. "This is a two-cylinder, in case you were wondering," But of course, he knew she wasn't. He stammered breathlessly. "Here we go! This is a momentous occasion, Janey!" Janey's attention was upon the teeming rain outside. "This two-cylinder steam Engine has an advantage above all others," he was explaining to no avail. "It's self-starting, see… Look, see how it's going! She's turning!" Janey's eyes flashed across to the kittens in the basket by the paddock. "Don't worry…" he said. "It won't rotate until I turn this wheel. Now, there… see! Here we go! Slowly…slowly! Now then, let's apply a little steam, shall we? And… we're… off!"

The old man bent down to examine the fire in the furnace. "Well, the boiler's still working." He was sweating now and frantic with fear and excitement all mixed into one. He slammed the furnace door closed. "Inside there," he began shouting, "are tubes. They are the first to give way if there's a problem, so let's hope they don't! If they bust..." he said with great concentration. He stuck out his tongue while carefully topping up the boiler with more water. "Water will drip down here –" he was still explaining while tracing the potential track of water with his finger to demonstrate, "...and, it will put the fire out, so, we need to keep our eyes open for that, don't want that to happen, do we? But I think we're fine; we're in the clear. No, no leakage! Nope, we're in luck!"

A sound like a thousand crashing cymbals exploded in Janey's ears. The barn was awash with noise, smoke, plumes of puffy white steam clouds, dirty, smelly smoke and dancing shadows. Janey was scared. Then the pistons burst into action, monotonously moving up and down, up and down, steam whooshing and popping. Janey covered her ears; the sound reminded her of hundreds of flying gaggling geese. The magnificent Engine began to jolt and jerk. The old man turned the wheel, manoeuvring slowly forwards, leaning over impulsively to ascertain spatial distance around the beast's torso. Janey's heart sank, and her mouth fell open; she turned to see the old man hopping around insanely inside the cabin, one hand stoking up the fire and the other still turning the great wheel, his snowy white hair windswept and wild and his face contorted and covered in soot. Janey's thoughts were of nothing but the safety of her kittens. She sat quietly watching the basket from the cabin; the mother fled, abandoning her brood, running off to a safe distance. Janey thought Grandpops was pretending to look scary like that on purpose to make her laugh, then realised he wasn't; it was a genuine expression. She no longer recognised him. "Grandpops," she whispered. "I want my mummy." She looked up, tears in her eyes, shaking and confused as the noise assaulted her tender ears. The pops of steam made her jump out of her skin. She could no longer smell the kittens in the barn, just thick choking soot and smoke coming from the furnace; it was stinging her eyes, nose and throat, causing floods of tears to stream down her smut-covered cheeks, and her nose began to run. She covered her face, peering out at the basket of kittens between cracks in her fingers. She could see they were trying to escape. Janey knew, just like her, the kittens wanted their mummy too.

The Cabin 1937

The cabin was dark and held a variety of nooks and cracks; Janey thought the Engine didn't like children; it seemed to be angry; she imagined it chasing her over the fields into the woods where, according to Mummy, no one ever finds small children. She leapt to her feet and glanced up at the sky and down at the ground. The noise was thunderous, the wind was blowing, and the treetops waved at the Engine as it thrust out between the barn doors into the stormy night. While in the barn, time had passed unnoticed, and the gale had increased to storm force; cracking branches fell from old trees into the yard. Past caring about the Engine or the kittens, Janey stared at Grandpops wide-eyed, inwardly pleading for him to stop and take her home. She felt the inside of her head about to explode and tried to let out a scream, but fear held it in. The old man glanced around and saw the panic on the child as she sat cowering away from him. Staring at her uncomprehendingly, more in despair than anguish, he yelled, "What?" Janey backed away. "Hey, Janey, what's wrong? Don't you like it?" In his imagination, he saw his worst nightmare being realised over again and felt sure she was about to jump off and meet the same fate as Martha had done years before. He reached out a hand towards the child and grabbed at her dress. He held her tightly with one hand squeezing the front of her chest until he suddenly brought the Engine to a halt. It made a low growling noise as it stopped dead. When the steam cleared, the old man muttered. "Janey?" "I want to go home now." she was crying. Tears the size of diamonds were rolling down her soft cheeks. "You little tyke!" he said, stricken with relief. He threw his arms around her and held her as tight as he could as she cried into his shoulder—both black as the ace of spades; they remained quiet a moment longer. Until he finally released her from his tight grip and let her go. Trembling and clutching the kitten tightly, she sniffed and said, "I want to go home now."

The old man laughed. "You scared me to death. I thought you were going to jump. I'm sorry, little un'! Thank god you didn't jump!" He held her tightly again and sobbed. "Can I go home?" she whispered against his chest. The old man wiped tears from her soot-streaked face with the palm of his hand. "Yes, of course you can! Here, see this, this is my pocket watch," he told her. "Put it in your pocket. It will bring you luck. Now, let's take you home. Stay there; I'll get you down," The old man jumped out of the cabin and reached up. Just as his fingers secured a tight grip on Janey's tiny waist, there was an apocalyptic explosion.

The Clown is in Town (continued) 1937

Amy stood perplexed, looking over at the cottage from the gap between the doors and the old Elm trees on either side of the barn doors. Staring at the front door, she wondered why behind it, only hours before, had she awoke to find herself semi-naked, limbs aching and torn and frozen to the bone with the sound of an explosion of some sort still ringing her ears. The blast outside had hit the cottage like a tornado, causing the building to shake. Suddenly, Amy remembered the pressure of the Franconi brother's boot upon her chest as she lay beneath it; how he had pushed her away and surged towards the door, missing the iron handle and almost falling over her. He had thrown himself hard against the door and yelled at her not to move. The man was panting and sweating. Amy remembered how she tried to sit up, but he kicked her back down. "Shh!" he'd said before peering out of the door. She collapsed at his feet as he carefully opened the door, fingers slowly curling around the handle, hesitant and breathless. She remembered how she had laid on the floor with her entire body aching, trying to see through the gap in the door, but with each breath she took, a blackness pulsated behind her eyes, forcing them to go in and out of focus. The last she recalled, the man dressed entirely as a Clown had opened the door wider, just enough for her to see his whitewashed face momentarily illuminated by the moonlight. Then, before succumbing to a complete blackout, an explosion shook the floor beneath her. Her lifeless, violated body felt every ounce of pressure from the blast. Strangely, at that time, Amy had no strength to question the noise outside but remembered her father's last words. "Don't open the door to anyone, not a soul."

The Cabin (Continued) 1937

The old man awoke, some seventy or eighty yards from where he had been standing. He was lying beneath a piece of mangled metal; ten yards ahead of him lay Janey in a bloody tattered heap. He heaved himself to his feet, ears ringing, eyes and throat burning and knelt beside the tangled child who lay face down in the mud. The trunk of her body was cut deeply, exposing a mass of entrails, and one leg was pulverised. The back of her skull was smashed, and fragments of her brain were scattered. Carefully, the old man rolled Janey over and whispered her name, instinctively, scraping handfuls of flesh, trying to replace them back inside the torso. He began collecting mud, dirt, grass, and anything he could lay his hands on to cover up the mess. Scraping together parts of the body that could be peeled from the ground, soberly, the old man placed them into a small pile and looked around for a container. Finding an empty pail, he carefully began filling it. Some of the flesh was recognisable, parts of the child he had once caressed, as a loving father would his own child; a small forearm, part of a foot and hand. Filling the pail to the rim, he found a sack and began using that instead. As he knotted the top, nothing was further from his mind than seeking a way to end his own life as quickly as possible.

The Clown is in Town (Continued) 1937

The Franconi brother ran from High Oakham Cottage, stopping for no one. The evening's rainy mist made the heavy oils and metals in the face paint he was wearing stream down his face, merging all the colours into a dark corpse-like mess, which shone in the moon's grey light. His heavily segged boots skidded on the cobbles as he ran over the yard. Reaching the far side, he hesitated momentarily, looking back at the Engine and what appeared to be a massive hole in its flank. Then he realised the stream was lapping over the gated entrance, cutting it off from the farm and the lane. He slid down the embankment and waded through a torrent of water, where a babbling brook had once flowed and proceeded to scramble up the muddy slope on the other side. He ran down the lane and over the narrow stone bridge towards the village without hesitation. Due to the bad weather, a Welsh fella, a newcomer to the village, who was going by a name no one ever seemed to pronounce right, had rounded up his new flock of hardy Derbyshire Gritstones and was herding them to higher ground in the opposite direction? The Franconi brother suddenly found himself face to face with him. A crow cried as it flew from the shelter of a tree. The man jumped as the strange Clown like man appeared to come running out at him as though from nowhere. Offering no apology, he tore through the shepherds flock, knocking them from side to side and causing them to skip off in all directions; then, he disappeared down an embankment at the side of the lane, leaving the shepherd scratching his head in disbelief.

Nottingham Fair 1937

The Fair in Nottingham spread was out and more significant and louder than ever. The energy around the city was positively charged. Despite the torrential and perpetual rain that had reportedly flooded many parts of the country, an extravaganza of excitement, frantic gaieties and visitors, wealthy citizens mainly, hovered around the streets of Nottingham, watching the Circus' every move with wonder and excitement as they prepared for the long weekend of events. The whole troupe excitedly anticipated an excellent run. "It's going well," Leo said, ducking beneath the opening of the temporary structure. "What are you two up to again?" he asked with an exaggerated suspicious tone. "What you reckon, guys? I've got a good feeling about this place." Dan jumped up, slapped his brother on the shoulder, and watched Faye stride over. "It's great!" she said, glowing. "Isn't it?" Leo laughed, then looked from Dan to Faye, his brow furrowing, and then he forced another laugh, rubbing his hands together with nervous anticipation. "We should do back-to-back shows while we are here; make the most of it; what do you think, Faye? You up for it?" "Of course," Faye tossed her golden-brown hair over her shoulders. "Can't wait." "I'll protect you if things get rowdy," Jack said, with one arm through his shirt as he walked towards them with a strapping young lad that no one knew strutting beside him. The young lad nodded at everyone, buttoning up his shirt as he walked by. Jack, distracting their attention away from him, by placing an arm around Faye's neck. He slipped into the rest of his garment, and began buttoning it up from the collar. She shifted gracefully, causing his arm to drop away from her shoulder. "Course you will, Jack, but that's not likely to happen. Where have you been?"

The vibe changed instantly, as it always did when Jack arrived with lads from other camps.

"You know you drive the crowd's wild," he said, slapping her bottom. Dimpling, she looked at Dan, curtsied and walked away.

"You never know who is watching," Jack called out after her.

"Jesus, look at you. Where have you been?"

Dan asked him as soon as Faye had disappeared outside.

Jack shrugged, laughed and hurried after his wife. With the entire Circus thrown into a frenzy, no one had time to question Jack further. The horses were groomed and decorated, the erection was finally up, and the girls dressed in garlands, silver, sapphires and high colourful head plumes always drew a breath from crowds. Readier than ever, men draped and decorated looked terrific and equally sumptuously. Dan smiled, pleased that the stop-off in Castleton had paid off as anticipated, even if it hadn't all gone to plan. Leo and Faye finally announced that they were tolerably satisfied with everyone's appearance, and Dan considered the small people's observations were as good as any, so with that, everyone agreed they all looked and felt great, even Jack, who had finally emerged late as usual, but clean and prepared. "Ready to fly?" Faye asked rhetorically. She threw up her arm and ran out before the crowds. She pirouetted gracefully; purple silk flowed around her body like water, and the silver bells draped at her wrists chimed as she angled her body in the direction of her team, gesturing for their grand entrance. one by one. "You're on, you're on!" Leo was yelling as he moved his troupe along. Jack, rolling up his sleeves and just about to go out, felt Leo pull him back slightly. "Here, pin that strap up on your sleeve with this; it's loose."

"Is that mum's brooch?" Jack asked, taking the delicate piece of jewellery between his fingers. "Where did you find it?"

"Take it. I dunno, it was lying around."

Dan thundered up, breathless with excitement and anticipation. "Ready?"

He looked at Jack, watching closely as he pinned the glistening brooch on his arm.

"Let's have a look at that. Is that what I think it is? What's this doing here? I gave it to Amy."

"I dunno, it was lying around. It'll bring us good luck. Come on!" Leo said, pulling back the curtain.

Jack ran out and circled the circumference of the arena bare-footed. He stood on the back of his Shire as the horse trot developed into a gallop, then leaned over and lifted Faye onto the animal's back. They circled a few times more at high speed before Dan joined them on the Apache. He took Faye swiftly and gracefully from Jack's horse to his as rehearsed a million times before. On their third or fourth lap, Leo sent out ponies, one by one, from the back and watched as they fell into line obediently to the audience's cry of "Aaarrs" and "Aws". Faye dropped gracefully onto the leading pony and reared it up. The pony remained on its back legs, circling for the audience until others followed suit. Jack and Dan drew their horses beside them, falling in line from larger to smaller; together, they all reared up and completed an entire 360-degree circumference on their back legs with as much grace and elegance as was expected. The audience, growing thicker around the sides of the arena, cheered and whistled. Dan preferred doing theatre and menageries when not in the ring, and this show was on the road with a vengeance. Dan's heart thumped at the commotion of the fanfare, but in the back of his mind, he longed to return to Castleton. He couldn't stop thinking about the brooch and Amy, his newfound friend, a gorgeous woman, and his soul mate; he was sure his mother would be proud of him. Picturing her at home with Amy, both waiting for him by the fire, he suddenly realised he was indeed in love. Never before had he wished his mother could meet one of his girlfriends. Amy was the one. He missed her like he'd missed no other, and it felt exciting. Breathless and flushed, Jack, now back on the Shire, drew him around to Dan's left flank. "Hey, you with us or what?"

"What?"

"Focus, bro, come on!" Dan's attention snapped back to the ring. He tried hard to refocus. He was present, but his heart wasn't in the show. Distraction was just something you could not afford; even Jack knew this, not in the Circus. Loyalty, dedication and especially concentration kept colleagues alive, simple as that. "Sorry, bro!" Dan shouted and snapped the reins to bring the horses about. "On your mind, is she?" He threw his Shire around to face the other way. The brooch on Jack's sleeve flashed in the lamplight. Dan smiled embarrassedly and shrugged; his brother knew him well. "How come you have that?" Dan asked Jack as he flashed by. "This?" Jack asked, pointing to the brooch. "Recognise it?" "Yeah, it belonged to mum. I gave it to Amy three days ago before we left." Jack gave a cheeky wink before waving at the crowd and galloping off. "Maybe you should stop making promises if you can't keep them!" The crowds cheered and rose from their seats. "What?" Dan shouted over the din. "Amy's obviously seen through you and brought it back, just like Rebecca did."

Nottingham Fair (Continued) 1937

Rain pressed against the wooden structure, made of narrow planks about 5 inches wide. There was no footrest, so the audience's legs had to hang down. It was common for young children to fall through if parents weren't careful. Dan didn't really like this setup, but there was nothing more they could do in the short time they had to prepare and with minimal funds available. He screwed up his eyes and groped around in the half-light, trying to plaster the bluey-white grease-based paint onto his tired-looking face, then tied a toggle around his loosely fitted pants. Faye flopped back on the bed and put on her bra. She rolled onto her stomach to fasten it, cradled her chin in her hands and watched Dan with amusement. "That will get the kids flocking in, I'm sure." She laughed mockingly. She knew Dan hated putting on the slap, and although he was no stranger to wearing it, she was having difficulty persuading him it was the best tactic to increase customers over the weekend of festivities. There was so much competition out there now.

Don't you have a husband to go to?"

"Oh please!" she groaned, turning her head sideways. "I hope he's lost out there somewhere." The roar of the wind grew louder through the wooden structure.

Faye sighed, "The Fair's been shortened from four days to three due to the high winds."

Dan shrugged. "It's probably for the best.

In the dusky light of the fresh morning the Fair was taking a breather, relaxing and catching its breath in preparation for the remaining few nights, and spirits were high. "Having three clear nights is acceptable. People seem to be flocking down just in case it is cancelled at the last minute anyway."

Faye watched Dan donning his ridiculous wig.

"The people of Nottingham will be forgiven if they are led to believe you aren't an actual person at all." She laughed.

"We aren't. Haven't you learned that yet? We are all freaks, Circus freaks! Nothing natural about any of us at all."

"Is that why you're dressed as a Joey today?"

"Hmm, thank God it's only for three shows."

"Leo's doing the same, so you're not alone."

"Yeah, I saw him. It was like looking in the mirror. We all look the same, don't we? By the way, don't be trying any triples out there tonight. My heart can't take it!"

"Na, I won't."

"I saw your rehearsal."

"What did you think?"

"Good, good."

"I saw some of yours. Two clumsy Clowning chefs, trying to deal with your wretched, weak-kneed kitchen hand." Faye laughed and flicked her hair back. "Good storyline." She laughed sarcastically loudly.

"That's the best I could come up with."

"At least you're not a fairy on top of the cake, like me."

"No, that should be Jack's part."

"Dan!"

"The other girls are dressed as otherworldly celestial beings; they love it! And they look great, don't they? Did you see us in our best-spangled muslins and pink tights?"

"All for the audience's delight! You should take them through a series of evolutions; as a narrative. Not that I'm criticising."

"We do follow a narrative."

"Well, while the small people perform as harmonious, gentle musicians, are you supposed to be telling the story through dance?"

"We are. We do."

Dan laughed. "Okay, it could be tighter, though, just saying. It doesn't run long enough. Hence, the reason I am donning this getup for you."

"Hmm, I think it works fine, a very different twist on our usual act."

Faye sighed and rolled over onto her back, leaning her legs against the boards. "But it's Fair time, isn't it! What ya gonna do?"

"Well, Jack certainly as the best part, the most fitting, I think."

Faye laughs. "He deserves special notice. He'll love it when he's met by a chorus of hisses and boos."

"If he plays the part right."

"Jack, the villain? How can he go wrong?"

"Have you seen him, dressed, I mean?"

"Yeah, have you?"

"Works well for him, being so tall and gaunt and all; he looks very—"

"Imposing?"

"Yeah, he carries it well. The proper majestic villain."

"I saw him in rehearsal, looked demoniacal with all that hair, shocking!"

"That's the point. Dressed like that, Jack will give all the little boys and girls nightmares for weeks."

"That's the plan."

"He had my mother's brooch on. Do you know anything about that?"

"No, why?"

"No reason, just wondered where he got it from. I gave it to Amy before we left, so –"

"How has he ended up with it then?"

"I've no idea." Dan continued to prepare for his afternoon performance in total silence, inwardly wondering how Jack had ended up with the brooch he had given to Amy before leaving for Nottingham. Counting down the hours now, he was waiting for the last show of the season to finally declare to the troupe and all the travelling community that he was through, retiring, turning his back on Circus life for good. The rest of the crew were busy making plans of their own; most were planning winter at Eastwood, while some would continue to travel under the Franconi name, minus three-quarters of the family. Faye and Jack had made plans to part company to pursue their own Theatre Company, which Dan was glad to hear. They hoped to continue until the following summer, where they'd perform in their own elaborate facade in a much worn-out old tent lit by coal oil flares. "Theatre performances beneath canvas are fast becoming a thing," Faye had said, and the play was the thing, with scripts by Faust. The public loved the sequence of scenes in various settings, such as Murder in the Red Barn. It was all the rage, and Faye wanted to move with the times. A good idea, of course, Dan thought. He was fast accepting the end.

"He's not mentioned you to me," Faye said, rolling back onto her stomach. "I feel sorry for the fucker, don't talk about him to me." Faye screwed up her nose and placed her hands on her stomach. "Okay!" she sighed and rolled over again with her back to him.

Pendulum 1937

Looking for another lantern in the darkness, Amy prized open the barn door to let in what little light was from outside, but the wind was pressing against it so firmly that it was hard to keep open; it slammed shut again. Amy felt herself swallow hard as a rope swung slowly back and forth, in and out of the lamplight; in and out, like a slow and steady pendulum. An eerie creaking sound high above the cavernous roof space made her stop and glance up. Her eyes trailed a curve of pale light, which sliced across the loft space from a solitary lantern perched high above her on one of the oak rafters. The creaking of the wooden structure resounded in the darkness. A black mass swinging gently on the end of a spinning rope made Amy gasp and stagger backwards. She looked away, then back again. Closing her eyes, instinctively, she knew. She saw a foot—then two feet, one shoe on and one off. They were hanging in half-turning motion, then the tiny flash of a belt buckle, a hand, and an arm hanging loosely from the coat sleeve confirmed what she thought she had seen. She watched in horror as the face and body of a man swung slowly into view stared down upon her.

Flooded by a tsunami of emotion, Amy froze and momentarily could not comprehend what it was she was seeing; then she felt anger and anguish; she was traumatised and afraid while at the same time searching, pacing through sobs and screams. In all that time, she began to develop a desire to run, get out, as far away as possible and not look back, but how? How could his daughter leave her own flesh and blood hanging by the neck? Being a single breath away from screaming hysterically, she talked herself into being stronger; she took courage and looked upward at the corpse. Suddenly, her heart stopped, as did her capacity to think, breathe, see, and stand. Every thought process that had kept her intact fell apart; she lost her composure and collapsed. Dropping to her knees, she pleaded, "Why, why?"

Glancing upwards again, she caught her father's eyes, staring wide like stone marbles. His face was stern, fierce and contorted into a fearful cry, an expression she never saw nor would ever forget. It was a look of sheer horror, as though he had witnessed the purest of evil before the fatal moment. In the direction of his glare, Amy wondered if there was a clue to suggest what had made him do such an act—she looked around at things she thought he may have seen moments before his death—was there a clue within the barn? A letter, perhaps, something in his line of vision that could offer answers. Whatever it was, whoever it was, Amy felt it was present in the room still. She remembered how he had cried when he confessed to accidentally killing his wife and wondered if he could no longer live with that guilt, but she knew her father well. He had promised to put things right, and she believed he would. He wouldn't hurt her this way. She felt she was being choked through heart-rending cries and sobs that broke so deeply inside; after an eternity of trying to breathe, she began searching for something to cut him down with. She stumbled upon a sack that she had never seen before. It was neatly stitched with new, fresh twine and leaned against the wall beside the basket of kittens. She looked away and upwards again and wondered if it was that he had been staring at during the last moments of his life. She tried to listen for words, a voice, his voice. She pleaded with him in her mind to explain himself. "Why? Why did you do this? Why?" Praying to God for a sign, anything that would indicate why he had done this. What was she supposed to do? Do something, do nothing, what? Returning her thoughts to the sack and the kittens, she didn't know why she was so drawn to them but was. They were all she could think of, to find the thing that had driven her father to take his own life. She walked around them again, thinking of Janey, of how she had planned to take the kittens home the last time she saw her. Amy steadied her thoughts and reached down, taking a firm hold, her fingers ripping through the coarse fibres of the sack. She tried to lift it but couldn't. It was much heavier than expected. Suddenly, feeling something moist and disgusting, she let go and stepped back quickly. The barn had several high windows shining in straight lines creating pools of hazy light on the ground. Instinctively, she dragged the sack into the light to examine it. A sticky substance covered most of the sacking; evidently, it was soaked in something black and tar-like. She stared at the dark imprints in the palm of her hands and backed off a little further. A cold, hot flush seemed to rise and fall from head to toe and back again, and as the realisation that she was no longer crying suddenly occurred, she also realised the substance in the palms of her hands was blood. Wiping her hands down her front, the thought of what she had discovered disgusted her. Any fear she had drained away, leaving the strangest sensation of nausea, shock and anger, a vast screaming void like nothing she had ever experienced, hollowed out a place in her chest where her heart once pumped love and joy. Looking back down at the thick viscous substance on her fingertips made her feel suddenly numb. Now slightly on the verge of passing out, Amy retched a few times before carefully sitting to take a breath. She felt sweaty, hot and cold all at the same time. After a moment or two, her nerves steadied again. She began unpicking loose stitches in the top of the sack. The top parted and fell open as each stitch began to pull into flexible hoops.

"Oh shit," she breathed and turned away. Whatever her father had done, if he was responsible for whatever was sewn into the sack, Amy decided she would defend him, maintain his innocence and protect his memory. Then, as quick as that thought came, another flustered in. There was no comeback. If she ran to the village now, she could declare she had found her father dead. Nobody could press charges; after all, he had taken his own life. All she had to do was report the incident to the police. Such a declaration seemed the easiest way out, and in some ways, she was glad her father was dead—she didn't yet know what was in the sack, so at this point, her father was still innocent. She pulled the sack open slightly wider at the top and peered inside. "Jesus…no…" She fell back. Then taking one last deep breath, she paused before tearing open the sack. Soft blonde hair, matted with dried blood and a mash of flesh, lay beneath a shallow nest of straw. Immediately, Amy knew her father could never have done something like this, not to Janey or anyone. He couldn't, and he didn't—Jack, on the other hand, most certainly could and most definitely did.

"No, no, no. Dad! Jack!" Amy screamed up into the concave roof above her. "Janey, Janey, no, please…No! "At the moment of Janey's death, Amy surmised that her father must have witnessed it taking place. He must have caught Jack in the act and tried to defend her but couldn't; why else would he take his own life? Obviously, Jack, dressed as a Clown, tempted Janey away from Dad; he had to, just like he had done when he lured her away before at the Circus. Janey knew Jack; she trusted him, but so did Dad. Dad would have protected her, but he couldn't, nor could he bear the pain of what he must have witnessed. As she tried to rise slowly to her feet, she scrambled to the plume of light and screamed into the universe, "You will pay for this!" Crying and sobbing upon the floor of the barn for hours, the deadly silence around her was suddenly broken by the sound of a cheerful robin with its sweet refrain and trusting nature; the tiny bird could be heard chirping to its heart's content somewhere in the loft space above where her father's body still hung from the rafters, now creaking under the weight of his body. A glorious slither of warm crimson sunlight creeping in between a gap in the barn doors slowly slid across the floor to where she knelt. Glancing down at her bloodied hands that lay shaking in her lap, she watched the light gradually crawl over her legs, illuminating and warming the palms of her hands with its soft peachy glow. As dawn broke, it warmed the darkness around the barn, completely transforming the cold, dank atmosphere with its magnificence, like a phoenix rising from the ashes of its smouldering grave. Morning poured its light into the wooden structure, penetrating the darkest corners, bringing Amy to a sudden stark awakening. She watched the light as it scaled the walls and crept over the highest rafters, covering everywhere with a golden haze. It was only a matter of time before Greg Price arrived searching for his daughter; descending upon her with a large pack of angry villagers, who had most certainly been out searching for days not only for the missing child but for Rebecca and the other woman who had been washed downstream in the storm. Amy remained on her knees until the sun had engulfed her in its warm embrace.

The animal's internal clocks had sprung awake hours before; now hearing voices outside, they were agitated and fearful. Voices growing ever nearer were coming from the courtyard outside, and those congregating had surrounded all the buildings harmed with weapons of all descriptions.

Amy glanced up to see a flash of blonde hair in a tight bundle lifted into the arms of a distraught woman who assumed she was perhaps a sister or close relative due to her striking resemblance to Rebecca. Shocked by a flood of sunlight bursting in from the barn doors, which were now wide open, Amy watched as a young man in his early twenties, wearing a flat cap and wire-rimmed glasses, was helping the extremely brittle and grievous Gregory Price into a carriage outside in the yard. Amy sprung away from the open door as their heads suddenly turned towards her. The young man cocked up his cap and strode across the yard towards the barn. There was no polite introduction before he marched in.

"This is so painful," he said, removing his cap. "The Prices will need you to accompany them to Nottingham. They need you to identify those involved." Amy nodded. The man lifted her to her feet, pulled a small object from his pocket and held it out to her.

"This was found in the child's pocket."

She took it and held a pocket watch up into the light with a shaking hand and watched it spin back and forth on the chain before wrapping it around her finger and squeezing it tightly in her hand. Then the man helped her to her feet, took her by the elbow and led her outside. A party of strangers were staring at her but said nothing. They remained frozen there a few minutes longer, whispering amongst themselves; they headed back towards the village one by one.

"May I?" Amy cleared her throat. "May I… see my father…?"

"One last time?" the young man asked. He led her to the cottage, where he opened the door and gently allowed her to enter alone before shutting the door behind her and locking it with the key.

The old man had been laid in a pine box on the bed. Amy lifted his hand and placed the watch between his stiffened white fingers. "They'll swing for this," she said, kissing her father's hardened brow. "I'll hunt down the Franconis, and I'll kill them. I'll kill them all!"

Last Day of the Fair 1937

Faye jerked away from Dan as Jack walked into the tent. Looking up and down at Dan in his Clowning attire, he laughed and pulled Faye closer to him. Jack turned, forced a cocky sneer to Dan and placed his arm over Faye's shoulder.

"So, what did it feel like joining the Jossers? Finally donned the costume to slum at the bottom with the rest of us."

"There's no shame in it." Dan's eyes flashed at Faye momentarily as she squirmed awkwardly beneath the weight of Jack's arm.

"Just doing my job like the rest of you. It's been a great Fair!"

"She's pregnant!"

Dan was flummoxed. Of course, he knew immediately who his brother was referring to, but for his life, he couldn't put the declaration into the context of what they had just been discussing.

"Did she tell you?" Jack said, forcibly turning Faye around to present her before his brother and waiting for her to offer validation to Dan.

Dan shrugged, shook his head and looked away, unable to stomach the bizarre spectacle his brother was making of his wife.

Glancing back, he sighed. "Pregnant, hey?" Dan forced a smile and looked up at Faye. As his eyes roamed her body, he wondered if the baby was his own. "No, I didn't know," he tried not to sound too shocked. When their eyes met, Faye knew Dan was clearly calculating, not counting this day, but how many months it had been since they were last together. Dan wondered if Faye had thought about that too, but of course, she had, and she knew that question would be the first one Dan would ask had they been alone. Embarrassed, she mumbled a few inaudible words and wrapped herself tightly in her gown.

Jack turned her towards Dan. "What? What did you say?"

Indignantly, Faye sighed. "I said, I didn't want to tell anyone, not just yet. I've only just found out."

Dan smiled and shook his head. "That's your business, Faye…" he said, reaching out a hand for Jack to shake. "She'll tell us all about it when she's ready … but hey, that's great news, congrats!' He took a step forward and slapped his brother's shoulder, then raising his hand to Faye, he waited for her to shake it.

"I'm really pleased for you," he said.

Sheepishly, Faye took a slight step forward. "Thanks." she bit her lip before wrapping her arms tightly around her body and stepping back towards Jack. She felt his arm fall about her neck again.

"Great news." Dan was still saying. He turned his hand back to Jack again. "Great news, Bro!"

Jack shook it with a self-assured chuckle. Faye gulped as though she'd felt her heart leap to her throat. "Let's…er… have a drink, shall we?"

"Yeah, that's exactly what this calls for," Dan said, looking around for something to start them off. He quickly procured a bottle of something. Bottles were soon flowing, and once Leo was informed, the whole troupe were ready to be part of the celebration.

Faye went to stand beside Dan. She clamped her neck. "I can't breathe," she whispered; Dan ignored her and moved away; he felt the walls closing in. He headed for the exit.

"So," Jack said smugly, coming up behind him. "By the time you return to Castleton, we will have ridden off into the sunset to become parents. What do you think, Bro?"

"The winds of change are certainly upon us," Dan said, chinking his glass with Jack's. What will you do without us?"

"Live my own life, finally! And about time too," Dan punched his brother playfully. Jack grabbed his fist and held it tight in his.

"Let go," Dan said playfully. "That's enough, Bro, eh?"

Jack's grip tightened before he let go. He backed off laughing. "Just messing."

"No shit!" Dan shook his painful fist loose.

Jack leaned in and dropped his voice. "You can let Faye go now, bro; leave her alone!"

Dan shook his head, "I've plans of my own. You don't need to worry about me."

"Well, don't bother going back to Castleton. Amy's not waiting for you. The brooch is proof of that." He moved in more closely, "Let's just say that spit and a promise you left her with, the one you give all the girls, didn't hold water with Amy. You should have given the girl more credit."

Dan shrugged. "No idea what you're talking about, Jack, but great news about Faye? You're going to be a Daddy."

"Have you spoken to Amy?" Jack dropped his head to one side as a show of sympathy.

"No, you know I haven't; why? I'm sorry, Jack, but you've lost me; I'm not with you. I don't understand what you're trying to say, Bro."

"That old technique of yours, the old divide-and-conquer? You thought you'd got it mastered after years of worming your way into everyone's lives to manipulate everyone to get your own way; it didn't work for you this time, did it?

Dan shrugged. "Ain't got a clue what you're saying, man, not a clue!"

"Did you hear on the grapevine? Amy is easy; she's really easy! Those good old Machiavellian tactics, keep your friends close and your enemies closer? Well, it backfired this time. You should look to those closest to you to know your real enemies, zingaro!"

"What are you going on about?"

Jack flashed the brooch at his brother again. "You said you gave this to Amy before you left?"

"That's mum's; yeah, you know I did. I told you that. How come you have it?"

"This means a lot to me, this old brooch. It means a lot to Leo too. We cherish our mother's memory, and these old trinkets are all we have left of her. We'd never use them to con over any old slag that flashes her tits at us. Leo was right about one thing; he told me to sort the girl out before you do. He said it would make us all even."

"What?" "I bet you're wondering now if any of us took that liberty, aren't you? Well, I guess you'll never know. It's all over, bro; no more secrets, no more sneaking around; we are all on an equal footing! Imagine when we leave here tonight, we'll each have a clean plate. If you decide to go back to Castleton, you can tell Amy from Leo and me, her secret's safe with us!"

"Secret? What have you done? You lying little bastard!"

Jack spat at Dan's feet. "Ask Amy. She brought this back for a reason. I'm sure she'll tell you how good it was." Jack laughed loudly and began walking away. You'll never know, mate. You'll just never know!" Laughing, he sent a kiss through the air. "Mwah!" Jumping around, he did a half twist with his body, laughed, and licked his lips suggestively.

"What have you done, Jack? Give me that brooch! Give it here. I gave Amy that brooch in good faith; she trusted me." Dan forced a laugh. "She hated you; she'd never go near you in a million years. Just give it back to me."

"You want it, here, get it!" Jack stretched his tightly clenched fist high above his head. "Take it. Let me see if you can get it off me as easily as we got it off, Amy. You should have shagged her when you had the chance!" Jack laughed as Dan snatched out at his clenched fist.

"Give it to me!"

"Whoever shagged your girl probably took that Engine an' all!" Jack turned to walk away, laughing loudly at his own joke.

"Liar! They sold the Engine!" Dan realised how childish they were both being. "For fucks sake, man…just tell me how you got the brooch?"

Walking away, Jack shook his head, waved a hand, and laughed.

"You stole it, didn't you? Just like you stole the watches!"

Jack turned and spat. "Stay away from Faye!" He threw the brooch at Dan before dipping beneath the canvass fold.

Dan struggled to stop himself from chasing after his brother and diving onto him from behind. He wanted to kick his head in, but he managed to restrain himself, slammed his drink down, and stormed out. Before Dan got free of the tent, like a bull to a red rag. Suddenly, Dan found himself square on with a crazed mob; evidently, he could tell by their accents that they were all from Derbyshire and still approaching from all directions, red-faced, eyes burning insanely, and each brandishing sticks, scythes, metal bars and bats, anything they could get their hands on before leaving the village in pursuit of the Circus. A lamp was suddenly thrust into Dan's face; squinting through it, he quickly looked for a weapon.

"State your name!" a voice yelled in his face. Dan could see a silhouette of a colossal man standing before him.

Reflex took over as he threw up his arm to cover his face.

"State your fucking name…now!"

"Daniel! Daniel Franconi!" his words delivered in short blasts between the yells and screams from the crowd tightly gathered behind a wall of lamplight.

"That's not Daniel; it's not him," a female whispered.

"Amy? Is that you?"

"Are you sure it's not him?" the man asked her.

"It's not. Dan doesn't...he doesn't dress like that— he never wears face paint."

"We are all wearing it."

"That isn't his voice."

"Are you sure? So, is this the brother? Is this Jack Franconi?"

"Yes, it must be. Dan never dresses like that... He isn't a Clown. That isn't his role in the Circus; he's a trapeze artist, not a Clown. Please, let me go find Dan!"

"No! Stay where you are!"

"Amy! Is that you? It is me, Amy. I am Dan!"

"Dan, is it you?" Amy thrust herself free of the man's grip. "Is it you, Dan?"

"What's going on?" Dan dropped his arms so that she could see him.

Amy gasped and backed away, seeing the grimacing painted face up close in a wash of flickering light emanating from the hundred swinging lamps. "It's not Dan! That's Jack! I think he's the one who killed Janey and my dad; that's him, that's him right there, I'm sure of it."

"Amy, no, no, it's me! Listen, it's me, Dan!"

"You are under arrest for the murder of young Janey Price, my daughter, and Mr Peter Harley—this lady's father...."

"Damn it, Amy! It's me, Dan!" He tried to run towards the sound of her voice, but someone held him and forced him to the ground. He heard a gun cock in his ear. Suddenly, he felt a searing pain in his right side. He was shot. The blast reverberated around the canvas structure behind him. Dan felt the shockwaves from the blast rumble through the ground beneath his body as he lay writhing in pain.

The man holding Amy spun her body around towards Dan, "Look! Look at him! If this is the man who raped you, then take the gun...Take it!"

"Yes, it is him...No, I can't do it... Don't make me do this, please...."

"Shoot the fucker! Here, take the gun!" The man continues to push the weapon into Amy's hands. "Shoot him!"

"No, Greg! Please, I can't."

"Kill him! Kill him!" The crowd began chanting, repeatedly, baying for Dan's blood. Satisfied only if Amy herself pulled the trigger to show her remorse and prove had she had not been part of the heinous crime as everyone in the village of Castleton suspected. There was a cheer from the crowd when she finally succumbed and took the weapon from Greg.

"I can't. I can't!" Greg pushed her towards Dan; she staggered and fell.

"Get up! Get her up! Lift to her feet!"

"Let me find Dan, please, you promised, Greg. You said you'd let me find him to prove we weren't involved."

"Shoot him!"

"No!"

"Get off her, please…Amy, I'm here…it is me; please, you have to believe me!"

Strong hands were forcing Dan's face into the wet ground. He spat grass and soil and heard Greg mumbling a much calmer tone.

"Shoot him, so we can all go home. He's just an animal. He killed my daughter, your father… and he raped you. This is your chance to get revenge. Your chance to prove to everyone here you weren't involved with them. "Upon hearing those words, Dan exploded with rage. He rose up from the ground like the devil himself.

Greg and the others fell upon him, forcing him back down. He was hit by an almighty strike from the butt of the gun into the wound in his right side, causing him to fall and squirm in pain.

"Turn him around, please, let me see."

Greg and other men began kicking Dan and stamping on his head as he lay rolling and contorting in agony. "Show her your face."

Suddenly, having heard a gunshot and Dan's cries, pandemonium let loose, and all hell broke out as the Circus troupe came rushing out of the tent in all directions to meet the mob, armed with weapons of every description. A fight broke out among them.

Dan struggled to break free from Greg, who was still forcing his face into the mud.

"I'll snap your fucking neck!" Greg was yelling and slamming his foot harder into Dan's head. "You're a dead man. You fucking bastard!"

A fireball of flames racing upwards hit the tent and sank through the canvas like a hot knife through butter, making a great plume of black smoke. The tent crackled into a massive inferno within seconds. Voices from those trapped inside could be heard, men, women and children screaming, inches from Dan's body, but he couldn't do anything. He heard screams from grown men struggling to get out while attempting to rescue loved ones still trapped inside, innocent bystanders burning to death deep within the furnace that raged on like the bowels of hell.

"Fucking hell!" Greg, still standing over Dan, was transfixed by the spectacle. Semi-deranged now with his foot firmly planted into Dan's head, he looked around agitated, unsure what to do.

"We're off!" He heard someone shouting.

"No, wait! I'm ordering you." Greg yelled through the black-amber smoke engulfing the field and trees beyond. "Don't go! Stop!"

"We're all gonna hang for this!"

"No, wait, all of you, please…wait!"

Not wanting to be arrested or charged, the mob hurriedly began disarming themselves, throwing their make-shift weapons into bushes and hedgerows and running off to a safe distance, mingling and disbursing within the crowds and neighbouring streets to make themselves sparse. Through burning eyes, Dan saw Jack, almost in slow motion running towards him. Seeing Amy with the gun pointing at Dan, Jack changed direction and made a sudden beeline for her instead.

"No, Jack!" Dan shouted.

Amy, paralysed with fear, still held the gun pointing down at Dan. She glanced up momentarily to see Jack running towards her. Realising she had made a grave mistake, she turned the gun towards him and took aim. Greg was shouting at the top of his voice. "Shoot! Shoot him!"

A stray spark blowing in the super-charged heat drifted from a small fire that had engulfed a child, who lay burning like dry kindling beside the tent. Its corpse had been dragged out by someone who had been brave enough to attempt to rescue him but had failed. Suddenly the long dress Amy was wearing caught light, flames spreading from the hem, up and around her thin form. She began thrashing wildly, trying to put out the fire that had now taken hold and was lapping up her arms and into her face, her eyes staring in horror, black, soulless, like the eyes of a great white shark she searched blindly for help. As her body burned, she screamed, still conscious that Jack was nearly upon her, and through sheer panic and fear, she turned the barrel towards him, closed her eyes and shot into the darkness. Greg ran towards Amy, tears streaming down his face; he staggered and fell. As his hands grasped her frail body, he forced her to the ground, rolling her in the cold, wet grass to extinguish the flames. Leo, as if from nowhere, suddenly appeared and stood over them. He had taken the gun from the ground and pointed it at the back of Greg's head. Amy saw him silently wording something and taking aim.

"Move…" he said again calmly.

Amy could barely muster the strength but knew it was imperative she obeys. Not knowing if the man looking at her was, in fact, Jack or Leo, she did as she was commanded. Crawling from beneath Greg, she heard the gun go off, its blast rattling through the air like a cannon.

Suddenly, Jack, trying to disarm his brother, charged into Leo, knocking him completely off his feet. The gun he had, still pointing at Greg, went off again with the force of Jack's body blow. Faye, who was running close behind Jack, saw Leo fall. When she reached him, she noticed Dan lying only meters away from Leo in a bloodied heap. She ran to him, scooping him up into her arms; she began sobbing uncontrollably. Dan's blood-soaked body lay helpless in her arms.

Faye, trying desperately to stem the blood flow and keep Dan from passing out, attempted to help him to his feet but couldn't lift him.

"Jack! Help!"

"Leave him; it's too late. We need to go!" He ripped his wife away from his brother, tossing her to one side like she was nothing more than a ragdoll. Now climbing to his feet, Leo rushed for the gun, but Jack got there before him. Stood like a demon in the firelight, aiming the gun at anyone who dared move, Jack turned to see Faye crawling back to Dan. Faye watched in the silence between each sob, muffled by smoke and fumes, as her husband rolled Amy's limp body over his boot; she was neither crying nor struggling. Her heart shattered into a million pieces at the sight of her injured brother-in-law and lover; Faye looked to Leo for help.

"Leo! Please…!" To disarm him, Leo ran at Jack; there was a struggle between them before he removed the gun.

"Go!" Leo commanded. "Both of you, just go!"

Jack tore Faye away from Dan. "Come on!"

"No, I'm not going without Dan!"

Jack tried to take the gun from Leo again. "Give it to me… I'm gonna end this right now!"

"No, Jack! Leave it! I'll take care of him; please just go!"

Faye staggered to her feet and looked at Jack but fell back down upon Dan, cradling him in her arms, "I can't leave him!"

Leo spun around and took aim at his brother." "Go, Jack! Get the fuck out of here." He quickly snapped another cartridge into place and retook aim. "Get your wife! Go!"

Leo watched as Jack pulled his wife away from Dan.

"No! I'm not leaving him…!" Jack turned and looked at Leo hopelessly.

"Just leave her!"

Jack took flight across the field, leaving Leo to persuade Faye to follow him. He pulled her by the arm, "Go on, get out of here!" Faye's eyes stared up at him as she tried to read his quizzical expression. She lifted her head in defiance. "You don't get it, do you? I love him. I love Dan! Not Jack!" She took the gun barrel in both hands and placed it in the centre of her chest. "Shoot! Shoot me please!"

Leo realised his efforts were in vain, he released his grip on her arm. He laughed and looked as though he wanted to cry but couldn't.

"I love you, Faye! I've always loved you," he said. "Surely you already knew that?" He sensed her body go rigid. "I know, Leo," she whispered. "I love Dan. I'm not leaving without him."

"You need to run, Faye, please. I'll take care of him, I promise! Now please; just go!" Faye rose to her feet, kissed Leo on the cheek and ran into the darkness beyond the burning inferno. Waiting until she was out of sight, Leo spun around, took aim and shot Dan. He stood a moment, staring at the blood as it oozed slowly from Dan's brain, watching as it dribbled down over the mass of white grease paint on his face and neck, forming a dark viscous pool in the mud. He remained a moment longer, wiping splats of blood from his face as he stared at his brother's body; then, suddenly hearing the sound of choking and coughing behind him, he pivoted his body around to see Amy struggling to get to her feet. "Amy!" He looked at his brother, who lay bathed in the flickering light from the fire behind them. He rushed to help her but slipped into the pool of blood beside his brother's body. "Fucking hell." He stopped and wiped off the blood from the sole of his boot on the long grass. "Fucking hell! He said again, throwing the gun into the long grass. Leo walked towards Amy, lifted her into his arms, kissed her gently and carried her away. "I'm here, Amy. I'll never abandon you, not ever."

Falling Apart 2020

Georgia walked into the kitchen. Len looked up from his paper. "Going out?"

"Yep."

"With Jake?"

"Later." She was angry and couldn't bring herself to look at him.

Len folded his newspaper, gave a sigh and rose to his feet. "Can I come…?"

Georgia looked up sharply and then realised when she saw him smiling that he was joking. He was sure she would be amused by his great humour and wit. She filled a glass with orange juice from the fridge, half smiled and offered him a drink.

"No! No thanks."

Joking aside, Georgia felt herself growing emotional. She wandered around the kitchen, tripping on a basket of washing and splashing orange juice on the stone flags; she forced back tears as Len laughed at the comedic way her anger was displaying itself. She felt betrayed. Len's, I'm as fresh as a daisy act, following a night on the booze, just pissed her off even more. Even a bird's song outside sounded contrived at that moment; its joyous whistling sounded ridiculously out of context to how she felt. Georgia just wanted to shoot it. Ever the perfectionist, Georgia had begun arranging the look of the place, getting it ready for holidaymakers, while Len had been drawing up ideas and plans for the new house with an architect online. So far, he had been the one arranging everything. The big dream, the big move, now the grand design, but they had made a pact together, and he was supposed to stick to it, but he hadn't; he had let her down again, and within days of arriving at the cottage. With this in mind, she believed she had a right to be pissed off.

"I didn't hear you get home last night." She drank orange juice and scratched the back of her head.

"You were fast asleep; I didn't want to wake you."

"Didn't take you long to get back to your old ways."

Len breathed out heavily but said nothing.

"Drinking again? Thought you'd hold out longer than a week. Suppose you're gambling again too?"

"Look, are you going out or what?"

Georgia stared out of the window, saying nothing; she drank more orange juice.

"If this chap of yours doesn't turn up, we can go grab lunch in the Travellers. They do a great Steak and Ale pie, by the way."

"Like the one you ordered yesterday?"

"Ahy, exactly, like the one you didn't return for."

"You said you wouldn't do this, not here. Not where we're supposed to be 'starting afresh'."

"I'm not drinking, nor gambling… not as much as last time—if that's what you're worried about? A pint or two with the lads isn't a crime. Neither is a game of cards, but thanks for the concern."

"But it is a crime, Dad; in my book, it is a crime. When I gave up my life in London to come here to help you recover… you were supposed to stick to your end of the bargain." Her voice faded. "…and like an idiot," she said, "I believed in you!"

"That was the old me… all that stuff … it's all in the past."

Georgia shook her head. "Feels like yesterday to me!"

"G, look. I'm trying. I'm trying to fit in; get to know people; it's important to us. We need friends and people around us. We might need help if we are going to do all the things we've set our hearts on –"

"We need good friends, Dad… not friends like him…that Mark, who just wants sad mates to give him an excuse to be a prick… He's probably ruined more marriages in this village …you can just tell."

"Well, you seem to be getting on well with what's his name…Jake? Which is great, by the way; I am happy for you! I truly am. Go, explore, go into town, meet people… you've got the car… use it. Let your hair down, G, and allow me to breathe, will you?"

"Right!" Georgia fell silent. She drank more orange juice and wiped her mouth on the back of her hand. "We're losing sight of why we came here…clearly."

Len frowned at the oxymoron but said nothing.

"Am I?"

"You are!" she said quietly. "I heard one of my Uni friends died last night in a car crash."

"Oh, Georgia, I am sorry. Sorry to hear that, honestly. Do I know them?"

"No. One of my friends on Facebook told me. I also spoke to Martin's mum, remember Martin? Martin Spalding!"

"Yeah, of course... I remember Martin; he's one of Nathan's best mates from that reality TV show-did well for himself!"

"Hmm, yeah, well, he's married now."

"Martin's married...and so young? Wow... shotgun, was it?"

"All my mates are getting married, Dad. They are all in their late twenties... and thirties; some are married now. They're not that young anymore."

"No, guess not! Wow, indeed... how time flies."

"We spoke about mum."

"Yeah," Len tried to look mildly bored. He sniffed and pretended not to appear bothered. "Did ya?"

Georgia could tell he was irritated.

"She saw I was online—Martin's Mum, so she asked if we could chat, then private messaged me ... she asked about you."

"That's nice."

"Yeah, it was."

"We got talking about Mum...and she said."

"...You going out or what?" Len leaned against the sink and gazed out over the sea of fields. His eyes came to rest on a line of fir trees in the distance. They reminded him of his late wife.

Christmas trees, that's what she called them. All fir trees were Christmas trees to her. She always wanted them in the garden, but he would never allow it. It's the roots, he'd insisted; they grow too quick... and they grow tall... they'd be a nightmare.

"A nightmare, trees?" he thought about the irony. The trees would still be there, but his late wife was gone; what could be worse? "Bastard..." he whispered to himself.

"What?"

"Nothing, just thinking out loud."

The faint morning sun tried hard to push through the clouds and burn off the haze. It made him feel restless like he had an urge to get out and enjoy the day before it was too late.

"She said she couldn't believe Mum had been dead two years."

"Aw, well, is it that long?"

"She said, seemed like yesterday to her!"

Len's reaction was as Georgia had thought it would be. He just couldn't talk about her mother with her or anyone, which really didn't help. He'd been born poor once. He was nice enough, or so that's what everyone imagined, but he was weak. Georgia had been thinking this a lot lately. He's weak, too weak to find the strength to quit his bad habits, too weak to talk about her mother, and too weak to ever become a good business partner as they had planned. In fact, Georgia thought her father had been too laid-back for most of her life. She sighed; he'd certainly been a weak husband too. His fatal personality flaw didn't remove the fact that he caused his wife's death, nor did it give him the excuse to drink like a typical Northern. His drinking was the one defining northern trait she believed was why her mother died, his love of booze. As a southerner born and bred, Georgia knew all the subtle differences observed between Southerners and northerners, and her father certainly fit the stereotype. His lack of Tube knowledge, to see no one, hear no one and definitely not speak to total strangers on the tube is essential Tube etiquette, something Len could never adhere to. He told Georgia, I can't sit next to another human being and not speak; it's just not my nature; I'm from the north. His northern generosity exceeded him, too, a trait never lost while living in London; he often complained about the price of a pint in the city but was always the first to buy a round of drinks despite the cost. Georgia slammed her glass of juice down hard and shook the spillage from her hand.

"I'd like to have been at Martin's wedding."

"Yeah? Didn't you get an invite?"

"I wasn't around, was I? Nathan was there; he asked about me, apparently."

"Martin's mum said Martin would have liked to have seen me at his wedding." Len lifted his glasses and rubbed his eyes. "Well, you dumped him when he went off to the army, remember? And of course, circumstances, G, your circumstances just didn't permit it at that time, you know the story."

"I know, but she doesn't, Martin's mum. She has no idea I was saddled with a mental breakdown, fucking flying high one minute and scraping the bottom of the barrel the next."

"You're hard on yourself, G; she would have guessed something was going with you. It's like that. You had just lost your mum, and bipolar disorder is hard enough to live with at the best of times. You're still not yourself, not properly; the doctor told you that."

"How could I ever be myself? And what about you? How are you supposed to feel normal when Mum lay dead in the cemetery? It was us that put her there, don't forget that. We both drove her to it! The gambling, the women, the drinking, me, me, and my bipolar. Imagine having to cope with all that!"

"Don't start, damn it!" Len thumped his hand down hard... He looked at her sharply. "Did you take your medication today?"

"It's not about me, Dad. It's always about you!" Len took a step back and tried to calm down.

"Right, okay... I'm not doing this, Georgia... just go take your tablets."

Georgia shook her head, held the glass of orange juice in two hands and gazed out the window. "We left the old house to combat our depression, both of us."

"Put it all behind us, yeah, that was the plan. Bury it, for god's sake. It was your mum's ailments, not ours, that plagued her.; she was a sick woman, and that wasn't our fault. It was hard living with her depression G. I lived with her illness for twenty-nine years...depression creates depression, especially if it goes unchecked and everyone else has to put up with it. It makes lives very difficult for everyone living in and around it. You know that, come on!"

"They don't tell you that in the TV ads?"

"No, they certainly do not! All this mental health awareness bullshit. Yes, they should help raise awareness, but they should help those who have to put up with someone else's mental disorder."

"Yeah," Georgia nods. "They should tell the world that it is okay to struggle with someone else's mental illness. It's hard, it's dark, and it's damn right lonely. If one person in the home has it, you can guarantee everyone else suffers from it."

"Of course, it's like that—when the one person you want to turn to for support is worse than you are...No one tells you how to cope with that.

"We should know!"

"Oh yes!"

"You had two of us—three if you count yourself."

"Now you've hit the nail on the head, my girl. It's a contagious disease. Indeed, if one person is miserable in the home, it causes everyone in the family to be miserable. Let's raise awareness about that, shall we… Support the carers too?"

"That's why I need for you to stay strong, Dad! Be strong, for me!"

"I'm here, Georgia."

"But, the home-grown DIY counselling from friends and so-called family didn't work though, did it, Dad?"

"I've heard it all before—None of it was your fault—Your wife was a sick woman—Your daughter is ill—blah, blah day in day out—How many times do I need to explain? That's what everyone said…and it was true. It took me a while to accept that—none of it was my fault, but now I know. Now I understand…It wasn't, it truly wasn't my fault, nor was it yours… So let's do this differently from now on!"

"Well, yes, exactly, that was the plan, remember? No drinking, no gambling this time, just me and you…we can do this, Dad if you stick to the plan!"

"And no dwelling on the past, G? I'm not going to dwell on it anymore; we are here, new house, new town, fresh start. This cottage is our project, our new beginning, Yeah?"

"Well, you know me, I feel guilty no matter where we go. I'll never feel any different. I can't just get back to normal. I am not like you…!"

"Okay, stop this! You just got to stop this. You're not listening to a word I'm saying… we're going around in circles. I only offered to take you for dinner if your friend didn't turn up! Come on … past is past, yeah. Get dressed; let's get out of this damn house …And let's eat. i"m starving! What do you say?"

Georgia forced a smile and instantly wanted to say sorry for arguing but couldn't. She wasn't even sure if she was the one who needed to apologise anyway. She killed the smile as soon as she left the room and bit down on her lip hard until it hurt.

Remember mum's pain, she thought, squeezing her teeth tighter until a droplet of blood trickled down inside her mouth.

Georgia headed off upstairs, squeezing down on her lip harder to relieve the guilt. She wasn't one to share her darkest secrets; who did she have to share them with? After all, Georgia wasn't the one who had gone off and left her mum and tore up the family. And she wasn't the one who had brought Judas into their home. Yet somehow, she was left with all the guilt, no matter what she said to her dad. The pain in her lip was having a strange effect. It felt like a punishment, which she thought she deserved, but at the same time, it made her emotionally exhausted. By the time she reached her room upstairs, she had stopped doing it and sat on the bed. She flopped back, arms outstretched like Christ on the crucifix. Old habits die hard, and here she was, still suffering for the sins of others.

Somewhere deep inside, she could hear her own sanity warning her. If I ever allow you to stop punishing yourself, Mum will be forgotten forever, but that is just your insanity speaking…

Len opened the door and leaned on the door frame. He lay his head on his forearm.

"Come on, you getting up," he sounded tired now.

"If I hadn't pretended to be ill that day," Georgia said. "…and wanted to go home from school."

"But G…" Len sighed heavily. "That was ages ago! You're dropping G; take your tablets, yeah!"

"Yeah, but let's just say right, if I hadn't pretended to be ill, though –" She continued even though she knew she had already overstepped the mark. "– And I didn't ask to go home, would Mum still be alive?"

"Oh G, come on, love, we've been over this."

"She wouldn't have found out about you and the affair with what's her fucking name?"

"And, you're guessing she wouldn't have killed herself?"

Len slammed his forearm against the doorframe and thumped the wood." He turned and left in silence. Georgia rose from the bed and followed him. She couldn't accept silence. Not like that. That was a powerful, effective exit. The arguments and self-harming were worse now than before, and the atmosphere between Georgia and her father, Len, was nearly as bad. It needed addressing.

"New house, new start," she said to Len as he turned to close the bathroom door on her.

"Georgia, I don't want to go back down that path. We've moved on. Call me when you're ready to go out. I'm taking a shower."

"You're repeating old habits, Dad," Georgia shouted at the closed door. Glancing over her shoulder, she was sure that visiting the past was literally resurrecting her poor mother; she could sense her there in the room. She had felt her mother's presence more lately since they arrived at the cottage.; either that or Georgia was going insane again, just as Len said. There was one thing for sure, Georgia undoubtedly was still not herself. She yearned to tell her father about her self-harming and the ghosts in her head but couldn't.

After an hour of resting on the bed, Georgia met with Len as they collided in the hall. Checking her phone for texts, she brushed past him. Len held her back by her shoulders. "Steady," he said, then turned her around to face him; nodding strangely, he sighed, "It's not happening again, Georgia. I've got the hang of things this time. I promise I'm not returning to old habits, and neither are you!"

She tucked her phone away in the back pocket of her jeans and shrugged, "We'll see. I don't want our life here to become a fallacy, some stupid joke!" Georgia knew how to wound her father, but he had hurt her deeply. "I wonder, is there any love left between us because sometimes I question it?" She brushed past him and left him standing alone in the hall.

"Indeed, on occasions like this," he said softly, as she headed downstairs, then yelled, "I search for it too…" he said.

Georgia heard his words as she put on her converse All-Stars downstairs, searched for money in her father's jacket pockets, brushed her hair in the mirror and threw on her denim jacket. "We're worlds apart, Dad, you and I. Worlds apart!"

"Indeed!" she heard him shout back, "Most of the time, but you're making it worse, and it doesn't need to be this way!"

Then suddenly, as she opened the door to leave, Georgia realised how ridiculous the conversation was fast becoming, how immature on both sides. She stopped trying to antagonise him, closed the door and left.

Georgia felt the phone in her back pocket vibrate as she quickly wiped her tear-stained face and headed off up the path. Taking the phone out to see who was calling, she tapped on the tiny blue envelop on the screen and read aloud. "Sorry, mate. Something's come up. Catch up with you later, Jake."

"Course you will!" Georgia tucked the phone away, thrust her hands into her pockets, and discovered she still had the car keys. She decided to take the car, then changed her mind and nearly turned to take them back inside, but decided against it. "I'll walk," she said to herself. "I'll go to the Traveller's and have a fucking drink."

The Traveller's Rest 2020

Breathless and cold, and around half-hour after setting out from High Oakham Cottage, Georgia walked across the car park to the Traveller's Rest. A girl behind the bar polishing glasses on a tea towel looked up. The music sounded pumping when she opened the door, but no one was in. She dumped her jacket on a table near the bar, the keys in her pocket fell heavy, making a loud clanging noise.

"Hi! What can I do for you?"

Georgia looked over and smiled. "You are open, aren't you?"

"Yeah, just about...not sure how long for, though, with all this talk about that Coronavirus."

"I know! It's in the UK now, isn't it? It's scary." The girl nodded.

"Can I have a diet coke, please... no, make it a cider..."

"Any?"

"Yeah, any... actually, do you have anything dry?"

"Apple County? It's a medium?"

"That's great, thanks."

The girl disappeared, crouching momentarily to procure a bottle from the fridge below the counter, then reappearing with an ice-cold one; she clipped the top off, poured the apple-amber fizz into a glass, and slid it over.

"Thanks."

"You're welcome. I'm Nikki, by the way."

"Oh, I'm Georgia, or G—most people just call me G," She lied. Her father was the only person to call her that, and she hated it. Searching her jacket pockets or her phone, she realised it was still in the back pocket of her jeans; she took it out, removed her card from the wallet, walked along the length of the bar and swiped the contactless machine. As she put the debit card away, she paused to look at a grainy old photo that caught her eye on the wall behind the bar. "Where's that?"

"It's your place, High Oakham Cottage." Georgia's eyes widened with interest. "I thought so. How do you know I live there?

"Oh, it's a village thing, everyone knows everything. Do you like living up there?" Georgia sipped the cider, "Hmm, it's not bad." Putting away her phone, she turned her attention back to the photo. Pushing the froth around on the cider with her finger, she leaned over the bar to look closer. Two women in the centre of the picture were dressed in 1930s clothing with heavy laced-up boots and neck bandanas. "Who are they?" One woman wore a striped pinafore with her sleeves rolled up past her elbows; the other wore a pair of high-waisted baggy trousers, which she'd rolled up over her boots and secured with a thick black belt strap that hung off her hips. Both girls had tied their hair high, secured with headscarves and bows. The girls stood like bookends, side by side in the cottage doorway, and even though it was a monochrome photo, Georgia couldn't help thinking they had the sun in their eyes. Looking closer, Nikki pointed at the image. "She's still alive." Georgia perched up on the stool, giving her more scope to lean over for a closer look. "Uh-huh wow!" Slurping the froth from the top of the glass, she could see Nikki from head to toe, and she couldn't help thinking how great she looked. Very chic for a barmaid in Castleton. Her tiny, impish features seemed to suit her slightly odd vintage taste in fashion. "Ooh, love the boots… and that top you're wearing; it's gorgeous."

"Thanks," Nikki tapped the picture frame again, "Inspired by these two lovely ladies… I do love m' vintage rags."

She bent over and took a large JW whiskey bottle from a case of six. "They look amazing, don't they?"

"Fashions may fade, but style is eternal." "Ooh, I like that."

"Yves Saint Laurent."

Nikki threw her head back and laughed. "Great. I'll use that in my next Insta vlog—Hashtag Fashion Nuovo." She laughed and turned to mount the bottle of whiskey in the optic behind her. A cluster of Edison industrial lamps encased in a glorious bunch of black glass and copper shades hung low behind the bar, picking up flashes of electric blue in the tips of Nikki's jet-black hair. Georgia loved her hair—the way it was cropped short in a silky black bob, framing her face perfectly, which made her sparkly blue eyes pop. "According to this article," Nikki said, putting the whiskey down for a moment to pull out a Town and Country from beneath a pile of magazines. "She owned High Oakham Cottage back then. She was called Amy. The other woman in the photo is the woman I know. There used to be two cottages on that land, High Oakham and Harley Cottage, and the Farmhouse, but Harley cottage was knocked down after the war. They were two-up, two-down cottages, like the one you live in. "Look, it's all on page 20. That's her, the one with my Great Gran… she's the one who lived in your place."

"Which one is your great-gran?"

"The other one, that's her. She's called, Faye" Nikki pointed out the women on the right in the baggy trousers.

"It's the same photo as that one on the wall, isn't it?" Georgia diligently observed.

"Oh, yes—it is. I never realised that."

"My great-gran joined the land girls in 1941 when she was around twenty-four, the age I am now. Apparently, they worked together for three, four years, or at least until Amy left. She left just before the war ended. That's when Gran bought the Hamlet further up the lane, do you know it?" Nikki lifted the whisky bottle and stretched on tiptoe to push it into the wall-mounted spirit dispenser. She secured it by clipping it into the optic, then relaxed and let go. Turning, she wiped her hands down her jeans and flicked the hair from her eyes. "Imagine being a land girl. I'd hate that. All that digging and shit."

"They had to do it back then though, didn't they?"

"For the war effort, yeah." Nikki spun the magazine around for Georgia to look at it, tucked her shirt back into her jeans and rubbed her eyes. "Says here that the cottage was built on a marsh and was susceptible to flooding? Does that still happen?" Georgia checked out the part where Nikki was pointing. "Dunno. The surveyor said there was an history of flooding but they never mentioned it in the auction." Georgia slid the magazine back over to Nikki. "No, they wouldn't tell you that – it's bought as seen, isn't it? I keep this magazine because people staying in that cottage always ask. There's a lot of history about the place., they always want to know about it. Here, read it. Just leave it on the bar when you've finished." Yawning, Nikki looked around, pulled a face to express her boredom, and then glanced at the clock. "I'd better get on; we've got bookings coming in, in fifteen minutes." She poured herself a coke from the dispenser, put the remaining five bottles of whisky back under the bar, and then kicked the empty box into the back. "Thanks," Georgia shouted. She rolled up the magazine and went to sit down. It fell open as she dropped it on the table, its pages parting in the centre revealing a black and white photograph of a row of beautiful quaint

English cottages covered with wisteria and ivy splashed across the pages. Roses lined the flagstone path from a field gate to the front door. Nikki's voice startled Georgia, "That's the Hamlet, the place my great-gran bought. It's a bit further up the road from you, have you been up? You should go! In fact, there's an updated photo of it on the other page. My cousins live there." She stopped polishing the glass she was holding, leaned over, licked a finger and flipped the page over. "There, that's it."

"Who are they?"

Georgia pressed down the pages with her thumb to loosen the staples in the fold of the magazine.

"Who?"

Georgia pointed again. "Oh, that's her, my Granny, Granny Faye. She was beautiful, wasn't she? And that… that's my mum with aunty Amy; Mum was around three or four years old then. Amy is the woman who lived in your place." Nikki flicked the page back.

"There she is again?" Georgia said, leaning in for a closer look.

"Oh, that's Amy with her husband, Leo… He was Granny Faye's brother-in-law.

"How come there are so many photos of them?"

Nikki smiled. "I told you, there's a lot of history surrounding that old cottage; that's why people like to stay there. My great-grandmother purchased this pub in the 40s. She lived upstairs for years before they moved her into the care home in town a couple of years ago. Gran hates it there, but what can you do? She's old. She's one hundred and five if you can believe that!"

Georgia spun the magazine back around to give it closer scrutiny. "How old? One hundred and five? Wow, what's her secret?"

"Hard work and whiskey, she says."

So, you've kept this place in the family?"

"Mum and Dad took it off her thirty-odd years ago."

"That's your cottage again, look. And that's Amy with her little boy, Leo. Her husband was called Leo, and so was her son? I heard the grandad was called Leo too?"

"Yeah, they used to do that back then, call their kids after their fathers and grandfathers."

"Imagine, it must get confusing, having a husband called Leo, the son called Leo and a grandad called Leo." Georgia laughed. "I wonder what they called the dog." She sat bolt upright. "Those names, though? There were three generations of Leos in their family." "Yeah, they were Italian, so it was a given back then, I think." "That's incredible." Georgia narrowed her eyes and looked up. Nikki shrugged. "My great-granny, Faye, and grandad Jack were Travellers before the war. They worked in the same Circus together. I think that's how she met my grandad and Amy met Leo." "Travellers, you mean like, Gypsies?" "Mum said my great-grandma Faye talked about her life in the Circus a lot. She told me all the history; that's why I know who everyone is." "My dad's name is Leo." "Is it? "Named after his dad." "Really?" "Don't know what my great grandad's name was, never asked, but I know they called my dad Len as a nickname. It is an Italian thing, you're right. My dad has Italian heritage. I never knew any of them. But keeping the male name running down the generations was definitely an Italian thing." "Right…"   "So, these two in the photo are both called Leo?" "Yeah, father and son – Leo Franconi." "Oh my god, no. I don't believe it!" Georgia slammed down her glass, splashing cider over the table. "What?" Nikki laughed. "That's my surname—Franconi!" Georgia's mouth was gaping. "Can you believe that?" "That's weird!" "I know!" "I know all of this because Leo, this little boy, used to play with my mum when they were kids. Granny Faye brought my mum up alone because my great grandad, Jack, died in the war." "That's really strange! Do you think we are the same Franconi family?" "Well, how many Franconis do you know? And if your dad was named after his dad, we could be related. Was it, Leonardo Franconi?" "Yeah! 'No shit, really. That is so weird?" "So, you think all these people in these photos could be related to me?" "It sounds like it!"

"The names are too similar… Len – Leo…"

"And you can't mistake the name Franconi?"

"No, definitely not—and that's my mum's maiden name!"

"Oh my god, so this Leo could be your great-grandad…?"

"And that kid could be my dad's dad? He lived around here as a boy but never knew where exactly."

"The Franconi's owned that cottage for years. The one that you're living in now. Amy Harley was born there before Leo moved in with her. Then she became Amy Franconi."

"If Amy was a Franconi, she must have been my dad's mum?"

"Yeah, your great-grandma. My great-grandma was the same age as Amy. How old is your dad?"

"He's eighty-five next."

"Oh, old then."

"Well yeah, Dad had me late in life, in his sixties. Mum was one of his Geography students. Scandalous"

"Wow, yeah. So it all sounds about right then."

"certainly, sounds like it!"

"Then we're related?"

"I think we are."

"Amy was my gran's best friend. They were more like sisters. Apparently, my granny Faye loved her. Mum told me all the tales. Faye is a legend around these parts because she was the Travellers' landlady for years and is now one of the oldest women in the village. Everyone knows her. Our Granny's met at the Circus, but the strangest thing is, they both fell in love with the Franconi boys! The boys were much older than them."

Georgia shuffled around on her stool. "Really?"

Granny Faye first performed in the Circus in Ireland when she was four years old, but in 1931 when she was only fourteen, her parents joined Circus Franconi. That's when she met the triplets and Grandad Jack. The triplets? The Franconi's were triplets?"

"In their twenties, much older than the girls."

"It's a shame you're working."

"Yeah, I could tell you all about it."

"Wow, this is so interesting. I wish my dad was here."

"Well, let me just tell you this—" Nikki said, sitting beside Georgia and putting down the glass she was polishing.

"Amy and Faye met through the Circus. Do you know anything about the riot that took place? You know, the Ringmaster story?"

"Vaguely…Oh, I wish I knew your great grandmother."

"I go see her most Sundays. Come with me if you like."

"That would be great."

"She loves talking about her life in the Circus. She'd love to tell you all about it. You can't shut her up when she starts. Anyway, she would tell you all about the Ringmaster."

"I'd love to hear it." Georgia curved the magazine back around to face Nikki.

"So, tell me again…that's Amy, possibly my great grandmother?"

"Potentially, you should ask your dad."

…And she lived in the exact same house as us…?"

"…Can you believe that! And she was my great Gran's best friend…who later became her sister-in-law."

"Wow, imagine. I can't believe this!"

Nikki looked closer at Amy's photo again. "She does look a bit like you."

The girls started laughing. Then suddenly, the door flung open as a busload of pensioners came pilling in, shouting orders and commenting on things they only found amusing.

A wiry grey-haired man stood waving his stick at the bar. "Have I got to pour myself a drink in this place!"

"Gotta go…" Nikki said, hurrying behind the bar to begin what looked likely to become a very long shift.

Georgia immediately began calling her dad. "Pick up…Come on…"

Bursting to tell him what she had discovered, she rushed out to get a better signal. As the ringtone changed from calling to engaged, she pushed the phone back into her jeans and returned inside to read the magazine. Georgia read the magazine with great interest. There was so much information about Castleton and the cottages; she even found a website to check out. Georgia searched the net using the pub's free Wi-Fi and found Castleton's Facebook group but was disappointed to discover it was full of adverts for hairdressers, plumbers and roofers—and a barrage of information regarding the onset of the Corona Virus hitting the UK, but no actual historical pictures, or details that she could sink her teeth into. Georgia thought this strange, especially since the place was renowned for its rich history, intrigue and natural beauty.

As she scrolled through snippets of village life via the modern context of social media, she was brought to a very stark realisation that the world was, as the world is, and life simply goes on even in a place that looks as though it is frozen in time.

"Georgia, Christ…What a surprise!"

"Jake! Hi!"

"What are you doing here? Didn't expect to see you…not in here,"

"I… I took your advice…" she laughed, her voice sounding nervous, even she could hear the quiver of nerves. "Went for a walk and ended up here."

"Good…great! Look, I'm er…sorry…you know… that I cancelled on you today, but…I …er…" He pointed off awkwardly at nothing in particular.

"That's fine…no problem…good to see ya anyway." She watched as he turned and walked towards the bar.

"Take care…" She said, then, regretting saying that, bit her lip.

He stopped and turned back. "I'll call ya, yeah…?"

Georgia nodded. She saw Nikki's eyes light up as he approached the bar.

"Hiya Jake!"

He winked at her. "Hey, Nikki!"

Bloody hell, Georgia thought. "He didn't just wink at her as well. I bet he's snogged her face off an' all—you bastard." She looked down at the magazine, licked a finger and flicked the page. She didn't want to think about him, but she couldn't stop. She flicked another page over and felt sick to her stomach. How had she ever allowed him to kiss her?

Dusting her phone down, having just dropped it in the Traveller's Car Park, Rebecca called Mark while pulling a reluctant James behind her.

"Mark, hi, it's me…you alright? Good, I'm just doing the shopping…yeah, nipping into Tesco now. They've been talking about a possible lockdown in the country; have you heard it on the news? I thought I'd stock up. Do you want anything? I'm not buying that much wine! I'll be popping into the agency on my way home to see if they're okay. They're short-staffed again with this bloody Virus. No, no, I'm only nipping in on the way back… Okay, see you later—yep, see you." She turned to James and pulled him close.

"Don't you dare tell Mark you've seen Daddy today, okay? Are you listening, James? He'll be angry…?"

Rebecca stopped at the door, wiped the child's face with her hand and flicked his fringe out of his eyes. He laughed.

"Are you listening? Do not tell Mark where we've been today!"

She checked her watch and tried to mentally time herself, imaging how long it would take to get around Tesco, nip into work for at least 20 minutes, and then drive home.

"Sorry, Mummy. I won't tell him. Can I have chips?"

"Yes, just be a good boy for your daddy, okay?"

Rebecca walked into the Traveller's, looking flustered with James pulling and tugging on her arm. He was trying to make a break for it, kicking and pulling until he broke free and ran off. Unable to call him back, he made a beeline for the bar. Seeing James heading for the bar made Georgia physically gasp out loud. She lifted the magazine to her face and sank behind it. To Georgia's surprise,

Jake rushed from the bar to greet him, hugged Rebecca and kissed her. He took her coat and bag and then led her to an intimate table in the far corner, where he sat down with her a moment before going off to the bar to order drinks. James ignored his mother's plea to join her instead of remaining by the bar, clinging to one of those Sorrento swivelling stools, with his whole body lolling over it, spinning one way then back to the other.

Georgia, was whispering under her breath. "You bastard!"

She watched as Jake took the child by the hand and made him sit on the stool.

"I want coke, Daddy!"

Georgia dropped the magazine down, her mouth falling completely open. She sat up bolt upright and strained to listen.

"…I want chips…Daddy, I want chips!"

"Behave, James, wait a minute, mate."

Jake pulled him off the barstool and made him go sit with his mother. "He'll have a coke, please, Nikki, and a small portion of fries."

Realising her mouth was gapping, Georgia closed it quickly, blinked back tears and hid away again behind the magazine. She saw Nikki pouring the child's coke. She popped a straw in it and handed it over the bar to Jake, who took it with a wink before hurrying off to give it to the excited child. Nikki prepared more beverages—a glass of Prosecco, a pint of Ale, and a bottle of something else. Stomach-churning with rage, Georgia felt so betrayed and embarrassed, but how could she have possibly known he was married with a child. She couldn't believe what she was witnessing.

Shaking her head, she tutted loudly and watched as Jake returned to pay for the drinks, leaving Nikki to put the bottle on a tray with an empty glass. Jake put his wallet away and returned to the table where Rebecca sat smiling. Before he sat, he turned and lifted his pint to Georgia and nodded. Georgia didn't know where to look. She threw the magazine up again in front of her face and slid down her seat, heat rising in her cheeks as she flushed with embarrassment.

"There you go, G," Nikki said suddenly. "Jake's bought you a drink."

"What? Why?"

Nikki was standing over her with a bottle of cider and an empty glass on a tray. "I told him you were on cider…is that okay?"

She placed the ice-cold bottle next to the one she already had and put her hand on her hip as though waiting for something.

Georgia looked down at the bottle and then back up at Nikki. "Why?" She asked again.

"I can change it for something else if you prefer?"

"No, no—that's…er fine…thanks…thanks, Nikki…?" Nikki shrugged.

"You know him then…Jake…?"

"Yeah, we're cousins. You know, he's Faye's great-grandson, the woman we were talking about?"

"Oh!"

"I know, it's mad, isn't it—small world."

"Weird world… Is that kid his then?"

"James? God, yeah. He's a brat!"

"Uh-huh," Georgia laughed. "He certainly is. I didn't know Jake was a Dad."

Nikki shrugged again. "Yeah, I know, he doesn't seem the type to be a Dad, does he? See you later. "Feeling wounded Georgia sat back, shaking her head in disbelief and sighing visibly at the bottle. Georgia held the bottle for a while, waiting for Dan to look over so she could thank him for it, but he didn't.

Glancing at the two bottles on the table, she needed to decide, should she stay and drink one bottle, the one already started, or just grab the one Jake had bought her and get the hell out of there, or should she just drink both quickly as possible, then get the hell out of there? She pulled her sweater down over her hips and got up to go to the loo, but before she rose to her feet, her mobile phone began vibrating and dancing on the table; the screen lit up with an incoming call from DAD.

"Hi, what's up?" She curled around the table and headed for the ladies' toilets.

Len stopped dead in his tracks. "You sound…happier…?"

"Well, not really, but I'm fine…listen…?" Georgia scratched her head.

"Where did you go?" Len cut in. "Have you got the car keys?"

"I have, yes…Listen… you're not listening…you'll never believe what I've discovered today?"

"So what the fuck are you after this time, money, because there isn't any?" Rebecca sat the bouncing James beside her and harmed him with a colouring book and crayons, hoping he'd sit still just long enough for the fries to arrive.

"Aw, Becky, not in front of Jimmy; keep it civilised!"

"Civilised, you?"

"Nah, come on, we can do civilised. We've been well civilised in the past, remember?"

"I remember it."

"Not that long ago, in my kitchen, if my memory serves me right!"

Rebecca tutted loudly. "Look, I don't have time for this, Jake; what do you want?"

"Don't be like this. We can sit here ten minutes before our son and talk like adults…Eh, what do you say?"

"I know you're after something, Jake, so you may as well just come out with it."

"We carried on seeing each other for ages, even after we'd split, for god sake, the least you can do is give me half an hour with my son, enjoy a friendly drink while we discuss my boy's life, seeing as I never get to know what he's up to unless someone in the village fills me in."

"Shh…James! What the hell are you talking about now!" She nodded at James and indicated with a finger pressed to her lips.

"We've been together more times since you married Mark, then we did when we split up." He laughed. "Or have you conveniently forgotten that too?" Rebecca glanced at him as he slumped back, arms folded, grinning.

"So? It's not going to happen again, not anymore. Where's James? Where is he?"

"Under the table."

"Is he? James get up. What are you doing under there? Is that my phone? Give it here!"

James's hand flew up to his face. "Don't hit me."

"Get up!"

"Fortunately, it won't happen again," Rebecca said, finally returning her attention to Jake. "Yes, I can remember the kitchen and all the other times before that!" She pushed her phone back into her handbag. "It was a mistake… a big mistake." She waved a suddenly empty wine glass at him. Jake rose and took the empty glass. "Did that even hit the sides? Was it? Was it a big mistake? He examined the glass and wiped off her lipstick stain with his finger. "We only stopped doing it because –"

"Because, because it didn't feel right anymore." Rebecca interjected, lifting James's empty coke glass for Jake to take with him to the bar. She glanced up at him briefly. She thought he looked just like he did when they split five or six earlier, perhaps even a bit fitter than before.

"It didn't feel right anymore?" Jake said, "Why, because Mark found out?"

Rebecca looked down at her handbag and shuffled slightly. "Yeah, well…"

"Took the excitement out of it for you, didn't it…?"

"Just a bit," she sighed and looked up. "You been working out?"

Jake lifted his glass from the table, supped the last dregs of beer, burped, winked then took the drinks to the bar for refills.

As Nikki prepared Jake's order, she nodded at where Georgia was sitting. "What a bizarre coincidence," she said. "She's related to you, to the Franconi's."

Jake looked over at where Georgia had been sitting, two bottles of cider, one still on the table un-supped; made him feel sorry for her. "Yeah?" As he returned from the bar with a set of fresh drinks, Georgia returned to the table from the ladies' toilets. Jake watched her as she sat and poured the second cider and sat back with the Town and Country magazine. He strategically placed the Prosecco and coke before his estranged ex and their son, then adopted an assertive stance beside the table. "I'll have this next one with you, then I've got tobounce. There's somewhere I need to be, alright, Jimmy lad?"

"Don't call him that."

"Why not? It's his name, isn't it?"

Suddenly, Jake leaned in slightly and whispered in Rebecca's ear.

"What did you tell Mark? Where does he think you are right now?"

"Does it matter? Sit down," Rebecca responded loudly, demonstrating that she had nothing to hide. Then she lowered her tone. "I am here with you in one of his locals, so there's nothing suspicious going on, other than that, for all he knows, I've popped in to buy James."

Jake smiled. "I see, well thought out."

Rebecca stared down at his black Doc Martens, firmly planted beside the table. His hands, flat on the table, looked rough and worked; three fingers had bruised, black nails on his left hand.

Jake took a deep breath, glanced over at Georgia then stood up straight.

"You're right; I do want something."

"Of course, you do, don't you always?"

Dressed in his long retro black and grey blended Mod coat, with traditional velvet collar and notch lapels pulled upright, he reached down and undid all 3 of the buttons down the front, allowing the coat to fall open, revealing the rich red lining and a thick white cotton grandad shirt, red braces and a red bandanna, which he wore loosely around his neck. "Hand over that bloody Engine, will ya?" He said bluntly.

"Do you have the papers?"

"Didn't think so?" Rebecca smiled, then sipped the Prosecco daintily.

"You took them. You got everything. You got a share of the farm, the car...the kid... Jesus Christ, Beck...what more do you want? What's Mark gonna do with that fucking Engine anyway, the prick."

Rebecca sat back and took another sip of Prosecco, and sighed.

Jake smiled, "What happened to you?"

His innermost thoughts just fell from his mouth.

"You used to be ...I don't know –"

"Nicer...?"

"Normal!"

Rebecca shook her head. "I grew up, Jake, as we all tend to do..." she looked up and down at him and breathed. "Well, most of us."

"Nah, that's not it..." he straightened and scratched his head. "You changed... as soon as you mixed with him and all his exemplary 'bourgeois' lot," he quoted the air. "... What with all their land, their horses and Mercedes."

"Audi, two, actually. So, you're just perfect then?" Rebecca said cocking her head slightly more than normal on one side. Thoughtfully, she examined him again, checking out his chest and muscular thighs, which she'd always admired. Then glancing up and down again, she casually did a half-turn towards Georgia. "You act like the whole universe should revolve around you, do you know that?"

"Yeah, well, maybe it should—you used to think so."

"I can't be doing with this, Jake."

Jake laughed, causing his lush brown curls to fall into his face. Rebecca threw back her head, closed her eyes and breathed deeply.

Jake took a sip of beer, his eyes tracing down her delicately tanned forehead and over her strong, straight nose and slender neck down to a flash of breast, just visible between a gap in the button placket of her coral silk blouse.

"I guess Mark's six-figure quarterly is more attractive to you nowadays?"

Rebecca opened one lavender blue eye and closed it again. "Of course." A tiny crease appeared on her brow as she chuckled to herself.

They were both silent for a while.

"Fries!" Nikki stood with a plate of piping hot chips for James. "They're hot," she said, placing the plate down carefully.

"There you go, mate," Jake said, pushing it across the table.

Both Rebecca and Jake suddenly jumped away from the table.

"Where is he?"

"For fucks sake?"

"He's over there, with G," Nikki pointed in Georgia's direction before spinning on her heels and heading off into the kitchen.

"Ah-hah…there he is…." Rebecca said with a sarcastic tone. She smiled over at Georgia, then turned back to Jake, snarling under her breath. "Why's he gone and sat with her, for God's sake!"

"Fucking hell," Jake said. Embarrassed, he began to stroll away from the table.

Rebecca rose too, then sat again. "You go," she whispered to him.

"I am going!"

Rebecca sat back down, scooped up the glass of Prosecco and wiped a smear of lipstick from the rim. "Well, there's a thing! She said, laughing into her glass. "It's about time you took responsibility for your child." Jake clenched his fist and turned to her. "He's a spoilt little brat… don't know if you've noticed? A proper spoilt little shit… Then again …"

"What? what do you mean, then again?" Rebecca shouted over the room, then stopped when she realised Georgia could possibly hear her from where she was sitting. She sat up taller and watched as Jake approached her.

Jake looked at Georgia and smiled. "Sorry about this."

Georgia shrugged. "It's fine; we've been chatting."

"Yeah? well, sorry, we'll leave you in peace now." He took James by the wrist and pulled him away. "Your chips are going cold, mate."

"See ya, James." Georgia was extremely relieved to see him go, though he hadn't been that bad for a change.

Jake returned and sat the child down to eat his lunch. "Careful mate, they're hot."

"I want ketchup, Daddy."

"What?" Rebecca sat back and folded her arms. "What were you saying…?"

"Aw, nothing, forget it… don't want to put ideas in your head."

"What ideas? Come on, what?"

320

Jake walked away to get the ketchup from the end of the bar, leaving Rebecca flummoxed.

She sighed and shook her head. "So, you were saying…?"

"Aw, nothing," Jake sat beside his son, shook red sauce over his chips, and replaced the lid. "I was just thinking… won't be too long before you pack him off to boarding school, will it?"

"And that is a bad thing because…?"

"I knew it!"

"So, getting a first-class education is wrong now, is it? There's been a conversation, yes! Perhaps, when he is old enough."

"Well, getting him away from Mark does seem the better option in some ways."

"He's better off there than with…."

"Than with who, me? I'm not good enough for him now, I see? Is he better off at some boarding school than at home with his own Dad? Is that it? Ah, of course, let's not forget that you already went to great expense to ensure that didn't happen."

Sensing a presence looming over him, Jake spun around. "Josh!"

"I've come for the latest episode!"

"Episode…?" Rebecca lifted slightly from her seat to offer a hand for him to shake over the table.

"You know he doesn't do handshaking."

"Aw, of course, how could I forget?" She laughed and sat back down gracefully.

Josh pulled up a stool and sat, sloshing his ale everywhere. "Hi, Jimmy, mate!"

"James." Rebecca reminded him.

"So, what's new in the Becky versus Jake saga?"

"We're discussing the Engine."

"Our Engine…Good! About fucking time. It's my Engine, and I want it back!" Joshua looked at Jake.

"It's over at High Oakham, in their barn—her barn," Joshua said, glancing at Georgia. Rebecca followed his gaze over to where Georgia was sitting and sniffed. "Yeah, well…"

Joshua, slightly intruding on Rebecca's personal space, leaned toward her. "That's our fucking Engine, and don't you forget it! I've been and had a look at it. Did you tell her, Jake? You did, didn't you…?"

"You're really not helping, bro… just sit there, will ya…"

"Giz a chip, Jim."

"Joshua!"

Jake looked into his ex's eyes, trying to read what she might be thinking. She curled the sleeves of her cardigan over and ran her fingers through her hair. He couldn't see anything behind those eyes other than wonder. He sensed she wondered how she appeared to other people in her Jimmy Choo boots, designer shirt, and expensive cashmere cardigan.

"Look, I'll talk to Mark," she said finally. Taking Jake and Joshua by surprise, they each put their pints down and raised their eyebrows.

Okay," Joshua said, almost alarmed. "Progress," Jake said, lifting his pint to his brothers and then squeezing his way between his ex, brother and son to pinch a chip.

Rebecca turned to him. "You'll need to get the boiler tested. Do you want to pay for that, Jake—didn't think so?"

"Joshua will do it; he's a qualified Engineer and a member of that club."

"…But what about the steam and hydraulic certificate?"

"Yeah, we are aware of all that."

"But, I'm not doing any of that until you hand over the papers. We're not that stupid?" Joshua said. "It was in good working order when Jake took it to yours …and you know damn well it was."

Rebecca nodded. "That's not the case now, though, Josh."

"There was nothing wrong with it. It has been in our family for generations… It's as much mine as it is his…!"

"Yes, Joshua, I know that, but your brother left me with a pile of debt to clear…so that Engine is repayment. He owes me!"

"That doesn't give you the right to take from our Joshua, though, Beck? He doesn't owe you anything…And, if I remember rightly, he paid the insurance on it last."

Joshua nodded. "I did."

"It's not insured now."

"No, it won't be if you didn't keep up payments."

"It's insured."

"I used Walker Midgley. Who you got it insured with now?"

Disconcerted, Rebecca shifted in her chair and began to clear up the things on the table. "You might have insured it with them, Joshua, but it's expired now."

"See, I knew she was lying!"

"You should have collected it, Jake, when you had the fucking chance."

"I know that now, don't I Josh? I didn't know Mark would steal it, did I?"

"He didn't steal it; he put it in storage."

"Of course, he did, like there's no room in your massive barns. He hid it from us, you mean?"

"Look…I would like to say yes, hire a low loader, go get it, but –"

"But what? It's him, isn't it?"

She nodded and sighed.

"Mark, of course, is it."

"What do you expect? He did bail me out of all your shit."

"Our shit!"

Rebecca smiled and nodded again in an attempt to ease things. "Two forms are needed before you can move it. You'll need to obtain them from the –"

"Yeah, we know," Josh said. "…the V627/1 and the V55/4, but we need those docs."

"Yes, but…"

Josh gave Rebecca a stern look and folded his arms. "But! But what? I've been in this business years, love."

"It's alright, mate…she knows!"

"I know more about these things than she does." Josh began rubbing his hands up and down his jeans, growing more agitated. He looked at Jake for backup.

"It's alright, Josh; we'll sort it, mate."

"I was going to ask, was the vehicle rebuilt by you?" Rebecca asked Josh directly.

Jake was stunned that she addressed Josh in that manner. She had always considered him a fool of sorts.

"What? You don't know the answer to that?" Josh nudged his brother. "Josh, don't tell her, mate."

Josh nodded. "That is what has tripped them up, Jake."

Jake smiled at his brother. "I know, see…there's always a solution. The truth will always prevail; what did I tell you?"

Rebecca regarded both men a moment, then looked at Josh specifically until his eyes met hers briefly. "I can't remember if you worked on the Engine or not?" She looked down at her lap.

"Well, you were there," Jake said. "How come you don't remember?" He was genuinely stunned.

"I don't remember, you had that many Engines... they were all over the bloody place ...they all look the same to me."

"You couldn't sell it because you didn't know its history?" Jake looked at his brother and winked.

Josh rocked slightly back and forth as he laughed, "That's why it got pushed off to storage, Jake!"

"Yeah, mate."

"The vehicle inspector didn't come out from the DVLA, did he? You know, for the inspection?"

"Ah, interesting point, Josh." Jake laughed and sat up, smiling into his pint and shaking his head. "See, he ain't no fool."

"No, so I see. Well, not exactly Josh; he was going to come out but then..." Rebecca answered softly, her voice growing cautious sounding. "But I couldn't fill out the form because I didn't know."

"If the Engine had been rebuilt or not...?"

"No, well yeah." She hesitated, head down. "I couldn't process the form because I didn't know if Josh had rebuilt any of the Engines...so the inspector never made it out to see if it was safe."

Josh looked up from his beer. "They're not safety inspections!"

"No, they're not." Jake agreed.

Rebecca blushed brilliantly at this point.

"They come out purely to confirm the identity of the vehicle."

"And it has nothing to do with safety."

"Nor road-worthiness..."

Rebecca nodded but still didn't look at Josh. "It's not that kind of inspection, Jake?"

"No, mate."

Rebecca feigned disinterest. "Oh, well..." she sighed.

"So, that's what tripped the bastard up...?"

Rebecca shrugged and scanned the room.

The rowdy party of elderly revellers had finally settled at their table, awaiting the last course of coffee and cake, when Nikki turned on the TV with the remote from behind the bar and turned up the volume.

"Hey, has any of you been watching this?"

The whole place fell quiet, turning their attention to a BBC News bulletin that was now blurting from the TV screen. Georgia, sipping the last drops of cider, looked up to see what everyone was looking at.

Like a Germanic Shrek with a florid complexion, Boris Johnson stomped across the TV screen at the televised BBC news conference carrying a pile of white papers. Tucking his shirt into his trousers, he approached the podium, placed the documents down and ran his chubby white fingers through his mop of milky white hair, making it look wilder and more windswept than it was already. Then, like an overgrown schoolboy, he began twiddling his crisp Salvatore Ferragamo tie, bought that day with taxpayer's money from Harrods, until it hung all askew, then ascertaining which camera to address, he looked about confusedly. Without further ado, Boris squared up to the press and flashing cameras to address the 26 million viewers waiting to hear his announcement about the government's decision to lock down the country due to the Covid-19 pandemic or not.

Boris's chaotic, scatter-brained demeanour seemed strange to have the exact opposite effect on his audience, for as soon as he spoke, his orotund tone and rather imposing broad shoulders and thick neck commanded instant respect.

"Good afternoon, everybody. I chaired a government's Cobra emergency committee meeting this morning on the Coronavirus outbreak. There have now been four deaths from Coronavirus in the UK. Our action plan, as you know, sets out four phases for tackling the Virus: contain, delay, research and mitigate. As things now stand, it may bear repeating that the best thing we can all do is wash our hands for 20 seconds… with soap and water."

In Georgia's mind, Boris's speech made no excuses. It was openly insincere. It did not deny the government's lack of knowledge and understanding about the disease, which somehow seemed to make him more authentic and sincere. She sensed he could have quickly delivered some highly effective rhetorical speech to hide those facts, but Boris, being Boris, didn't bother. The government could not offer advice at this stage because they simply didn't know enough about what they were dealing with, and Boris was far too clever and sophisticated to attempt to hide that fact. He had already proved to the Nation that he was not one to enter into political charades…and that's what Georgia loved about him, and she believed the majority of the Nation loved him too…after all, she thought, thankfully, he was no president Trump. Like everyone else in the country, she thought, time will tell. Playfully flicking a tea towel at the TV, Nikki returned to work. "Old Boris will work it out," she said as she switched off the screen.

Everyone returned to their banter as Josh stood up. "See!" He shouted, slamming his pint down on the table. "That's exactly why I wash my fucking hands!"

Rebecca pressed her hands to her eyes and laughed hysterically, her diamond rings flashing in the light. Jake did a 360 on his seat and shouted after his brother. "Keep washing, bro; the way this Virus is coming at us, you may never get out of the men's room again."

Rebecca wiped tears from her eyes on the sleeve of her cardigan and turned to Jake. "Just go and get that bloody Engine, Jake; it's more trouble than it's worth."

*

A car pulled up at the curb beside Georgia as she walked home from the Travellers. The window on the passenger side began to slide down slowly.

"Hey…Franconi!" Georgia stopped and ducked slightly to look in the car. "Jake, hey…" She was pissed off but happy to see him at the same time.

"Walking home?

"Erm, yeah." The humiliation and embarrassment were unbearable; she quickly tried to think of an alternative destination. She had no intention of getting into his car but didn't know the area well enough to think of somewhere local to use as an excuse.

"Yeah…I'm on my way home."

"Get in; I'll give you a lift."

"No, it's alright…I prefer to walk."

"Come on, get in. It's freezing."

Yielding to his persistence, she opened the door and climbed in. They hardly said a word as he drove out of the village into the countryside. He rubbed his stubble and glanced at her. "You're quiet today."

Georgia scowled. He'd only spoken to her on two occasions, and they ended up snogging in the rain on one of those, so how could he possibly know how talkative she was? They'd never really had the opportunity to get to know each other. She hated how presumptuous he was being.

"Thanks for the drink."

"Least I could do to apologise for letting you down. Sorry, I cancelled on you." Staring out of the window, he sniffed and rubbed his stubble again as though racking his brain to think of something else to say. "I...er..."

"It's okay, honestly."

"No, let me explain... I needed to discuss something with my ex."

"Oh, so Rebecca Price is your ex?"

"Becky, yeah, she is."

"...and James?"

"Yeah, Jimmie, the little 'un. He's mine."

"Oh, right. I didn't know that."

"No, well, there's no way you could have known."

"So, you were married...?"

"No! God, no! Thank god... we never got married... I love my lad, and all that, but ... she rarely allows me to see him... so I have to take any opportunity I can...It's hard, it's really hard, but he knows I'm around for him...When he's old enough to make his own decisions, I hope I'll be the one he wants to hang out with."

Georgia smiled. "I'm sure he will."

"And you? Any kids or exes?"

"Kids, me?" Georgia giggled. "That'll never happen...I hate kids...no, but there is an ex...just one—Nathan."

"What happened with you and this Nathan...I already hate him!"

Georgia laughed... "He went in the Army...Engineer."

"Okay, fair enough."

A small silence came. Georgia lifted her hand to her chin, leaned on her elbow and stared out the window.

Jake's forehead wrinkled as he eyed her. "Fancy a coffee?"

Georgia considered it but only for a second. No one could accuse her of being a homewrecker since the home was already wrecked, and Rebecca was with Mark now, they were living proof of that.

"Okay," she said, trying not to look too excited.

The invitation certainly wasn't a formal arrangement anyway, so she was glad of that, it made her feel less nervous around him, and the confession tilted the battle of wits somehow in her favour, though she never would have guessed he'd been in a serious relationship with that weird woman who had appeared and disappeared from her house on the first night when she arrived in the village. Georgia studied Jake's facial expression, wondering if she dared push for more intel on the elusive Rebecca Price, but was put off when he took such delight from her acceptance of his invitation. His demeanour appeared to change, becoming more content, as though a huge weight had been lifted.

"Right!" he said, rubbing his hands briefly before grabbing the stirring wheel again. "I know a great coffee place." He checked his rear mirror, chucked the car into fifth and sped off, leaving a Sunday driver in a cloud of exhaust fumes. He switched the radio on, which was far too loud until he adjusted the volume, then glanced over and winked.

"Alright, love?"

"Yes."

"I'm glad you know now about Becky and James."

"Rebecca and James? Why? It's fine."

Jake nods. "It's not what you want to bring up on a first date."

"Is that what that was, the other day…a first date?"

Jake laughed. "That kiss, you mean…?"

Georgia blushed. "What was that?"

Jake grinned from ear to ear. His gorgeous, straight teeth flashed white, setting off the bright navy blue in his eyes. "That was …er…" He blushed faintly, laughed again and shook his head… "Yeah…that was…er… weird! But great."

Georgia felt her cheeks burning.

"What?" Jake was teasing her now. He was embarrassing her, and he knew it. Georgia shrugged and glanced out of the window…

He tapped her leg. "So, what did you think…?"

"God…please. It's embarrassing!"

Jake laughed loudly. "I don't know how it happened. One minute we were talking, next, we were like –"

"Shut up!" Georgia's stomach fluttered with excitement. She loved how he was teasing her, even if it was becoming infantile.

Creases formed around his sparkly eyes, and his dark curls bounced each time he laughed. Georgia was staring at him, thinking he looked like the actor Aidan Turner.

"It's your fault…" he said. "You started it."

"What! Don't blame me! That was all you!" Silence fell again.

"I've been worried about you."

"About me, why?"

"Stuck in, in that cottage with your dad… He must be retired by now, your dad. What did he do for a living? Oh, by the way, I hear you're a Franconi; is that true? Nikki told me?"

Georgia flicked up one eyebrow and laughed. "…and so are you!"

"Yeah, fucking weird, eh?"

"It is a bit, yeah… So, to answer your question." Georgia cleared her throat and turned to him playfully. "My dad is… was… a Geography teacher—retired twenty years ago."

"So, what's he planning on doing with his retirement then?"

"Turn the cottage into a –"

"Let me guess, holiday home?" Georgia laughed, "Yeah, well, that's the plan."

"If he needs help with that?"

"I'll tell him."

"You know the barn at your place?"

"Yeah"

"We've been talking about it today, as a matter of fact."

"Why?"

"Oh, it's a long story… the Traction Engine is in there, as you know."

"Yeah."

"Well, Rebecca and Mark hid it there, and I want it back!"

"Well," Georgia sighed. She turned back to face the front. "We're planning on converting the barn into a house soon, so we'll need it moving."

"Ah, well, then, I need to get it moved. That was the conversation I was having with Rebecca today. She's finally allowing me to take it, so I'll be chatting with your dad about it soon."

"Georgia looked at him. "You'll definitely need to speak to him about that."

"I will, soon."

Jake seemed older, but Georgia wasn't sure if that was because she had just learned he was a father.

"So, how old are you?"

"How old do you think I am?"

"Dunno… 29-30?"

"Close. How old are you?"

"28…"

Jake nodded – snap – same!"

"Really, when's your birthday. I thought you were older."

"Thanks! I'm a Scorpio, the 02nd of November. You?"

"Aries. The 01st of April."

"Ah, the fool! You hungry?" Jake took a sudden left and bounced the car down a rough dirt track.

Georgia shrugged. "Now you mentioned it."

"There's a great restaurant up here."

Jake drove a short distance and turned off suddenly down a long private, and secluded driveway. A pair of black ornate wrought iron gates announced their arrival by opening electronically, the drive then leading them further to the rear of a 19th century Mill, with its water turbines still groaning in action, grinding and powering millstones hidden within, like work horses. The Mill sat within a Hamlet of the most regal robust design Georgia had ever seen.

More buildings of the same stature filed around the cobbled courtyard forming a complete U-shape. A small row of cottages reminded her of the ones she'd seen in the Town and Country magazine at the Traveller's Pub. A shop, a crafts centre, an art studio, and workshops for glass blowing, ceramics and woodturning and at its dead centre, a substantial Georgian house with a turret clock on one face on the upper front exterior wall, which just incidentally happened to chime at the very exact moment the car ground to a halt.

"There's amazing coffee and excellent vegetarian food in the cafe." Jake took off his seatbelt and turned to face Georgia. She stares around her, eyes as wide as her mouth.

"That's East Lodge, a two-bed cottage."

"It's beautiful. Is it Georgian?"

"Grade 11 listed. The clock house has 12 bedrooms—too big for Josh and me, so we let the rooms, but we use the kitchen for the restaurant. It's huge and really well equipped, a bit like me."

"So, this is all yours. You could turn this into a hotel?" Jake just laughed.

"It's tranquil and peaceful out here; very secluded."

"Come on, we'll eat, then I'll show you the garden. There's a private swimming pool."

"I don't have a costume."

"Who said you need a costume." He jumped out, walked around the car, and opened the door on the passenger side. "Allow me!" He said, stepping back. "This is my passion," he took Georgia by the hand. "High Peak Hamlet." He announced fiercely proud.

'Oh. It's lovely!" Georgia quickly glanced around, then back at him. "So, this really is your place, from your Great-Grandmother?"

"Nikki told you, I guess?" Georgia smiled and nodded.

"Well, I usually only cook for friends and family these days, but yes, we acquired the place from my great-grandmother, Faye Franconi."

Georgia turned and smiled at him. "Wow, lucky you!"

"Remember I told you Josh and I work in all trades.'

"Yes, I do remember; why?"

"We work all hours to keep all this afloat. It's become more of a curse than a gift. But, if Joshua decides to take that position in the States and doesn't go in the army, we'll be off to America soon. It's not permanent for me in the US. I'm just going to help him settle, you know?"

"I'm not being awful, but can Autistic people go in the army?"

"If you you're autistic your prospects of joining the military are slim; the conditions interfere with your ability to function under pressure. Josh can't stand to be touched or yelled it and the sensory over load – can you imagine with guns going off. However, because Asperger autism is a moderate disorder with little symptoms, things are a little different for him. He aced the exams and he didn't tell anyone, He's never been assessed or officially diagnosed. Mum didn't want him being held back because he is extremely intelligent. He's trying to work on becoming less sensitive. I'm teaching him to gain situational awareness and get used to being yelled. He just needs to try to stay in sync with everyone and control his emotions.

"So, you might be off to America?"

"New York, actually."

"New York, wow. That's amazing."

"Yeah. It is kinda cool."

"Who can blame you, so Josh accepted hasn't accepted the offer then?"

"He can't decide, but if he does so he'll be in charge of the American guy's total catalogue of Engines, cars, the lot.

"His Man toys?"

"This guy has a lot of man toys, boats, Engines, planes, you name it."

"Well then, absolutely, he should go and you too… definitely."

"We've both worked really hard on this place, but we need real customers to make a living, so…" Jake laughed to hide his disappointment. "I'm not doing very well at impressing you, am I?"…

She glances around. "You were doing really well until you just said you are off to live in America and own a failing business…wish I could help."

"Nah, I wish you could. If this place was busier, I wouldn't be making plans to leave, nor Joshua. We'd had this stupid notion; we thought we could encourage trade out here—walkers, bikers. We thought they would substitute their well-trodden paths for more uncharted territories. Why wouldn't they like to come out here where no one has been in years. Over the last two centuries, people have been denied access to all this. Only people who had access were the rich landowners and Millers who lived in these cottages, and they were just labourers."

Georgia looked out across the landscape. "It is beautiful."

"People lived centuries on these hills, farming, milling before being driven out—ousted for sheep farms, or forced into the Mills and coalfields in Yorkshire."

"Ah, the great rural exodus?"

"Yeah, they all left. Follow me," Jake said, pointing off somewhere over the yard.

"Are you sure most people voluntarily didn't just desert their land in preference for a better life, like in the towns and cities? If you ask me, the wonder is not why so many left the countryside, but why many stayed." "God, is it that bad for you out here?" Jake said, leading Georgia around the narrow causeway lined by the buildings that created the neat U-shape and enveloped the cobbled courtyard.

"Well, I don't live in anything near as grand as this… but I can see how people were attracted by new opportunities elsewhere rather than driven from their homes. Even now, urban areas offer better job opportunities, higher pay and a more appealing social life—especially for the younger generation. Rural life in these small communities is a bit, I don't know… boring, and to live somewhere like this, as a worker, would feel oppressive, even now."

Jake laughed loud. "Oppressive?"

"Well, you know, I mean… I don't know, I'm just finding the countryside all a bit…too quiet for me."

"It certainly isn't London, if you mean?"

"No, it isn't."

"Was London the magnet that attracted your dad away from here all those years ago?"

"You know about that? Did Nikki tell you? We think he lived here as a boy. When I say here, I mean literally in the same house where we live now… Isn't that insane? Nikki thinks it might be the same house; it belongs to the same family!"

"I don't think it's coincidental if you ask me." Jake stopped walking and sniffed. "You should ask your dad; maybe he knows more than he lets on? You're definitely related to me somewhere down the line."

"Maybe," Georgia sighed. "Is that weird?"

"Nah! It is a bit, don't put me off, though, if that's what you mean…?"

"No, me neither."

"So, what made you open a restaurant out here?"

Jake rubbed his beard, "Madness."

"Is that in a good way or in a bad kind of way…?"

"Madness is as madness does."

"I'm pretty sure that's Stupid is as stupid does if you're quoting Forrest Gump."

He shakes his head. "Come on, I'll show you inside."

He gently leads her around the square by placing his arm across her shoulder. A shower of rain starts abruptly but is short-lived. Light bursts through convective clouds, bouncing off each wet stone, giving the cobbles over the yard a glossy reflection as they dash towards the arch beneath the clock tower.

Georgia glances up at the construction of the vertical structure. The front of the building comprises four colonnades with a central vault rising from the base to create the entrance. The front of the building faces southwards, allowing the late afternoon sunlight to creep into every corner of the hollow masonry vault beneath the arch. There are doors on the left and right beneath the giant arch; opening to the rear is another double door that leads to a well-stocked walled garden. Georgia notices a tangible magic atmosphere about the place.

"It was all derelict when we took over."

"Was it? You've done an amazing job then!"

"Yeah, well, it's not just ours—not yet anyway… It also still belongs to my great-grandmother, Faye Franconi. She hasn't parted with it just yet."

"She's in a care home in the village, isn't she?"

"Sandhurst, do you know if? She bought this place just to preserve the bell tower. Campanilismo, she used to call it, meaning 'Our Bell Tower' she said, it's how Italians describe their local patriotism—that age-old rivalry between townships was represented by the size of their bell tower."

"Oh, well, you certainly have a huge one."

Georgia laughed. Jake just nodded but was inwardly thinking how damn sexy that just sounded. Turned on by her playful innuendo, he wondered if he should try his luck later.

"People's pride and loyalty to their locality was symbolised by the size of the bell tower; imagine that!"

"In which case, to date, yours is the tallest in the town?"

"Hmm…It is probably the only one in this town; I never thought to check. I continue to feel a deep, loyal campanilismo, especially since my family has lived in this region for generations. I think that's why we thought since there's been a surge in the antiques, why not utilise what we have here and keep it in the family."

Georgia looked up at the tower. "There's no time like the past."

"Well, we tried… we combined all the current fads: cycling, running, walking, teashops, crafts, antiques…you name it, it's here."

"Joshua's addition." Jake said as they turned the corner beneath the arch that led to the rear gardens, "Oh, a vintage traction Engine display!"

"There are a few more around the back that no one ever wants to see."

Georgia sighed. "Maybe the 19th-century rural deprivation is more difficult to eradicate than you thought?"

"Most certainly is; that's a fact."

"I thought at least the Arts and Crafts industries would have jumped at the chance of working in a space like this … I mean, just look at this location; it's perfect!"

"I know, the views are stunning…Well, until there's a substitute for the Internet. That seems to beat real-life hands down, and until there is a movement to reverse that, I guess we're all fucked."

"Have you advertised?"

"Internet, radio, press…done the lot."

As Jake pushed open the large oak doors on the left and waited for Georgia to enter, a moment of silence fell. Smiling up at him, she momentarily lost herself in his eyes, so blue and deep that she could almost swim in them.

"Maybe I can help? I specialise in digital marketing."

"Oh, do you?"

"Yep."

"Or…" he said, responding to her provocative gaze, "…we could just try that kiss again."

"Without the rain…?"

He led her back beneath the arch and gently pushed her against the door, and without saying a word, their arms folded around each other, Georgia buried her head deep into his hard steel chest that smelled gorgeous, like Mandarins. Then, gently lifting her chin, he stared into her eyes and smiled. "You're beautiful." His voice was low, deep and sensual.

"Get a fucking room, will ya!"

"I wish we could," Georgia whispered.

"Josh! This is…er…" Jake bowed away.

"I know who she is…."

"We've come for lunch."

"You've come for a shag; that's what you've come for!"

Timidly, Georgia touched Jake's arm, as if it was not her release from the warm embraces she wanted but his protection from Joshua.

'Georgia, you know my brother, Joshua?" She nodded, and he nodded back and rolled his eyes. "He speaks before he engages his brain, and I swear he has no fucking filter!" He turned to her with sincerity. "I'm so sorry about that…."

"Do you believe those stories about your house?" Joshua blurted.

"What? What do you mean?" Georgia looked at Joshua, half puzzled and half-amused and laughed.

Jake shook his head. "Georgia, please, take no notice of my brother… he's just fucking insane."

"It's supposed to be full of ghosts, your house."

*

In the High Peaks Industrial Hamlet kitchen, a breeze blew in through the open window: winter was only a few weeks away, still had reminiscence of a late autumn aroma.

"So," Georgia said, scattering things on the breakfast table to make way for an ordnance survey map she found in the reception area. She spread it out and tapped on a spot excitedly with her finger.

"We're near Edale—in this valley, right? That's the River Noe and the train station; sure you know it's the southern terminus of the Pennine Way?"

Jake turned and kissed her gently on the head. "Good morning you!"

"Morning…"

"Did you sleep well…?"

"Fine, did you?"

"Would have if a certain someone didn't snore –"

"So do you!"

Jake smiled, said nothing, just nodded and rolled up his sleeve to flip a sizzling egg in a red-hot frying pan. Joshua, drawn by the smell of breakfast, walked in.

"She still here…?"

He filled a bowl with soap and water at the sink, washed his hands in the usual methodical way, and then pinched the slice of toast waiting for its topping of a fried egg; Jake flashed Georgia a look, which she shrugged off.

"It's a 268-mile walk to Kirk Yetholm; from there," Josh said, spraying crumbs everywhere. He leant over Georgia to look at the map.

"I didn't know that," she said sarcastically before glancing up at Jake and shaking her head.

Jake smiled, "Joshua, sit," He threw a tea towel.

"Well, you do now!" Joshua said, eating loudly.

"Thanks …"

"It's alright… Kirk Yetholm is in Scotland, by the way."

"I did assume that," Georgia said, turning to Jake, trying to pick up where she left off. "…the station provides direct transport to the heart of the Dark Peak countryside."

"Manchester or Sheffield?" Joshua asked.

"Well, I did know that," Jake interjected as he walked over with the fried egg on a spatula. He shuttled it onto the empty plate and then returned to the stove to put another piece of bread under the grill.

"If you go over Mam Tor or Hollins Cross to Castleton or any of the caves, from here." Georgia put the tip of her pen in her mouth, removed the lid, brushed Joshua's spit and crumbs from the map, and then drew a broken line of dashes. "It is only a 30-minute walk to your place."

Jake quickly retrieved scorched bread from the grill, frisbeed it across the kitchen to the waiting plate, and then handed it to Georgia like the crown jewels.

"Is it? 30 minutes, is that all? From here?" He said, "On foot?"

Georgia looked for somewhere to lay the plate, as far away from Joshua as possible. "There, you see. I'm not just a pretty face, am I?" She smiled at Jake playfully.

"Hey, thanks, man!" Like a great white shark from the deepest darkest sea, Joshua rose and pounced on the plate, taking egg, toast, plate—the lot—gone in one fell swoop.

With toast lolling out of the corner of his mouth, he rose again, this time for a bottle of brown sauce on the side by the fridge, then he sat heavily to eat like an ogre. Exhausted, Jake wiped his hands on the tea towel and sat, totally dumbfounded, shaking his head in disbelief. "Hope you enjoy Georgia's breakfast, Joshua."

"Oh mate, sorry, was that hers?"

"That's your selling point!" Georgia piped up. "That's what you should be focusing on; forget advertising the restaurant and the Hamlet, just concentrate your efforts on inviting people to explore the surrounding area…There are at least 30 walks and biking routes in this radius. If you do your marketing right, this place could naturally become the 'go-to place' en route to the Pennine Way."

Joshua took the toast from his mouth and dunked it in Georgia's tea. "She has a point."

"That's Georgia's tea!" Jake Shout.

Joshua sprayed tea over the kitchen. "Oo, minging!"

Rebecca's Home 2020

Sunset embers burnt invitingly in the cast iron stove, offering warm, rich honey tones that spread like shimmering gold across the black marble hearth, where little James lay quietly, upon a luxurious grey-black Helgar sheepskin, like Clannad, playing in the background, filled the air with a smooth haunting monophonic chant.

"One of Italy's true greats," he had delighted in telling her when he first brought her to stay at his family's luxury Grade 1 listed Manor House, set within its own medieval knot garden on the edge of the Peak District. Rebecca leant dreamily against the large floor to ceiling Georgian window, watching rain patter against the glass. On the one hand, a warming, smooth glass of Emidio Pepe, Montepulciano, taken on the sly from Mark's 1980s Vintage collection. In her other hand, a gold-tipped Company's Treasure cigarette, which she delighted in stealing from yet another of Mark's most expensive vice collection: made, she was told, from the world's finest tobacco, though to her, it was just a cigarette like any other.

A sudden burst of tinkling vibrations emanating from a French Art Nouveau 18-carat gold and enamel dragonfly wind chime hung above the kitchen's French doors. She had bought it while on a yachting tour of the Mediterranean.

James looked up. "Mark's back!"

"Go to your room."

"Aw, do I have to?"

"Now…!"

"Don't bother." Mark's voice barked out from the kitchen as he removed his boots. "Stay where you are, James; I want to speak to you!"

Mark thundered into the room, tossed his keys on the table, walked up to Rebecca, removed wine and cigarette from her person, and then adopted 'the stance'; hands on hips, legs slightly astride. He knocked back the wine and puffed heavily on the cigarette. Rebecca knew she was in trouble.

"So, you gonna explain this?"

"Sorry…?"

"Sorry?" Mark laughed.

Rebecca knew that laugh; bitter—not good, self-important and hollow. She had come to recognise that that laugh was his demonstration of higher intelligence. He's drunk, she thought inwardly. Here we go.

"Do you want to explain this?"

Rebecca was puzzled. Mark took his phone from his pocket, swiped it, tapped it and did all manner of things until voices were audible—her voice and Jake's—as clear as day.

"Don't be like that. We can sit here ten minutes before our son and talk like adults… can't we? For God's sake, we carried on seeing each other for ages, even after we'd split."

"Shh…! What the hell are you talking about now?"

"…We were 'civilised', then, even after you married Mark, or have you forgotten that?"

"You've got your son to thank for that little gem," Mark said, throwing his phone at Rebecca.

"James?"

"I didn't know, Mummy!"

"Seems your son borrowed your phone and accidentally rang me while you were busy entertaining your ex."

"There are no secrets here, Mark…Jake rang me, and I ended up meeting him."

"No shit! You didn't go to work either. I know that because I rang them."

"No, I didn't; Jake wanted to see James and needed to discuss something important with me."

"At the Travellers?"

"Do you think I'd meet him somewhere public if I was going behind your back? You could have walked in any minute."

"You managed to screw him right under my nose last time, so what does it matter where you meet him? You're both still laughing about it—evidently! You lying, fucking bitch!" He took Rebecca by the arm and stubbed out his cigarette in the back of her wrist.

Rebecca screamed in agony. "Jake might have been joking; we weren't laughing…I didn't lie to you, Mark; I just chose not to tell you!" Crying now, she pulled her hand free and licked the scalded flesh. "I had James with me, for God's sake."

"So, what was so fucking urgent that you went sneaking off to meet him without telling me…?"

"Have you been drinking…?"

"Just answer the fucking question!"

"He is James's Dad, Mark. He does have rights…don't forget that."

"Forget it…how can I? I'm still paying out of the fucking nose for him and his little bastard of yours!"

"Aw, you didn't mean that, Mark; come on…please."

"So, what did he want?"

"The Engine!"

"Oh, right. Should have known that…!"

"It's not really Jake's, you see. It belongs to Joshua."

"Ah, he's using that old chestnut, is he? So now it's not Jake's…its Joshua's—that fucking idiots, who doesn't know his arse from his elbow, what's he gonna do with it?"

"You know, Joshua is an amazing Engineer. He's a whiz… Everyone goes to him."

"He's a fucking retard."

"He's not stupid; he's on the spectrum—slightly—"

"Where you going… Come back."

"I'm going to get ice."

"You'll be fucking autistic when I get my hands on you. Sit down! Listen, if they want that Engine back, they'll have to repurchase it. I want every penny that that bastard owes you!"

"I've tried to sell it; it's not that easy. There's been a lot of work carried out on it; I can't answer questions about that on the application or catalogue or whatever the DVLA want. I just can't do it. We can't put it in your name until the inspection has been carried out, and they won't come out to inspect it until the application has been filled out. You need to know what you're doing with these things, and we clearly don't have a clue. And you can't sell something unless you legally own it! Anyway, I've told Jake they can take it. I'll be glad shut of it."

Rebecca wasn't sure who had come out best from the exchange. She was shaking a little, but for most, if not all the way through the conversation, she was expecting Mark to hit her again, but then he just sat looking at the fire; his only thought was how on earth would he stop the Franconi brothers getting their hands on the Engine? He scrolled through his phone and then tipped the last drops of Montepulciano from the bottle into his glass.

"James, come here. Come on, I won't hurt you." James rose to his feet reluctantly and approached Mark without taking his eyes from his mum.

"Go to the cellar, fetch another bottle like this." He held out the empty bottle. James reached out and took it from him.

"Look, look at the label. It has a picture of a little angel, see? There are more bottles like this in a wooden case in the cellar—at the bottom of the stairs. Go get one for me, and don't drop it."

"He's not old enough to run errands like that."

"He's a spoilt little brat, isn't he? According to his dad... Yes, I heard him say that an' all. It's all on the phone. If he thinks like that about his own son, we'll have to start making changes. I'll put his son to work, get him doing chores, might even get him out in the fields with me... see how he likes that!"

"I'll come with you, James."

"No, no, you won't. Go on, kid, do as I say."

"Mummy, it's dark in the cellar." "I know, love, I'll go...don't worry!"

Mark jumps up objectionably. "I said no! Let him go! Who's in fucking charge here?"

Rebecca took James' hand and walked down the hallway to the cellar, opened the door, put on the light and allowed him to go down alone.

Rebecca's worst fears had been recognised. Mark had always been aggressive, especially since finding out about her affair with Jake. She'd been wondering how long it would be before he turned his aggression towards her son. A shadow fell in her heart as she watched the little boy climb down the cellar steps, his short legs barely long enough to reach each stone step as he disappeared into the darkness below.

"I can take the brutality, Mark," she said from the top of the stairs, "but I am not about to let you subject my son to it, not you nor any man."

Mark came thundering up the hall towards her from the living room. "I'm doing him a favour; he needs to man up."

"He's a child!"

"What does Jake want the Engine for?" He slammed the cellar door shut. "What's he got up his fucking sleeve this time?"

"I don't know!"

He pushes Rebecca to one side, opens the door again, switches off the light and slams it shut.

Blackness, as dark as night, falls around the cellar. Little James tumbles forward over boxes and crates. "Mummy! I can't see, Mummy, please Mummy!"

Rebecca threw herself at the door, trying to prise Mark's hand away from the handle.

"Mummy! Please…"

Mark leaned against the door, holding Rebecca away at arm's length. "You can tell Jake from me before he gets anywhere near that Engine, I'll blow the bastard thing clean off the face of this fucking earth…and his son with it… Understand? Do you understand?"

"Yes, Mark!"

"We'll see who's fucking civilised!"

Rebecca, reaching over, pushed herself against Mark, knocking him out of the way, threw open the cellar door and switched on the light. James came running upstairs towards her, arms outstretched, crying.

"Whoa! Whoa! Steady on there, young fella!" Mark said arms crossed, smiling.

Seeing Mark, James stopped short and held out the bottle of Montepulciano.

"See. No harm done." Mark took the bottle from him. "Now go to your room; Mummy and I have a business to tend to."

Jake and Joshua 2020

The weather had been excellent in the morning, cold and bright, but now it had clouded over. Jake and Georgia climbed into the car and put on their seatbelts.

"I've left my bag in the kitchen." Jake removed his belt.

"No, no, it's okay, I'll go. I know where it is."

She ran steadily across the cobbled yard towards the clock tower, dashed beneath the square arch and rushed into the kitchen. She heard a splash of water and turned to see Joshua standing over a basin, washing his hands while watching TV. The highly recognisable cryo-electron microscopic image of the biological rogue slowly bringing the world to its knees was spinning on the screen. A three-dimensional micro shot showing the whole volume of the deadly novel coronavirus on a molecular scale became the backdrop to all TV news channels.

"I should really catch up with the news," Georgia said as she began scouting the kitchen for her bag.

"Briefings are daily now," Joshua said.

"I know, it's getting scary, isn't it?"

Josh looked back for a moment over his shoulder at the TV, then, hatred stirring in him, glanced back at her.

"Jake should watch what he's doing —"

He reached for the remote and turned up the volume. They both stand staring and listening.

"This is the BBC News at midday… Today we are told the biggest impact on cases and deaths will come purely from social distancing. To protect our NHS, the elderly and other vulnerable groups MUST practice social distancing."

"The government advises we all stay home, keep our distance from each other," Joshua said, splashing his hands in the murky soapy water.

Feeling he was being commanded urgently to a halt, he reached for a towel, wiped his hands and turned to Georgia.

"What do you want? What are you looking for?"

"Oh, just my bag. I have forgotten my bag."

"So, what do you want me to do about it?"

"Nothing."

She was halfway across the kitchen, but Joshua didn't know how to prevent her from getting any closer. They were both alone in a small confined space, which made him feel agitated… and now the government was telling people to practice social distancing.

"Where's Jake?"

Joshua's voice sounded thin and worried. He knew nothing about women, just that they made him nervous.

"He's waiting for me in the car; sorry, can I just get past."

"No…"

"Sorry, if I can just –"

"No!"

"Please, Joshua, just jumps up, will ya please." Josh was looking for somewhere to escape.

"It's okay; I'll just … squeeze past." Georgia reached for her bag.

"Why are you here?"

"To get my bag."

"I'm not talking about the bag. I mean, what do you want from Jake?"

"Nothing…" She took a step closer and reached around him.

Joshua felt his heart labouring. "He doesn't need your help. He's got me!"

"O-kay…" Georgia snatched up her handbag and hastily stepped away from him. "Got it."

"He doesn't need you coming around here making changes. We're leaving soon anyway. We're going to the states …to live!"

"Right! So, you have decided to go then? Jake wasn't sure if you were joining the forces? He has spoken to me about it, so…he said he isn't going for good, anyway…."

"You should ask him to tell you the truth! Think you'll find we are looking for property over there. I have decided to go the States, so we don't need any delays!"

"You seem to know a great deal about it; I'll ask him."

"You do that. Jake should tell you the truth, so you can stop wasting your time."

"I've become very fond of your brother…and you, so I'm sorry you feel that way."

The sound of the car horn fragmented the tense vibe in the room.

"That's Jake…I'd better get going."

"Yeah, piss off then."

"O-kay, goodbye, Joshua. Great talking to you."

High Oakham Cottage Len's Visitor 2020

Len was walking into the lounge eating an apple when he heard a sound outside. He gave it a few minutes before walking over to the window. Surprised to see the barn doors wide open, banging repetitively in the wind and disinclined to venture out, Len decided to call Georgia. She didn't answer, so he hung up. He tried again, then rang off. He was about to try one last time when the display on his phone faded. He switched it back on, but it just died. Despite being on charge all night and having only been used once that day, Len couldn't believe the phone was out of power. He tutted, shook his head at it, tucked it away in his pocket, and then ventured outside to close the barn doors.

As he hurried across the backyard, he tripped on something. Twisting mid-air to avoid the object beneath his feet, his ankle gave way, and he slammed onto the ground. Sat there, in agony, he managed to lean over, pull his trainer off and assess the damage. His ankle was throbbing, bright red and bruised, and looked like it was already starting to swell; then, he heard a scream as he tried to get to his feet. He scrambled up and looked around, then down at what he tripped over; a tiny, black and white kitten, the size of a large orange, no more than six weeks old with its mother's milk still fresh on its whiskers. It was wreathing in agony as its tiny body contorted and twisted.

Len stared at it, wondering where it had come from, then, with great regret, realised it was he who had probably injured it. Bending to look closer, the scream came again, like a child waking amid a night terror. Len didn't know where this was coming from. His brain was telling him something was not right and to get back to the house, but the kitten, so poorly injured, just couldn't be left to die in that way. He needed to tend to it, burry it, or something. He carefully picked it up, held it close to his chest, and then slowly began to hobble towards the barn with one shoe on and one-off.

As he approached, he heard the scream again, coming from inside the barn, but this time it was closer and even more bloodcurdling than the last. He stepped inside, eyes wide and a little afraid; the smell of warm diesel and smoke filled his nostrils and lungs.

"Who's there? Hello?"

The kitten in his hands suddenly felt different, its fur coarse and dry. He glanced down; the silk of its warm coat had hardened. It was spiky now, with fragments of tiny bone, brittle and sharp, sticking into the palm of his hand. It was crumbly, rotted, and obviously dead—dead a long time, then its carcass began to crumble, turning into fine powdery dust, which fell loosely between his fingers and blew away on a gentle wisp of freezing cold air that appeared to whip up from nowhere. Astonished, Len staggered backwards, rubbing his hands frantically down his shirt, wincing and swearing, "Jesus fucking Christ!"

As he twisted in disgust, daylight washing down the wall from the tiny windows in the roof illuminated a small child. She was sitting in a pool of golden haze. She saw him and looked up sharply. Her mouth fell open in a scream that rang through the air. Her eyes were gouged, her hair burning, and the flesh on her cheeks peeling from the bone, melting, scorched and black. Her skull was bashed entirely open on one side, exposing a mass of her brain. Slowly, she rose, arms outstretched, moving in silence towards him, bringing a putrid smell of singed flesh and dead rot. He watched her coming, shrinking in horror. He tried to move, but something was holding him on the spot; a rope tightened around his neck, then suddenly snapped its grip taut against his windpipe and yanked him completely backwards off his feet. He sensed himself slowly being hoisted; the rafter above creaked beneath the weight of his body as he hung from the rope's end. His feet thrashed wildly; he swung, spinning one way, then back the other. He scratched at his neck, trying to get a grip of the rope, forcing his fingers beneath it to loosen it, but the more he flinched, the more his weight pulled him down upon the rope. He kicked and struggled as a warm gush of piss ran down his legs. His nose was streaming, his eyes bulging, and his head was about to explode.

Something in the Air 2020

The car was swept along the narrow lane and around the foot of Mam Tor. The road had obviously been built when traffic on roads was far less.

"Have you been listening to the news?" Georgia said, switching on the radio.

"I've just heard it while you were getting your bag…insane!"

"I know; they're talking about social distancing now."

"What does that even mean?"

"I know, right? Is it even possible?"

"They're saying to work from home if you can."

"It's a good job; this weekend's open day."

"Listen, Jake, about that… Joshua just told me you're both moving for good."

The car slammed to a sudden screeching halt.

"For Christ's sake, you nob!" Jake was screaming at the car coming in the opposite direction. "He could see me, but he just kept on fucking coming… Reverse, you twat!" A guy in a red Audi took no notice and kept inching forward on a bend that was not designed for one car, let alone two. Jake yielded to the guy's alpha gorilla ego and practically ditched his vehicle to allow the idiot in the red sunglasses that matched his car and the leather jacket he was wearing to squeeze past.

As the two vehicles drew side by side, Jake caught a glimpse of a sallow face with a sly slanting grin, a collar on a pink polo shirt turned up to his ears, and a blonde-red fringe swept up so high with a gallon of L'Oreal hair spray, he was at risk of taking out an eye on the spikes. Then, he was gone, leaving nothing more than a cloud of dust and exhaust fumes in Jake's rear-view mirror.

'That was Mark! I'm sure that was fucking Mark! See what he did? Nearly drove us off the fucking road! And what the fuck was he wearing?" Jake turned to Georgia quickly. "What were you saying?"

"Oh, nothing…"

"So, what are you planning for the open day with all this social media stuff… don't get me wrong, it all sounds interesting, but…you don't have to do this, not for me."

"Well, that's what I wanted to talk to you about. If you are still interested in getting more people out to the open day, I can ask a friend of mine, Martin Spalding. It would be great for your socials, get numbers up, attract more people out on the day."

"Who is he?"

Georgia laughed. She tapped images on her phone and presented a picture of herself with some bloke.

"You do know him. Martin Spalding. You'll definitely recognise him."

"I know him, yeah. I've seen him on the telly."

"You will have done after he won that reality TV show; he went on to do loads of TV after that. He just got married, so if he does come, he might bring his new wife with him. They'll need somewhere to stay, though."

"That's fine; they can stay at the Hamlet, but not sure I can afford a celebrity if I'm honest."

"Don't worry, he's my absolute best mate. I met him through my ex, Nathan. He helped me get over him, and I've helped him in the past with a few relationships that went sour on him. So, we go way back. Apparently, we played together as kids, but I don't remember him. We used to paddle in the sea at Brighton, naked. Honestly, I have no recollection of this, but he does."

Jake's eyebrows shot up. "Really!"

"When we were toddlers, honestly, your mind!"

Jake laughed. "As long as it was that long ago since you paddled together in the duff."

"Trust me, he loves me; he'll do anything for me."

"I'm sure he will!. Okay, I'm joking. Go for it."

"Are you sure, because… I do need to know."

"What? What are you looking at me like that for…?"

"Are you like, fully committed to this opening day? I mean, do you have any other plans?"

"Like what?"

"I don't know." She began stroking his leg. "If the open day does work out, is there a future, a foreseeable future?"

"For us, you mean…?"

Georgia slid her hand slowly higher up his thigh, her fingers tracing creases in his jeans until they reached the folds around his crutch. Jake stroked her hand, his penis slowly rising and hardening on its own accord beneath the fabric.

"Well, I like to finish once I've started if you know what I mean? Don't like leaving a job half done. Why do you ask?"

"Why?" She started moving her hand up beneath his T-shirt and rubbing the hairs on his stomach. She pulled the top of his jeans until the button popped open, allowing the zip to separate until her hand fit inside his jeans and around his ever-increasing erection.

"I don't want to involve Martin Spalding; if you're just going to shut shop and leave…what would be the point?"

"Leave, for America, you mean…? I'm coming back; I told you that."

Very gently, Georgia began to knead his testicles and rubbed the shaft of his penis up and down rhythmically with her other hand.

"Are you sure you're not going to live in the States with your brother for good, leaving me wondering when you're coming back?"

Jake nodded. "I see where this is leading." He sounded breathless but kept his eyes on the road. He parted his legs slightly to give her more room.

"You been talking to Josh? What's going on? You have my full attention now." His head fell back slightly. He wanted to pull over, so he started looking for somewhere to stop—somewhere discrete. He swallowed hard, clasped his hand down upon hers, and began thrusting up towards her warm, caressing hands. "No, I'm not going to run off." He was bulging to the capacity of his jeans now, but the conversation prevented him from exploding.

"I am going for a month, maybe two… help him set up. He needs support; I owe him that much at least…" then, moaning quietly, he clasped Georgia's crotch. "I'm coming… back…."

He sat up, leaning over the steering wheel, then leant towards her to kiss her quickly on the cheek. He indicated and pulled over.

"What have you gone and done." He was laughing, going through the glove compartment, looking for tissues.

"Here," she said, delving into her bag. She pulled out a packet of Kleenex. She threw the bag on the back seat and turned back to look at Jake as he cleaned himself up.

"Don't listen to Josh," he said, mopping up the mess on his stomach and jeans. He pulled up his zip, sat up straight and threw the tissues out of the open window.

"Look, Josh wants me to give up everything and live with him in the States… Sure, you've noticed, he has his weird idiosyncrasies, but he ain't no idiot. Josh can cope alone. Josh has coped alone in the past, so… And there's no way I've invested all this time and money into the Hamlet to leave it; besides, it still belongs to our great-gran while she is still alive. I also have a son to think about. I can't just go off and leave them. You've just seen what a twat Mark is… such madness… he absolutely requires a gun to the back of his head, but still…." He turned and smiled, returned his eyes to the road, indicated and pulled out. "What are you doing?"

Georgia smiled and then looked away with her phone pressed against her ear. "I'm ringing, Martin Spalding. Hi Martin. It's me. What are you doing at the weekend? Great. Fancy joining me…well, me and my…" she paused, "boyfriend?" She glanced at Jake, watching for his response; nothing had ever been mentioned about whether or not they were an actual item. She popped the phone on mute… "Does having sex three times in one night constitute boyfriend and girlfriend?"

Jake laughed. "Three times, is that all? I've got to up my game. I don't know, you tell me."

Georgia put the phone back on the speaker. "Yes, I have a boyfriend." She winked at Jake and laughed. "Well, you can vet him when you meet him, come up at the weekend, I'll fill you in then…Ring you later. Oh, how's Lindsey? Great. Okay, speak later; love you too."

The road took a sharp incline and flattened out into a long mile of the narrow lane. Jake flicked on the radio:

…And yet, social distancing was not recommended then. That day, 12th March, after hearing with disbelief the government announcement that didn't include widespread social distancing, I suggested to my team at Imperial that they should work from home for the foreseeable future. Indeed, I have not been to my office since.

"This shit is getting serious."

"And I laugh at Joshua when he's washing his fucking hands."

"The enemy is upon us. It's like we were back in 1939."

"At least they could see their enemy—knew what they were dealing with."

Jake pulled up at High Oakham Cottage. There was no time for further news. The sight of the place seemed to stir something deeply suspicious within Georgia's subconscious; she knew instantly there was something wrong…

"Coming in?"

"I did want to ask your dad about taking the Traction Engine," Jake said, smiling. "I'll finally have the papers for it at the weekend; Rebecca's bringing them to the open day."

"Oh, she's coming, is she…?"

"With James, yes. We thought he'd enjoy a day out. That's what I spoke to Becks about in the Traveller's when I saw you."

'You'll need to gauge what sort of a mood Dad's in before asking him about that Engine. He did buy the house with the Engine as part of its contents."

'I know, but when we spoke about it last, he said he'd reconsider if I had the right papers."

"Good. I don't know why, but I feel there's something wrong today. You know when you get that feeling?" She sat back, rubbed her forehead and glanced over at the cottage. "It worries me because Dad is old. He's eighty-five." She sighed heavily. "When I found my mum, I had this same weird feeling."

"What?"

"Never mind… The front door's open."

"Hmm, and the barn doors are. He's probably in there."

"He hasn't been answering his phone all day; I hope he's okay."

Jake climbed out of the car, moving around to the rear, popped open the trunk and reached in. Georgia took her bag from the rear seat and looked briefly to see Jake pull out a bolt action rifle. He slammed the boot shut, cocked the gun and laid it over his right arm. "You ready?" Georgia watched as Jake began loading cartridges into the chamber, then closed the breech by re-locking the bolt against the receiver.

"What are you doing?" She closed the car door behind her.

"Just in case," Jake said, nodding at the cottage. "It's the Gypsies; you never can tell."

"Gypsies?"

"You just gotta keep your eyes open out here. They're all over the bloody place. If something's not bolted down, they'll have it… Go on, I'm right behind you."

Georgia walked towards the house and went inside, leaving Jake on the doorstep. She returned moments later, looking a little concerned, but amused at the same time.

"He's not in; he's probably in the barn."

As they walked over the yard together, Georgia kept looking at Jake, shaking her head and giggling. "I'm not sure we need to be that dramatic," she said, laughing. She opened the large wooden door and peered inside. "Dad!" Her voice echoed back from the vastness of the old wooden building.

Len heard his daughter's voice, a dull pulsating sound carrying upon the vibration of his fading heartbeat.

"D-a-d!" Georgia shouted again.

There was a man's voice also; Len was sure it was Jake between each heartbeat in his chest.

Jake stepped into the barn behind Georgia, holding the shotgun steady before him; he pointed it downwards towards the ground, eyes searching the darkness, half expecting someone to jump out. Suddenly, without warning, Georgia darted forward. Suddenly seeing Len hanging by his neck, Jake dropped the shotgun and ran after her. He pulled her back and wrestled her to the ground before rushing beneath Len's swaying body to take his weight. He wrapped his arms around his legs to alleviate the strain on the rope and tried to hold him there long enough for Georgia to find something sharp. She climbed a pair of rickety ladders and started to hack at the rope with a blunt knife. Struggling beneath the weight above him, Jake felt his stomach muscles were about to rip apart. The effort of holing Len's weight upon his shoulder took every last drop of his strength. It seemed to take Georgia a lifetime to cut through the rope.

As the blade began to tear through the fibres, the rope snapped suddenly. Len dropped upon Jake; both men fell to the floor. When Len hit terra firma, he fell unconscious. Jake thrust his arms under Len's and pulled him up across one knee, hauling him into a seated position.

"Fucking hell." He was crying out. Georgia was backing away, standing by the door speechless.

Jake, trembling now, looked up at her and saw she was in a state of existential shock. He began yelling, "Georgia…Georgia! Call an ambulance! Call a fucking ambulance!"

Hands shaking, Georgia made the 999 call; the reception was clear as the woman at the end of the line talked her through the process and assured her the ambulance was on its way. Remaining on the phone, Georgia walked towards both men, dropped on one knee and gingerly touched her father's face; it was vacant; eyes like pebbles, bloodshot and glazed, staring at nothing. She gently removed a strand of rope from his hair. He looked like a corpse; his face was the same colour; Georgia suddenly remembered, like her mother's, the last time she saw her. Hearing the ambulance siren somewhere off in the distance, Georgia quickly loosened the noose from about his neck and threw it across the floor. Jake lay back, leaning on one arm, the flat of his other palm caressing Len's forehead.

"He's warm; he's breathing," He whispered. Uttering a prayer, he removed his Jacket and adjusted it carefully around Len, straightening his limbs beneath it to ensure he was covered. He cared for Len with such a shocking tenderness it terrified Georgia. Never before had she witnessed her own father so frail. She began to absorb what had just occurred and broke down, sobbing uncontrollably.

Hospital Run 2020

Georgia lit a cigarette outside the hospital, leaned against the wall, and looked at Jake. His eyes fell down upon her. "I'll remember that for the rest of my days," he said.

"So sorry! It's not something I will erase from my mind in a hurry, either." She swallowed hard as though pushing the memory to the pit of her stomach. Jake placed the heel of his boot against the wall and leaned back. He took her hand in his. "He'll be fine… don't worry."

They exchanged a glance. Georgia drew heavily on a cigarette and blew smoke down to her feet.

"I thought you didn't smoke?"

"I don't…I got it from him –" She pointed to a man in jogging bottoms smoking grass, his trouser legs tucked into his socks. Jake looked down at his own trainers and ripped T-shirt.

"I can't think why he would do something like that. He was fine before I left him."

Jake placed his arm around her. "Sometimes, you just don't know what's happening in people's heads. I mean, look at that bloke; what the hell is he thinking, tucking the bottoms of his Trackies into his socks like that?"

Georgia smiled. "He would never do something like that, though… I just don't understand."

"I thought my fashion sense was shit, but fucking hell!"

Georgia laughed again. "I'm talking about my dad!"

"I know you are…" he ruffled her hair and kissed her cheek. You know what's baffling me? Not why he did it, but how did he do it? There were no ladders near him or anything to climb up. Fucking mystery!"

Georgia began to cry. "It's my fault!" She threw both hands up to her face. "It's all my fault."

Various reasons for Len trying to take his own life were battling inside her mind. "We had an argument."

"It's not your fault. Stop blaming yourself."

"I accused him of killing my mum with his drinking and roving eye. A daughter should never say a thing like that to her own Dad! I totally humiliated him! I never should have said that!"

"Come here" Jake moved closer to her, pulling her into his chest.

Georgia choked back tears and lowered her voice; her tone was hushed. "In the ambulance, he kept saying a child did it… a little girl when he came around. He said she tried to kill him."

Jake looked down at her, shocked. "A little girl…Is that what he said…?"

"…No idea what he was talking about?"

Noting Jake's evident pique of interest, she blotted her tears on the back of her sleeve and glanced up at him. "Do you know what he meant by that?"

Jake pulled her close to him again and buried her head deep into his chest.

"No, I don't… Ask him when he's feeling better." As he held Georgia securely within his warm, loving embrace, his stomach twisted in knots; his conscience no longer contained within the island that was the pit of his stomach, the lucid memory of the child he saw on the Peaks only days earlier had privately haunted him ever since. The very mention of the word ghost eroded his disbelief, like a dark mire lapping at the shores, reclaiming every inch of his repudiation, which had taken twenty-eight years to erect around his fear of the subject. To his prior knowledge, the murky existence of such matters was waded through only by priests and lunatics who believe they are privy to a secret world beyond death. Only they had a much deeper understanding and intuitiveness on the matter, and good luck to them. Perhaps, Jake said inwardly, it is yet another conversation to be had with Len if the opportunity should arise for a private audience with the man.

Run Rebecca Run 2020

When Rebecca awoke in the morning, she stretched a leg across the bed but didn't bother rolling over to see if Mark was asleep beside her. Relieved to discover he wasn't, she rose quickly, put on her faded Persian silk dressing gown, walked to the window and peered down at the forecourt below, where Mark's pillar box red Audi would typically have been parked, but there was no car, which meant he was already out somewhere. She looked out over the expanse of glorious Derbyshire countryside for one last time and sighed. A sea of golden-green fields washed back and forth in the breeze.

The view from that window always took her breath. She counted her lucky stars each morning since the day she had first arrived at the house. Mark would wrap himself around her and whisper sweet nothings in her ear, planning romantic ways of spending their day together, breakfast in bed, coffee by the pool, a drive to the lakes, lunch at South Side's Tennis Club, followed by long sexy afternoons with hand-rolled Belgian truffles, pink champagne and freshly laundered silk sheets. It had been that way for at least eighteen months of their five-year marriage, but for some reason, unbeknown to her, the relationship took a turn for the worse and slowly began to fizzle in ways it never had done with Jake. Rebecca tiptoed across the hall and checked in on James, who was still sleeping, wrapped beneath his navy-blue rockets, moons and stars duvet that he'd had since he first left her side to sleep in his grown-up bed. She closed the door gently, showered, tied up her hair, leaving it in a high wet messy bun, threw on Jeans and a loose T-Shirt, and then ran through the house collecting oddments, things she thought she might need urgently. She had been packing a few boxes and cases for quite some time and had managed to hide sufficient amounts of clothing and essential items, along with a fair amount of cash, which she literally hid under the bed, around the house and in places where she thought Mark would never find them.

She had been planning this day for quite some time, but part of her had hoped things would improve and that Mark would somehow change. However, it was only getting worse over time, and now it had reached the point where life in the house with him was unbearable. The incident with the cellar had been, for her, the last straw. There was no way she was about to stand by and allow him to humiliate her and hurt James in the same way he had been treating her of late.

Recently, there had been bruises, scrapes and bumps on James, leaving her with growing suspicion. She knew James was hiding something from her, his behaviour had gotten increasingly more disruptive, and she feared that whatever he was hiding, he was too afraid to share with her.

The cellar incident had to be the catalyst, confirming that her suspicions were justified. Inwardly, she could still hear her child's cry for help and couldn't believe how long she had stood by and allowed it to take place. How could she let Mark treat her only child in that way? She had to get out of there quickly before he grew suspicious of her. She had planned to use the open day at the Hamlet, which Jake had invited James to attend, as an excuse to leave with James alone. The open day at the Hamlet gave her the best reason to go out. And now, especially with Mark out of the house, she could quickly get away without raising any suspicions. The car was packed; she had to find the papers for the Traction Engine, which she had promised to return to Jake. The documents also served as an excuse to get closer to him. She needed help, Jake's help. He was the only person she could trust with the security of their child.

*

Jake stood stiffly with his arms folded, looking out of the kitchen window that overlooked the walled gardens at the rear. Behind him, cupboard doors slammed, and pots and pans clattered in the background as the kitchen staff prepared for the special event.

"We'll change things here for the better," Jake explained to his brother. Seething at Jake's obdurate reluctance to move with him to the States, Joshua looked around at the kitchen staff who were everywhere. "What would be the point of trying to change things here when it can only get worse?" He said, pushing pieces of cold ham into his mouth.

Mrs Winters, a plump Liverpudlian woman in her forties, came towards Jake carrying cartons of chopped vegetables and homemade soup she had already prepared. Smiling through crooked teeth, she nodded at the fridge, "Open left side, will ya, love."

Jake spun and flung the door open, then waited as she pushed each carton into their respective shelving space.

"We don't need this stupid open day!" Joshua was saying. "We're leaving for the States soon."

Jake was embarrassed. "We are all doing what we can to make this place work, Joshua." Overhearing their conversation, Mrs Winters gave Jake an odd look, then waddled off to collect more things to stuff into the fridge.

"Who's we?" Joshua said, slapping his thighs repeatedly, clearly growing anxious. Thanks to Joshua's outburst, a chorus of me and me came from the ensemble of chefs and waiting staff who were all busy going about their work, all now aware that the special day might be their last.

"Well. Georgia's using social media to get us where we need to be. She's put posts everywhere on country magazines, cycling groups, walking groups and every social platform, and we have Martin, whatever he's called, coming to open the event."

There was a rise of Oohs and Ahhs from the women in the kitchen.

"Are you still refusing to agree with me? Forget her, I said!"

"Forget who?" Jake felt like a spare part in the room. He had promised to help but wasn't quite sure how. He began tying up a brimming bin bag and carried it off round the back.

"That lass!"

"That lass? Who, Georgia?" He opened the back door.

"Come on," Joshua was pleading now. "Live with me in the States; you'd be insane not to."

"And where would we be without him?" Mrs Winters said, returning four boxes of chocolate gateaux that had been sliced, and were now ready to be put back in the fridge. "Open the t' other side, make yourself useful?" She said to Joshua.

Jake nodded to his brother to do Mrs Winters' bidding, then slipped out with the bin bag.

Joshua breathed heavily, went to the fridge, flung open the right side that contained dairy products and cakes and waited for her to slide the boxes in before reaching in over her to procure a carton of milk. Looking around for a glass, he spotted one on a tray by the dishwasher, poured milk into it, and then returned the carton to the fridge.

"Look," Jake said, coming back through the back door, "this has to be regarded as the right thing for me to do. You're moving to the States, not me!"

He unravelled a fresh bag, pushed it into the bin, and then quickly washed his hands at the basin. "You have to learn to take other people's views into account."

He shook his hands dry. "I'm obliged to do the right thing by people who rely on me, like all these guys."

"Like who?"

"Like my son, this lot, Gran and Georgia!"

"Her again, what is it with you and this girl? You don't owe her anything! You barely know her!"

"Ssh, please. Georgia is the future for me – a new beginning."

"Excuse me, love, can you just find the whisk? It's under that counter somewhere in a container."

Jake bent and began looking beneath the stainless-steel counters.

"I've worked so long to make many worlds better for other people; it's never just been for me. Coming from this background working with Mum and Dad in pubs and bars, it looked like all I had to offer was these hands. It's an Italian thing, I think. It goes back to Gran's days in the Circus with Grandad Jack and old Leo; it's always been about graft and family. It's a Franconi thing!"

"La Famiglia!" Mrs Winters chimed out mockingly. Jake handed her the whisk. "Ta, love!"

Jake shouted over the noise of the whisk as Mrs Winters set to work on the fresh cream.

"It's the most important aspect of my life, Joshua, to provide and support. I'm just being straight with you, bro!"

"So, I'm no longer family to you then?"

Joshua began washing his hands in the basin, lathering them with 5mils of hand sanitiser. Jake secretly despaired at the waste and cost but said nothing.

"You are, mate, of course, but you need autonomy and independence. Even Italian kids move away from their family ties."

"Imagine if your theory rang true today, especially amongst the elderly, like the first-generation Italian migrants?"

"You mean like the Franconi lot?"

"Well, yes, like Grandad Jack, had he still been alive today."

"Yeah, well, he died in the war, so what's your point?"

"I know, but what would he have said if he knew we had put his wife in a care home?"

"It couldn't have been avoided; she's one hundred and five years old, Josh! And with mum's deteriorating health, we had no other option, even though I hate Care Homes and still view them negatively; it's in my DNA, but what's your point?"

"Times have changed. That's my point. Not even granny Faye resisted being placed in a care home."

"No, she didn't, neither did she apply any of this Gypsy morality pressure and guilt thing you're putting on me, now! Unless you're deliberately trying to be a hypocrite, I don't get your point?"

"What I'm saying, Granny Faye, didn't complain because she knew what was good for us!"

"You mean she didn't want to become a burden? Oh, and, by the way, you shouldn't have laid any of that bull shit on Georgia yesterday."

"Her again…"

"Whatever you said the other day was bang out of order, mate. If she ever became family, just saying like, she'll play the most crucial role in your life, she'll be the only person creating cohesion and a sense of belonging for you in our family, if ever you want to return to the UK. So, don't go around deeply wounding those who may be all you have at the end of the day. Look, go to America or go in the Army, whichever. Start a life for yourself. You'll be happy in the States, working on your Engines and doing whatever you love, and you might even meet a nice girl." He tapped Joshua on the shoulder and then wished he hadn't. "Sorry, mate."

Joshua recoiled dramatically.

"A nice American woman, and with that accent, man, come on!"

"I prefer middle European."

Jake laughed and shook his head. "What! You've thought about this already; why, you dirty little thing!"

Anyway, if you decide to go in the Army instead, I won't be able to come with you, now will I?"

The boys glanced at each other; Jake laughed and shook his head again. "Mate, honest, you crack me up; middle European women, I never thought you had it in you. "

Mrs Winter's popped her head around the door. "There's a bit of a traffic jam going on outside; I just thought I'd say."

"Come on then, mate, let's get this show on the road!"

Jake opened the door and went out to find a long stream of cars, jeeps, vans and trucks, some heading through the gates towards the Hamlet, those who had already arrived were parked or parking up, and one or two vehicles had somehow found their way beneath the clock tower and were trying to park in the walled garden.

"Hey, hey, where you going? Not in there, mate! There's plenty of parking out here! What the fuck are they doing…?"

Jake helped him reverse back into the courtyard and wondered how they'd managed to get through in the first place.

"Mrs Winters!" Jake yelled into the kitchen. "Get some chairs across here for me, will ya! Just block off this entrance before another joker tries that!"

Joshua was now with Mrs Winters, finding chairs to place in a neat row across the arch below the clock tower, while Jake went over to organise the rest of the oncoming traffic. Once the first car from the convoy had passed through the iron gates, a bird decided to run out in front of the second vehicle; it changed its mind, ran back towards the rhododendron bushes, then changed its direction and ran back across the road again. The second car, a brand new shiny black Mercedes GLC, hit the panicking creature full-on, leaving a plume of feathers and guts in its wake. Two guys, falling about in hysterics, staggered out of the car and inspected the murder scene.

"Jesus Christ, man! What the fuck!"

"Stupid fucking bird!"

"Good job, it was only a pigeon and not a stag."

"Grouse, actually." Jake rolled his eyes and walked over with his hand extended. "Hi, welcome! You must be –"

"I'm Martin, Martin Spalding…"

"And this is…?"

"Nathan…"

"Oh right. You're er—"

"G's ex, yeah. I am!"

362

"Well, hey, hiya. I was going to say friend…but okay. Nice to meet you, Nathan."

"Hey, sorry about this mess; this stupid fucking pigeon just ran out!"

"Yeah, Grouse tend to do that. So, Nathan. You're the Engineer, Georgia's…."

"Georgia's ex! Yeah, mate."

"I was going to say Georgia's soldier friend."

Nathan almost shot to attention. "101 Royal Engineer Regiment EOD&S, South East London!"

Jake nearly laughed. "Georgia did mention your name a time or two." He turned to shake Martin's hand again. "And yours too, Martin; great to meet you, man. Listen, I'll get Josh to show you around; this is Joshua, by the way, my brother. Where is he? Oh, there he is, Josh mate!"

Joshua walked over, mumbling under his breath about the prick who had tried to park in the walled garden.

"Josh, this is Martin Saunders and er…"

"Nathan!"

"It's Martin Spalding, actually. Hi Josh. Pleased to meet you." He leaned in to shake Joshua's hand.

Joshua threw his fists up towards him.

"He doesn't do handshaking, sorry about that! Forgot to say."

"I thought you were gonna swing at me, mate…." Martin laughed, and then suddenly, as if from nowhere, Nathan's fists were out before him like two striking cobras.

"W-a-a-a-y! What's going on? That's a bit belated and unnecessary; come on, dude, what's up with you?"

"Oh, sorry, automatic reaction, sorry. It happens sometimes. I was on tour recently in Afghanistan."

Bosh! Josh swung a punch, thumping Nathan right in the face. His nose burst like an orange, splatting blood all over the place.

"Fucking hell! Josh! What's going on?"

"Automatic reaction, sorry." Joshua was clearly taking the piss.

Jake wanted to laugh, but Nathan squared up to Joshua, and all hell broke out. Chest pumped, blood dripping from his nose, he began snarling abuse, his aggression spitting out like bullets from a machine gun, covering everyone in splats of fresh blood and spit. Seething, he growled like a Neanderthal, with no concern for his broken nose, just a desire to rip Josh apart. Joshua didn't care much about the empty threats; his only problem was washing the dirty bastard's blood from his hands and face.

Martin and Jake both jumped in and pulled the two guys apart.

"This was a mistake, coming here today, clearly! I should never have brought Nathan with me, sorry. Tell Georgia I'll ring her, yeah!"

"Yeah, sorry about that, mate. God! I don't know what happened."

"Go on, go get washed up, you daft bastard," Jake said, turning to his brother before walking back towards the Hamlet. "What did you do that for?" Josh leaned his arm over his brother's shoulder and laughed.

"I didn't fucking like him!"

Jake watched Martin struggling to get his mate back in the car from the kitchen window and was still working on getting Nathan back in the car when Joshua reappeared, washed and redressed. "Shall I give him a hand?"

"No-o-o!" Jake was on the phone with Georgia. "Look, Georgia. I've apologised to Martin. Yes, and the Neanderthal. Sorry, I mean that fucking Nathan, what the hell-!" Jake burst out laughing when he heard Georgia give a little laugh. "I'll ring ya later."

"Where is she?" Joshua said, drying his ears on a towel.

"Still at the hospital with her dad. They're discharging him today, so, with any luck, she'll come later. I'll see them after the event, and ask Len about the Engine, yeah?"

"I know loads of people who've bitten the bullet due to PTSD. It's the mind, man. It's our worst enemy."

"What are you talking about?"

"I've been thinking. I reckon that guy has it, PTSD. Anyway, look…"

"What is it?"

"His tooth. It was stuck in the back of my hand."

"Err, fucking hell, Josh. Throw it in the bin, mate."

"I'm here to help."

"With what?"

"Anything. With Georgia, if you need it?"

"Okay…" Jake was gobsmacked. "Okay, mate. Great, well, I er…need to get on, so, help Mrs Winters in here, will you? And don't go punching anyone else's lights out unless I give the order, yeah!"

A stout man stood at the door. He was just about to knock when Jake opened it.

"Jake?"

"Yeah, I'm Jake…"

"Pleased to meet you. John, John Hurton, the security guy!"

"Hi, yeah, of course. Pleased to meet you. Thanks for coming out yesterday to get familiar with the gig. Sorry I missed you. My girlfriend's Dad was rushed to the hospital, so it's all been up in the air."

"No problem. Looks like I should have gotten here earlier. Do you want me to sort that out?"

"Are they still out there?" Jake spun around to see Nathan finally climbing back into the black Mercedes.

"What happened there?"

"Hah, just a bit of a misunderstanding."

"Yes, well, as I explained on the phone, as a leading supplier of event security, we understand the role you're expected of us today, so don't worry. I'll be making sure your guests, staff and performers have a successful and safe event, and that kind of thing won't happen again today, not on my watch."

Jake watched as Martin's black Mercedes sped off towards the electric gates, which weren't entirely opening fast enough for his exit. "Great," Jake said, half-smiling to himself. "I leave you to it then?"

"Absolutely, sir."

"Feel free to use the restaurant today. It's open all day, so you're all welcome."

"They'll be too busy for that, and they all have their own drinks and lunch, so it won't be necessary, but thanks anyway."

"Jake!" Recognising the voice instantly, Jake spun on his heels to greet her, "Becky, hey! … James, hiya matey!"

He knelt to greet his son with open arms. "Alright, buddy?" Smiling warmly, he folded his arms around his boy's tiny frame. "Missed you mate."

"What's up?" Without another word, Jake knew there was something wrong. All Rebecca could do was nod.

"Is everything alright?"

"Can he stay with you tonight?"

"'Course he can!"

"No, I mean, both of us?"

"Yeah, why, what's up?" Rebecca could hardly look at him. "Has something happened?"

She did a half-turn, whispering over her shoulder into his ear, "I've left him."

"What you've done that for?"

"It's been coming a while. "sighing, Rebecca quickly reached into her bag and pulled out an envelope.

"The papers—for the Engine."

"Oh, wow, great! Thanks! This really means a lot. I'm going to sell it to help Joshua to help get him settled in the States!" He rubbed his hands over his face and gave out a little groan, "So, what's been going on then?"

"Shh, let's not...not now."

"Hey matey, look, it's the Circus."

A vibrantly painted convoy was approaching through the iron gates; wagons were painted to replicate an old-fashioned early 19th-century Circus with a carefully orchestrated stream of horse-drawn wagons and carriages. At its flanks, a modest number of otherworldly people danced along to shimmering trumpeters in an explosion of petals, fluttering scarves and banners. The fanfare was not just a spectacle for a grand entrance into the Hamlet but a celebration; a festival of life and art, all methodically rehearsed with the precision of a Roman Legion returning home triumphant from battle. The whole ensemble was strategically choreographed for the sole purpose of stimulation; to arouse the imagination. Designed strategically to stir up misalliance in the souls of even the most conservative of village folk.

Trailing behind the procession were elaborately dressed horses and carriages decorated in beautiful bright fabrics, trimmed exotically with ribbons of red and green, golden silks and laces woven in a silvery gossamer thread. A line of walkers and cyclists dressed in Lycra followed on slowly behind. Comic acts and fire eaters took up the rear, bounding in with juggling tricks and cartwheels. A few children with parents were incredibly intrigued to discover where the excitement was taking them.

Bare-chested, sun-baked Circus men blew kisses to adoring women as they all came from the kitchen and craft shops to see them strutting by like peacocks. Exotically dressed women in silver bangles and amethyst necklaces danced alongside mysterious carriages, showering the narrow, cobbled drive with biodegradable confetti. Long swishing skirts seductively reveal smooth, toned calves and jingling bells about delicate ankles, drawing interested men from the

Mill, craft centre, cafe and workshops. The Circus, graceful, mysterious and skilled, elaborate and explosively introduced itself to the High Peaks Hamlet, bringing excitement and the anticipation of a day. Once the Circus had established its allotted performance space, people began milling around the field, waiting for them to set up. Jake was happy to see people behaving as intended. The staggered arrival of the attractions had allowed time for the public to hit the cafe and restaurant but not meet and greet the famous Martin Spalding as they anticipated; many wondered who the hell he was, and some did ask questions to that effect. Most people just had a wander around the many workshops taking place around the Hamlet. It was all going nicely to plan.

*

The rest of the morning passed with little opportunity for Rebecca to speak to Jake privately. Leaving James to enjoy his father's attention alone, she wandered around the Hamlet. She had checked her phone a million times for fear of the many screaming voice messages she knew would be lined up waiting for her ear, but there were none. In her mind, Rebecca worried that Jake would not help her and wasn't even sure if she should spend the night at the Hamlet.

She saw Jake and James a few times walking and laughing, and on the last occasion, she saw them going into the kitchen, so she took it upon herself to follow them.

"Mrs Winters, do you have something James can eat now? There's a huge queue in the cafe."

"Is there? Oh, wonderful! Yes, of course! Now, let's see." She opened the fridge on the left, which Jake knew was full of cakes and cream.

"Yeah, I think he needs something more nutritious," he said. "His mother is around somewhere. We'll get into trouble if she catches him eating crap. You can have ice cream after lunch, mate, yeah?"

'Well then, what can we find? Come with me, young man…?" Taking James by the hand, Mrs Winters led him off to the dining room, allowing the swing doors between the two rooms to waft closed behind her.

Rebecca peered moments later around the kitchen door, searching for James and Jake, her face drawn and worried.

Jake, who was now busy editing the week's kitchen rota, looked up. "Alright?"

Cautiously looking around to see if he was alone, she stepped inside.

"I shouldn't say anything, but I know I can trust you. Where's James?"

"Oh, Mrs Winters took him for lunch. Coffee?"

"Yes, please."

Jake rose to put the kettle on. He prepared two mugs of instant coffee and a couple of packets of Lotus Biscuits.

"I do have cash. How much is it?"

Jake winked. "We only take Card."

Rebecca let out a long sigh. "Oh, I can't use Card. Mark will see the purchase on his phone and know exactly where to find me."

"I'm only joking." Jake laughed and handed her the steaming cup of hot coffee. "Wow, it's that bad, eh? So, why have you left him?"

"God, yes…" She walked around the long silver bench in the centre of the kitchen and sat on a stool by the back door. She dropped her bag on the floor, pulled her top down to cover her hips, folded her arms, then leant over towards him and peered at his laptop.

"So, you've really left him then?" Jake said again, closing the laptop down.

"I had to, for James' sake."

"What! Why?"

"I don't like how Mark has been treating him."

Jake jumped up. "Why, what's been going on…?"

Rebecca shrugged, and her eyes dropped to the coffee. "It's not been good." She swallowed, her eyes rising to meet his. He saw tears welling, so he looked away, slightly embarrassed for her. Rebecca sniffed, swallowed back tears and sipped from the hot mug.

"If I find out he's been hurting that kid, I swear to fucking God!"

Rebecca laid her hand on his arm. "Don't worry, we're not going back."

Joshua breezed into the kitchen bringing in a strong gust of fresh air behind him. "They're touching everything. I keep telling them to look, don't fucking touch! Why is she here?"

Rebecca moved away from Jake, wrapped her hands around the mug of coffee and leaned against the eight-ringed cooker.

"She's brought the papers for your Engine, look. They're in my laptop case. You can collect it any day now, just need to clear it with Len."

"It's about time!"

"I think thanks are in order."

"I think not. She should thank me for not calling the cops."

Jake laughed and shook his head. "Cops! He thinks he's in New York already. Look, mate, we're just in the middle of something; would you mind just —"

Josh took a packet of Lotus Biscuits from Rebecca's saucer and opened it. "Is that why Mark's outside! He swearing and shouting."

"What!" Jake bolted for the door. "Where is he?"

"Oh, for fuck's sake, no…!" Rebecca slammed down the mug of coffee and followed.

"He's gone now!" Josh said. Taking the envelope from Jake's briefcase. "Oh, he said he's taking James with him. He told Mrs Winters to do one—"

Jake collided with Mrs Winters at the door. "A man just took little James, dragged him off like he was nothing more than a rag, said he was his dad…but you're his dad?"

"Joshua, get security! Get them to lock down the gate. Rebecca, call him, tell him to bring him back, now!"

Jake ran over the yard towards the security pavilion; his phone buzzed. "Nikki…yeah?"

"Jake! Hi. I have Granny Faye with me. I was bringing her to the open day, but she's insisting I take her to see Leo."

"Who's Leo?"

"Georgia's Dad."

"Oh, Len!"

"She keeps calling him Leo. She's adamant; what should I do?"

"Take her! Nikki, there's an issue here at the Hamlet; I've got to go, love, sorry. Anyway, it's a good job you're taking her there. Keep her occupied, yeah. Don't bring her here, for God's sake, not yet; we have a situation, okay?"

"Okay, I'll take her to High Oakham. Is Georgia there?"

"She should be home by now. Look Nikki, gotta go."

"Okay, see ya. Wait! If you see Mark's car, give me a shout, will ya?"

"Why, what's happening?"

"I gotta go Nikki. Just let me know if you see him."

"Okay."

High Oakham Cottage Revisited 2020

"Knock, knock, may I come in?"

Pushing open the door uninvited, Faye leant on a white stick and waited to be asked inside. Clumsily, she grabbed the doorframe with her free hand while trying to place her walking stick in a safe place for support. She looked over at a Len, a tired man who looked like he had seen much better days. He glanced up from his seat beside the fire, where he sat reading and drinking tea with a fleece throw draped over his knees.

"Now, now, who do we have here then?" Faye said mockingly as she began to shuffle over the threshold and walk towards him. Nikki, following behind, steadied her great grandmother a little and smiled at Georgia as she appeared from the kitchen, wiping her hands on a towel.

"Hiya G!"

"Hello?" Len said quizzically as he rose slowly from his easy chair. He looked at Georgia for some indication as to who these people were.

"Can we help you?"

Faye laughed loudly. "You were a mere child this big when I saw you last."

Still trying to place the woman, Len stepped forward, offering a shaky, fragile hand. "I'm sorry, have we met?"

Georgia laughed and wiped a stray tear from her cheek. "Don't you know who this is, Dad?"

"I'm afraid I don't. Sorry!"

Faye indicated for him to sit. "Please don't get up" Len looked to Georgia to explain. "It's no good looking at her."

Georgia smiled reassuringly at her father and then closed the door behind them. She waited with her hands clenched excitedly for the penny to drop.

"You know who I am; you've just forgotten," Faye said.

"Can I take your coat?" Georgia hurried over to offer assistance.

Len glanced over his spectacles. "Sorry, I just can't seem to place you. Where do I know you from-?"

"I'll keep my coat on, dear; I feel the cold." Faye laughed again and let out a deep sigh. "From this very room, as a matter of fact," she said in response to Len's question. "My goodness, it's not changed a bit! Do you mind?" She was flopping into the chair opposite Len's before anyone had time to respond.

"No, no course, please, do sit." Len looked at Georgia again as he turned to sit opposite the old woman.

Faye let out another deep, long sigh before sinking back into the armchair. Peering over the rim of her lenses, she studied Len, then removed them from the tip of her nose and tucked them away carefully in the pocket of her blue-hooded parka. "There! Know me now?" She lifted her head deliberately for Len to look better at her. "Well? Do you remember me?" She raised both eyebrows in anticipation of his response. "Hmm?"

Len shook his head and rubbed his hands over his mouth. "I'm… I'm afraid I don't. I really am sorry."

"Well, let's see." She turned to Nikki and pulled her forward by the wrist. "This here; this is my great-granddaughter, Nikki."

Nikki was gently coaxed out from her safe zone behind the armchair. "Hi. Pleased to meet you, Mr Franconi!"

Georgia smiled and gave a little laugh. "Oh, and this girl, your daughter, knows my Great Grandson, Jake, very well, or so I hear. Is that right, dear?"

"This is Nikki, Dad, the girl I told you about from the Travellers? Your alright, Nikki?"

"Not bad, G, you?"

Georgia nodded and smiled at Faye.

"Of course, you don't know Nikki," Faye was still reassuringly to Len, "but you know her mother, my late daughter, Clara? Ring any bells?"

Len's facial expression remained blank.

"And –" Faye said, turning to Georgia to shed light, "Now, I hear your lovey Georgia is a very good friend with my Great Grandson, Jake!"

"Yeah, Gran, you said that already."

Len looked at Georgia, trying desperately to connect the dots.

"Who, I believe, you have met. My Great Grandsons Jake and his brother Joshua live up at the Hamlet. Do you know it? Do you know the place?"

Len scratched his head. "I know the boys. They did a few jobs around here …and they read palms too, by all accounts."

"Dad, they were only messing with me. They don't read palms, not really!"

"Well, I don't know anything about that, but you won't remember Jake, Josh or Nikki. And you certainly won't remember them growing up because you'd left this place years before any one of them was even born, but, like I said, you used to play with my Clara. God rest her soul, right here in this very room. God bless her!"

Everyone proceeded to look about the room in silence. "Your mother, Amy…."

Len's eyes shot up to Faye. He nodded emphatically. "Hmm?

"She knew me. She was my sister-in-law, and for the best time of my life, she was my best friend. I, my dear, am your aunty. I'm your Aunty Faye! I'm Faye Franconi!"

"Oh, my bloody good God!" Len jumped up. "Of course, you are…Aunty Faye! Well, well, well, well, well! I never…!"

"Ah, so you do remember me, see?"

"Yes, of course, I remember you!"

"We all lived together in this house, you, your mother and I until she left with Leo, my brother-in-law. For the best part of your infancy, your mum and I were land girls in 1941 during the war; you were only a nipper then. We farmed this land together with our bare hands. We made a good team and did a good job of it, your mum and I! Well, like I said, that was before Leo came on the scene. He was a triplet, you know? There were three, all boys! And I was married, Jack. He never made it home from the war, unfortunately."

Faye opened her mouth and shut it again. She sighed heavily. "Danielle, well, he died in the great tragedy." There was a long pause before her tone changed up a gear. "…And so, when Leo returned home after the war, naturally, he came looking for me and got taken up by your mum. In every sense of the word, my dear Amy, what a lady she was. What I would have done to be even an inch of the woman she was."

"So, I lived here in this house until I bought the Hamlet."

"You'd be around three years old, I imagine. I went on to live at the Hamlet and lost touch with you both, but such is life…."

"Is that when Mum took me to London?"

"That's right, for reasons unbeknown to everyone but your good mother."

"For school, I suspect?"

"Most likely, you were a bright boy, and your mother always wanted the best for you. It all seems like yesterday to me. You would have been around ten when you left us?"

"You just said he was three, Grandma, not ten."

Len nodded. "If my memory serves me right, I was about three or four, but memories of my childhood here are all terribly vague. I didn't even realise I'd already lived in this house. So, I actually grew up here?"

"Strange you have no memory of it…."

"My mother wouldn't share any information about my life before London—this house—growing up here. It's like the whole thing never existed to her. I honestly don't know why she never shared any of that knowledge with me."

"No, but I supposed your mother had reasons for not wanting to preserve those memories. She didn't tell you anything?"

"Nothing. And there are no photos, no documentation—nothing."

"Ah well, those were very different days back then. I hate to be the bearer of bad news regarding your real identity; sorry if it all seems vague."

"Bad news…?"

"Well, Nikki says you think Leo was your father…?"

"Gran!"

"Oh, should I have not mentioned that?"

"I don't think so…no, maybe not!" Nikki shook her head at Georgia. "Sorry."

"I'm just trying to shed some light…."

"I'm sure Dad would love to know the truth, wouldn't you, Dad?"

"Well, not quite sure how much truth I need to know, but it would be good to hear about my life here."

"Oh, I remember it all. I can tell you everything, warts and all!"

"Gran, honestly!"

"Of course, yes, please tell me whatever you know, Aunty Faye; I'd love to hear it from you. But I think I did wonder if Leo was my real father."

"Well, that much is at least true; he wasn't."

Despite the roaring fire, the air was still and chilled. Faye shuffled in her chair and sat forward.

"You know, your mother didn't have a great start in life, but I'm sure perhaps at least you already know that much?"

"No, I didn't, but carry on."

"Well, truth be known, your conception wasn't... let's say... a pleasant experience for her."

"She was raped, you mean...?"

Faye sniffed, "Sorry, is this a good time to expose you to all this?" Anxiously twisting the rings on her fingers, she looked to Georgia for permission to continue.

"He wants to know."

She took in a deep breath and sat forward. "Your father was, in fact, my husband. I know how bad that sounds, but...."

There was an audible gasp from everyone in the room, but no one dared question what she had just revealed or wished for her to repeat it. Instead, there was an exchange of silent glances between them all.

"Jack, my first husband, Nikki's Great grandad, was, let's just say, of a violent nature. He was a Gypsy, so he liked his boxing, as did they all...and he was a Circus performer, one of the first Italian immigrants to bring their show to England—an exceptional Equestrian performer, one of the best in the business in fact, and not a bad aerial acrobat either, which is how we met. He was a marvel in the Circus, handsome, but let's just say he didn't fit in socially; he struggled, like most Circus folks. Life for Jack was, at times, a little overwhelming. Whenever things didn't quite work out, where most would try to sort things out, Jack would just take off—disappear for days. No one ever knew where to. I guess now there would be some label to describe his affliction, some kind of syndrome, spectrum, genetic disposition perhaps, anyway, back then people like Jack were just odd—and Jack was strange and gay."

Nostalgia caused Faye to pause momentarily; she stared into the fire briefly, then snapped back with a sharp intake of breath.

"What!" Nikki sat up straight on the arm of the sofa. "Did you just say your husband, my great-grandad was gay?"

"Oh, yes, it wasn't unusual for gay men to marry women back then – lead a double life for peace and quiet, I suspect!"

"Anyway, his relationship with his brothers Leo and Dan, who I am sure you now know, worked together in Circus Franconi?"

Len shrugged. "I had no idea. It was never mentioned to me."

"Well, they had some argument, some kind of discord—"

"You need to explain all the story, Grandma, because I don't think people know what kind of discord you refer to. The discord, you see, was her...." Nikki laughed and pointed at her Great-Grandmother.

Faye sighed. "What can I say? I loved the Franconi boys."

"All of them?" Nikki shook her head and laughed.

"True. Yes, I did love all the Franconi boys, and they loved me. It was an embroilment, let's just say. I danced with the devil; we all did, but Leo was the lord of the dance. That's how it all began, and it all got a little out of hand. Regarding your poor mother, let's just say, Jack, being Jack, took it upon himself to take his revenge on his brother Dan for loving me."

"Wait a minute, wasn't Dan Jack's brother?"

"Yes, that's what I just said, but Dan and I were once in love, well before I married Jack, and before Leo and I were... Oh, never mind...either way, Jack could never live with all that past hanging over us, so to get his revenge, he waited until Dan fell in love, I mean truly fell in love and attacked and raped the girl who he knew would do the most hurt to Dan."

"And that girl was my mother?"

"yes, your poor mother, Amy."

"Oh my God!"

Silently, Len removed his glasses, wiped a tear and pulled his handkerchief from his pocket to wipe his nose before letting out a long sigh.

"Of course, everything spiralled out of control, Leo."

"Indeed..."

"Your great grandad, Jack, joined the army after that. Eventually, they both were drafted; apart from Dan, it was too late for him."

Silence fell in the room as everyone took stock of what they had just learned.

"So, long story short, I ended up here with your mother and the rest you now know."

Len stared at the floor a moment. He had the impression that a great deal of vital information had just been eclipsed from the whole story.

"I never knew that." He turned to Nikki and nodded. "But yes, I did think Leo wasn't my dad; they never married. I never knew how or why I had the same name; I just assumed I'd adopted it from him. But I really don't remember that much of Leo either, so... I guess it doesn't make that much difference to me now. Like Jack and me, Leo was much older than your mother."

"That's right, he was twenty years older."

"Hmm."

So, what happened to Jack? Did you ever find out how he died?"

Somewhere Near Dunkirk May 1940

With a heart hardened in so many ways that no reasonable man living should ever understand and nerves as rigid as steel despite the regimented life he was now leading, Leo slid clumsily through heavy clay in a waterlogged dugout beside a canal somewhere between Louvain and Dunkirk. His boots were so tightly laced he could barely feel his feet. Stopping in a shaft of daylight to light a cigarette, he caught a pair of eyes staring up at him from the darkness.

Leo took a slight step back. "Soz, mate."

A deep, low voice whispered gruffly from beneath a wet trench coat doubling as the windbreaker. "You heard?"

"What's that?"

"They're getting us out."

Leo burped loudly and laughed. "Is that right?" He took another drag and picked a piece of tobacco from his lip. Reluctant to say more for fear of offering false hope to those eyes that appeared to gaze up with such longing through the wind and mud. In Leo's nine months of duty in France and Belgium, it was just yet another child's face that Leo knew for sure he'd never likely see again. Leo drew deeply on his cigarette and handed it to the youth. The lad pushed his arms over his trench coat, sat up and leaned on one elbow. Taking a drag, he flashed a youthful smile and handed it back.

"Frank, the name's Frank!" His voice was clearer now; it sounded hopeful and bright. "Heard they've got some rescue mission planned in Dunkirk?"

"Where are you getting all this intel?" Leo nodded. He took a few more long drags and then flicked the nub into the mud.

"Don't believe everything you hear, mate. I've been here nearly nine months, and I'm still digging fucking holes. Their idea of your rescue is that you'll dig yourself home by the time this fucking war's over... You know all the allied troops, the Belgians and the French are all cut off; we're surrounded by fucking Gerrys!."

Frank laughed, flashing a dead straight line of strong white teeth, instantly confirming to Leo he was a kid no older than eighteen if a day.

"Don't they know we got land creepers now?"

"I don't know about creepers or Brens…." Leo laughed and shook his head. "Gerrys will see them coming long before they'll see your gun! Mate, just divvy up where you're better off. Lay doggo while you've got the chance. My advice—keep your powder dry and your head down. No one here cares if you get the fucker blown off!"

Rubbing the back of his aching neck, Frank laughed. "Funny, my old man told me before I left…." He sat up, put his trench coat on, slapped mud from his knees, and laughed. "Here do you think it's true—my old man told me the French girls are like… right up for it. What do you reckon?"

"Is that so?" Anyone with a sense of humour was alright by Leo. He flipped open his cigarette pack and held it out.

"I like the sound of your old man. If I were you, I'd keep that dick of yours in your pants for now. You never know whose side those lasses are on…this war ain't going to be over for a long-time, mate. They still think we're two opposing fucking armies going bang, bang at each other like it's 19 fucking 14."

Shakily, Frank took a cigarette, placed it in his mouth, and then searched his pockets for a light. Leo reached out and lit it.

A rustling noise from around the sharp curve made the men freeze, acutely aware that someone or something was closing in. Frank stood bolt upright, stunned for a moment, listening intently.

Leo pulled the strap of his rifle over his shoulder, his eyes flashing down at the kid; he drew in a breath and held it in. Waving his hand and touching his lips with a finger, he indicated that the kid remained still.

"Mister Franconi!"

Leo spun around to meet the voice, his physical reaction kicking in moments before his mouth had time to engage. He slammed his rifle down and threw up a salute, Jumping to attention. "Sir. Yes, Sir!"

Frank jumped up to follow suit.

Relief washed over Leo, but he showed no such emotion. The badge was a solid six feet or more who spoke softly, like a real English gent, despite looking as though he might be a man made of iron. Leo thought this unusual for a man his size, especially since he was a Scott stuck in a shit pit with a good thirty or more English men.

"You are one of the Macaroni brothers?"

"Franconi sir. Leo Franconi."

"Franconi, yes, yes, of course. Had a convoy drive in this morning, Mister Macaroni!"

"Sir?" Leo found himself clenching his fist, wanting to do nothing more than take a swing at the bastard, yet at the same time, he found himself strangely converging to the Sergeant's accent. Something he'd noticed himself doing a lot while in the confines of the trench with a band of men from every region in Blighty.

"Spoke to a chap who reckons they were driving towards the Channel when they were stopped by the Military Police at a crossroads to allow movement the other way."

"Sir?"

"The boys had been given no information about where they were supposed to be going, other than to follow the vehicle in front, but when they were allowed to continue, they had no vehicle to follow, so they ended up here, lucky, eh?."

"Lucky, Sir? Not so sure about that."

"Could have been worse, Private; they could have ended up in enemy hands."

"Aye, yes, of course, Sir! So…none of these lads had any idea where they were supposed to be going, you say, Sir?'

"Seems not!"

"Well, no disrespect Sir, but if they don't know where they are going, how the fucking hell am I supposed to know…." Leo smiled smugly. The Sergeant nodded; no man's fool, he knew only too; well, the banter was for the sheer benefit and entertainment of the young lad present, but it was more than his job was worth to let it slide.

"Very funny, private! I was informing you of this, Macaroni, because this fellow goes by the title Lance Corporal Giacomo Franconi! Ring any bells?"

"Jack! Yes Sir."

"Ah, thought that might be interesting to you, Macaroni. Your brother by chance?"

"Jack is my brother, Sir. Sir, where is he, Sir?"

"We don't fucking know where he is!" The youth blurted, then instantly recoiled. "Sorry, sir."

"Injured, I'm afraid. An error of identification as it happens. Civilian fire from the rooftops in Louvain, mistakenly taking out the driver of one of our 15 cwt trucks and twelve men, wrongly believed to be the enemy. You'll be glad to hear that your brother was one of the lucky ones."

"Fuckin' hell!" Leo threw his rifle over his shoulder. "Permission to go to him, Sir?"

"Yes, yes, of course, granted, go! Have a quick word before he is taken to a hospital."

"Hospital? Here in Belgium, Sir?"

"No, you'll be pleased to hear in the UK."

"Sir! Does that mean he's very seriously injured, like…?"

"Ordinarily, yes, he would need to be quite bad to warrant a ticket home, but as his brother, you're one of the lucky ones who gets to be in charge of taking him home to Blighty!"

"Me, Sir?"

Frank's eyes shot open. "Fucking hell, mate. You lucky bastard! …Sorry, Sir."

"And you can bugger off an' all, Private."

"Sir? Me Sir?"

"Aren't you one of the Koyli lights?"

"Light Infantry, Sir! Yes Sir! Frank Burton 7510!"

"Then you'd better make haste, Burton, before you miss your boat."

"Boat, Sir? We're going home…?"

"German forces have trapped the British Expeditionary Force; there's no point in denying this; the remaining Belgian troops and three French field armies are trapped along the northern coast. General Viscount Gort has ordered all troupes on the ground to withdraw to the channel; Dunkirk is the closest good port."

*

The patter of light rain in the canopy woke the birds earlier than usual; their song grew louder as the sun inched between the leaves and branches as the early dawn mist crept silently around the sleeping camp. A river raged somewhere in the distance as floodwater from the previous night's storm rushed into it from nearby streams and dykes. Frank Burton rubbed his face and leaned against a tree to remove his left boot. Philippe Aaron, an extremely tall, balding Belgian farmer, who always seemed to be awake before everyone else, looked up over a plume of white smoke sputtering from a campfire made up of damp foliage and wet bark. He balanced a pewter mug on a stone in the fire and hoped it would warm its watery content.

"Morning," he said brightly—too brightly for Frank's liking.

Frank nodded but said nothing, just sniffed and spat into the earth beside him. Philippe had offered his services back in Lille when he discovered King Leopold III had surrendered to the Germans. He looked down where Frank had spat, looked up again and smiled.

"Fuck off," Frank said. He began teasing the tight lace from the eyelet of his other boot. His fingers were so cold and wet that he could barely bend them.

According to Leo, as the story goes, on the morning of 28th May, Philippe read somewhere that Leopold had surrendered to the Germans; the Belgians surrendered because they hoped their country would remain a unified and semi-autonomous state within a German-dominated Europe. Phillippe, like the majority of his countrymen, didn't believe for one minute that this would happen, so distrusting both King and the nation's political agenda, he feared for the future of his country, his family and his livelihood, so he decided to take matters into his own hands. He sent his wife and daughter into the dense forest under the guise of mushroom pickers to approach a camp of infantry Brits hiding in the woods. Phillipe had seen Leo and his men and suspected they were starving and needing supplies. A meeting with Leo was quickly set up, and soon a group of locals and French resistance fighters were procured to guide them to safety using their aids and contacts.

Philippe took the lead of the mission and announced he would be the best person to guide the men to Dunkirk via some backwater route where it was thought to be free from German troops. He swore no German would ever tread this route.' And for the best part, he was right, but Jack and Frank opposed the intrusion. They had openly pleaded with Leo not to trust them, but Leo felt he had no other choice but to accept Philippe's support, and so he joined the band of men despite their resistance against him. Philippe nodded at the tree where Frank sat, making some garbled comment about it. Frank ignored him, but Philippe was insistent, pointing and mumbling under his breath. When he started laughing, rage boiled in Frank, and he jumped up.

"What! What you looking at...?"

Frank hated the man, didn't like him, didn't want him near him, didn't understand him and certainly didn't trust him.

"What's he on about now?"

He sat again, pulled off his boot, and peeled his sock away from his foot like a second skin. Jack, laid on a stretcher in the back of the lorry, heard the commotion and opened his eyes. Leo, who had also been sleeping, lifted his coat from his head. "He's talking about the tree."

"What fucking tree?"

"The one you're sat under!"

"What's wrong with it...?"

"Dunno." Leo pulled a quarter-sized lump of cheese from his coat pocket and bit down on it, but it was hard, and nothing broke away. He tossed it in the fire and watched it sizzle.

"Noisetier ja!" Philippe stood up, placed his hands on his hips, and beamed at the tree like it was about to take off.

"Noise...ey what? What is he fucking on about now?"

Philippe made a gesture like a squirrel gnawing on nuts.

"I can't fucking stand his charades."

Philippe picked a few fragments from the ground and offered them to Frank.

"I think he's trying to show you something."

"What! What, you daft bastard...?"

"Frankie!" Leo stood up and looked at the pieces of fragments in Philippe's hand. "Hazelnuts!" He placed his pewter mug in the fire next to Philippe's and poured a drop of water into it from a canteen.

"What? There are nuts? Where?"

Frank stood up and stumbled around, trying to put his boot back on while looking for nuts.

"No, no... he's telling you that the tree is a Hazel. There won't be nuts... it's too early for nuts."

"Too fucking early for nuts; you can say that again!" Frank reached for his rifle. "I'm gonna fucking bury the bastard." Leo jumped up and dived up on the gun and swiftly disarmed him.

"It's his fault we missed our fucking rendezvous, the lanky fucking, bald bastard."

"Come on, Frankie mate, the man's kept us alive. You've heard what's happening."

On 24th May, when Leo set out to lead the small convoy of injured troops to Dunkirk, one of the soldiers among the wounded being his own brother Jack, the

382

Belgian, British and French soldiers had all been cut off and surrounded, making all routes incredibly difficult. By the time they reached Dunkirk, the Dynamo operation had already rescued many allied soldiers from the beaches and the harbour. Leo walked off to piss against a tree. Frank watched him go, then broke the silence.

"Winston Churchill called this whole BEF campaign a colossal military disaster, saying the whole root and core and brain of the British Army stranded at Dunkirk would have perished or been captured."

Philippe nodded thoughtfully.

"Where do you get your fucking Intel?" Leo shouted over his shoulder.

"Churchill said the rescue was a miracle, a miracle of deliverance."

"This is what I hear too," Philippe said, nodding.

Leo strolled back through the undergrowth, striding over a few sleeping bodies under trench coats and pieces of plastic sacking. His eyes unseeing, and his thoughts were in turmoil.

Frank picked up a stone and tossed it into the grass. "If all the British have withdrawn, what about us? Eh? What about us!" Philippe watched Leo sit opposite. "Two divisions are remaining still in the south."

"Yeah, I heard that, and a further 40,000 British troops reported to have been left behind in this vicinity alone."

"Fucking hell...So does that mean they're coming back for us then?" Frank's face cleared as relief spread all over it.

"I'd not expect it myself," Leo said.

"I've put the word out," Philippe said, trying to offer comfort and hope.

"So, those lucky bastards who made it back are being hailed as heroes in Blighty?"

"Heroes, who said that?"

Everyone turned to look at the lorry. Jack's voice rang out as though he was sitting beside them. "For what?" He shouted. "It's not over yet. We haven't won... This war is still raging on here for us."

"It's raging on for at least 300,000 or more fellow soldiers out here," Leo shouted back to his unseen brother lying in the lorry.

"Do you reckon we've been forgotten?"

"I don't know, bro."

Frank rummaged through his kitbag, looking for something, anything to eat. "Brits are being rounded up and machine-gunned down like dogs all over. That's what I hear."

"Have some respect, mate. He doesn't need to know that. And Philippe here is risking his neck for us, and no one asked him to do it."

Frank sat back down on his kit. "We're the lost fucking legion of Rome; that's who we are."

Jack lay in the darkness beneath a makeshift canvass sheet. He tried to roll over but couldn't muster the strength. He let out a groan.

A loud crack in the undergrowth made everyone freeze. Everyone grabbed a firearm. Philippe held up his hand. "Shh!" He whistled tunefully and lightly.

Eventually, a reply came back, succinct to his own. There were two further exchanges before a young lad slowly emerged through a cluster of distant elms. He was no older than sixteen and appeared with both hands high above his head, his rifle strung over his shoulder.

Philippe laughed, threw open his arms, and then ran to greet him. "Nephew, my brother's son. I told you he comes!"

"Did he?"

"Dunno, he might have done." Once Leo had ascertained that the visitor to the camp was an ally, he allowed him to share his news.

"Belgian Army surrendered...." The lad said, eyes wide and fearful.

Frank flicked his cigarette into the fire pit. "Tell us something we don't know already...Are we lumbered with two of them now?"

Leo scratched his beard, listening intently. He looked over at the truck where his brother lay beside two more injured soldiers. Jack had developed an infection of sorts and had declined rapidly over the past two days.

"France has lost 24 infantry divisions...six of seven motorised."

"Fucking hell... We're all fucked!"

"Frank, give it a rest, will ya."

"Alan Brooke, he returns to France."

"Brooke's back... in France, well, at least that's something."

"He commands British units, yes?"

"Good, good, yeah, we know him. We're back under command; did you hear that, Frank... Brooke's back?"

Frank, peeling a piece of grass to chew, raised an eyebrow and nodded.

"Okay, okay…now this is sounding promising." Leo began rubbing his hands together. The group sat now, nodding in agreement and hitting each other playfully.

"No. No good."

"Hey, why? Why no good?"

"Brooke say, the situation here un…ten…ten…ul."

"Untenable?"

"Yes, that's the word—un-ten-ble…."

"He's organising more evacuations then?" Frank looked at Leo with that naive innocence that Leo could only wish to one day gratify.

"No. Your Churchill, he says British presence here in Belgium and France is still needed… It's needed to make French feel good."

"Feel good? What's the fucker on about…?"

"My nephew, he means you British soldiers make us feel supported!"

"So they're not coming back for us then?"

Philippe's nephew shook his head. He understood more English than he could speak, and his uncle spoke more English than he understood—strangely.

"Brooke, say to Churchill—not possible to make corpse 'feel'."

High Oakham Cottage Revisited (Continued) 2020

"Leo was Killed in action in Dunkirk on 27 September 1944."

"Too bad, sorry."

There was a pause as everyone turned to Len and watched him throw a log on the fire, "I had no idea when I purchased this cottage from the auction that I had once lived here."

"No, but obviously, there must have been something buried in your subconscious to attract you to the old place?"

Len shrugged. "Indeed, guess so."

"Goodness knows why your mother left without saying a word to me. I will never know, I suppose."

"She must have had her reasons."

"Thought I'd never see you again. Why did you not stay in touch, Aunty Faye?"

"Indeed, that, my dear, is a long story."

"Georgia, go to my room. There's a shoebox beneath my bed; bring it to me, will you, please? Len rose from his chair. "Please forgive me for not having remembered you." He hugged his aunty delicately. "I am a fool; I've not been well."

"Oh, poppycock! I know all about that! There's absolutely nothing wrong with you, man. If you think that incident that occurred in that barn was somehow of your own doing, then you must be—"

"Mad?"

Georgia glanced at Nikki, eyes and mouth wide, but was glad someone had dared to bring up the elephant in the room. She slipped upstairs, trying to listen while searching beneath Len's bed for a shoebox. When she returned, the two were sat again, staring into the fire.

"Ah, thank you," Len said, taking the box from her and removing the lid delicately like it was about to explode.

"Can you tell me anything about these? Found them in my mother's flat when she died. I saw them years ago, and she told me they had belonged to Leo." He pulled a cloth bag from the box and shook it, letting its contents fall into the shoe box. A pile of golden fob watches fell in a tangled heap.

"They are all engraved. There's one gifted to Jack, dated 1937."

Crying, Faye turned her head away. "Not sure how your mother got her hands on these." She sniffed, wiped a tear on her handkerchief, looked at the pile of watches in the shoebox and wept. "They belonged to Leo, you say?"

Len nodded.

"Do you mind?"

"No, please, help yourself."

Faye carefully took the box from Len and read each inscription. "I can't believe it," she breathed out a curled choke as though in shock. "So, Leo took them! It was him. I should have known. After all these years... I really can't believe this...." She pulled the corners of her mouth down and nodded to herself.

"And this too?" She quickly removed a golden brooch from the tangle of chains and watches. "This was Jack's mother's. Dan gave it to Amy, your mother, the last time he saw her... before he died."

She raised her hands in a hopeless gesture. "Amy told me that Jack had torn it from her...that night he raped her..." she sighed heavily... "I don't quite know what to make of these; I'm not sure how these ended up in Leo's hands. Jack was supposed to have stolen them, all of them and flogged them all, or so we were made to believe! He always claimed his innocence, but... Is there anything else in the box?"

"An old photo of three very creepy-looking Clowns."

"Let me see. Ah, I remember this. I took this photograph. It was the last picture of the three brothers together at the Nottingham Fair, just before the fire."

"In fact, it was our last show together." She had to stop to swallow back her tears.

"So, they were a band of brothers?"

"Oh yes, for all their foibles, Leo, the eldest, Jack, the middle born and Dan, the last baby to be delivered."

Deep in thought, Faye polished the broach on the sleeve of her coat and looked up. "I don't know how to say this..."

"What, what are you thinking...?"

Glancing down at the brooch again, she gave a little sigh. "In light of these possessions, there is a possibility that Leo is your real father, not my Jack."

There was a long silence; Len stared out the window, shaking his head. Georgia noticed his eyes watering with tears. Faye shook her head and dropped her eyes to the brooch again; cherishing its memory, she discretely gave it a tight little squeeze in her hand, then placed it back into the box.

"I never knew all this!" Nikki said, finally breaking the silence. "You didn't tell me any of this, Gran."

"No one ever really spoke about those things, not in those days." Faye turned her attention to the photo, looked at it over her lenses, and laughed.

"They do all look the same, don't they? You'd be hard-pressed to tell them apart.

"Indeed, they do, exactly the same."

"Nikki, would you like to help me make tea?"

"Yeah, of course."

The girls headed off into the kitchen, giggling.

"This is so fucking weird!" Nikki leant against the door, laughing.

"Ssh, don't let them hear, I know, so weird... So, Faye is Dad's real aunty then? It's bizarre...for Jake and me, I mean."

"I don't know." Nikki laughed again, shrugging dramatically. "I can't believe it."

Len had one memory of his aunty Faye; he remembered the day precisely because it was the last time he saw her. Being a land girl, in Len's vague memory, she had always worn the same working clothes, same old beige blouse, muddy boots, and men's baggy trousers pulled up to her chest and hair tied up in a knotted headscarf, but on this occasion, she was dressed differently, in a dress and heels. Faye had let her hair flow down her back in ringlets, making her look younger somehow. Even as a child, that memory had always remained with him; how she paraded before him, pirouetting and asking how she looked. Now, sitting before him, at nearly one hundred and five years old, just as spritely in both spirit and in mind, but he couldn't help but wonder where that younger woman had gone? Where had she been all those years? Was she still the same person inside? Perhaps he could see an element of the younger Faye somewhere in the eyes, hidden behind the veil of time's cruel mask. If she was still the same person, where was he, the young boy she had once loved as if he were her flesh and blood? Even if they were now nothing more than complete strangers, with all those long years eroded away by the seriousness of life, were remnants of what they once shared still bubbling beneath the surface? Faye moved awkwardly towards the edge of the chair and leaned on her stick, her tone dropping practically to a whisper, "Would you allow me to be frank with you, Leonardo?"

"Please, feel free."

"I can't afford to mince words here, dear, especially these days. Outings like these are a rare occasion and now most certainly numbered too, so I shall just come out with it and say exactly what I came here to say. That situation you found yourself in, in the barn?" Len shifted awkwardly. "Yes, I think I know what you're referring to."

"That shift from knowing oneself completely with a sense of self-awareness and preservation, to suddenly being faced with, shall we say, a deep desire to take one's own life?"

Len's brows furrowed, and his face flushed with embarrassment. He wasn't aware anyone knew about his experience in the barn. He certainly wasn't ready to discuss it.

"Hmm...?"

"Was it orchestrated to the highest of degree? I mean, did it happen so quickly you barely had time to react?"

"It all happened against my will, if that is what you mean? Despite what others may think or may have told you!"

Faye hung on his answer awhile, then looked him up and down, she nodded. "Hmm, sounds like the Ringmaster at work to me."

"The Ringmaster?"

"Your weakness, dear, inevitably, it is your weakness that leads to a tragic consequence. As your own life story's protagonist, your faults were integral to the plot. Your misfortune was determined by the nature of your frailty. You allowed the Ringmaster to seek your weakness tragically, and he found it in you. If there is a will for a tragic downfall, the Ringmaster will find a way."

"So, if what you say is true, what was my hamartia that caused the Ringmaster to seek me out?"

"Attempting to run away from your past, maybe? Your misery; perhaps failing to manage your frailty? I don't know Leo, but your hamartia allowed the Ringmaster to manifest swiftly and with great precision, as though you took the rope and placed it about your neck yourself." Faye paused. "Is that how it felt for you?"

"It certainly was. "

"Yes, I thought so, orchestrated to the highest degree of accuracy, like that of a high trapeze artist."

"I don't know about any hamartia or high trapeze artists; what attacked me in that barn was something evil, like a bolt out of the blue, like some demon! I haven't spoken of it to anyone."

"No, no one would understand! You aren't wrong; what happened to you happened between your world and his. It isn't unheard of to find somebody already taken in this house by what would appear to have been of their own accord, but I know the truth." She looked around the room and removed her spectacles. "I know how the Ringmaster works. I know how this house works."

"I knew it; the place is haunted, isn't it? I never believed in that kind of thing, such nonsense, but now I see."

Faye laughed. "It's not haunted, dear, not the house nor the barn. It really is that simple; what attacked you, Len was your frailty."

"Hmm? How's that then?" Len did not sound convinced, nor did he grasp the theory of the Ringmaster.

"The Ringmaster has been waiting to pounce upon your human error. He knew your soul was broken; you'd snapped and reached your lowest point, so the subsequent drama was inevitable. There was no way he'd let a priceless piece of drama like that slip between his fingers."

"Wait. What? Are you saying this Ringmaster is a ghost or devil or something, but the house isn't haunted? I don't understand.?"

"Hmm, yes and no –"

"Are the stories true? I've heard about the Ringmaster. There was a

festival surrounding the folklore just the other day in the village. I thought the old folk story was based on something that happened here years ago, in Castleton, not on an actual entity?"

"Ah, yes, the village still hasn't let go of that; you know about the Franconi Circus disaster? Well. I think it goes back even further than that, to the time of the plague in Eyam? Still, what does it matter? The festival draws in the crowds, which pleases the Ringmaster enormously." Faye laughed. "It is strange, while our own mothers scold us for displaying our weaknesses, the Ringmaster sweeps us up into his arms, feeds our imperfections on gigantic and enormous applause;

and for our sweet human faults, provides the wind and the wings, points us in the direction of the stage and encourages our most sublime performance. My dear, tragedies make the best theatre, but you are still yet to take your final bow."

"I'm still not sure I know what you mean? So, who is this Ringmaster?"

"If you like, he is the agent, the director, the producer, the advance man, who knows. Without promise or contract, he waits to turn our downfall into our finest performance, our weaknesses into our greatest finale, but in time, he is merely life! While we get caught up in the embroilment of our lives, he stands in the wings, his Circus shining like a mirage in the sun, waiting for us to fail and eventually fall. That, my dear, is the beauty of theatre, the beauty of life; the Ringmaster is merely an usher. who shows people to their seats."

"You're speaking though he is real! Like he is somehow attached to me, if not this house?"

"Not the house, per se; he visits us all from time to time. The deeper we fall, the more frequent his visit. But somehow, that Showman's Engine in the barn keeps him here."

"What? That machine?"

"Your curtain call would have been obvious, you know? There would have been indicators and signs had you been attuned to them. The Ringmaster loves a good old build-up before the main feature.

"Not to me; it wasn't apparent to me. I never saw or heard anything before that day in the barn."

"No, but he would have been in your nightmares. He'd have been lying there weighing heavy, feeding on any morsel of off-beat emotion, depression, anxiety, jealousy, anger, all by-products of loss and grief. He knew exactly what was lurking within your heart, within your soul. He loves a sad story to tap into. It makes it easier for him to pull

on those heartstrings, make you pliable, easy to manipulate. Did you see a child, by any chance? It's all part of his dramaturgy."

"Well, now you mention it, I suppose I did experience a few of those afflictions and, yes, I did see a child just before it happened. And now I think about it; Georgia has had awful nightmares since we moved here." "Ah, you see, all those occurring instances are signs."

"Signs?"

"Each an indication of the applied talent of mediumship. You've been in rehearsal for days, my dear. You just never knew it."

"Seeing ghosts, you mean?"

"Tea!" Georgia walked in with a tray laden with teacups, a teapot, biscuits and teaspoons. Nikki followed behind carrying the sugar; she perched it on her Grandmother's armchair and watched Georgia handing around brimming cups. "Don't be surprised; it's within your DNA and potentially Georgia's."

"What's that?" Georgia sat at the table and poured herself a cup.

"Gypsy gibberish." Len laughed. Faye looked offended.

"I thought, only moments ago, you were a converted believer? And one with a genuine experience."

"Well, I certainly experienced something, but not sure how it has anything to do with being of Romany origin. Gypsies are just, well, ignorant, most of them. They can't even read or write."

"A Gypsy, even if ignorant, has given you a key that allows you to see beyond this plain. You just need to learn to understand the symbols. You clearly possess the talent."

"Hmm, not too sure."

"Well, I bet you didn't know some Gypsies over the years have been famous for their contribution to the arts and to society, although you would never know of their background. Charlie Chaplin, Sir Michael Caine and Bob Hoskins, and let's not forget the adorable Mother Theresa, and she was a Nobel Prize winner."

"Really!"

"And your footballing stars, like Eric Cantona, he's a Gypsy."

The old woman was getting quite irate.

"Well, I didn't know that!"

"Oh, you'd be surprised. Many Gypsies out there have become stars, even David Essex."

"I don't know him either," Georgia whispered to Nikki.

"What about Elvis.?

"Elvis Presley!"

"You've heard of him, haven't you? He was another."

"I can't explain what happened to me." Len pulled a handkerchief from his pocket and rubbed his nose.

Georgia went to sit beside him and placed her hand over his.

"I'm alright," he said, tucking the handkerchief away and sliding his hand out from beneath hers.

"It is not a sign of weakness to admit to seeing something you know others can't understand. Unless they've experienced it themselves, how would they know?"

Nikki snatched a biscuit from the tray as though someone was about to slap her hand.

"Believe? Believe what?" Biscuit crumbs fell from her mouth, making her laugh as she wiped them away on the back of her hand, looked over at Georgia, and laughed again. "What are these two going on about?"

"Ghosts, Nikki" Faye raised eyebrows and dropped her eyes to the floor.

"Well, folk stories, really." Len, looking mortified, annoyed this was no longer a private discussion.

"Everyone has them."

"Ghosts?"

There was a quick exchange of looks between Nikki and Georgia.

"If you have lived, you have a past; if you have a past, you have a ghost or two."

"Aunty Faye! What are you saying now?" Nikki reached for another biscuit.

Faye explained the folk tale about Gypsies being able to commune with the dead in ways others can't.

"Like it is supposed to be a Gypsy thing?"

"Psychic, you mean?" Faye drank from her teacup and clattered the cup back into its saucer. "That's exactly what I mean. Gypsy by blood, Gypsy by nature…like you, dear. You've seen things around this place, haven't you? I'm sure you have? Nikki does."

"I told her about your nightmares," Len said, gazing off into the fire. "But you said the house isn't haunted."

"I have horrible nightmares; not sure it has anything to do with ghosts, but….." Georgia stopped and put her mouth near her father's ear. "I have seen things here, Dad."

"Things? Like what?"

"I can't explain; I've heard things –"

"You never said anything!"

"Would you have believed me?"

Len sniffed. "I never saw anything here, and it's not something my mother ever discussed with me either, so –"

"You've not seen anything until recently, you mean…?" Faye's eyes blinked in annoyance. "The house isn't haunted. It is your past that is troubled, that's what I am trying to tell you."

"Well, indeed, that's different. That is something I can relate to."

"Wasn't your mother a Gorger?" Faye leaned her chin on one elbow on the arm of the chair.

"A what?"

"Not the best term to use, I know; I do apologise, old habits –" Faye sighed and considered how to rephrase. "What I meant to say is your mother wasn't Gypsy. The boys were, of course, God rest their souls."

"So, anyone who's not Gypsy is a what?"

"Oh, never mind. It was a poor turn of phrase."

"Right, going back to this Ringmaster then, what…who…was he? Some sort of Clown…or…?"

Georgia put her cup down and leaned on one elbow. "We saw a picture of him, didn't we, Dad?"

"Did you? Where?"

"In a shop in Castleton."

Ah, yes, I think I know the place. No, the Ringmaster isn't; he wasn't a Clown. It's funny, people have this idea that a Ringmaster should be loud and bombastic, but in truth, they are quite the opposite; maybe some are, but in my experience, on a deeper, more personal level, I've always found them to be quiet, observant; they see all, hear all and say nothing, as the saying goes. Leo, of course –" She stopped to sip tea, then clattered the cup down in its saucer again. Nikki lunged forward to help her locate the saucer with her cup before its scalding contents spilt all over her.

"I'm fine, dear, thank you."

"Leo, you say?"

"Leo? Oh, yes, he was exactly like that…."

"He was a Ringmaster…?"

"Ah, you didn't know? The Ringmaster of the Circus Franconi, yes he was, before the war, of course."

"I most certainly did not know that."

"Something else to add to your list of revelations today."

Georgia sat rolling a strand of hair around her finger, listening and observing Faye. She was suddenly struck by a strange revelation herself. Something about the very old woman was different from anyone she'd ever met. Yes, she was old, but she miraculously had this very young persona. Then, she realised Faye was probably the first older person she had ever really spoken to in-depth.

"Well, before he married your mother, Leo was the Ringmaster at a few Circuses before taking up the role in his dad's company. His father told him to go away, learn all the trade tricks, and return and take over his position when he was ready, and that is precisely what he did. Leo didn't get along with his father, so he left shortly after and didn't return to join the brothers until his father passed away. Leo was good at his job, the best. He worked in different ways than what his brothers were used to. It took time before they all clicked. He knew exactly how to manipulate everyone. He'd keep you at the top of your game if you were in his show. If you were in his audience, he would keep you on the edge of your seat. He ensured whatever you saw at the Circus would stay with you forever. No one knows why he is linked to that damn Showman's Engine, but somehow, he is, and through it all, he still uses human circumstance to manipulate his existence."

"Sorry, what? What do you mean, he's linked to that traction Engine?"

"You've read the stories about the Castleton Ringmaster, you said yourself, well, sometimes, I believe it is a portrayal of him to some extent."

"Yeah, but I've read the literature about the Ringmaster; there's nothing to suggest Leo is like the actual one from the stories. And nowhere did we read he is linked to that Engine."

"That Traction Engine in the barn?" Nikki said, flicking an eyebrow up to Georgia and Len.

"Yes." Georgia laughed.

"You never heard anything about Leo being the real ringmaster, Nikki?"

Nikki threw her head back and laughed. "I've heard stories about the Ringmaster but never knew he was related to me!"

"Ah, well then, you might need to ask in the village."

Nikki screwed up her face and shook her head over at Georgia.

She silently mouthed the words so only Georgia could read her lips. "It's not true."

"Oh, but it is, dear."

Nikki jumped. Faye suddenly sounded stern. That was another thing about Faye; she was as blind as a bat, but somehow, she knew exactly what was happening around her.

"Ask, in the village," Faye said again, turning to Nikki.

"I'm not going to ask people in the village say, by the way, did you know I'm related to the evil Ringmaster?"

"Anyone will tell you! You only need to ask. Did you never stop to wonder why that damn Engine is still in that barn even after all these years, despite being sold off, blown up, raided for parts? I've lost count of how many times that Engine has found its way back here. It just keeps on coming back, like a bad penny!"

Faye handed her cup and saucer to Nikki without looking at her. Faye said again, "Ask anyone around here; they'll tell you, they'll tell you stories that will make your skin crawl. About the debauchery; every sin in the book of Solomon, just as in 1 King 11, 1 to13."

"What is the Book of Solomon? I've heard of it but never read it."

Len laughed at Georgia. "Well, there's a shock. What book did you ever read?"

"Oh, shut up, Dad." Georgia flicked her fringe from her eyes and pulled a face at Nikki. They both smiled.

"We have this debate regularly," Len said, looking up at his daughter. "Georgia is an English grad who has never read a book in her life."

"For your information, you're wrong; I do know about that book, just never read the verse. The Book of Solomon probably dates back to the 14th or 15th century Italian Renaissance."

"Not entirely correct, dear," Faye says moving to the edge of the seat.

"The Book of Wisdom, or the Wisdom of Solomon, is a Jewish work written in Greek and most likely composed in Alexandria in Egypt. Generally dated to the mid-first century BC. The work's central theme is wisdom, appearing under two principal aspects."

"True, true," Len affirms his knowledge too, "but I don't understand how it links to that Engine."

"Every verse can be depicted in that machine."

"Now I've lost you," Len said, looking over at Nikki, puzzled.

"Well, dear," Faye says, "Every desire, every sin of those who have ever found their lives embroiled somehow in that machine, the Ringmaster has plucked out so grotesquely to create such convoluted disharmony and conflict. If I told you the stories, it would make your eyes water: the lies, the infidelity, the incest."

"Incest? Wow! What?" Nikki sits up laughing. "Now, this is getting good." Georgia put down her cup quickly before spilling the tea. "Who's that then? Do we know them?"

Len sniffed. "Not related to us, I hope."

"See, desires of the flesh stir the imagination like no other and non-normative behaviour runs through all walks of life, all societies; that's why the Ringmaster roots it out for dramatic effect, every last dark seed. Every sin is everyone else's fascination, and no one is immune or perfect. As I said, Len, the human hamartia provides the best drama!"

Nikki shook her head, confused. "But the Ringmaster is part of the Circus, not the theatre."

"The Circus is the most grotesque form of theatre, where each performer reaches their own destination, rather than their intended one, they each create their own unique dramatic performance. That Engine is to the Ringmaster what a pack of tarot cards are to any Gypsy, except it is more powerful. It allows him not only to foretell the future but dramatically create it. All the Ringmaster need do is exercise his talent to exhibit yours: Lust, love, hate, desire, you name it, that Engine inspires it."

"Indeed, sounds absurd."

"Oh, it is! To him, it is comical, depending on how dark your humour is. He doesn't care about the human response as long as he achieves one. He doesn't care what you might derive from his theatre; the Ringmaster just wants your story, so he may bring your human hopes, desires and fears to the surface. That is the job of a Ringmaster. But you should already know that. Where there's guilt, there's drama. Nikki, I'm exhausted, darling. I would like to go home now, dear."

"Of course, Grandma." Nikki helped her Great-grandmother to her feet and handed her the walking stick that was leaning against the arm of her chair.

"Well, darlings," Faye said, holding Len's hand as she stood. "If I was you, I'd sell that damn machine sharpish." She placed her hand upon Len's cheek. "Goodbye, my dear. Look after yourself. And don't forget, always wear sensible shoes, because you never know when you might need to run."

The Chase 2020

Mark's car bounced at breakneck speed along the dirt track from the Hamlet to the main road. He glanced at James in the rear-view mirror. "What's your name? Hoy, I asked you a question; what's your name?" "James."

"Your full name?"

"James Franconi."

"It's Price, you fucking idiot! James fucking Price! Jesus! What's your name?

"James Price."

"We got rid of that shitty name. Why do you keep forgetting?"

"James Price. My name is James Price"

"For Christ's sake, you've had my name for three years! It's your mother's fault; for taking you to see him behind my back at every chance, she gets. You're not going to see your dad anymore, do you understand? Forget him!" The car reached the T-junction at the end of the private dirt track and then whipped a right as the satnav started up again of its own accord having just found its signal.

"Where's your mother?"

"Don't know."

"What do you mean, you don't know?"

"Mrs Winters took me for lunch."

"Why didn't your mother take you? Where was she?"

"She left me with Daddy. I don't know where she went."

"So, you were with your dad, then Mrs Winters took you for lunch?" "Yes."

"By yourself? Why didn't your dad take you for lunch, James? I said, why didn't your dad take you for lunch?"

"I don't know."

"You don't know where your mum and dad are?"

"No."

"Well, that sounds fucking suspicious, doesn't it? Doesn't it, James?"
"Where are we going?"

"You want to know where we're going? I'll tell you where we are going. I'm going to take back what's mine, that fucking Engine for a start, then my wife, and as for you, you little shit, you're going away."

"Away, with Mummy?"

"No, not with Mummy. We're gonna get you booked into one of those good schools away from home, far, far away; how does that sound, hey? Mummy won't have an excuse to keep going to see him then, will she? That'll fucking teach you both. Neither of you appreciate anything I do! Especially you, you little fucker. You and your dad are causing trouble between your mum and me. I'm sick of it."

High Oakham cottage stood off the road to the left; its two chimneys were visible over the fields at the front and beyond the ancient dry-stone wall and hawthorn hedge that ran the entire circumference of the land. Without indication, Mark's car screeched through the field gates and parked abruptly outside, where he found Len and Georgia standing on the doorstep waving off Nikki and Faye; their car doing a complete lock turn in the yard before coming to a stop in front of Mark's Audi. As the two vehicles came tete-a-tete, Nikki recognised him, smiled, and then slowly manoeuvred her car alongside his. "What is he doing here?" Waving, Nikki watched as Len and Georgia stepped back inside.

"Lord knows." Nikki wound the window on her side and waited as Mark drew down his. "Alright, Mark?"

"Not bad, Nikki, you?"

It was one of those rare occasions when Nikki saw someone she knew outside the context of the Traveller's Rest. She'd only ever seen his face in poor lighting over the bar. She was surprised to see he had a flurry of freckles, like tiny specks of gold running over his nose and high cheekbones. A patch of sunlight squeezing down between the two vehicles revealed flashes of silver at the roots of his wiry blonde-red hair. He looked angry, but Nikki had only ever seen him drunk, never stone-cold sober. She looked at him a moment longer, then turned to James, who, strapped in his seat in the back, smiled and waved.

"Hi, James."

James liked Nikki. He thought she was friendly. She often gave him lollies and colours from the kid's table in the pub. Nikki thought about how tired he looked, as though he had been crying a lot.

"Alright James?"

"Not bad," Mark said sharply.

"Okay." Nikki paused. "Sure you're alright, James?"

"He's fine!"

"Great, good seeing you, Mark. Probably catch up with you later in the Traveller's?"

"Possibly." Mark forced a smile. Nikki was no psychiatrist, but she definitely got the hint that they both seemed on edge, distressed, like something was wrong. Nikki accelerated and began slowly moving away. "Okay, see you later! Bye! Bye, James! Do you think they're alright, Gran?"

"Who, who was it?"

"Mark, Grandma! With James, our James."

"Who?"

"James was in the back of Mark's car, Gran."

"Oh, so who was he then?"

"He's James' stepdad, Gran. Have you forgotten? Never mind..."

"He's obviously here to see Len because of the accident."

"Well, maybe," Faye said, putting on her sunglasses. "Let's hope he takes that machine from them."

"Well, as a matter of fact –" Nikki laughed and turned to her Gran, smiling. "Oh, Gran, nothing gets past you, does it? I heard Mark does want that Showman's Engine, but there's a bit of a war over it."

"Of course, there is. That's exactly how it works. How it picks its next victims. Well, let's hope he takes it soon. I didn't like him. I think the Ringmaster will have a ball with him."

"The Ringmaster, oh Gran!"

"He doesn't have anyone to plague now he's had his fun with Leonardo. Let's hope he has done his worst with him."

"You mean Len? Oh Gran, surely you don't believe in all that, really?" Turning the car through the village, Nikki took her grandmother's hand in hers, smiled and drove along Millbridge, down How Lane and slowly up the narrow curve leading to Castle Street; then, without warning, she stopped the car, leaving the Engine running, jumped out and ran into the chip shop, only to return moments later with a piping hot fish supper. "Salted and vinegared, Gran, just the way you like it."

"Not too many chips, I hope, dear," Faye said, taking the sweaty hot bundle from Nikki as she climbed back into the car.

"Can't eat too many chips. I hope that man takes the Showman's Engine away from the cottage tonight. Do you think that is why he's gone there now?"

"I don't know, Grandma. You mean Mark?" Nikki pulled the belt over her shoulder, indicated then pulled away. "So you believe it all true about that Engine then, Gran? Where did it all begin?"

"It's a long story, but I hope that Mark takes it as far away as possible from Leo and our James." Nikki twisted briefly in her seat, glaring at her Great-grandmother and then back to the direction they had driven in her rear-view mirror. "Shit! James! I need to tell Jake that I've just seen him."

"Gran, if any of that rubbish you said about the Ringmaster is true, which I don't think is; do you think that's why Amy took Len away from that house all those years ago?"

"Because of that Showman's Engine? Absolutely, dear! After Leo rebuilt the Engine, Amy couldn't sell it, nor could she give it away. No matter how she tried. The Showman inside the Engine had found himself a perfect host in Leo, the Ringmaster. After all, he was the one who rebuilt it; put the show back on the road. Together, they made a formidable force, and Amy knew that."

"Okay, this is crazy. We need to go back for James!"

Dunkirk (continued) 1940

Jack slowly sat up, resting on one elbow beneath a canvas roof that dipped and waved in the wind just inches from his head; he pushed it up with his forearm and looked beneath it for cigarettes. He was laid on a stretcher in the rear of a Fiat 626 truck with three other injured men. The makeshift roof, a stinking wet canvas hanging loosely covered in patches of black mould and Engine grease, kept dropping annoyingly above their heads in the wind. According to Philippe, who made the coverage,

"This Lorry," he told the small band of British infantry in his booming Belgium accent, "is a good one, my friends."

Leo and the guys didn't care less if they had been presented with a dozen donkeys, just as long as they could all jump aboard, grateful to the man for having rescued them from their inevitable ill fate. Philippe and his French companions were on their side; the Lorry was just a bonus.

"It's amazing," Frank said. "It's like the cavalry has arrived, and all our Christmases have come at once."

Philippe was a giant of a man who practically lifted Jack into the back of the truck himself with one hand.

"This truck is good for military operations, good for the Italian army, is good for me!" Jack wasn't sure how the truck had made its way across two borders from Italy to Belgium during the war and didn't much care, but he was glad of it that night. All the Brits who climbed aboard, injured or otherwise, thought they were home and dry, which was still the dream they kept in their hearts; the one thing that had kept them moving on. The pile of shit had left them by the road at least six times that they could remember, or at least while those injured had been conscious long enough to keep count. Jack rolled over carefully, trying not to touch the sides for fear of pulling the sheet down upon his head. The way he was feeling right now, he would never fight his way out if it did. The truck shook suddenly as a massive blast of howling wind whipped up around it. He stopped searching for cigarettes in the kit bag and waited for the wind to drop. One of the injured men raised his head slightly to see the commotion, then dropped it back down again. The exertion caused Jack to break out in a cold sweat; frustrated with the constant pain in his stomach and legs, he thumped his forehead with the heel of his hand and lay back down again, waiting for the pain to subside. As he drew a breath to pull a damp, prickly blanket across his chest, he saw his brother's kit bag lying opposite. Lifting the canvas above his head, Jack leaned over and dragged it towards him just close enough to claw out a few items. He spotted a few grainy photos in the dusky light from the truck's rear on the top of the bag. He smiled, instantly recognising the picture of three Clowns, leaning into each other, side by side, laughing with himself positioned in the centre with his arms wrapped around his brothers' necks, as they stood shouting rude comments to Faye, who at just that precise moment before clicking the flash to freeze them all in time forever, commanded them to call, "tits and bits!" Then, pulling another photo from the bundle of garments and cans, he found another photo of a naked woman lying on her side with one leg outstretched and one arm behind her head like Cleopatra. Now distracted from his tobacco craving, Jack took the photo and was just about to tuck it into his shirt pocket when Frank lifted the sheet above his head and climbed aboard. He checked up on the sleeping injured before sitting heavily beside Jack. Jack tutted at the flap of canvas he'd left open to allow the elements to rip through the precarious structure. "Feeling better, I see?" Snatching the photo from Jack, Frank studied it closely. "Well, now I see why. Who is this babe?" "My wife!" "Sorry, man!" "No, no, keep it. Don't know why my brother has a photo of her in his bag anyway." Frank glanced over at Jack in a, are you fucking serious kind of way. Jack, flinching in pain, groaned before lying back to laugh. He reached up to lift the sagging canvas with his forearm. Frank pushed his rifle up beneath it and took the weight from Jack. "Leo is the one with the camera." Jack laughed. "You reckon? How do you know?" "Just do" "So she's posing for him?"

"I guess she must be, and I'm the only fucking idiot who didn't know it was going on behind my back."

"Well, let's just put it back in his bag, shall we?"

Frank stood the bag up and began burying the photo beneath other items. "You can ask them about it when we return home to Blighty."

Rubbing his hands together, Frank sat again, quickly thinking of ways to change the subject.

"They've got a route mapped out, you know?"

"Oh, aye? Won't make any difference, not in this pile of fucking junk. I don't know why they just don't leave us on the side of the road for the fucking Gerrys and be done with it."

"Truck's running sound now, mate; they've secured us a safe route, there's a boat waiting to escort us back to Blighty, and there's a lift waiting at the other end—happy days, mate, happy days!"

Wiping sweat from his forehead, Jack rubbed his face and sighed heavily. "Get us a smoke, will ya?"

"Where?" Frank kicked Leo's kitbag with his boot. "In here? Are you sure your brother won't mind, mate? I mean, we shouldn't be going through his stuff like?"

Jack tried to stretch for the bag himself, but Frank stopped him with his hand and made him lay down. He placed the bag on its side and searched through it, pushing his arm down to the bottom. He dragged out a blue and white pack of De Troup Cigarettes.

"What's that?"

"Cigs."

"Not the cigs, them? Pass the bag here, will ya?"

Frank took out the French cigarettes and slid the bag over to Jack. "You can't light one in here; you'll go up like a zeppelin with all the paraffin soaked up in this canvas. Here, just put one in your mouth for now."

The cigarette tasted great as Jack rolled it around in his mouth, soaking up the tobacco with his lips and the tip of his tongue.

"Not sure you should be doing that, mate. Nicking a cig is one thing, but raiding your brother's kitbag is out of order, don't you think?"

Clenching his stomach, Jack rolled over onto his side to pull a coil of watches out from the bag and began examining each one, read inscriptions on the back and flipped them open.

"What are they? Watches?"

The cigarette lolled from the corner of Jack's mouth as he squinted in the half-light to read each inscription. "Yeah."

"Here, how come he has so many?"

Jack put the cigarette behind his ear and began collecting the watches together. Frank took them from him and put them back where Jack had found them. "Don't think your brother will appreciate you routing through his stuff, mate. Honestly, I'm telling you, he's gonna be pissed off."

"He's always pissed off."

"He might be your brother, but he's my badge. Come on, hurry up, put them back. He'll have me court-martialled for this."

Jack delved deeper into the bag until he found a small item wrapped in a handkerchief. A timeless piece of jewellery began to reveal itself as he unpeeled layers of tightly bound silk. "After all this fucking time! I fucking knew it. I knew it was him!"

"Here, put them back, mate!" Frank tried to take the brooch from Jack. "You're sick. You should be resting, yeah!"

"No, I need to see these. Give it back to me now!"

"What, this old brooch thing? It's just a piece of old jewellery; mate probably belongs to his missus."

Frank stared at Jack as he examined the back of a watch. He read from the inscription, "Circus Franconi. To Jack..." Jack laughed to himself.

"After all this fucking time, it was always him." He stretched for the bag to search some more, but Frank kicked it away with his size 10 boot. Jack, trying to sit up again, caused the muscles around his infected wound to contract. Flinching, he dropped the watch and the diamond and ruby-encrusted brooch beside him on the stretcher and lay back, squirming in agony.

"Told you, mate, you really need to rest. We're off to Blighty tomorrow; you need your strength for the journey. Look, ask your brother everything when you get back home, yeah? Here, have a fag!"

Frank looked around for the items that Jack dropped but couldn't find them. The van dipped and creaked under the weight of someone climbing into the cabin. They heard the doors slamming shut and the Engine starting up.

"We're parting waves now, mate. Come on, lay doggo, yeah!"

Pulling the blanket over Jack, Frank put a cigarette in his mouth, lit it, and then offered it to Jack. "Careful mate, with all the paraffin on this canvas, the whole thing could go up; we'll be roasted like ducks in here. Just a few drags, yeah!"

Jack took a long deep drag before Frank took it from him and stubbed it out on the soul of his boot. Exhaling a plume of hot grey smoke from his lungs, Jack closed his eyes and threw his hand up to his head in a salute. The items beside him fell unseen from the stretcher to the floor. Frank gave Jack a quick two-finger salute, laughed then jumped out of the vehicle. He ran to the front of the truck, shouting for the driver to wait; their mumbled voices and the sound of Frank climbing into the cabin indicated to Jack that movement was imminent. Once seated in the front of the wagon, Frank glanced over his shoulder to check on the rear, then hung his arm out the window, banged on the side of the truck and shouted back to Jack and the other passengers, "Wagons rolling!"

Jack was in agony; he was confused, emotional and shivering with fever when he awoke hours later. Gangrene was setting in with many different bacteria and yeast feasting on his wound, giving off an odour like a wet dead animal. Leo was sat beside him, holding a steaming hot tin cup in one hand and the distinctive brooch tucked away unseen in the other.

"Here, looks like you need this."

Jack, struggling to focus, tried to sit up. "Where are the others?"

"They all out on deck."

"On deck?"

"Don't. Lay still. Here, drink this. You'll be happy to know we've made it to Dunkirk. There's a boat waiting to take us home." He flashed the brooch before Jack's eyes and dropped his voice to a whisper, "Did you find what you were looking for, you devious little fuck?"

Jack sighed. "So, it was you who stole the watches in Castleton?"

Leo laughed at Jack's quizzical expression. "Just a practical joke, Bro, honest. I did mean to give them all back, but what with everything that kicked off."

"And the brooch? How do you explain that?"

"Ah, you're referring to Amy, the girl you conveniently tried to kill." He clapped his hands. "Well done! That was an impressive performance, by the way."

"I panicked; she killed Dan; what was I supposed to do? Why did she come after us with a lynch mob? And what about Mum's brooch? How did that end up in your bag?" He shook his head and put the cup down. "Tell me that? What the fuck did you do to her, Leo?"

"Me? Nothing! We need to get our story straight, Jack. The less we talk about this, the less we put ourselves at risk. Do you understand?" He gazed into Jack's eyes, lost for something further to say on the matter. He cleared his throat and shook his head. "Let's just say we found ourselves in a gregarious mood a couple of times." Smiling widely, he scratched his chin. "I don't know why she sent the mob after us."

"Amy wanted Dan killed?" Jack sighed. "I just don't understand; why?"

Staring down at his hands, Leo shook his head. "I'll find every single one of those bastards."

"You made a habit of screwing Dan's girlfriends, didn't you, Leo?" Leo looked up, shrugged and smiled.

"And always in my name. You think I didn't know that all these years?"

"Do you blame me?"

"You better not have said you were me to Amy. She hated me anyway, and she'd have known that you weren't Dan, so-?"

"Aw, the lass was easy. Threw herself at me."

"So you did!"

"Yeah, but that still doesn't explain why Amy wanted Dan dead."

"What did you do to her, Leo?"

"You want the truth, I'll tell you the truth; if Dan hadn't come up with those watches when he did, there would have been a mutiny; they'd have risen up and taken everything away. We would have lost everything."

"But we did lose everything! You're the fucking Hermes; you stole Poseidon's trident from under his nose. I know what you did to Amy. As soon as I saw that brooch lying on the floor that night, before the lynch mob turned up, I knew you had done something to her. "

"So, why didn't you say something? You knew what I was planning; why didn't you stop me?"

"I thought it was the drink talking. Never in a million years did I think you'd actually –"

"– I'll tell you why you didn't try to stop me because you hated Dan as much as I did. He was always shit and roses, mate. Shit and fucking roses! You've got to hand it to him; who else could find a jeweller to coax into a poker game?" Leo was laughing and nodding with self-certitude. Jack looked on, listening, too ill to protest.

"Dan was the fucking Isis child...he always was."

Jack nodded his head. "but we loved him, right?" Reaching out, he placed his hand over Leo's. "I understand, mate, I do... I get why you would feel the need to avenge our brother; God knows I tried. I love you, bro, yeah. God help me, I do, but tell me, why do you have a photo of my wife?"

"The naked one?" Leo laughed. "You're dying, man. Does it really matter? I just took back everything that was mine, mine before you and mine before Dan took it …and I had to be ready…."

"Ready?"

"I knew it was all falling apart, and I knew if I didn't take back what was mine, you'd get there before me, so I just took the lot, the jewellery, the watches, the women, everything, everything! What else was I supposed to do, walk away with nothing?"

"But Faye's my wife; the rest was history, water under the bridge, bro. Amy didn't just fall into your arms, did she? What did you do to her?"

"…Nah, she didn't." Leo smiled, then laughed. "Let's be honest; it was only a matter of time before you got in there before me."

"Woh-no! Why, why would I, to spite Dan? No, no, I wouldn't do that!"

"You thought about it, though, didn't you? That night Dan was with Faye; we said we both agreed the only way to get back at him would be to screw the love of his life."

"Like I said, I thought it was the booze talking. Do you think I was capable of raping my own brother's fiancée? Coz that's what you did, didn't you, Leo? You raped her! That's why the lynch mob came after us."

"One brooch doesn't mean I raped her…no, no, I didn't rape her! She was consenting. Once she learned about Dan and Faye, there was no stopping her."

"That one act of revenge cost the lives of hundreds of innocent people, including your own brother. Dan died for something you did! And your wife, your kids? Where are they now?"

"So, what! Do you want me to say sorry? I'm sorry! Okay!"

"Are you? I sure as hell am."

"Of course, I am… I am! I didn't know the repercussions would be of that magnitude, did I? Who expected that to happen? None of us saw it coming!" He drummed his fingers on his arm and looked out at the dark sea over the port of Dunkirk. "Na, I never really loved my missus; it was a marriage of convenience."

"That's horrible, don't say that." Jack lay with his mouth hanging open, appalled. "And your kids, where are they?" Jack looked at Leo pleadingly, too choked to say anything else. He shrugged and shook his head. "What did you do, Leo?"

"The Kids got out alive, don't worry about that. I made sure of it. Look, you always took what belonged to Dan. You were jealous of him, always had been since we were kids. And Faye, she was never your type, but you had to take her. Why? Why did you have to take her away from me?"

"That's what all this is about, isn't it? When Faye split with Dan, you asked her out, and she refused; she told me."

Leo swallowed hard and looked away. Shocked to see tears forming in his brother's eyes, Jack tried to sit up. "You loved her, didn't you? You always did!"

Leo heard Jack take a sudden breath.

"Right, it needs saying –"

"What?"

Leo chuckled to himself. "Faye always knew about you."

"Knew? Knew what?"

"I'm just going to come out and say it…we all knew. It was never a secret."

"What!"

"Women were never really your type, were they, Jack? Let's be honest! Before Faye, it was always boys for you, wasn't it? Well, this is what we heard. Faye said it was your experimental years." Leo laughed, "But you still had to proceed to fuck the arse off her."

"Oh, for fucks sake."

"I was in with a chance with Faye, but you just couldn't stand the thoughts of losing her to me."

Jack flopped back. He felt the warmth of fresh blood oozing from his wound. "I guess…" he breathed. "None of this matter anymore; we lost everything in the fire. I don't know where she is, so… it's over… it's all over."

"No, not quite. After the fire, I sobered up, went back; you'd pissed off by then like you always do."

Jack lifts one eyebrow. "I was in hospital –"

Leo shrugs. "No, you ran because you couldn't find courage enough to deal with it."

"You know where she is, don't you? Where is she? Where's Faye?"

"I caught up with her by the Trent river. I walked down to the jetty and saw her climbing into a boat with some bloke. I had Amy in my arms. She was…she looked dead, I dunno. There was a high tide; it was dark. I lifted her into the boat, wrapped in some sheet. Everywhere stunk, stunk of oil, burning flesh. It was horrible. It was raining. I couldn't even see; it was too dark. I wanted to shout out to Faye, ask where she was going, and tell her to look after Amy, but I thought she was dead, so I just left her there. I couldn't expose us. Do you understand?"

"But Amy killed our brother, Leo. It was her fault he died. Why did you try to help her? What if she wasn't dead? She could still come after us. You should have left her? Do you think Faye went back to Ireland?"

"I am hoping she's in Castleton with Amy. That's where I am heading after all this is over. 'He laughed. I hope they are both there because I'm going back when I get home, and you're not coming this time! I'm taking back what's mine, the girl –"

Spitting with anger, Jack tries to get up. "Don't you dare go anywhere near my Faye!"

"Don't flatter yourself, bro." If she is still alive, I'm returning for Amy, the house and that Engine. So, if you make it, you're off the hook; you can go anywhere you like; just don't go back to Castleton."

"I'm going to find my wife in Ireland. Faye turned you down before, Leo, so do not think about going to find her. And Amy, she'll never let you step foot through the door. again." Leo laughed, "Oh, she'll have me."

"Are you insane? She wants you dead."

"Funny, I remember her calling your name when I took her on the floor. She didn't even know it was me. You see, the thing is, the time that passes between moments of insanity and moments of reality are just so fucking unbelievably boring. I can't bear to live alone with my insanity. It's too fucking lonely." He kissed his brother gently on the forehead, then quickly placed a pillow over his face and pressed down with both elbows.

"I don't know what I want, Jack. A man like me never knows what he wants; I've always had a burning desire to take from you what I can't have. I don't even know who I want, but you're not gonna fucking take anything else away from me."

Jack squirmed and fought beneath the pressure of Leo's weight bearing down upon his face. His fight for life was more potent than Leo had anticipated. When Jack's strength began to wane, Leo lay across his midriff, trying to avoid the blood oozing from Jack's wound, watching as it spread slowly in a circular stain.

A corner of the canvas suddenly lifted, allowing a burst of natural daylight to flood in.

"Sir! Sorry, Sir! Didn't see you in here." Frank's voice trailed off as he witnessed the very last throes of Jack's life fading, his legs twitching and his mumbled cry falling silent.

"No, Burton, you didn't see me here!"

High Oakham Cottage
Unwanted Visitors 2020

Mark climbed out of the car wearing a bright pink cotton shirt, jeans with a stiff crease down the front and a costly-looking brown leather jacket. Georgia could smell washing powder, soap and aftershave from where he was stood. A totally different look, she thought, from the last time she had seen him at the Engine Rally. She glanced at his brogues as they crunched towards her in the gravel.

Nodding and smiling, Len held out a hand. "Afternoon."

"You sound jovial," Mark said, smiling.

"Visitations from so many unexpected guests have been quite the tonic," Len had certainly been craving company, and Georgia couldn't help but notice his mood slowly lifting after each visit.

Mark checked out Georgia before he spoke to Len. "Afternoon yourself, good Sir. How are you today? Heard you had a bit of a scrape? Thought I'd pop around; I was just passing, so is there anything I can do? Hello love," he said finally to Georgia as he approached the door.

"Hi."

"Not over at the Hamlet, then? They're having some sort of Circus day, aren't they?"

Len shook his hand vigorously.

"You're looking very well, Lenard."

"Oh, his name is Leo! It's Leo Franconi, everyone thinks he's called Lenard, but it's actually Leonardo." Georgia wished she hadn't offered so much info and wanted to bite her tongue.

"You're a Franconi, eh? Ah, well, now there's a name. Funny, Rebecca never said anything. It's a very well-known name around these parts. Strange though, don't know why Rebecca never said –"

"She did ask, but I thought there was no connection at the time; it turns out there is; I just found out today."

"Interesting, I suppose the old lady filled you in, Faye Franconi. That was her in the car, wasn't it?"

"Yes, yes, she explained the connection to me. It's a small world. Please, please come in." Len stepped back and allowed Mark to stride past him into the cottage.

"It certainly is. I won't keep you long," Mark said, rattling car keys in his pocket. "Got James in the car."

"Oh, would you like me to bring him in?"

"No, no, he's sleeping. He'll be alright for a minute."

Georgia looked back at the vehicle before stepping inside; she saw nothing but the high side of the child's car seat.

"Take a seat," Len said, indicating Mark to sit opposite him.

"Oh, go on then. So, what's this I've been hearing?"

"Hearing?"

"Georgia, close the door. Make us a brew, will you, love? Tea, Mark? Or would you prefer coffee, or something a little stronger perhaps?"

"No, no, nothing for me, thanks, I'm good, honest, thanks."

The smell of his aftershave was honking the place out when Georgia returned with the tea. She poured a cup from the pot and handed it over.

"Oh, okay! Thanks. One sugar then, please." Mark inspected the tea before taking a swig. He placed the cup down on the hearth, balanced his elbows on the arm of the chair and studied Len. Then clasping both hands together, he leaned forward, smirking.

"So, is everything alright now?"

"Yes, had a bit of a mishap in the barn, but ...er... I'm okay."

"Thank goodness. We rarely have ambulances with their lights flashing, tearing up the back lane. Beck and I, we did hear something. We thought something had happened but didn't like disturbing you."

"Oh, it was nothing. Just climbed up for something in the barn on an old ladder, you know how it is, should have checked it, should have known I couldn't trust the rotten old thing."

"Well, if there's anything I can help you with, you only need to ask. I could start by taking that Engine. You know, the one you've got in the barn? Get it out from under your feet. It's probably cluttering up the place, I suspect."

"Dad, I think Jake wanted to talk to you about that."

"About the Engine, why? Damn, thing's no good. It doesn't work, it's only good for scrap, and everyone knows the scrap price isn't what it used to be." Mark sighed and sat up straight. "No, tell him not to bother. I put it in there, so I suppose I'm the one who should get it moved." Mark laughed. "It's gonna cost me more to get rid of the damn thing than what I'll make back on it for scrap." He forced another laugh. "Honestly, tell him not to bother; I'll get it moved. I can do it today if you'd like. Only need to make a call."

*

Eyes fixed on the cottage's front door, James waited patiently from his car seat for Mark to return. Part of him wished he'd hurry, so they could go home, but the best part of him was dreading his return. It would mean he'd be alone in the car with him again, being forced to listen to him saying angry, unkind things about his mummy, something he didn't understand; either way, James knew he had to be brave, brave for himself and brave for Mummy.

Sitting a while longer, he started to need a wee. Fidgeting and wriggling, he pressed his nose against the window and breathed a white plume of warm breath up the cold glass. He drew a cat in the steam with his little finger from two rudimentary circles, dots for eyes, triangles for the nose, tongue, paws and ears. He thought the cat looked as though it was begging like a doggy, then he panicked. Mark might see it. He'd be cross with him for making a mess on the glass, so he quickly wiped it away with his sleeve. There was a real cat, sitting opposite beneath an Elder Tree, in almost the same position as the one he had just drawn. Totally forgetting about his desperation for the toilet, James unclipped the seatbelt, slipped quietly out of the car, and crept towards the drowsing animal. He held off a few yards so as not to frighten it away. James had enough space between him and the cat to study its black-coloured fur and long slender form. It looked like an old British short-haired: mostly black with just a little patch of white on its stomach and neck, his favourite. He had learned all about different cats from a book Santa brought at Christmas. His mummy said Santa would have given him an actual kitten if kittens weren't so afraid of flying on sleighs.

James stood perfectly still, with his hands on his knees, watching from afar as the cat awoke, slinked and scratched around the tree before slowly strolling across the yard towards him. It began curling around his legs, purring so loudly James could feel the vibrations through his ankles and hands when he bent down to stroke it. Suddenly, James felt an ice-cold breeze about his legs and a strange tugging sensation in the fold of his arm, as though he was being pulled to one side. Suddenly, a girl appeared, smiling down at him. He glanced up, wondering why he hadn't seen her before, as she coiled her tiny fingers around his arm again and began pulling him gently towards her; James straightened up and watched as she turned and ran towards the barn; obediently, the cat trotted along behind her. Stopping by the old barn doors, she glanced back over her shoulder and slipped away inside. Before James could catch up with her, the girl had disappeared within the huge cavernous interior of the barn. She was just about visible when he stepped inside. She stood a moment longer in a hazy shard of daylight slicing through a hole in the roof. James pulled the doors a little further apart and stepped inside. "Hello!"

Smiling, the girl beckoned him over and bent to kneel beside a basket. Hesitantly, James took another step. She lifted a tiny kitten from the basket, showed it to him, and held it close to her cheek.

"Kittens!"

James ran to join her and knelt beside her.

Immediately, he counted five, maybe six tiny pompoms of fur in all colours: Locket, his favourite, Mitted, not so much, Tuxedo and Magpie and even a Harlequin, which he'd never seen before, but had always wanted to. He remembered that word, Harlequin, because Mummy said it meant all colours, just like the costume worn by his Harlequin Clown on his dresser at home, and this kitten was very colourful.

The barn doors slammed shut in the wind and rattled against the wooden structure, making James jump out of his skin. Quickly realising it was only the wind, he watched the girl as she carefully lifted another kitten from the basket and handed it to him. He inspected its colouring and placed it against his cheek like she had done with the others. The wind howling outside suddenly lashed against the barn whipping a spattering of rain across the dusty floor before them and covering the wooded decking with splashes of rainwater, which very quickly began to form a small puddle. Scuttling cockroaches, the size of small rats, scurried from dark places to where a pair of leather riding boots stood off in a dark corner. James's eyes trailed from the scurrying cockroaches to the boots, then moved slowly upwards, revealing a tall thin man. James fell back onto his heels. The man also wore a long black leather tailcoat, velvet top hat and black breeches. He took a step forward, performed a rolling bow like a jolly jester, and then smiled. He jabbed the ground with his cane and took another step, bringing him out from the shadows.

Following each heavy footstep was a tap as the cane stabbed at the hard-wooden floor: thump, tap, thump, tap, thump. James scrambled to his feet and stood back a little. The man stopped, cocked his head weirdly on one side and scanned the room. When he saw James alone, his yellowing teeth grinned from behind a mask of white-washed face paint that had visibly crackled and flaked off, leaving grey-blue streaks from the corner of his eyes and mouth.

As he moved in closer, James noticed an odour of fresh manure, a familiar smell, living in the country, but it usually blew in from the surrounding farms during mid-summer, when his mother would complain and run through the house closing all the many Georgian windows.

"Poor beggars, they'll drown here if that river continues to swell." He laughed loudly.

Heartbroken, James glanced up at the strange man, then quickly lifted a kitten from the cradle of its mother's warm breast and held it close for protection.

"Don't let them drown."

The man's smile turned to a scowl. He reached down and ruffled the child's hair. "Now, wouldn't that make quite a spectacle? We would not want to miss that!"

As James gently rubbed his cheek against the kitten's tiny paw, the man watched silently with great amusement.

"Aw…" he said pitifully. "Pleased to meet you, James," he held out his hand. "I am the Ringmaster." James took the Ringmaster's hand in his. "Time to get this show on the road." He pointed at the Engine at the back of the barn. "Shall we…?"

The Ringmaster reached down and lifted the children one by one into his arms, seating them beside him inside the cabin of the Showman's Engine. "There, children, ringside seats!"

James glanced down at the kittens as they sat purring warmly in the basket beside their mother.

The Confrontation 2020

Jake was careering at breakneck speed from the Hamlet down country lanes towards the village with Rebecca beside herself in the passenger seat.

"Here, do me a favour, get my phone out of my pocket. It's buzzing."

"Who is it?"

"I don't know! It could be Mark. Have a look!"

Stretching over, Rebecca felt inside Jake's many pockets until she found it and pulled it free.

"Who is it?"

"It's not Mark. It's her –"

"Who, Georgia?"

"What does she want?"

"Answer it."

"No! You answer it. I'm not talking to her!"

"She may have seen Mark or James."

"Why would she have seen them?"

"If she's driving towards the Hamlet, she could have passed them. She can tell us which way they were heading!"

Rebecca grimaced at the phone and dropped it like a lump of red hot coal.

"No, I'm not talking to her!" The phone cut off. Jake reached into the footwell, picked it up and dropped it when it rang a second time.

"Aw, for fucks sake, Becky, answer it, will ya!"

Rebecca reached down to retrieve the buzzing phone and sighed. "Mark's probably just taken James home, anyway. Hello!"

"Oh, sorry, it's me, Georgia; I'm looking for Jake. Is he there?"

"Yes, he is!" Raising an eyebrow at Jake; she smiled.

Jake looked sideways at her and shook his head.

"He's driving."

"Put it on speaker, Becky. What's up G?"

"Hi Jake," her voice sounded shaky, trailing off to a quiet whisper. "Mark's here."

"Is James with him?"

"He's left him sleeping in the car."

"James, sleeping at this time of day. I doubt that!"

Jake shot a look at Rebecca. Rebecca's face, easy to read, expressed her thoughts in every crease and frown. She looked shocked but more annoyed than anything. "What's Mark gone to her house for?"

"The Engine," Georgia answered, having overheard Rebecca's question to Jake.

"Right!' Course he has!"

"Of all the places for him to take James, he had to take him to her house."

Georgia could hear everything that Rebecca was saying but chose to ignore it. "He's talking to Dad now; he's saying he wants to take the Engine today."

"Today!"

"No, no way!" Rebecca was shaking her head and silently mouthing. "Fucking hell!" She threw up her hands. "I can't believe it!"

"Look, tell your dad I have the papers right here to prove it's mine, Okay? Whatever you do G, don't let Mark leave with James, okay? Try to keep him there. I'll literally be there in two minutes."

"Well, I'll do my best, but I don't know what to say to him. Jake, Jake, are you there?"

Rebecca laughed a little, "Yes, he's here."

"Oh, okay, bye. Love you, Jake?" With Rebecca present, Georgia thought it was the perfect time to set out a test to judge Jake's commitment to her. She waited a moment for his reply. "Jake?" The pause was far too long; he failed.

"Yep." He heard you!" Rebecca said, clasping a hand over her mouth to hide a childish giggle.

Georgia slammed the phone down on the side of the kitchen and returned to the living room, where Mark was still talking to Len.

Rebecca raised an eyebrow at Len and glanced out of the window.

*

"So...?"

"What...?"

"Are you kidding? She loves you?" Rebecca said sarcastically. "Since when?"

"Yeah, well…"

"You're at that stage already? You've only known the girl a week! Seriously?"

"See, I knew Mark would head straight for that Engine."

"But why, and why today? And worst of all, why take James there. I don't get it."

"I do; it's a possession thing, his way at getting at us, both of us. Have you thought about what you're going to say to him?"

"To Mark? Dunno, why? I'm not going back to him if that's what you mean?"

"Put your hair up, brush it or something. You look, I dunno, unruly. Mark might suspect something."

"So, what if he does? It's not like he hasn't just kidnapped my son, our son! What do you mean unruly? Of course, I look unruly!"

"You look like you've been rolling in the hayloft."

"With you? Like we used to?"

"You don't want him thinking that."

"I don't care. I'm not bothered by what Mark thinks anymore. Wait, you're more worried about what Georgia will think; aren't you?"

"Don't bring her into this, or me!"

"But, you said –"

"I said what? As far as I was aware, you just dropped my son off; that's as much as I know. How was I supposed to know you two were having issues?"

"Aren't you going to back me up?"

"I agree he shouldn't have taken James without consulting you, or me for that matter, but, technically, no, how can I back you up!" Jake sighed and eyed Rebecca with a degree of discontent. "Mark is James' legal guardian, and you gave him that legal right, so!" He threw his hands up. "He is James' stepdad, so technically he hasn't broken any laws."

"Hmm, guess not." Rebecca's eyes dropped to her hands. She looked up again, spread her arms, wrapped them around the back of the seat and glanced out. "But…" she said, returning her attention to Jake, "He didn't consult us."

"No, he didn't! And if he says one fucking word, just one fucking word to me, I swear to God!"

Becky looked back sharply. "What?"

"I'll fucking kill him!"

Wiping dried tears from her face, Becky smiled, assured that she had won back his respect. She placed her hand over his on the gearstick. Jake knew he'd always been putty in her hands, but he was over her; it took him years, but he was finally dubious of any attention she attempted to throw his way, and likewise, Becky knew his affection for her had gone. Flipping down the sun visor, she tried to tie her hair into a quick, neat bun, then ran a dark red lipstick over her pouting lips. Leaning over, she pulled Jake slightly towards her, then planted a kiss on his cheek and laughed. "Perfect," she said, examining the scarlet kiss impression. "That'll keep him guessing."

"Get off, will ya." Jake rubbed away the lipstick smudge in the rear-view mirror, causing him to narrowly miss an oncoming car careening around a sharp bend on two wheels in the opposite direction. He slammed his foot on the brake and slowed down, just in time to indicate and swing left into the drive that led to the cottage.

Becky had calmed herself down by the time the car pulled up behind Mark's, but Jake was secretly seething. He jumped out, leaving her waiting for him to open her door chivalrously until she recalled she was with Jake now, which wasn't going to happen.

Climbing out, she waited for him to knock on the door, but he was busy doing something in the boot. When he eventually emerged, he held a rifle across his chest to Becky's amusement.

She laughed. "What are you going to do with that?"

"Protecting my property."

"What, you want to risk going to prison over some old Steam Engine?"

"No, my son, my wife, well, ex!"

A twinge of excitement roused in the pit of Becky's stomach; Jake's ego had always turned her on since they were kids at school. Being partial to a good old scrap, always looking for trouble, and if he didn't find it, it would inevitably always find him, and Becky loved it! She pulled him back by the arm.

"Come on, put the thing away. There's no need for it, honestly. Mark might be a wife-beater, but men like him are terrified of men like you, with or without guns."

"Well, we'll see about that; he needs to be taught a lesson. Jake need only look at the purple scar on the back of Becky's hand to be reminded that his son would probably be Mark's next victim, and there was no way he would sit around and wait for that to happen. "No one takes my son from under my nose like that." He glanced down at the back of Becky's hand again as she reached up to remove the gun; the cigarette burn still fresh on her flesh reminded him how much hatred he had for any man who commits such cowardly cruelty against the fairer sex, let alone his child.

"Get out of my way, Becks; I don't care who the fuck he thinks he is!"

As they walked by Mark's car, they instinctively glanced in to see if their child was sleeping in his car seat, but as expected, he wasn't. He wasn't even in the car. Together they walked towards the door, Becky suddenly dropping back through fear, afraid of what might kick off once Mark came outside. Jake knocked three, four times, but there was no answer.

*

Music sprang out from the machine, slowly at first, slurring like an old record on slow speed, then gaining momentum along with the Engine's speed; yellow lights grew brighter around the canopy until it was glowing like a birthday cake beneath a hundred burning candles.

The Ringmaster glanced up at James, then said, "Folks will kill to see this show."

What began as a low hum along to the machine's haunting melody soon developed into manic laughter as the man burst into a show of deranged hysteria, and combined with the volume of the rising noise of the Engine's mechanism, the barn was awash with smuts, plumes of puffy white steam, stinking black smoke and dancing shadows. With pulsing light coming from the furnish and the sound of a thousand crashing cymbals exploding in James's ears, the machine's pistons burst into life monotonously, pumping up and down, up and down, pushing, throbbing with hot steam through valves, like blood coursing through the veins of a dragon, stirring it from his deep sleep. The whooshing and popping of the Engine resounded off the walls, making them literally shake and vibrate. James closed his eyes and covered his ears.

Leaping around inside the cabin, the Ringmaster's snowy white hair, windswept and wild beneath his top hat, wrapped about his contorted face, which was now covered with a spattering of soot and grease.

Shaking and confused as the noise assaulted his tender eardrums, James felt he had awoken in the depth of a nightmare. "Mummy!" Tears streaming down his sooty face, he looked up a few times as the loud pops of steam made his heart pound. He spun around to look for the little girl who sat beside him only moments earlier but was now nowhere to be seen. Plumes of thick grey clouds of black ash choked out from the furnace with a splattering of hot soot flying like sparks stung his eyes, nose and throat. When he looked up again, the Engine was out into the world, and the man beside him was now no stranger. James only dared to peer out between the cracks in his fingers a few more times, covering his face again. Trees lining the yard seemed to be waving and bowing their heads. He leapt to his feet and glanced quickly at the sky and down at the ground. The gale outside had increased, cracking branches that split and crashed around him. Inwardly, he pleaded for the ride to stop, but fear held his words in the back of his throat. He wished for nothing other than his mother's love, warmth, and safe embrace. He wanted for nothing, only to jump down from the lumbering beast, so he may run to his mother before the inside of his head exploded.

*

The Showman's Traction Engine had emerged in all its glory, gleaming brand new and sparkling in the cold light of day.

Hearing the commotion, Len opened the cottage door.

Jake spun on his heels and walked towards the machine, "Who's that?"

Len stepped out, his eyes narrowed, and they looked almost closed. He pushed Jake to one side. "Nothing to do with me, he said, striding across the yard.

"We just got here, mate!" Jake said, looking equally as confused.

Georgia followed out; seeing Becky, she paused at the door and held back, then finding the courage to speak, she directed her questions carefully to Becky, embarrassed to even look for Jake.

"What's happening?" She leant out further around the door with arms folded defensively across her chest.

"I don't know; we just got here." Becky looked up at Georgia, then up and down again, head to toe. "Jake's going to find out what's going on." She flicked her hair over her shoulder and shrugged. Georgia couldn't help but think she looked like a cocky little schoolgirl.

The word 'we' seemed to linger in Georgia's mind, hanging there like a barb stinging her several times with layers of ambiguous meaning.

Everyone looked to Len for answers.

"Dad? What's happening?"

"Don't look at me. Mark's got to have something to do with this, obviously. I didn't even know the damn thing worked."

*

"Daddy!" Seeing Jake striding towards him, suddenly feeling safe, James swung open his arms, shouting with newfound confidence. "Daddy, I want to go home now."

Mark came to the door and watched as Jake made his way towards the Showman's Traction Engine; he knew with each step he took he had every intention of rescuing his son by force, while he himself had no other thought at this point but to retrieve the Engine, but then suddenly spotting Rebecca walking after Jake, arms folded, withdrawn, it drew Mark's breath to the pit of his stomach. She looked detached, remote almost, as she had done once before a lifetime ago when they were teenagers. They'd all grown up together. Mark was a skilful hunter, a man of the field, while Jake was a quiet man, fond of music; living in tents, and tepees, strumming guitars in the same fields tended by the hard-working Mark. While beneath the glittering moonlight, Becky lay in Jake's arms as Mark slept, waiting for the break of dawn so he may toil in the same fields where the two lovers shared their communal existence with a load of others, unshaven, unruly, long-haired hippies. Becky's so-called rejection of the established social rule that Mark's middle-class family represented destroyed any hope of him being with her. Mark loved Becky, even though she clearly doted on Jake, buying into his hippie tribe lifestyle, and still often, decades on, still claiming to relate to her former hippie liberal years, calling them the best days of her life. Mark had always had a particular predilection for marrying the women of his dreams if only to destroy Jake and his controlling bombastic father's wishes, whose life's teachings were based around the importance of a good work ethic. Secretly, Mark wished to be free, too, just like Jake and Rebecca.

Mark glanced over his shoulder to see the expectant child, eyes wide with excitement, then over at Jake, who was nearly upon the Engine. Then Mark saw the Ringmaster laughing and smiling with a forced, erroneous look of sympathy at James.

"Oh dear, doesn't James like the show? Stamp your feet, you little shit, perform your tantrums now, scream and shout, beg until your eyes bulge; you'll soon get all you deserve!"

Jake flung his arms toward his son to symbolise his intention to protect him. "I'm coming, buddy. I've got you!"

"Have you?" The Ringmaster shouted and shook his head. He laughed loudly. "Have you, though? I don't think so. What will you do to get your son back, Jake? What a fine example of hatred and violence you portray right now, though you pertain to be demonstrating just the opposite. Can you win him back, Jake? What's the matter, James?" The Ringmaster turned suddenly towards the child, taking him by the wrist and forcing him to look at his father. "See! Look at this show of dominance!" He was yelling now over the mighty roar of the pistons. "Who will win your affection now, Mummy or Daddy? Coz, it sure as hell isn't going to be poor Mark Price. Poor old Mark. He just wanted to be loved by your mummy, but you had to get in the way, didn't you? What's wrong, don't you like this show? Don't worry; it isn't over yet; the best is still yet to come! Mark is jealous, but your father's finale will be amazing!"

*

Jake was upon the Engine, swinging out with punches from every angle. Shouting at the Ringmaster. He climbed aboard, "Who the hell are you?"

The Ringmaster laughed. "I'm the protagonist, the main man! I am the character in your nightmares, Jake. You, Sir, are the tragic hero that leads everyone to their downfall. And as for the rest of the ensemble, they are merely defects, weaknesses, the ones everyone will talk about saying, they all had their part to play, but they were innocent nonetheless."

Hanging loosely from the side of the Engine, Jake took hold of the Ringmaster and tried to heave him over the side of the cabin. A scuffle broke out, and the two fought to control the Engine. While the struggle between Jake and the Ringmaster continued, Mark took James and held him tightly in his grip.

The machine inched ever nearer to the cottage. Becky turned to Len and whispered under her breath, "Who is that?" She walked towards the Engine, confused and shaking her head and shouted to Jake, "Who is that, Jake?"

Len looked at Georgia, exchanging a look of complete bewilderment.

"I have no idea what's going on!" He walked towards the Traction Engine, each step innocently placing him closer to the lumbering beast as he tried to ascertain what was happening.

Rebecca stepped up her pace to catch up with Len. They exchanged looks; she turned from Len to Jake and shouted, "Is that the Ringmaster? Is this supposed to be fucking funny, Mr Franconi?" Her face turned a sickly shade of white as she realised the driver, whoever he was, was now out of the Engine trying to pull her child away from Mark by the wrist as though he was about to hurt him.

"Stop him! Jake, stop him."

Joshua, running over the yard from the road, was shouting. "Jake! That Engine's not safe!"

Georgia waved frantically to Joshua. "Stop them, Josh!"

Jake, Len and Becky reached the Engine before Joshua had time to finish his sentence." There was an almighty explosion. Everyone near was sent hurtling through the air. The thundering noise was intense. It rolled across the sky for eternity, rumbling through trees, hillsides and valleys.

When silence fell, Georgia picked herself up from the ground, ears ringing; she ran through the debris and smoke, eyes stinging, as the fumes were so acidic it hurt deep inside her lungs to breathe. Leaping over burning fragments of twisted steel, ash and flames, she spotted Jake partially buried beneath a large shard of metal ripped from the Engine and dug into the ground like an axe blade. His body lay submerged beneath it in the grass, far from where he stood only moments earlier.

"Jake!"

"I'm okay," he said, dazed, "I'm alright."

Georgia wiped a trickle of blood from a deep gash over his eye. Suddenly, he staggered to his feet, taken by a surge of adrenalin. "James! Where's James?"

Georgia had seen him but dared not look again. She tried to hold Jake back. "No, don't – Jake…!"

"Call someone!" He pushed her aside. "Call someone! Oh God! Jesus…"

Georgia tried to hold him away from where James lay. But Jake pushed her away. "Get off!" He struck her in the chest; she couldn't physically breathe for a moment.

"James! Falling beside his son's body, Jake knew there was nothing he could do in an instant. "Help! Help him!"

Sirens somewhere distant assured Georgia the authorities had already been called; some neighbouring farmer or passer-by must have made the call. She tried to go inside to find her phone but saw Becky lying face down. She looked asleep, almost perfect; though a mass of red blood at the front of her skull revealed the extent of her injuries, Georgia felt sure they were fatal. Pulling herself together soberly, she tried to walk towards the gate, looking out for the authorities. Then stopped, turning her attention to her own father.

"Dad?"

Not knowing where to turn, she looked back towards Jake, who was no longer the man she once knew. His screaming was uncontrollable, his cry nothing but a blur in Georgia's brain as she tried to deal with her own sense of bewilderment and unbelievable state of shock.

Flashing blue lights flooded the yard, though Georgia didn't remember seeing them arrive on the scene; police, ambulance, fire Engines, and air ambulance, hovering above the wreckage, found a safe zone and landed in a nearby field. People in uniforms appeared running in all directions, some with dogs, others with guns and rescue services, officials of all descriptions still arriving in droves. A paramedic, dressed in green combat trousers and fern green fleece, was pulling Jake away from the remains of his child, but then Jake punched him hard in the face; the man flinched away and walked off, leaving Jake in a state of bedlam.

The barn doors were open. Crows cawing and fighting on the barn roof brought Georgia's attention to the open countryside around her and back to the stark light of day. A tall thin man standing in a half-bowed position, with his arms open wide as though making some reference to all the chaos around, gave her a broad smile, revealing yellowing teeth stretched from ear to ear. He took another low bow majestically, performing a rolling wave with his arms, over his hat, like that of a gesture, then suddenly disappeared.

Frozen with a cold sense of reality, Georgia suddenly stood between two policewomen. They were talking to her and leading her away from the scene. She looked back in horror at the chaos and realised they had taken her back to the cottage. As she began to walk towards the front door, she saw Len smiling, arms open wide. She threw the policewomen off and rushed towards him. Then throwing herself into the folds of his strong arms, she sank into the safety of his warm embrace.

Suddenly, from nowhere, a gun sounded off. Len fell with all his weight upon her. They both lay collapsed on the ground. Looking up, Georgia could see a silhouette above her, a dark shadow of a man against the bright afternoon sky. He was hovering over them with a rifle held up against his chest. Squinting, trying to bring the man's shape into focus, Georgia heard the cock of the trigger click back and again, she saw a sudden flash from the barrel of the gun as it exploded a second round into the back of her father's head. The lifeless body dropped heavier upon her; she heard his life sigh away on one last breath.

Police fell upon the man with the gun and wrestled him to the ground; the two policewomen removed Georgia from beneath her father's lifeless body. She called out her father's name.

"It's not your father, Georgia. It's not your dad." The policewomen shouted, "It's not him!". They dragged her away, supporting her weight between them as they carried her to a vehicle nearby and helped her inside.

"Help my dad, please!"

Clicking her seat belt, a policewoman sat heavily beside her, removed hair from Georgia's wet face and tried to reassure her.

"You're mistaken, Georgia. It isn't your father." Georgia could see the woman's lips moving, but she didn't understand. She had lost all sense of rational thought and couldn't make out a word of what the woman was saying over the ringing in her ears. A policewoman in the front of the car glanced over the backseat.

"Any idea why Jake Franconi would kill all the Price family, including his own son?" She asked the same question repeatedly. When Georgia tried to speak, her voice slowly became audible.

She looked up through stinging tears. "What, what do you mean?"

"Any idea why Jake Franconi would kill all the Price family?" the policewoman repeated.

"Jake hasn't killed anyone."

"I know this is very difficult for you right now, but it is better for us if you can tell us everything you know about what has occurred here today while it is all fresh in your mind; we'd like to get to the bottom of it. Do you know why Jake shot his little boy James, his estranged wife, Rebecca Price, and her husband, Mark Price?"

"No, no one shot them; my dad's been shot!" Georgia's cries seemed to be unheard. "Someone shot my dad! You saw that; you all saw that!"

"No, dear, Jake Franconi just shot Mark Price at point-blank range. None of us saw it coming. We couldn't stop him. Mark Price was shot in your arms. Can you explain why? Why do you think Jake killed Mark and his family? Do you believe it is an act of passion? Were you and Mark passionately involved?"

"No! Someone shot my dad! And there was an explosion. The Showman's Engine exploded! Mark was on the Engine!"

The policewomen exchanged a strange look at each other. "Yes, there was an explosion, and we are looking into that, but...."

The other Policewoman sat in the back of the vehicle, shook her head and made it clear she wanted the interrogation to end, but the other Policewoman ignored her and continued, "Miss Franconi! You are mistaken! Mark was the one who called the police and the ambulance service when his stepson, James, was shot by Jake; then, when you ran to Mark, Jake shot him too. Why? Can you tell us why he would do that?"

"Where's my dad?"

The two women exchanged another glance but ignored her completely.

"Where's my dad? Where's Len Franconi? He is here; I couldn't find him. Please, let me get out; I need to find my dad." She tried to get out of the car, but it was locked.

"I don't think that's wise, dear."

"Go! Drive, drive." The Policewoman sitting with Georgia in the back of the car began taping the back of the driver's seat again. "I said, go!" The driver switched on the engine and put the car in gear.

"No! Please. I'm begging you! I need to find my dad. My dad is here. I need to see him, now!"

The Policewoman in the front of the vehicle cleared her throat. She turned in a deliberate fashion to address the driver, "She should definitely go by ambulance. Look, we'll explain where your dad is, but I think we should get you to a hospital, okay? Just get you checked over."

"I agree." The other Policewoman said. She placed her hand sympathetically over Georgia's. "It's alright, dear. Everything will be okay." She unclipped her seat belt, climbed out, and called over a paramedic. There was an exchange between the police officer and a paramedic. The paramedic opened the rear door and leant into the car.

"Coming for a drive with me, love. Come on, I think it's best. Let me help you."

Georgia climbed out willingly and took the paramedic's hand. Seeing a body in a black bag being wheeled into the back of an ambulance, she stopped dead in her tracks. "Is that my dad?"

"No, love, it isn't your dad."

Without hesitation, Georgia broke free and ran as fast as she could across the yard to the barn. She flung back one of the heavy doors and stepped inside. Looking for a source of light, she pulled the other door open. An eerie creaking sound high above the cavernous roof space drew her eyes upwards then along a curve of pale light, slicing across the loft space from a solitary lantern perched high above her on one of the oak rafters. She swallowed hard as a rope swinging so slowly back and forth, in and out of the light, hung like a slow and steady pendulum. The creaking of the wooden structure resounded in the darkness as a black mass swinging gently on the end of the twisting rope made her gasp and stagger backwards. As she looked away, then back again, she closed her eyes, instinctively knowing exactly what was above her. Seeing, as she had once before, a bare foot; two feet, one shoe on and one off. In the grips of deja-vu, a body hung in a half-turning motion, a flash of a belt buckle, a hand and an arm hanging loosely from the sleeve of a coat confirmed what she thought she had seen. She watched in horror as the face and body of her own father swung slowly into view. An officer dressed in white protective clothing walked up behind her as a further two stood back by the door.

"I'm terribly sorry, madam; I must ask that you remove yourself from the crime scene."

"Please, just give me a minute alone with him."

"We can't leave him like that, we need to get him down and carry out our investigation, and you're potentially contaminating the area."

"It's okay, it's okay. Madam, I am the head of this investigation. Give her a minute, come on, it's fine, just leave her alone for a minute. Please don't touch anything or walk further into the marked area, okay? Come on, everyone, step outside. I'll close the doors, yeah."

"Yes, please, close the doors; thank you."

Voices could be heard outside as the two massive doors met, plummeting Georgia into ashy-grey darkness.

"Yes, Sir, I realise it's highly unusual, but she just needs a minute. Let's just give her a minute."

Sensing she was not alone, Georgia stepped carefully around the yellow and black tape that ran on steel rods in a perfect arena-like circle beneath the hanging corpse.

"Make yourself known to me!"

The Showman's Engine began appearing in all its glory, as perfect as the day it was built. Georgia had no heart or fear left in her to react. She moved slowly towards the back of the barn, listening into the depth of the silence for movement.

"You're a coward," she whispered with bated breath. "Why didn't you take me, you coward? Come out, show yourself!"

A slow clap resounded in response, then another and another.

"Coward? Not I, nor be poor death!"

"I know who you are; you're the Ringmaster! Come out and fight like a real man. I'll fucking kill you, you fucking coward. You prey on vulnerable souls and thrive on their death like a vulture!"

"All but theatre. The performance dies not, nor yet canst thou kill me. From life, which, by thy arrangement be, much pleasure, then from all, much more must flow for all to see, and soonest, in their proudest hour, all men do take their last bow; rest tired bones, and thus their life's work, their soul's performance be by far, their best and final show – a theatre's 'must see!'"

I'm Back
High Oakham Cottage 1941

A figure of a man dressed in full military BD, leant, almost camouflaged, against a dry-stone wall that ran the entire perimeter of High Oakham Cottage. A Red Admiral butterfly flicked from flower to flower in the Elder tree beside him. From a distance, the khaki colouring of the uniform: trousers, close-fitting open-necked jacket, shirt and tie, made the slender figure blend into the Derbyshire backdrop, allowing him to watch unseen for signs of life at great length. When the coast appeared still after quite some time, he decided to make his move upon the unsuspecting occupants of the sleepy cottage. Suddenly, Faye Franconi came from the barn; weighed heavily by a basket of freshly chopped logs, she strolled towards the cottage. The man backed away behind the wall and hid beneath the thorny branches of a hawthorn tree. "Isis dreams," he mumbled as he carefully lifted the spines from the crown on his head and wiped a trickle of blood from his brow.

"A life full of magic, magic full of life!" He laughed at the irony as he waited for her to go inside, then tilted his beret a fraction over one eye and headed towards the door. He knocked, then paused. Amy, busy making butter inside, licked grease from her hands, wiped them on her apron and opened the door…

"Good God! Leo!" Leo stood proud, relaxed; removed his beret and wrung it through his hands.

"Hello, Amy! I'm back!

High Oakham Cottage 2022

The day was warm, too warm. Georgia balanced her mobile phone between her ear and shoulder as she tried to pull open the freezer; eventually, cold air wafted as the door released its icy vacuum. She took out an ice lolly and cut it loose with scissors from the top drawer.

"So –" she said as she slid the ice lolly around her neck and chest. "Where are you now?"

"Just turning up your lane. Are you sure you're ready? I know what you're like. You say you're ready, but you're not! You know I don't like hanging around up there. You still want to go to the Traveller's?"

"Yes and yes, any more questions, Mother!"

Nikki laughed, "We can go somewhere else if you like?"

"I'm fine, honest! Stop making a fuss! See you in a minute?"

"It's the anniversary, you know? Thought you might not want to go anywhere near the Traveller's."

"Why?"

"It might remind you, yunno?"

"Nikki, it's been two years! Honestly, you need to stop worrying about me!"

"I'd feel better if you sold that damn Engine."

"I will, anyway; I don't want to talk about it; hurry up! I'm dying for an ice-cold beer" As she glanced out from the window, a Red Admiral butterfly flicked gently at the glass on the window.

Nikki was less than a mile away from the cottage. She threw a left on the sharp bend at the bottom of the long lane, then headed for the right turning that led to the top of the road. She glanced over the trees to her left and saw the chimneys from the cottage.

"I'm nearly at yours; make sure you lock the barn. It is locked, isn't it? Make sure it is because I'll just drive off if I see it open. It gives me the creeps."

"It is! It's locked! I don't even go in there anymore; it creeps me out too. Last week, I put the Engine back online and got a few inquiries. Got phone calls almost immediately."

"From who?"

"Weird people. I don't know who they were; strangers. Had an overseas number ring two days ago. It rang for hours. It kept ringing, then hanging up."

"Can't you just get some salvage person to come and collect it?"

"I dunno. Nikki, do you ever wonder if the life you are leading right now has been played out before?"

"What do you mean?"

"Yunno, same story, same old shit, just a different day, different time, but same people, same context, like we've all been here before, reincarnated, like?"

"I don't know."

"Just like we are living over the same shit until someone down the line gets reborn and does something different to break the cycle?"

"You been smoking something?"

"No", Georgia laughs, opens the door and waits for Nikki to arrive.

"I think the heat is getting to you. Are you sure you want to go to the Traveller's.? We can go anywhere you like, just say."

"It's okay; I'm fine, honest, just wonder about stuff like that, don't you?"

"No! Not anymore, not since Granny Faye died. She promised me that if there's an afterlife, she would return and let me know somehow; she never did, so it's all bullshit!"

"But that's my point; I think she will be back, but not as a ghost, as a baby reborn; it's called transmigration. There's a whole religious philosophy about it."

"Okay, this shit is just getting too weird now. I'm nearly there. You better be ready because there's no way I'm coming in."

Nikki indicated and pulled into the top lane.

*

Returned from the theatre of war, where his main job was to restore and fix broken-down armoured vehicles on the edge of Ukraine in the little city of Przemysl, less than 10 miles from the Polish-Ukrainian border, a figure dressed in military terrain camouflage is hiding. Almost invisible to the naked eye against an ancient hawthorn hedgerow that runs parallel to the dry-stone wall around the entire property where High Oakham Cottage sits nestled in the Derbyshire Moors; the seemingly tired figure leans lazily against the wall to watch the cottage intensely, waiting for a flicker of life. Juxtaposed entirely against the serenity of the lush countryside, the soldier holds still, dug in, steadfast, unseen, unheard and like a flashback from the movie, Went The Day Well, a narrative begins to unfold in his mind. Not too indifferent to his own story, a Soldier returned home to a sleepy village, recounts a memory of how a day very similar to this one, arrives in the small English village. Like the character in the movie, he too returns, not along with a group of seemingly authentic British soldiers like in the film, but as one solitary loner returning to where life, even much quieter than the one in the movie, exists to almost non-existent proportions. Life in the village of Castleton goes by at a snail's pace, the soldier had missed the serenity. Unlike the soldiers in the movie, this lonesome soldier knows he is not welcome, nor is he ever likely to be. He is aware that he should never have attempted to return, especially since the murders that took place only two years previous are still being mourned on this very same day. The date has now become a notoriously remembered one. The memory of that fateful is etched in the minds of all who knew him and his family well. This day feels, even to him, like only yesterday, and is undoubtedly the same for all who recall it. Though the sun is high in the sky and hot, the soldier shivers at the mere the memory of it. Shockwaves of the horror seem to slice down his spine; he senses it from every tree around the village, every hill, wall, and brick. Though he does not fear retribution, like the villagers in the movie, this soldier does fear his identity and connection to the murders could be exposed. He certainly would not like that. Like the character in the film, he does not want to end up writing messages on eggs to hand over to the local paper boy pleading for his freedom, or attempting to contact the village squire, a long-time collaborator with the enemy, and nor would British troops swoop into the village of Castleton, like they did in the fictitious town of Brambly End to rescue him. It wouldn't be he who will be rounded up by the villagers, like the Germans in the movie, and without a shadow of a doubt, be shot if he tries to sound the alarm bell in the Hamlet Tower. He is alone and unlike the movie, his story is real. This soldier knows how this narrative will end; he knows it all too well. In fact, he fears the Ringmaster's version of this tragedy will be far worse than the movie.

From a distance, the soldier's khakis make his slender figure blend into the mise-en-scene, allowing him to remain hidden most of the day, concealed, deceiving the human eye until eventually, with the sun beginning to sink over the hills, he builds up enough courage to make a move upon the unsuspecting occupant of the cottage.

Just as the soldier is about to spring from his hideout, a car pulls up outside the cottage. The soldier steps back into the shadows and waits. Georgia, a face he knew well once upon a time, hearing the car's engine, comes to peer out of the door. She takes the soldier's breath away. She is a ghost from the past, licking sticky red syrup from her hands like blood as the ice lolly she is eating begins melting down her fingers.

"You coming in or what?" She shouts to a woman who is now climbing out of the car.

"Aren't you ready?" Nikki responds, as she turns to face her friend.

"Not yet; just need to wash my hands and put slap on my face!"

"Bloody hell, G, I thought you'd be ready by now."

"Come in; I won't be long."

"Oh, for God's sake! You know I hate this place!"

Nikki climbs out of the car and, pulling her shirt down at the back, walks across the yard, glancing nervously at the barn.

"Are you sure you want to go to the Traveller's today, of all days?"

"The Traveller's do the best cold ones; I'm dying for a pint."

"Okay, it's up to you!"

Georgia closes the door behind Nikki while wiping her hands on a tea towel.

"Lock it!"

"Why? Oh, for fuck's sake, okay. It's broad daylight; there's no one out there."

Nikki circles the room like a nervous dog, flinching at every nook and cranny. "I hate this place. It creeps me out! I don't know how you can carry on living here."

She picks up a book from the table and flicks through the pages as Georgia applies the last finishing touches to her make-up with loose compact face powder, which she'd been refreshing throughout the day. The translucent powder glides over her tired complexion on a soft cotton pad, gently reviving her short-lived beauty with a false healthy glow.

"The Revenge's Tragedy, what's this you're reading?"

"Ugh, oh, a play, it was first registered in 1607. The Revenger has the desire to purge society of evil."

"Oh, I see. Are you sure you're okay, G? What are you reading something like this for?"

"I'm fine," she laughs. 'Of course, I am; it's just a play." She laughs again through O-shaped lips, pulling taut as she applies a glossy blood-red lipstick, and then kissed a tissue. "A good old tragedy helps keep oneself intact. You should try it!"

"I have plenty of tragic stories of my own, don't need to go reading other people's." Holding back the crease in the centrefold, Nikki reads aloud in a throbbing voice, "False!" Georgia smiles as she looks for her keys and prepares to leave.

"I defy you both: I have endured you with an ear of fire; your tongues have struck hot irons on my face."

Georgia was still smiling at Nikki's satirical throbbing voice and exaggerated tone, as she reaches for her bag and keys and opens the door. The Red Admiral butterfly has fluttered from the window and is now hovering at head height by the door. Georgia steps aside to allow the butterfly to dip in and out of the house before drifting off on a whip of cool fresh air.

"Mother comes from that poisonous woman there!"

Laughing, Georgia turns to step outside. "Josh! Oh, my God, It's Josh!"

Joshua stands proudly and still at the door. He relaxes slightly, removes his beret and wrings it through his hands.

"Hello, Georgia! I'm back."